The Invitation

Three Lives, Two Secrets, One Invitation

Clare Fryer

The Invitation

First edition independently published in the UK in 2024.
ISBN (Paperback): 978-1-3999-7138-6
Typesetting & cover design: Matthew J Bird.

A CIP catalogue record of this book is available from the British Library.

For further information about this book, please contact the author at:
clarefryer.co.uk

This book is dedicated to my parents,
Jean and Jeffery Wheatley.

Dad encouraged me to write and would be so proud that I have joined him as a published author.

Mum was the first to suggest I extend a short story to tell what happened next, and so *The Invitation* short story grew into this book.

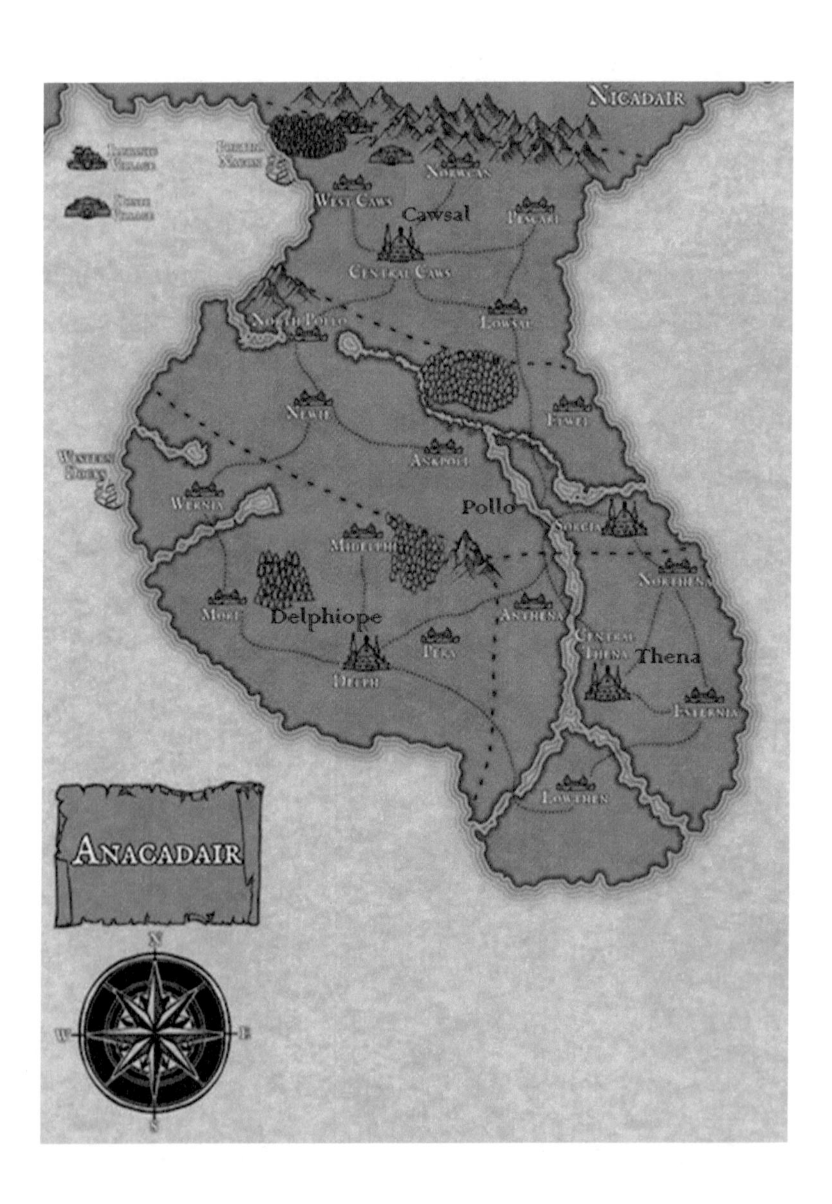
NICADAIR
WEST CAWS
Cawsal
CENTRAL CAWS
NORTH POLLO
NEWIL
WERNIA
Pollo
Delphiope
Thena
ANACADAIR
N
W
E
S

Anacadair

Anacadair is the peninsula of the Cadaira continental plateau. When King Anlan, the last true king, was the victor in the Blood wars over 200 years ago, he decreed Anacadair be segregated into four districts: Thena, Delphiope, Pollo and Cawsal. Those of King Anlan's Bloodline and heritage were centred in Thena district along with the seat of government, the High Council and the Legal Octon. The purity of the Anlan Bloodline was carefully monitored to protect the power that came with it. Pollo district was the centre for science and healing. Delphiope district was home to those whose talents lay in entertainment and performance and those of sporting prowess. Manufacturing and skilled workers were also focused in Delphiope. Cawsal was left for those of low status who cultivated the earth, mined the mountains and fished the seas.

Today, the districts have changed little since King Anlan created them, and there is still much prejudice against the Cawsal people. However, they are not without skills and talent. While King Anlan valued those with knowledge of weapons and warfare and brought them together in Thena, those with other talents were dismissed to Cawsal. Their particular skills and abilities are only now becoming known. Most commonly heard of are dreamers, usually children who can see the future in bursts. It is rare and inherited from the maternal line. Sadly, this ability drains their spirit, and often, they don't live past childhood—those who do become highly revered as seers.

The Anlan Seal

Last revised for King Anlan after the end of the Bloodline Wars. King Anlan was a King of Cada, an ancient people whose origins have been lost in time. What history there is indicates that the Cadan people arrived from the other side of the known world with weapons and technology unknown on the Cadaira Peninsula.

High Council and Octons

The High Council is the governing body of Anacadair. Today there are six Octons of government. There were eight originally, but two Octons were consolidated after 100 years of peace. Each Octon has a Councillor to the High Council plus a district Councillor representing each of the four districts. The Legal Councillor is also head of the High Council. At the beginning of this book, the following people had been elected to the High Council.

Legal Octon

Responsible for all laws governing Anacadair, including Anlan Bloodline Law.

Legal Councillor and Head of the High Council – Maxim (Max) of the Anlan Bloodline line.

Thenan Legal Councillor – Rush of the Anlan Bloodline.

Pollo Legal Councillor – Marc of the Anlan Bloodline.

Delphiope Legal Councillor – Anton, 50% maternal Anlan Bloodline.
Cawsal Legal Councillor -Targo.

Healing Octon
Responsible for Healers and wisewomen, including those of the former Pharmacia Octon who have specialist knowledge of medicines.
Healing Councillor – Otto (Delphiope) 20% Maternal Anlan Bloodline.
Thenan Healing Councillor – Aldion, of the Anlan Bloodline.
Pollo Healing Councillor – Kiron, 60% of the Anlan Bloodline.
Delphiope Healing Councillor – Triope.
Cawsal Healing Councillor – Oldron.

Education Octon
Covers all schools and colleges of education.
Education Councillor – Professor Hog.
Thenan Education Councillor – Professor Ben.
Pollo Education Councillor – Professor Ankharl.
Delphiope Education Councillor – Master Polombus.
Cawsal Education Councillor – Professor Lebartin.

Faith Octon
Responsible for all three faiths in Anacadair; Singularity, Quartive and Fatalism.
Faith Councillor – Father Anberto (Cawsal, Quartive faith).
Thenan Faith Councillor – Senior Steward Mica (Singularity) of the Anlan Bloodline.
Pollo Faith Councillor – Steward Elon (Singularity).
Delphiope Faith Councillor– Senior Leader Boldun (Fatalism).
Cawsal Faith Councillor – Father Garten (Quartive).

Militaria Octon

Responsible for the guards and the army. Guards support the legal Octon in enforcing laws.

Militaria Councillor – Stratagon Wiklon (Stratagon equivalent to General).

Thenan Militaria Councillor – Strato Caldo (Straton equivalent to Major) of the Anlan Bloodline.

Pollo Militaria Councillor – Nauticon Zartus (Nauticon equivalent to Sea lord) of the Anlan Bloodline.

Delphiope Militaria Councillor – Nautico Lautus (Nautico equivalent to Sea Commander).

Cawsal Militaria Councillor – Strato Bogdo.

Industry Octon

Responsible for agriculture, manufacturing, and trade. It also includes performance arts.

Industry Councillor – Norbarto.

Thenan Industry Councillor – Folke.

Pollo Industry Councillor – Debor.

Delphiope Councillor – Agrimo.

Cawsal Councillor – Toba.

Character List

(Primary characters in bold)

Name	**District**	**Role & Notes**
Father Garten	Cawsal	Cawsal Faith Councillor (Quartive)
Kayden	Cawsal	Friend of Amelie
Luzi	Cawsal	Housekeeper for Thea
Mother Kron	Cawsal	Wisewoman
Oldron	Cawsal	Healer, Cawsal
Silph	Cawsal	Dreamer
Toba	Cawsal	Cawsal Industrial Councillor
Bard	Cawsal	Captain of the Cargo ship Dolphus
Ollee	Cawsal	Book seller Married to Katja
Katja	Cawsal	Married to Ollee
Bogdo	Cawsal	Rank - Strato (Major), Cawsal Militaria Councillor Married to Petia, Nephew to Toba
Kayde	Cawsal	Parents – Ollee and Katja
Flit	Cawsal	Sailor on Dolphus
Petia	Cawsal	Wife of Bogdo
Salai	Cawsal	Wife of Toba
Brother Lori	Delphiope	Quartive
Senior Leader Boldun	Delphiope	Delphiope Faith Councillor (Fatalist)

Dorcana	Delphiope	Friend of Amelie, married to Ando, Mother to Orlan
Ando	Delphiope	Married to Dorcana, Father to Orlan
Orlan	Delphiope	Son of Dorcana & Ando
Malic	Pollo	Driver of Conveyance
Mother Plumb	Pollo	Wisewoman
Mother Pod	Pollo	Wisewoman
Suzi	Pollo	Nursery Maid for Thea
Yan	Pollo	Friend of Millie, Father is Kiron
Marc	Pollo	Pollo Legal Councillor, Father of Elon
Wiklon	Pollo	Rank - Stratagon (General), Father of Jak, Militaria Councillor
Kiron	**Pollo**	**Pollo Healing Councillor, Father of Yan Professor of Healing at Sorcia Quintarea Hospital, Pollo**
Zillah	**Pollo**	**Married to Max**
Mother Lib	Pollo	Mother to Thea, Wife of Father Jonca
Anke	Pollo	Friend of Amelie, Sister to Kiron
Elon	Pollo	Friend of Rush & Jak, Faith Octon (Singularity), Son of Marc
Frodel	Thena	Driver for Rush
Mica	Thena	Senior Steward of the Singularity Faith

Professor Hog	Thena	Tutor for Rush and siblings
Thea	**Thena**	**Parents – Father Jonca and Mother Lib, Married to Rush**
Amelie	**Thena**	**Parents – Max and Zillah**
Barti	**Thena**	**Parents – Max and Zillah, Married to Deeala**
Brig	Thena	Parents – Max and Zillah
Cid	Thena	Parents – Max and Zillah
Max	Thena	Parents – Max and Zillah
Rush	**Thena**	**Thena Legal Councillor Parents are Max and Zillah, Married to Thea**
Millie	**Thena**	**Parents - Thea and Rush**
Amillia	**Thena**	**Parents – Thea and Rush**
Cam	**Thena**	**Parents – Thea and Rush**
Edi	**Thena**	**Twin of Jami, Parents – Thea and Rush**
Elia	**Thena**	**Parents – Thea and Rush**
Jami	**Thena**	**Twin of Edi, Parents – Thea and Rush**
Jak	Thena	Friend of Rush & Elon, Son of Wiklon, Legal Octon
Maximus (Max)	**Thena**	**Legal Councillor, Wife – Zillah, Head of High Council**
Rosa	Thena/Delphiope	Friend of Amelie

Part 1 - Present day

1

Millie

My name is Millie. I'm told I am slight for my age, with a mass of long, dark, curly hair that frames my features nicely. Tomorrow is my sixteenth birth anniversary, and I'm looking forward to meeting my friends for a big party to celebrate. In Anacadair, the sixteenth anniversary marks the end of school and the end of childhood. After we leave school, we go to college to learn skills and trades. I want to take performing arts and vocal training in Delphiope, but Father expects me to stay in Thena and follow the Legal Octon. Legal is so boring, I can't bear the thought of being stuck with it. I live with my parents, three brothers, a sister, and grandparents. Cam is fourteen and generally OK. Elia is almost thirteen and a pain; she wants to do everything with me but is too young to tag along when I'm out with my friends. I like having a sister to share things with when we are alone, though. The twins, Edi and Jami, are five. I enjoy playing with them, but Grandma and Gramps are usually there and don't want me near them. Gramps scares me; he and Grandma spy on me when my parents aren't around, checking up like they don't trust me. Grandma and Gramps are Father's parents and live with us to help Mother care for the younger children. My father is Rush, and my mother is Thea.

My family and I live in Thena, the primary district of Anacadair. The country of Anacadair is on the continental peninsula of the Cadaira plateau. We live in a house surrounded by tall hedges, typical of Thenan houses where privacy is essential. Thena is a dull, stuffy district with so many laws and rules it takes all the fun out of everything. We have rules for how we dress, what people we can meet, who we can talk to, where we can go, and who must go with us. We even have rules for what we eat. Families like mine have a whole bunch of extra laws to follow, making life even more boring. It's all because we are of the Anlan Bloodline (descendants of King Anlan, who won the Blood War hundreds of years ago). My father, Rush, is Thena district Legal Councillor to the High Council, the ruling body of Anacadair. The Legal Octon handles law, including those specific to descendants of King Anlan. Gramps is the Legal Councillor to the High Council. It is the most senior Legal role and Head of the High Council. My father is expected to take Gramp's place when he finally retires. As a family of high status and of the Bloodline, we're supposed to set an example. Father and Gramps are very strict about that. It's easier at school, where I can forget some rules for a while and be treated like everyone else. Like most Thenan women, my mother doesn't work and is pregnant again. I didn't think she'd have any more after the twins, but I guess I was wrong. As a Thenan wife and mother, it's Thea's role to raise the children. I sometimes wonder if she is bored at home, although she never complains and she has her garden.

Standing in the kitchen doorway, I flip through the post that arrived this morning. I sigh as my green/brown eyes take in the typical family breakfast scene. *I wish my life was more like those I read about in books. There's still nothing from Yan. Yan is amazingly good-looking and so clever. Not the legal type of clever like Father, but a scientist. He's funny and makes me laugh; he likes my curly hair and the colour of my eyes. He makes me feel special and important, not an irritation like I'm treated at home. Yan wants to be a Healer like his father. His father is a Professor of Healing at the prestigious Sorcia Quintarea Hospital in the Pollo district.* I walked around the table handing out the post. One for Grandma, two for Gramps, and one for Cam. *I bet that's from Jaz; I'm sure that's her writing. I knew I was right when I saw her eyeing him last week. She's got no chance.* Arriving at the space between Mother and Father, I smiled as I greeted them and gave them their post.

"Good morning, Father, letters for you." I put several envelopes on the table beside him. They were from the High Council; I had felt the triangular Anlan Seal embossed on the back. He didn't look up from his newspaper or acknowledge the letters, *miserable old frog.*

"Good morning, Mother, your 'Garden Moments' is here." I put the glossy magazine on the table beside her. Mother nodded before swallowing and said thank you. The last letter stayed in my hand. *I wonder who this is from,* I thought, as I propped it up against the salt pot. I took my seat and reached for the silver coffee pot to pour myself some coffee. It was strong and dark, just as I liked it. Adding a little milk, I stirred as I looked at the envelope. It was expensive paper, and I didn't recognise that beautiful script on the front. Giving in to my curiosity, I took the letter opener and opened the envelope. As I slid out the contents, I sensed Mother stiffen beside me and glanced around. *Whatever's wrong*?

Mother had stopped mid-chew; her face drained of colour. *I hope it isn't the baby; she looks very pale, and it isn't due for at least another month.* I turned back to the envelope in my fingers and finished extracting the contents. In my hands was a white card of good grade with the Anlan Seal embossed in gold at the top. Written diagonally across the middle in bold black letters was the word INVITATION. The card has a crisp fold, and there seemed to be something inside. Opening the card, I saw delicate pink pages filled with the same beautiful script. Mother took a sharp intake of breath before saying.

"Give it to me, Millie, just give it to me p... please." Her voice was thin, quivering like a reed as her shaky hand reached towards me. Pale, bony fingers, nails buffed to a deep gloss, stretched out like a ghostly apparition. Her quivering voice sent shock waves around the table and hit me like a slap to the face. Instinctively, I pulled away, not wanting to let go of my letter. Silence descended like a cold shower as everyone stopped talking and turned towards us. Even Father lowered his paper. The expression on Mother's face was intense, boring deep into me. I felt compelled to put the card with the pages into the outstretched hand.

"What is it, Mother?" I asked as a cold shiver ran down my spine. I was afraid, she hadn't asked to see my post since I was small. The card had said 'Invitation' on it, so it couldn't be bad, could it? Invitations *had* arrived for me before, although not as fancy as this, but they caused no fuss at all. All the same, I had a deep sense of foreboding.

The silence stretched before Mother slowly opened the card and placed it on the table. She unfolded the delicate pink pages with shaking hands and laid them flat on the card. She put a hand over the words as if to hide them. Tears welled in her eyes, and I watched as they overflowed and trickled down her face. She swiped at them with her hand. My sense of foreboding grew further as Father reached across in front of me and placed a hand on top of Mother's.

"What's the matter?" I asked, "What's going on?" my words hung in the air before Father spoke, but not to me.

"We don't have to do anything," his voice was soft, but the tone wasn't, and my parents locked eyes. Gramps looked over, his face stony. Cam put down his spoon and found something fascinating on the table. Beside him, Elia sat with a coffee cup frozen in mid-air. Even five-year-old twins Edi and Jami stopped their fighting to watch the silent discussion.

"Mother, Father, what's the matter? Who is the letter from?" I asked, aware my voice was rising. My mind buzzed with so many questions, and I couldn't help the irritation in my voice. *It's my letter!* A voice screamed inside my head.

"Millie, silence!" his voice was firm. His hand on Mother's pressed down so hard her fingertips were turning purple. Mother looked at me briefly before fresh tears flowed down her colourless cheeks. Shaking her head, she looked down.

"Millie, your father and I need to talk about this." her voice was fragile, each word forced from her. I want to scream back at her, at him. *It's my letter, what's the big deal*? I tried to calm my voice before I spoke.

"I don't understand. The letter's addressed to me. Why do you need to discuss it with Father? it's addressed to me." I could hear the frustration in my voice. Father looked at me.

"Millie, go to your room until I call you. Cam and Elia, you too. Twins, stay with Grandma and Gramps." he delivered the instructions in a sharp and final tone. His frown was so deep his eyebrows almost met in the middle; his mouth flattened to a thin line. A deep red stain was rising on his cheeks, warning his temper was reaching a dangerous level. His dark eyes glared at us all as we sat in stunned silence before we began to move.

"Millie, I know you don't understand. Please do as Father has asked. He will send for you later, and we will explain." Mother's voice was weak and resigned; although it was morning, she sounded tired. Usually, she had energy in the morning despite the late stage of pregnancy. I felt tears prickle in my own eyes. *It's not fair.*

"It came to me. Why can't I read it?" I asked in a small voice, and I couldn't help a note of petulance creeping in. For all of my fifteen years, eleven months and twenty-nine days, I felt like a little child at this moment. *What's so wrong? What have I done or said*? Father's expression and Mother's tears sent a cold knife of fear deep inside me.

"Not now, Millie, P... Please, not now." Her wavering voice stumbled over the words that seeped from her bloodless lips. They washed over me like iced water, and I stood, not knowing what else to do, and walked to the door. I caught my breath as I bit back words that would inflame Father. Instead, I turned to Mother.

"Could I stay with the twins, please, Mother?" I pleaded. I couldn't bear the thought of waiting alone in my room, not knowing what was happening. At least the twins would be distracting. Everything has gone wrong today. *Why should I be sent to my room for a stupid invitation? I didn't even know who it was from. There wasn't even a letter from Yan to read. He had probably changed his mind and didn't want to see me anymore. I bet Juda, the tarty girl from Cawsal, has draped herself all over him, digging her claws in. I wish I didn't live in Thena with all these stupid laws.*

"Millie, p... please just go." Mother's voice is resigned. I didn't know what else to do, so I turned and ran upstairs.

"My study," he said as his hand closed over Thea's, crushing the pages as he gripped her tightly. Pulling her hand away, she snatched the pages as he whisked away the card. Awkwardly, she eased herself from the chair, pausing momentarily to lean on the table as she caught her breath. Straightening, she walked towards the door with slow, deliberate steps. Her body was erect, posture perfect, befitting her status. One hand protectively covered her huge belly, and the other held the pages scrunched in her fist. Despite the late stage of pregnancy, she still walked with dignity, her head held high. Her midnight black hair, scraped into a neat chignon, was secured with a neat green clip. At the end of the hall, she stopped beside an elegant door of carved dark wood. It was the entrance befitting the study of a

Councillor. Rush held the card as if it were something unpleasant. His other hand took a brass key from his pocket and inserted it into the lock. His face was set in a grimace; angular shoulders and straight back supported his tall, proud frame. There was no place for weakness, he knew from bitter experience. He pushed the door open and ushered Thea inside.

2

Millie

Sometime later, I heard the study door open, and Father's voice boomed up from the hall.

"Millie, come down to the study." He must have waited for me because I didn't hear the study door close. Reluctantly, I got up and left my room. I descended the stairs, my thoughts whirling around my head. He was standing there all pompous and full of himself, waiting for me as I knew he would be. *I hate him. Why can't he let me live my life without interfering? I bet that letter has something to do with those stupid Anlan Laws. Well, see if I care.* But I had been worrying about it since I was sent to my room. I was sure it must be about Yan. What else could be so bad? I had rehearsed what I would say and how I'd argue for the right to choose a boyfriend. Now, those brave words seemed less brave and less convincing.

Father silently directed me into the study, closing the door behind us. He gestured to the dark green leather chairs facing his desk, then sat in his black leather chair on the other side. Mother was sitting in the chair beside me, her face pale and eyes watery. Awkwardly, I perched on the chair. The leather was smooth and well-worn to my touch. On any other occasion, I would enjoy the privilege of settling back in one of these chairs, but not today. I sat stiffly, waiting to see what would happen next, my hands tucked under my legs to stop them shaking. *I hope Mother's OK. He can be so cruel.* Father picked up the pages, then put them down again and placed his hands on top. He stared at his hands, his expression unreadable. Mother, her hands white from their desperate clasp, gave a tiny squeak as if trying to hold back a sob. I still sat in silence as I watched the silent conversation. *Was I supposed to say something?* As I opened my mouth, his voice broke the silence. He spat the words as if they were unpleasant, poisonous.

"This Invitation is for your Introduction." Mother gave a half cry and clasped her hands even tighter, fingers dug deep into her knuckles. Her distress was more frightening than Father was at that moment.

"My introduction to what?"

"The Invitation is from your mother. It is for your introduction to the boy named on your Promisary Agreement." his words were delivered in a voice devoid of emotion, stilted and precise. They chilled me to the bone. His hands were firmly placed on the desk as if propping him up. The room began to spin as I took in the words. *Why would Mother write to me and then be all weird about it? What Promisary Agreement? Why haven't I heard about it before? Why is Mother so upset? Wasn't a Promisary Agreement supposed to be a good thing?* My thoughts spun faster and faster, then suddenly crashed with realisation.

"Mother?" I asked in a small voice, looking at the woman beside me. Even as I did so, I saw a tear escape and trickle down her cheek. I didn't have time to think because Father was talking, his voice cold as ice.

"Your birth mother was your age when you were born and didn't know how to look after you. We took you as our own until you reached your sixteenth anniversary." The bottom fell out of my world, and the room began to spin faster and faster. Sounds echoed in my ears as I slumped back into the chair, and my eyes closed. *It couldn't be true. Why hadn't I been told before?*

“I’m sorry, so sorry, Millie,” Mother, or the person who was no longer my mother, said, bringing me back to the room.

“Please say it isn’t true,” I whispered.

“We wanted to tell you, but it wasn’t possible.” her voice quivered and gave way to silent sobs. Her shoulders shook as tears rolled down her ashen face. *It must be his fault. Why wouldn’t he let her tell me*? Then, it dawned on me that my sixteenth anniversary was tomorrow, and I had plans. A cold dread trickled down my back.

“So, are you, my father? What happens when I’m sixteen?” my voice rose as I spoke. Hot, angry tears stung my eyes. *I was seeing Yan tomorrow. We were meeting our friends for the party. The party Father had agreed I could go to. HE HAD AGREED. How could he ruin yet another anniversary? He has spoiled every single one I could remember. Couldn’t I have one that was OK*? As he spoke, I balled my hands into fists and dug them into the seat.

“Tomorrow, you will go to the National Introductions Agency, where you will meet your birth mother and the boy from your Promisary Agreement.” His eyes were hard and cold as he looked at me. I looked back, and my eyes burned with hate. *How could I have a Promisary Agreement? Nobody had mentioned it before. Amba had been told years ago. It was bullshit. Why didn’t Mother tell me any of this?* I didn’t have time to think further because he was talking again.

“We agreed to tell you on your sixteenth anniversary in our own way. We didn’t know this would happen.” *Oh, funny, ha-ha*, I thought bitterly. *It’s a cruel game where I was the one nobody wanted, and everyone tried to get rid of.*

“So, do I get to read my letter now?” my voice held a note of defiance as I turned to Mother.

“And if you knew I had a Promisary Agreement, why didn’t you tell me? If you knew, why didn’t you say something, anything? I hate you; I hate you both." my blood was boiling now, and my voice was venomous.

"Listen," his voice had become a strangled growl. I glanced over at him, then back at Mother as she began to speak.

"Millie, it's true I'm not your birth mother. Your birth mother was just a girl." Her breath caught in her throat, and she took a deep breath. "She was just a girl and not ready to raise a little one. We thought we were doing the best thing for you." For one mad moment, I thought I would burst out laughing. How could this be the best thing?

"I don't believe you," I said.

"Your birth mother was only sixteen when she gave birth to you. Not old enough to know any better. My parents, your grandparents, asked us to raise you." *he was trying to be nice!*

"Bullshit!" the words escaped before I could stop them. I stood and lunged for the letter, but he slapped his hand down before I could reach it. My hand landed on his, and I pulled it back as if scalded. I stood back.

The room was suffocating. I had to get out of here. I have to get away. I turned, taking the few steps needed to reach the door. Grasping the brass handle, I turned it and pulled, yanking hard. *Come on, why won't you open?* Then I realised he had locked us in.

"Let me out!" my words fell like snowflakes into the icy silence around me. I looked around wildly. *There had to be another way out. The window behind the desk? It was closed, locked too, I bet, and he would get to me before I could escape, even if it wasn't.* I looked around again and saw the patio door. *If the bastard hasn't locked it, I could go out that way*. Running over, I tried, pushing and pulling in vain, but it didn't budge. *Could I break the glass with something? But I couldn't see anything and was afraid to use my hands.*

"Why won't you let me out? You can't keep me here!" I cried as I sank to the floor. Gathering my legs, I wrapped my arms around them, and hugged them, resting my forehead on my knees. My breathing was ragged; a deep agonising cry welled up inside, my eyes moist with unshed tears. *My life had been one whole lie. How could he? It was all his doing. Why was this happening to me? I didn't understand. I wished Yan was here. He would know what to do. I wished a hole would open and swallow me right now. There would be no point living if they forced me to meet some other boy. I don't want to live if I can't be with Yan.*

"Get back here now!" his voice was harsh, like a captain to a foot soldier.

"Millie, please, my love, come back over here." Mother's words struck like needles through my heart. In a few words, my whole life had become meaningless. Why should I care what they said now?

"You've lied to me all my life. Why should I listen to more lies? You're not my parents." I cried, my voice breaking. I gulped back tears and pushed my head further into my knees.

Deep wounds opened in my heart. A cry escaped as my body heaved against the urge to let go, to grieve, and to rip itself apart. I couldn't speak. I couldn't do anything. I clung to my legs and rocked, completely lost.

"Millie, I'm coming over, OK?" I heard fabric rustling as she moved, and then soft steps came towards me on the thick carpet—gentle sounds beside me as she eased herself into a sitting position with her back to the doorframe. A waft of her perfume reached me, sweet and floral, but today, it was nauseating, and I turned my face away.

"Millie, I know this isn't easy for you. I can't imagine how you feel right now," she sighed. "We thought we were doing the right thing. She was just a child; you needed parents who could love and raise you. I do love you, Millie. I didn't give birth to you, but I am proud to be your mother." The words rang true, but I didn't want to hear them.

"Who's my mother?" I mumbled.

"We... er... well... she was cut off from her family... when it happened. The disgrace... it was too much for the family." *Huh, what was so disgraceful about having a child at sixteen?*

"Is that what happens when I turn sixteen? You throw me out? Is that why there is such mystery around my sixteenth anniversary? None of my friends will talk about it, not even Amba." Finally, the unshed tears poured from my eyes and seeped into my jeans as my head rested on my knees.

"No, I wouldn't throw you out, Millie. When Thenan daughters reach their sixteenth anniversary, they are introduced to the boy from their Promisary Agreement. It is their mother's right to choose a boy from a good family and agree with his family to register the Promisary Agreement after their daughter is born. A Promisary Agreement was made for you when you were born as it was for me."

"Why didn't you tell me?" I was frozen to the spot. My voice was barely a whisper now. I'd passed into nothing where I could no longer feel. I wished I could sink through the floor and disappear.

"This is difficult for us too. We didn't know your birth mother had made a Promisary Agreement. She never told us, and it wasn't registered in Thena. Your father hasn't heard from her, from his sister, for sixteen years. Seeing her handwriting on the envelope when you brought it to the kitchen was a terrible shock. The Invitation with the Anlan Seal on the front was my worst nightmare come true." Her hand reached out and rested on my shoulders. "Please believe me..." The hand burned like fire, and I shook it off.

"My mother is his sister? I didn't know he had a sister." It just gets worse. *How much worse could it get?*

"Yes."

"Why didn't you tell me?" then another thought struck me even more laughable, "Are there two Promisary Agreements? Was I to be a bigamist? Why should I go there to meet people I didn't know and didn't want to know?"

Suddenly, I felt very, very angry. *How dare these people meddle and control my life? How could they keep my birth mother a secret all this time?* Anger filled the space where sorrow had been, and my breathing burned deep and fierce.

"So, what about my father? My birth father, why didn't he marry my mother? Why did he leave me a bastard? Is that a big secret, too?" I hiss, spitting each word, drops of saliva spraying onto the carpet in front of me.

"Your mother lay with a boy from Cawsal if you believe what she says." It was him talking now. The words were distasteful on his tongue. "He died in the prison mines."

"Why was he in the prison mines?" a sick fear gripped me, sour and burning. *Did he send my birth father to the prison mines?*

"It was a year after you were born. The boy was caught a few months after your mother could no longer hide her pregnancy. The High Judge of Thena tried the boy for defiling an innocent of Anlan birth. His punishment was to be sent to the mines for sixteen years. He was in an accident around the time you were born." Ice filled my veins as I took in what he said. *Was my father sent to prison because he had forced my mother? It's too horrible to imagine. My poor mother, and then they took me away, too. She wouldn't want me anyway if he forced himself on her. But why was it so terrible to have a child before marriage? Maybe it was a mistake. Somehow, perhaps, he had loved my mother.*

"I know plenty of girls who have babes young and kept them. Some even marry the father." I said coldly. "There was one girl in my archery class. It was the only sport she could do with a fat belly." I gave a mirthless laugh.

"They are not Thenan." Mother says. *I remember then. Thenan meant Anlan, which meant the Bloodline Laws. Ancient and rubbish. How could I forget that horrendous afternoon here as he gave me 'the talk' on all the stupid Anlan Bloodline Laws? The laws for Procreation and Education of Female children. It had been so embarrassing and as dull as the water flowing by the street.*

"Tomorrow, we'll take you to the gates of the National Introductions Agency. Your mother, Amelie, will meet you there. Your things will be packed and sent to your new home." He sounded as if he was conducting a business transaction. Cold and matter of fact. Then I realised what he'd said, and I cried.

"What? Why couldn't I come back here? Where will I go? Will I ever see the others again?" I paused for a breath; I can't describe how I felt.

"Slow down. We'll have to do this one step at a time. Your father and I know nothing of the boy she's chosen for you or where you will live. Once everything is settled, I'm sure you can visit us. Amelie will owe us a deed of gratitude for raising you." Mother's voice is soft and pleading.

"So, I'm supposed to turn up and go with strangers?" Mother took a sharp breath at my mocking tone.

"I want to meet you halfway. This has been a terrible shock, but we must respect your birth mother's wishes. It's the law." Mother moved her feet in circles, clearly in discomfort.

Without thinking, I said, "Can I help you up from the floor?" automatically, I stood and took Mother's hands, gently helping her up. Our arms reached around each other. I hated myself for giving in so easily, for accepting her comfort. Together, we stood for a long minute, hugging tightly as silent tears rolled down our cheeks. I drew comfort from the warmth of her arms that had always been there to pick me up and comfort me. Then, the moment was gone, and we returned to the chairs. I drew my legs up, hugged them, and rested my feet on the seat. *If he doesn't like it well, that's tough. I didn't care anymore*. Softly, Mother began to relate her story of meeting the man across from her. She described how it was a shock for her to discover what would happen, just as it was for me. *At least she knew who her mother and father were,* I thought bitterly. *I bet she was also told years before she reached her sixteenth anniversary*. Mother continued saying that the Promisary Agreement registered by Amelie must be honoured. The laws were in her favour.

The matter was not settled, but as she spoke, Thea saw her daughter, the girl she'd accepted as her own, begin to listen and nod. Gradually, she felt a glimmer of hope that the crisis had passed. Her daughter, for that is what Millie would always be, would accept her destiny as she had done many years before. Accept yes, but would she be happy? She hoped she would. I sat listening, showing the face they wanted to see, while I thought of Yan and our plans to run away together.

Well, they can plan all they like, but I was leaving. I'll go tonight. Until then, I can play the dutiful daughter for a little longer.

3

Millie

Tears silently slid down my face. I had to get away from here. I tried to sneak through the kitchen last night, but Gramps was there; he stepped out of the darkness in front of me. I nearly died of fright. I said I was getting a glass of water, and he watched me take it upstairs. I tried my bedroom window next. I could drop down onto the roof below, across and down by the backdoor. But my windows were locked. They are never locked. *I feel like a prisoner. I can't bear it. My whole life is a lie.* Mother wasn't my mother, Father wasn't my father, my birth father was dead, and an aunt I didn't know I had was my birth mother. Hot tears ran down my face as I curled up on my bed facing the wall. I let them form damp patches on the pillow, and gooey snot dribbled down my cheek to join them. I didn't care. I wrapped my arms around myself, holding my aching heart. Today, I must meet my birth mother and the boy in the Promisary Agreement. I felt sick. I've vomited twice already. I had to bathe and wash my hair like it was some special occasion and not the end of my life. There was no choice; Mother and Suzi fussed around 'helping' me on this special occasion. *If they say that one more time, I'll scream. So, now I've bathed and washed my hair, but I'm not dressing up. Why should I? I don't want to go, and it's not my special occasion.*

There was a rustle of fabric and soft footsteps approach. *Who was it now? I didn't want to see anybody.*

"Millie, are you awake?" it was Mother. She sounds nervous. Slowly, I turned my head. *Oh, what in all the Gods has she got in her hands?* A cream fabric was draped over her arm, and my heart sank.

"I bought an Introductions Dress for you last week. It's your size and looks perfect." *She's holding out a dress, which under any other circumstances might have been OK, but right now, I hate it. I hate everything it stands for*. I rolled back to face the wall.

"Do I have to wear it? Can't I choose what to wear*?"* I was trying not to argue, but I really, really wanted to rip it to shreds.

"It's traditional to wear an Introductions Dress, Millie. Several of your friends have had lovely dresses made for them. I'm sure you've heard about them at school." *I had, but I wasn't going to say so.* "I was going to ask the dressmaker, but I saw this one and, well, here it is." *does she have to sound so pleased? I couldn't care less who made it.*

"Can't I wear jeans or something? It's not like I've had time to try it on or have it fitted anyway." *Psh, that was stupid. Now she'll make me try it on.*

"Why don't you try it on then? If it doesn't fit, then we can find something else for you to wear." *Knew it. She had that smile on her face. I knew she was trying, and I was being horrible, but it wasn't fair.* Sighing, I rolled over and sat up. Slowly, I stood and faced her, wiping my face with a sleeve of my night shirt before I threw it back on the bed.

"Do I have to?" I kicked the bed with my heel, my towel held tightly around me. The pain in my heel felt good, and I kicked a little harder each time while my mind ran through possible ways to escape.

"Yes, you do, dear. I know this is a lot for you to take in. With all my heart, I wish I could have prepared you for this, but…

well... please know I understand. Now let's see if this fits you." *I wish I knew what she was trying to say. How could she possibly understand how I felt?* Then, the wind slipped from my sails, and I sagged like a spent balloon. *I couldn't see a way out. They've won.* I allowed her to clean my face before helping me into the new undergarments and the dress. They fitted like a glove. A tiny part of me glowed at my vision in the tall looking glass. Then I stamped on that traitorous thought.

"Oh darling, it fits you so well," she said, sounding relieved. It was a traditional Introduction dress, fitted at the top, with a skirt that flowed from under the breast just past my knees. Its cream, silky folds flowed around me like water. Tears welled up in my eyes, and I let them fall unchecked.

"Oh, Millie," Mother pulled me to her, and I let her hold me as I sobbed. *I feel so alone. Will I ever see Yan again? How will he know where I am?* My heart broke a little more with every question.

Eventually, as my tears stopped, I sank into myself. She gently released me and took my hands, looking deep into my eyes.

"There's nothing I can say to make today easier, but I promise I will find a way to help you." Her voice was firm. She looked so fierce and protective; I'd never seen her like this.

"Here are the shoes I bought to match the dress." They were traditional flat maiden shoes in deep cream silk. Obediently, I slipped my feet into them. They fit, and I might even have said they were comfortable if it wasn't for the occasion. Mother put her hands on my shoulders and gently pushed me down onto my chair. She brushed my curls until they shone, and then she produced a floral clip in a matching fabric. Drawing up my hair on one side, she fixed the clip just above my ear. The effect was good, but I was beyond caring. I was in a place so dark it hurt. I was watching through a lens as events took place. My body obeyed instructions automatically, but I was beyond words.

The conveyance purred softly as it carried me to the end of my life. Outside, the day was grey, perfectly matching my mood. The conveyance stopped by an imposing building with a large wall around the outside. Massive iron gates worked in scrolls, and intricate patterns stood open with the word 'National Introductions Agency' in curved letters above. A small group of people stood inside. Were they for me*?*

Mother helped me out of the car and straightened my dress. I could barely remember what it looked like. Every thread and stitch burned my skin. I hated the dress and what it represented. We stood waiting for an unspoken command. The floral hair clip pulled at my scalp, and the new shoes bit into my ankles. I welcomed their sting. Father walked round to join us. *He's wearing BLACK! Funeral black.* It matched my dark place today. It looked as if we were going to a funeral, and in a way, we were. This was where my life ended. I couldn't bear to look at him. The lies of the past sixteen years were like open wounds in my heart. He could have prepared me for today, but he did nothing to prevent the pain I felt. He started to walk forward, but my legs didn't want to move. It felt like walking through thick mud, each step a struggle. Mother put her arm around me, and I leaned into her. She smelled warm and comforting. I accepted her comfort and hated myself for doing so.

We stopped between the gates, and a woman in bright green came forward. She was beautiful and looked straight at Father. *I'm sure I've seen her somewhere before. Was she my birth mother?* Father joined her in the void between our two small parties. They spoke, but I couldn't hear. I suppose it was some formal greeting; there was always some stupid formal stuff in Thena. He signalled to us, and Mother's hand gently but firmly pressed on my back pushing me forward, she matched her footsteps with mine. I felt my life slip away with every step. Her touch was a burning reminder of all that I'd lost. We stopped beside Father, opposite the woman in green. Another woman and a tall young man have joined her. I couldn't bear to see their faces and keep my eyes cast down, wishing the day would end. Father began to speak in his formal voice, devoid of emotion, a business deal concluded. A tear escaped, burning a hot path down my face to the tip of my nose before it fell. Others followed, falling like pieces of my life crashing to the earth.

"Amelie of Delphiope, formerly Thena, daughter of Anlan. I present Millie, your daughter placed in our care for these past sixteen years and now returned to you." he said.

"Rush of Thena, son of Anlan. I thank you for your care of my daughter and her return to me on this, her sixteenth anniversary. Your obligations are now complete." Amelie turned to look at Thea, "Thea of Thena, daughter of Anlan, I thank you for nurturing and mothering my child for the past sixteen years. Your responsibilities are also now complete." The formal words were spoken like a woman of Thena, without emotion. *She didn't want me; I heard that in her words*. More tears escaped, following the others. *I was to be abandoned by the only parents I knew and unwanted by the woman who birthed me. What hope was there? The pain in my heart was unbearable, aching and empty.*

"Millie of Thena, daughter of Anlan. I welcome your return. Your given name when you were born is Tilda. From this day forward, your formal name will be Tilda Millie. Informally, you may choose what name to use." There was a softness in her voice. I couldn't look at her, I didn't want to see her pity.

"Orlan of Delphiope, son of Dorcana, I present my daughter Tilda Millie. You and Tilda Millie were named on the Promisary Agreement registered with the National Introductions Agency according to Anlan custom." *He must hate being landed with me, the unwanted child.* Mother's hand pressed discretely on my back. I was supposed to look at him, but why should I? I didn't choose to be here.

"Tilda Millie of Thena, daughter of Anlan, I greet you. Today is a great day, a new beginning for us both." His voice was soft and gentle; he sounded kind. Mother leaned down and whispered in my ear. She wanted me to look up, but I couldn't. I was supposed to say something, but the words stuck in my throat. Mother straightened and, with a squeeze of my arm, spoke the words for me. A small part of me heard the pain in her voice and the tremor that betrayed her emotion.

"Orlan of Delphiope, I greet you this day on behalf of Tilda Millie. Today will indeed mark a new beginning for you both."

Finally, it was over, but the woman in green was still talking. She moved forward as Father turned.

"Rush, I know this is not the time, but perhaps we could..." She stopped mid-sentence, leaving the words unsaid. I couldn't move. My feet were rooted to the spot, and my legs were as immovable as great tree trunks. It was Mother who stepped forward and spoke quickly before she left. I was left alone, beyond tears, totally lost. I wanted to run, but my legs wouldn't move. Finally, the betrayal was complete. My hateful body had betrayed me as everyone else had. *I wish the ground would open and let it entomb me.* As the moment expanded, the woman approached me and put an arm around my shoulders. I hated myself as I leaned into her; my strength had left me, and I had nothing left.

"Today must be tough for you. Why not come home and have a cup of coffee with me? I know coffee won't solve anything, but it might taste good." The last bit was said as if she was smiling, but I could only see her feet. Pretty pink toenails peeked out from elegant bright green shoes. I couldn't reply, but I didn't resist as she gently put pressure on my shoulders, and we walked away from that place.

Part 2 – Twenty Years Earlier

4

Thea

Father Jonca took me aside when I was fourteen and explained the Bloodline Laws and the Promisary Agreement they had made for me. The boy named in it came from Thena, a good family, but according to Thenan tradition, I would only learn his name when we met. At first, I was frustrated. I wanted to know the boy's name. Later, as time went by, it faded into the background. Mostly, I forgot all about it and threw myself into school life. I became friends with a boy from Delphiope who hoped to become a healer like me. We discussed the future and my Promisary Agreement and planned to run away together at the end of the school year, just before my sixteenth anniversary. We would then have our school certificates, enabling us to attend an academie. We planned to go to another district, apply to an Academie away from Thena, and study healing. How naive we were; from the moment I was told of the Promisary Agreement, my family began to watch me. I didn't realise initially, but it all changed six months before my sixteenth anniversary.

Dylen and I had arranged to meet at the lake near our house. It was a nice place to walk and have a picnic, and we looked forward to a lovely afternoon together as we had done many times before. I was bringing the food, and Dylen would bring something to drink and a sweet treat. Father Jonca had begun to pressure me to stop seeing Dylen, so I'd told him I was meeting a friend for a picnic. When I reached our usual spot by the lake, I spread out the blanket and cushions for us to sit on while I waited. It was a lovely, warm, sunny day, and I looked forward to our picnic. When Dylen arrived, he was flushed and had so much pain in his eyes. Something was wrong, and I filled with dread as I stood to hug him. When he pulled away, he tearfully told me he was stopped by someone on his way to meet me. The man told him to stop seeing me and threatened his future as a Healer if he saw me again after today. We hugged and cried together but couldn't see how to change anything. Our only option was to run now, and so we did. We quickly crossed the parkland and turned towards Cawsal. We knew we could disappear in Cawsal. People there would help us hide from family and friends until it all blew over, as it surely would. We heard them when we reached the main crossroads about to take the road towards Cawsal. Footsteps came fast from behind us, and a conveyance was approaching from Delphiope.

We ran on, and at the same time, I saw a friend of my parents coming along the Cawsal road. He was asking me to stop. I sighed with relief, feeling sure he would help us, but I couldn't have been more wrong. We had forgotten the footsteps behind us as we slowed to let the conveyance pass. I felt arms close around my waist, and I was pushed into the conveyance headfirst. I landed in a heap on the floor and heard the door slam shut. After scrambling up and sitting on the seat, I realised I was alone and looked out the window for Dylen. To my horror, I watched him pushed to the ground by a group of thugs who surrounded him and began to beat him. I screamed through the closed conveyance window and begged them to stop. The door was locked, and I was trapped. The family friend, who was now seated beside the driver in the front of the conveyance, said I would be taken home. I didn't understand why he wouldn't help me. Tears poured down my cheeks as I banged the windows with my fists to no avail. I pulled at the door latch again, but it didn't move. I was trapped. My panic rose as my poor, broken heart thumped, trying to break free of its confines. I'd had a recurring nightmare where I was trapped and couldn't escape. I always woke covered in sweat before discovering where I was or how I got there. Now I knew the moment was here and now. I was trapped and powerless in the place of my nightmares.

When we reached Father Jonca's house, I was hoarse from screaming. I lapsed into silent sobs, my arms wrapped tightly around myself. I was trapped in that nightmare; it didn't feel real. I was taken to my room and told to stay there. I fell into a dark place and lay curled up on my bed. Father Jonca and Mother Lib spent a long time trying to talk to me, but I didn't want to listen. I stayed in bed for days. I refused to eat and just took sips of water. I felt betrayed and heartbroken. There were so many more emotions I couldn't find words for. Eventually, I left my room. I was told life had to go on, so I did my best. Later, although I asked, I never found out what happened to Dylen after that night. I didn't even know if he was alive, although I couldn't allow myself to think he wasn't. After those early days, the deep feelings became a constant pain that never healed. I resigned myself to my fate, promising that one day when the opportunity arose, I would take back my life. Then I would try to find out what happened to Dylen. Somebody must know.

5

Thea

I met the boy from my Promisary Agreement on my sixteenth anniversary. We were introduced at the National Introductions Agency (NIA) according to tradition. After the formal greetings, we went inside the imposing building. There, we were told how the Introduction Process would proceed. So much detail was given, and it went straight over my head. There were formal steps to help us get to know each other and lessons in our responsibilities as adults in Thenan society, as man and wife and later as parents. Rush was a good-looking boy who took me to dances, for walks and the theatre. He always wanted the best for me, and I enjoyed his company. Later, I even grew to love him in a way, although not like my love for Dylen.

After completing the requirements of the National Introductions Agency (NIA), a date was set for our wedding. We were married on my twentieth anniversary in a big ceremony. His father, Max, was very high in the Legal Octon and scared me. I always felt he looked down on me as inferior, not good enough for his son. Rush's mother, Zillah, was a stern woman who permanently looked as if there was a bad smell under her nose, and I always felt it might be me. Rush's parents gave us a beautiful house as a wedding gift. Zillah helped me find a housekeeper to look after the house and help with the children when they came along. We were expected to have children early in our marriage. My duty as a wife was to bear the next generation while I was young and strong. Sadly, it seemed the Gods had other ideas because despite the act being performed, there was no swelling in my belly. I didn't enjoy those nights; behaving in such a way felt disgusting and unladylike. Yet, all women who bore children had gone through this act, so I accepted Rush's attentions and hid my revulsion behind smiles and kisses. I prayed to the Singular God (God of the Singularity faith in Thena) every week at the temple and at home daily. For good measure, I also secretly prayed to the God Sange (God of life in the Quartive Faith). Strangely, I've always felt an inexplicable pull towards the Quartive Faith. I hoped one of the Gods would hear my prayer.

Almost a year after we were married, our prayers were answered in quite an unexpected way. Rush told me a young woman from a good family could not raise her baby and would like a good family to raise her child. He knew how much I wanted to be a mother and have our own children. He thought this might be a way to start our family. We talked it over, and even though it felt as if I was giving in and admitting my failure, I couldn't deny this child a home. Zillah and Max brought her to us the day she was born. She was a tiny mite, but I loved her from the moment I saw her. The soft, smooth face, little rosebud mouth and eyes with delicate brows drawn above. I took the fragile bundle in my arms and counted her fingers and toes in amazement. She was so tiny I was afraid I would drop her; I had no idea what to do. It was then that Zillah and Max come to stay with us. Zillah was fantastic, and I quickly learned how to feed and clean the babe. Rush named her Millie. According to tradition, we found a boy of similar age who was an excellent bloodline match for Millie. Together with the boy's parents, we registered the Promisary Agreement at the NIA in Thena. When Millie reached her sixteenth anniversary, she would meet the boy at the NIA just as we had done. Millie grew into a delightful child with a mass of dark curls and deep green/brown eyes that twinkled with mischief. Zillah disapproved of her curly hair; it wasn't a desirable trait for Thenan children, and neither were her green/brown eyes. She became increasingly harsh with Millie, as did Max.

When Millie was nearly six months old and beginning to crawl, I discovered I was finally pregnant. It was the most amazing feeling as the child developed inside me, and my belly began to grow. The butterfly fluttering was magical as life inside made its presence known. Rush was so excited when he first felt the baby kick. I'd never seen him so overwhelmed by emotion. He was like a child with a new toy and kept returning to me to lay his head on my belly. We felt so close in those days. Millie was too young to understand she would soon have a little brother or sister. Even so, we tried to prepare her for the new arrival as best we could. When the wisewoman, Mother Plumb, arrived, Zillah took Millie to their rooms at the back of the house. I'm afraid, even after all the preparation with Zillah and Mother Plumb. *I was terrified when the time came. How would the babe ever leave my body?* My body struggled for what felt like a lifetime as it tried to expel the babe. I thought it would go on forever. I didn't notice time passing except for the increasing fear that I might not be able to give birth to the child. I was so scared, but Mother Plumb's calming tones eventually helped me trust nature. I relaxed enough to let my body do its work.

I was overjoyed when it was finally over, and I was presented with the tiny creature. Rush was too, when I told him he had a son, we had a son. The months that followed were full of feeds and changes of napkins. Millie was fascinated by him and wanted to be wherever he was. She was a little clumsy, as all toddlers were, and needed gentle guidance as she got to know her new brother. Rush named our son Accam, Cam as he became known. He had soft, expressive brown eyes and rich dark brown hair. Millie and Cam were close and went everywhere together. I was so pleased for Millie after such a difficult start. Two years later, we welcomed Elia to our family. Millic and Cam adored their little sister. As Elia began to walk, Millie showed the first signs of jealousy and irritation. As they got older, she asked for a lock on her door to stop Elia from entering when she wasn't there. Following a particularly distressing incident when Elia tore a book Millie had been reading, Rush agreed. A lock was put on her door, and she was given the key with strict instructions. It was only to be locked when she left the room.

Over the next eight years, I lost three babes, which was the most awful time of my life. I felt such a failure even though we had two beautiful babes and Millie. I was reluctant to keep trying; the heartbreak was so hard to bear, but Rush felt we should. We were expected to have a large family and were still young. I began to feel as if I was just a baby machine. Although we only had three children, our small family felt complete. As the children grew older, we enjoyed spending time together and took family holidays together, travelling around Thena. We went on outings to nature reserves with animals of the hills, mountains and plains. Rush and I agreed that children should learn about the country and district they lived in. When I finally became pregnant for the third time, I knew something was different. I seemed to expand at such a rate. Mother Plumb came with the Healer, and together, they examined me, confirming I was carrying twins. She visited me frequently to ensure everything was progressing as it should. It was a very long pregnancy, and I was tired for much of it. Thank goodness for Zillah and Max, who cared for the other children and allowed me to rest. Millie and Cam had started school, and Millie was doing very well. Cam was a little slower at his lessons. He also immediately took a dislike to one of the boys in his class. It was a while before we finally got to the root of the problem. Cam had been placed next to the boy, but he was from Cawsal, and his family lived on a farm. The boy always smelled of the farm, and Cam disliked the smell intensely. He was a very fussy child where smells were concerned. After talking with the class tutor, it was agreed to discretely move the boy to another seat away from Cam.

Although it was good to have Zillah and Max on hand to help with the children, I wished I had my house to myself. They seemed particularly hard on Millie, for some reason, and always implied she was up to no good. After the twins, Edi and Jami arrived, they felt their presence was justified again, and so it was in a way. They took on the twins, and apart from the time I fed them, I never had to worry about them. It was frustrating that the baby cuddles and special times I'd enjoyed with the other children were taken from me.

Zillah developed a habit of silently stalking the halls and corridors. She seemed to seek out the rooms where one of the older children or I might be trying to steal a few minutes of quiet time and eavesdropping on conversations. Their continued presence became a constant source of argument between Rush and I. He naturally defended his parents, but eventually, even he noticed their secretive behaviour. They listened to private conversations, even those between Rush and I. Our arguments became increasingly angry, and Rush exploded into terrible rages. At first, it was furniture and walls that felt his wrath. Later, I also felt his anger. He was always careful to ensure my face was never marked. I must look my best in public with no blemish or mark that might cause the wrong question to be asked. In truth, it was known such things happened, and women who appeared in public with a visible mark were whispered about in drawing rooms across Thena.

Part 3 – Three months earlier

6

Thea

The months before Millie's sixteenth anniversary were an anxious time. She still didn't know she had a Promisary Agreement and had no idea she would meet the boy on her anniversary. I had no idea how she would react, but I knew she was sweet on a boy from Pollo, which would make things difficult. She even told me he would be quite a good match. His father was a Professor of Healing at the most prestigious hospital in Pollo. I tried to discuss it with Rush a few months ago, but he wouldn't entertain changing anything. The match we had made was political, of course, to gain the support of a Councillor from the Legal Octon. The Councillor concerned was highly influential and would further strengthen Max's position. It would also help when Max retired as Legal Councillor and Head of the High Council since Rush would be the natural successor to Max. Unfortunately, support from the Healing Octon didn't carry the weight that the Legal Octon would.

Rush thought I didn't know about the political move. He often underestimated how much I knew; keeping it that way was advantageous. Poor Millie wouldn't understand these political manoeuvres, of course. After all, who would want to be a political pawn? I was disappointed when Rush told me of the match, and I had guessed the reason behind it even then. I wished we could prepare her; it would be such a shock, but Rush had been clear that she must not hear until her anniversary. Now, though, I must find her an Introduction dress and shoes. A traditional Introduction dress has a particular style, although minor variations were permitted to reflect changing fashions. In Central Thena, two shops provided ready-made dresses, and this was where I would look. I would have preferred to have a dress made for Millie, but it wasn't possible under the circumstances. So, a readymade dress would have to do, but it would still be of high quality. I knew Zillah would have something to say, but since they put us in this ridiculous situation, there was no choice. Furthermore, I was sure Max would be behind the decision not to tell Millie of the Promisary Agreement until her anniversary, although Rush never admitted that. I would go into town this week for the dress, shoes, etc. and, of course, something appropriate for me. My wardrobe was so limited while I was heavily pregnant.

A few days later, I took a conveyance into town. Central Thena has tidy streets with shops of a similar nature located together. Each shop had a sign outside stating the name and opening hours in a standard format. There was a hierarchy of shops, with the more prestigious shops allowed more window display space than those of less prestige. It made shopping and finding what you were looking for easier without travelling too far. Occasionally, I shop in Delph, the primary city of Delphiope, but the shops were scattered and there was no clear plan or design. Shopping was much more laborious although the chance of discovering new and unusual shops was always a possibility. That reason alone made the trip worthwhile. In Central Thena, it was easy. Tailors, seamstresses and shops to buy readymade clothing were all together in the Silk Quarter. Nearby was Cotton Bolt Row, where quality sheets and other items for the house were found. There was another smaller Furniture row close by for furnishing and upholstery services. All the shops you needed for stitching homeware, clothing or furnishing were in one place. It made sense.

The conveyance stopped near the shop I wanted to go to. 'Sarte Formale-Y' was the 'Sarte Formale' young person's department. I opened the heavy, dark wood door and entered the light, airy shop. Formal wear was grouped by occasion and, of course, by gender. In the middle of the shop floor were stands of cream dresses in traditional styles for Introductions. Some were decorated with lace and beads; others sparkle with gems. I knew none of these would be suitable for Millie. She needed no adornments to look beautiful. With her slight figure and dark curly hair, I was looking for something simple yet elegant. I explained what I wanted to the assistant, who led me to a stand with dresses with less adornments.

There were simple cotton dresses, but although the styling was good, the fabric was too simple for a Thena child of our status. The following rail had dresses that were too fussy with frills and lace. The third rail of dresses took my breath away. The first dress I saw was simple with a fitted bodice, modestly styled. It was made from beautiful water silk flowing from the bodice to just below the knee. It was exactly what I wanted, and they had one in the correct size. I bought simple cream flat shoes in matching water silk and a pretty silk floral clip stiffened to show petals. It would look perfect in her dark, curly hair. The bill was charged to our account, and the outfit would be delivered tomorrow. I was relieved my task had been accomplished so quickly. I hoped Millie would accept the dress and shoes when the time came. Now, to find a dress for myself for such a significant occasion, generous enough for my child-filled belly.

A few doors down was Silk Emporta, where my favourite dressmaker worked. Luckily, she was available and showed me some lovely fabric in a pretty pale green/blue water silk. I chose a smart pattern with a lightly fitted bodice but enough material to flow around me, which was perfect. She would make it up and bring it to the house for a final fitting in a few days.

Millie was so excited and full of plans to celebrate the end of school and her sixteenth anniversary with friends. I tried to prepare her, even suggested we might be planning a celebration for her, but she would have none of it. Even Rush was unable to sway her from her plans. In the end, I suggested they wait until later in the afternoon. It would give us time to go to the NIA in the morning and meet her friends later. I knew how important her friends were to her. It would be hard enough when she found out she had a Promisary Agreement. It might be good for her to have a chance to let off steam later. I knew too well that she had a fiery temper like Rush, although she didn't lash out, thankfully. We must carefully plan that morning to avoid confrontation and allow the essential formalities to occur.

7

Thea

It was a bright, sunny morning five days before Millie's sixteenth anniversary. I was lying in bed thinking as I put off the task of hauling my body out of bed. I didn't like this part of pregnancy; it really was too much. Pressing the bell, I waited for Suzi to help me rise. She worked with Mother Plumb and had come to stay with us until it was time for the birth when Mother Plumb would return. Her smiling face popped round the doorway, and she greeted me as usual.

"Good morning, Mrs Thea. How are we this morning? It's a lovely day already." she bustled in and began opening drawers and closets, selecting garments for me.

"Oh, I don't know, Suzi. I feel quite exhausted just thinking about rising." I said with a smile. Suzi came over and helped me sit on the edge of the bed while she presented the selected garments. I chose a pretty floral dress that was simple yet elegant and perfect for my planned talk with Rush. With Suzi's help, I bathed and dressed, then coiled my midnight-black hair into my signature chignon style. I had settled on this style years ago and could arrange it in minutes. I needed little makeup with the pregnancy bloom, but I always made an effort. Finally, with a squirt of my favourite perfume, 'Luninos', I was ready to greet the family.

"Thank you, Suzi. I don't know how I'd manage without you. Are the children up?"

“Yes, Mrs Thea, they are. The twins were early risers today. The older three are already at the table and ready for their studies. The conveyance will arrive for them in half an hour as usual.” Suzi knew what was happening in the house better than any maid. She seemed to have eyes and ears everywhere.

“Well, I had better join them at the table. Is Mr Rush with them, or has he left for work already?” I wanted to catch Rush. I was kicking myself for not rising earlier.

“No, Mrs Thea, he left early for the Legal Council offices today. He didn't say if he would return before the evening.” She hadn't managed to catch him either, I thought. She knew I liked to know when he might return and usually tried to ask him.

“Never mind,” I sighed as I rose and walked to the door. “I'd better greet the family.”

Later that evening, I finally had the opportunity to talk with Rush after supper. He was relaxed and cheerful throughout our meal, and I guessed it had been a good day. It meant I had a better chance of catching him in the right mood to discuss Millie's Introduction. We retired to our private parlour for coffee. It was a cosy room where we would be undisturbed.

“Rush, would you mind if we talk about Millie's Introduction?” I looked over, hoping I wouldn’t see the shadow cross his face. His face was relaxed and calm as he looked at me over his coffee cup. I allowed myself to relax a little. Perhaps it would be OK.

“Of course, what should we talk about?” he said before taking another sip of coffee.

“Did you know Millie has been making plans for her anniversary?”

“I did hear something, but she must know we will have plans. Have you spoken to hear about that?”

“I have. She's quite determined to meet and celebrate with her friends...” I broke off. I wasn’t sure if Rush knew about Yan, and was this the right time to bring it up? But it was too late. He had caught my hesitation and asked.

"What is it?" I took a deep breath. "There's a boy in her class at school that she's sweet on..."

"Is that all? It can't be serious. I've spoken to her about Promisary Agreements; she'll know she has one. It's expected for someone of her status." His words were in the same pleasant tone, but there was a sharpness underlying it now.

"I don't think she does. We haven't specifically told her. Isn't there a way to prepare her?" there it was. A shadow flashed across his face, and a hint of dark red began to rise on his neck.

"She'll find out soon enough. It's out of our hands. You know that." His words were sharp and staccato.

"I wish you'd tell me why we must keep this from her. It seems so cruel."

"There are things you don't need to know. There were conditions when Millie came to us. I agreed to keep to them, and so we must do as we agreed." The dark red was flashing on his cheeks now, and I knew I shouldn't push any further, but I had to continue now I'd come this far.

"Rush, could we make a compromise?"

"No!" he snarled, rising from his chair and approaching me. He roughly pulled me from my chair and shoved me to the door, and his fingers dug painfully into my arms.

"You must be tired, dear. Go to bed, and don't worry about things that are not your responsibility." he spat the words at me as he pushed me out of the room and slammed the door behind me. Staggering, I reached for the hall table to stop myself from falling, but it was too delicate, and we tumbled to the floor. I lay with broken pieces of the table, digging into my arm and back. There was no sound from the parlour, but he must have heard my cry and the crash as we fell. Tears pricked my eyes, and I tipped up my head. What was the point of tears? It wouldn't help anyone.

Slowly, I rolled onto my side and then to my hands and knees. It was awkward and painful as I knelt on broken pieces of the table. Gradually, I managed to rise onto my feet and using the wall, and stood shakily. I don’t think there’s any damage to me or the baby, although I can’t say the same for the table. I’d have to get that discretely cleared away. With a sigh, I slowly moved the pieces to the side with my foot. It would be OK to leave them for a while and return later. No one else comes down this corridor unless invited in the evening. I made my way towards the stairs, using the wall to support myself. All the time, I was thinking about how to explain things to anyone I might see. Fortunately, I managed to get to my room before meeting Suzi. She’d heard me coming up and had come to help me prepare for bed.

“Oh, my Mrs Thea!” she exclaimed when she saw me. “Whatever happened?” concern was written all over her face as she took in my appearance.

“I stupidly fell against that little table in the corridor by the parlour, and we tumbled to the ground together. I fared better than the table, it would seem.” I said, giving what I hoped was a wry smile.

“Well, I don't know. You have a nasty tear in your dress just here,” she said, touching my side, and I winced.

“Ah, that must have been a table leg, perhaps.”

“There are cuts and grazes on your arms and legs, too,” I hadn’t realised that either.

“Come now, let’s get you cleaned up and into bed,” she said briskly. She was no fool and well aware that there were secrets in families. She helped me bathe and dress for bed. There would be bruises in the morning, but at least the baby was okay, which was more important.

8

Thea

The big day was tomorrow, and I was a bag of nerves. I could not imagine how Millie would react when she heard about the Promisary Agreement. She would be upset, angry she hadn't told before. I had no answers; only Rush had the answers, but I was sure she would get none from him. Although Rush would never say so, I was sure his father was behind it all. Max was so vindictive and cruel, but I couldn't begin to guess what he had against poor Millie. As Suzi helped me dress, my mind circled, trying to find the right words for Millie. I was wearing a green water silk dress that flowed over my shape without billowing like the sail on a ship. The green clip I put in my hair to secure the chignon matched perfectly.

When I entered the kitchen, Rush was seated behind his newspaper. The twins were sitting with Max and Zillah at the far end of the table. There was no sign of the other three yet, which was hardly surprising. None of them were early risers, even on a school day. Greeting the twins and their grandparents, I took my seat near Rush. I poured myself a cup of herbal tea and took some fresh fruit slices to have with oat porridge. Eating oat porridge these days was old-fashioned, but I liked the comforting familiarity. Adding the fruit made an excellent start to the day. Shortly afterwards, Cam shuffled in, followed by Elia. Cam hated mornings and was never fully awake until halfway through the day. Elia was growing up fast; it seemed only yesterday when she took her first steps, now she was quite the young lady. She might even be taller than Millie. Her beautiful dark hair, with its hint of lilac, was straight and sleek. It was unusual for a child to have a touch of lilac in their hair, but it was very becoming on her. Like Cam, she usually struggled in the morning, but today, she was awake and smiling.

"Good morning, Cam and Elia," I said as they sat.

"Morning," replied Elia.

Followed by, "...ning." from Cam.

"Speak properly, can't you." Rush snapped briefly, lowering his paper to scowl at Cam.

Cam didn't respond, but as the paper rose, he turned and rolled his eyes at Elia, and they stifled a giggle. The gentle sound of spoons on china bowls resumed, and we descended into the usual quiet of breakfast time. Only the twins made a noise as they played with their food and chatted to Zillah.

A little while later, I heard footsteps descend the stairs. They paused at the front door, and then Millie appeared in the doorway; a mass of dark curls topped her slight figure. She scanned the post in her hand. She was hoping for a letter from Yan, I thought. Millie walked around the table, distributing the post. When she arrived at the seat between Rush and I she handed me my gardening brochure and passed several official letters to Rush. It seemed she was in luck. A letter remained in her hand as she took her seat. She propped the letter on the salt pot in front of her. It was rather fancy handwriting for a boy, more like a woman's hand.

Millie sipped her coffee as she studied the envelope before taking the letter opener and quickly slitting it open. She slid her fingers inside as I glanced over and pulled out a white card. Then my heart stopped, and I felt sick as I saw what was on the card. *It couldn't be, it can't be. Not after all this time...* My breath caught. There was a letter inside. *What if it was a letter with the things Rush had refused to tell me?*

I stretched out my hand and asked for the card. I heard my voice tremble. Millie looked at me before slowly putting the card and contents into my hand. She asked what was wrong. *What can I say?* It was my worst fear. An Invitation to join the boy named in the Promisary Agreement not made by me but by her birth mother. The birth mother I had never known. Yet that handwriting was so familiar even now. She'd been so proud as she perfected the elegant looping script. *It has to be from Amelie, but how could that be?* Opening the card, I saw it was no mistake. It was from Amelie in her beautiful handwriting.

Tears filled my eyes as I placed the card on the table with the letter on top, covering it with my hand. Then I felt pressure, and through my tears, I saw Rush's hand covering mine. The pressure on my hand increased as I heard Millie ask what was happening. *The poor child had a right to know, and I wished I knew what to say.* Rush spoke before I found the words. He said we must discuss it together first, and my heart sank, but I agreed. The pressure on my hand was so great; my fingertips were turning deep red, and the pain was unbearable. The hurt in Millie's eyes was deep and raw. *Will she ever forgive us?* Rush told the older three children to go to their rooms and ordered me to his study. The hand that had painfully crushed mine closed around my fingers, grasping for the card. I scrunched my fingers tightly around the letter and let him take it. *Perhaps I'll have a chance to read it. I wish I could destroy it, but I must know what it says first.* My head spun as I rose from the table and paused momentarily before walking. Holding my head high, I waited by his study door. Despite my tears, I would not let him see how much it had affected me.

In the locked study, we sat facing each other across the desk; each lost in the past for a moment. Then Rush spoke, his voice low and measured.

"This does not need to change anything. She's dead to the family. She..."

"Is she, is Amelie, Millie's mother?" My words burst from my lips unbidden as tears spilled down my cheeks. I was so hurt and angry.

"Yes, she..." he began, but I interrupted.

"I can't believe you didn't tell me; sixteen years and you never told me."

"I couldn't tell you. It would have made no difference. Millie is better off not knowing." His words were soft, but his dark eyes flashed as the red stain rose on his neck.

"I don't understand. Why hide it from me?"

"There are things I cannot tell you."

"Am I so weak and untrustworthy? I am your wife, Rush. For something as important as this, you should have told me." Rage blazed through me. *I want to unleash the fury, but I'm afraid I might never regain control. It was so strong this time.*

"Enough," he moved round the desk so fast I didn't have time to think. His hands gripped my arms, fingers dug painfully into the flesh at the top. "There is no more to say. You must accept that I cannot discuss everything with you." His words were urgent. I'd expected them to be full of anger, but there was an intensity I hadn't anticipated. My anger subsided, and I sank back into the chair. As I did so, the pressure on my arms eased as he watched the fight leave me. He took the letter from my hand and returned to his chair.

"We must decide what to do," he said, his tone was softer now and more business-like. "The law's with Amelie. It's her right to make the Promisary Agreement, although I hate to admit it. I know nothing of this boy, and there's no time to investigate, which I'm sure was her intention. She wouldn't want any challenge to her choice."

"Can we deny receiving the Invitation? It wasn't a delivery that required acknowledgement. It arrived with the regular post."

"No, I don't think we can." his voice was resigned. His legal knowledge was usually a bonus, but at times like these, it was a curse.

"How will we tell Millie that her birth mother is your sister? She doesn't even know you have a sister. She thinks we are her parents."

"These are tough questions."

"But when would she have been told? Her sixteenth is tomorrow." My voice rose, and I couldn't help it. *When would the poor child have found out the truth?* I screamed in my head.

"It's out of my hands," he shouted, then a little quieter. "The legal tape is extensive."

"I wondered when the legal tape would come in. It's so convenient to hide behind a wall of legal tape. Is this your father's doing*?" I'm so angry at the unfairness of it all.* Deep inside, the fury fed off my anger and began to stir.

"You cannot ask me about this. I'm asking you not to. It's enough that my parents are in our house." I knew the truth then in those words; his father was the architect behind everything. They inhabited our house, spying on us to ensure their plan was followed.

"Millie has seen the invitation and the letters, although I don't know how much she read."

"It changes everything. I'll tell Father after the NIA tomorrow when it's done. He knows the law; he'll know it's her right. Now, we must tell Millie." I'm surprised at the change of direction. *Can Millie be told today now? How will she react? I can't bear to think about that. What will his father do when he knows the truth is out? That worried me more.*

"What about the other children? Can we tell them?"

"We can talk about the Promisary Agreement we made for Millie. Hopefully, they won't ask about the Invitation Millie received."

"Cam and Elia will guess there's more going on." There will be some tough conversations over the coming days.

"I don't like this any more than you do, Thea, but it's not the time for discussion. We have to prepare for tomorrow."

"I've made arrangements for her Introductions wardrobe, as you know. Do we have a conveyance scheduled?"

"The conveyance was scheduled for midday to give maximum visibility to the match. Let's travel later now and avoid the crowds." he said.

"I agree. Was the match with Luca political?" I didn't expect an answer, and I was surprised when he spoke.

"Luca was my choice, but Father supported it. Luca's father, Anton, would have been a good ally for Father. I don't know what will happen now."

"I might have guessed. These poor kids are just pawns in the games of power. Have we learned nothing from history?" My heart ached for the children treated like possessions and nothing more.

"This is not the time to challenge the way things are done. It would not do for the High Council, or Father, to hear rumour of such views." He was right; now wasn't the time with his father under our roof. Would we ever be rid of their interference?

"I understand," I said with a sigh. What else could I say? He went to the door, and I heard him call her name, then her footsteps on the stairs. It would be a difficult conversation, and I wasn't looking forward to it. I hoped Rush could hold his temper when Millie lost hers, as I'm sure she would.

It was every bit as painful as I thought it would be. Poor Millie was devastated, broken-hearted. I couldn't imagine how I would ever regain her trust. After she returned to her room, we sat silently for a while. Slowly, Rush stood. He seemed to have aged in the hours since we rose this morning. His head and shoulders were hunched over like a broken man as he approached my chair. He took my hands gently in his, and we drew strength from each other as he helped me to my feet.

"You look tired. It's been a traumatic morning. Why don't you rest for a while? We'll talk later." I nodded; he was right. I was drained emotionally. We walked from the study together, and I retired to my room to rest.

I woke late in the afternoon, and the sun was already low in the sky. *Why hadn't Suzi called me for lunch?* I wonder. Perhaps Rush gave instruction not to disturb me. There were times when I saw a different side to him. Which was the true Rush? I wondered. Downstairs, I found Cam and Elia in the drawing room. I picked up my book and sat in my favourite chair, flipping to the page with my bookmark. I didn't really want to read, but it gave me a reason to be here with my children. Perhaps they'd hoped to find me here. I often read in the afternoon. It was Cam who broke the silence.

"What's happened? Why's Millie in her room?" his voice was full of concern, and I could see from Elia's pale face that he spoke for them both.

"Do you remember hearing about Promisary Agreements at school?" They nodded. "Elia, your father will talk to you when you are a little older. The same is true for you, Cam. Today, Millie received an Invitation to meet the boy from her Promisary Agreement. She will meet him at the National Introductions Agency tomorrow."

"Why was she so upset? She knew about the arrangement, didn't she?" he said.

"She does, but as you know, she's also fond of Yan, the boy from school. She's upset she has a Promisary Agreement and is unlikely to be able to see Yan again. It's unfortunate, but as you both know, it's the price we pay in Thena for carrying Anlan blood in our veins."

"Why do we still have to follow such old-fashioned laws? What would happen if we didn't have a Promisary Agreement?" I understood how he felt. It was entirely justified, but I must set the example for now.

"I'm sorry, but as a senior family in Thena and of Anlan heritage, there are laws we must follow, as you know." My words felt formal and false.

"That's rubbish, and you know it, Mother. We should set an example by eliminating these antiquated laws. No other district has them. Some districts allow free choice, and a couple may marry for love or not at all as they choose."

"Cam, that's dangerous talk. You must not speak of such things. Walls have ears." *Were Max or Zillah nearby, they always seem to be where they aren't wanted.* I held my breath, but no one appeared in the doorway.

"Walls don't have ears, Mother, this is our home. We don't have any spies here unless it's Father spying for the Legal Council," he said sarcastically.

"Walls can have ears, Cam. We must always be on our guard." I warned, "Millie will go to the National Introductions Agency tomorrow. She will start the formal Introduction process straight away. Why don't you talk to her this evening and explain our conversation? She might be pleased to see you. Suzi and I will be busy getting her ready tomorrow morning, and there may not be time to talk."

The following day, Rush and I had a quiet breakfast together. He told me his father had found Millie in the kitchen during the night. She said she was just after a glass of water, but he saw her bag and thought she may have been trying to run away. It broke my heart to think she would run away, and I said so. Rush was quiet and non-committal. The morning passed slowly, and I moved from room to room, trying to keep myself busy. Millie stayed in her room and wouldn't come out. Finally, the time came to begin her preparation. She needed to bathe and look her best. It wouldn't be easy, and I had asked Suzi to help. Millie liked Suzi and, under any other circumstances, would have loved to be pampered. Today, I was expecting her to be difficult and uncooperative. We heard the music thumping from the top of the stairs. It was deafening. Rush must be able to hear it, too, but perhaps he was giving her a little leniency today.

I knocked firmly on the door and called, "Millie, may we come in? It's time for you to get ready."

There was no reply. I guessed she was pretending not to hear me. I left Suzi in the doorway as I went over to the bed. She was lying with her back to me.

"It's time to get up, Millie. You need to get ready." I put a hand on her shoulder, but she shrugged it off roughly. She wrapped the bedding more tightly around herself.

"Please, Millie, don't make this any harder." she sniffed but didn't move.

"I don't want to force you. It'll be better if you accept what must be," my voice trembled.

"I don't want to. Why should I do anything for you when you've lied to me all my life?" came a small voice full of pain.

"I'm so sorry. Until yesterday, I didn't know who your birth mother was."

"Like I'm supposed to believe that?" she sneered, then sniffed again.

"There's a lot I don't know, and even more I can't explain. It's not easy being a high-ranking family in Thena. Being of the Bloodline on top makes it even more complicated. Please, believe me, I do understand."

"Huh, I wish I could let all the stupid Anlan blood flow out of my veins. I'd be free then. Free of the stupid Bloodline Laws and free of this family." she cried miserably. I sat beside her on the bed and gently pulled her into my arms. She let me hold her as she wept, and my heart ached for her.

"I do understand. My life isn't the life I imagined when I was your age. After your father and I married, the expected child didn't arrive. When you came along, it was a miracle, and I honestly thought we were giving you a good home. I've always loved and treasured you as my daughter." I kissed her tousled hair as I gently rocked her.

"How can I do this when I love Yan?" she said. Suzi appeared with a handkerchief, which Millie took and blew her nose loudly.

"Talk with the boy. If you agree the match isn't right, it can be dissolved. It doesn't happen very often, but it is permitted."

"Really?" she sounded disbelieving.

"Yes, if you both agree. No boy will want to force you to marry them if you don't want to."

"So, I can say no when we get there, then come home?" she sounded hopeful.

"It's not quite that simple. You'll need to meet the boy and show you have allowed enough time to get to know him. But it is possible. Trust me."

"So, I spend a few days with him, then we say it won't work, and I can come home. Right?"

"Something like that." Sitting up for the first time, she pulled away from me, "How about bathing and getting yourself ready?"

"I still don't see why I have to go through all this," she said as she rose from her bed. She went to the bathroom, followed by Suzi, and I sighed with relief. At least I'd won that battle. There was still the dress, and I feared that would be another battle. *I hope she remembers the formal words I taught her last night. Even if she does, will she say them when the time comes*?

A little later, Suzi entered the drawing room where I sat and said Millie was bathed and ready to dress. She was lying on her bed again, wrapped in a towel. I could hear her crying as I came into the room and went over to her.

"Millie, you need to get dressed?" she asked again if she could wear her jeans and T-shirt. I repeated what I had said before about a formal dress. Eventually, she rolled over and stood, kicking her heel against the bed. I looked away as she picked up her nightshirt and wiped her nose and face on it. It was disgusting and designed to irritate, I'm sure. I said nothing. Suzi could take it for washing after we left. I showed her the dress I had over my arm.

"It's a traditional Introduction dress, and I have some shoes for you, too." Finally, it seemed like the wind had left her sails, and she sagged before quietly saying OK. She dropped the towel from around her, and Suzi scooped it up, laying the clean clothes on the bed beside her.

After she was dressed in fresh underclothes, I slipped the dress over her and watched it flow around her body and legs. It was perfect. I caught her give a slight swish of the skirt before she remembered herself. I laid the shoes before her, and she slipped her feet into them. Suzi passed the hairbrush to me, and I brushed her hair until her curls shone. Finally, I took the pretty clip and secured a section of hair above her right ear. Turning her towards me, I looked at her. She was lovely. It would be perfect if it weren't for her gloomy face. I escorted her downstairs and out to the conveyance. We sat together in the back, side by side. She'd retreated deep inside herself and moved as if sleepwalking. A shell of herself, all animation was gone. My heart broke again for her as I took in the depth of her misery. Rush sat silently in front. There were no words that could touch our emotions today.

The conveyance pulled into the bay when we reached the tall, elaborate gates of the National Introductions Agency. The driver helped me out before helping Millie from the vehicle. I checked her dress and hair, giving her a final once-over before I looked up. Rush joined us, and then I saw what he was wearing. He's wearing funeral black! How humiliating, how could he? Poor Millie, it was the ultimate insult.

9

Rush

Thea had the child all dressed up as if it were a special occasion. It was such a farce. I chose a black suit. It felt appropriate for the occasion. There was no joy in this event, only pain. Another life ruined by Laws that bound us so tightly we could barely breathe. A small part of me looked forward to seeing Amelie, though. It had been so long since I last saw her. She has done well for herself; I had followed her in secret, tracking her rise to seniority in performing arts. She was always talented, yet had she not fallen from grace, she could never have realised her dreams. For this, I was happy for her. I never forgave Father for his actions. One day, I hope I can make amends for the part I played.

When we arrived at the imposing building, which had been the beginning for Thea and I, it was with a heavy heart. Thea fluttered around Millie, tweaking her dress and re-clipping her hair. She was nervous. She loved Millie as her own and hated to see her upset. After yesterday's arguments and fury, she knew Millie didn't want this. We walked slowly towards the gates with their elegant scrollwork and lettering. It was an impressive building with its grey stonework stretching beyond the gates. Amelie was just inside the gates, elegant and beautiful in glowing jade. Perched on top of her rich chestnut hair was a sophisticated cream hat. I'd know that curly hair, anywhere, bubbling down over her shoulders, even after all these years.

She looked well, but I caught her nervous smile. We fell back on formality, wrapping our emotions in the security of its bonds. Those stupid words that trapped us in ceremony stole the day, leaving nothing but pain in their wake.

Part 4 - Sixteen years earlier

10

Amelie

I'm Amelie, and I've had fifteen anniversaries. I'm not a typical Thena girl; I have rich chestnut curly hair with too much red, not enough dark, and too bronze. To make matters worse, it's far too curly, which I like, but to be a true Thenan, I should have straight black hair. My eyes are greeny brown, neither one nor the other. Mother never fails to point out these failings as if they were things I could change. I'm quite small for a Thenan, which further compounds my failings. Thenan women should be tall and slender with glossy, straight black hair and no hint of a curl. My mother is Zillah, and my father is Maxim (although most people call him Max). I have five brothers; Rush is six years older; twins Barti and Brig are four years older; Cid is two years younger; and Max is six years younger than me. No prizes for guessing who he's named after.

My closest brothers are Rush and Cid. They are the best brothers you could wish for, although Rush has been getting very stuffy since he went into the Legal Octon. I could count on Rush if I got in trouble with Father, which was a little more often than even I could wish for. Cid and I had a lot of fun and always got into some sort of mischief, although he was too sensible to let us get into serious trouble. It wasn't difficult to trip up when there were so many silly Laws to follow in Thena, plus those stupid ancient Bloodline Laws. Father said it would reflect poorly on him and our family if we broke the law because he was Head of the High Council. I didn't see why he couldn't change the law, especially the stupid Bloodline Laws. I was supposed to be preparing to study Legal after my sixteenth anniversary. I didn't like Legal, it was so dull. I wanted to perform, to sing on the big stages across Anacadair. I loved singing. I was always singing or humming a tune to my parent's despair. Unfortunately, becoming a performer was unsuitable for a child of Thena. If you were of Anlan Bloodline, you were expected to follow one of the high-status paths: Legal, Militaria, or Healing. But I didn't care. One way or another, I would find a way to perform.

A month after my fifteenth anniversary, Father called me to his study. He said he wanted to talk about the laws to protect the Anlan Bloodline. The study was warm, and Father's voice was the right tone to float over my head while I let my thoughts drift to Kayden. Unfortunately, he noticed.

"Amelie!" he said, raising his voice, "This is important. Listen while I'm talking. It relates to your future...blah blah blah," he droned on about why Thena children couldn't just marry anyone.

"Blah blah blah...purity of the Anlan Bloodline blah blah. Parents choose a boy, Blah blah blah. …match is registered … blah blah blah." *Honestly, in this day and age, why would anyone believe it was right to arrange their child's match at birth? It was ridiculous.* Father went on and on through the most intimate details. It was so embarrassing. *I would make a deal with the devil if I could escape a minute sooner.*

Finally, after an hour, he stopped talking and looked at me. He told me I must remember everything he had said. Then, I was sent to my room to consider my responsibilities carefully. No need to ask twice, I bolted from the study and flew up to my room, shutting the door behind me. I stood with my back to the door and slowly slid to the floor, exhausted. Trying to keep half an ear on what Father was saying while dreaming about Kayden wasn't easy. Kayden was tall with gorgeous curly fair hair and was the most amazing boy I'd ever met. Like almost every girl at school, I would sell my soul to talk with him for just five minutes. His silky voice flowed like chocolate from those delicious lips, and it was intoxicating. The only slight problem was that he came from Cawsal district and was considered low-born in Thena. It doesn't matter to me, of course. All this stupid status stuff was just that, stupid. People were people, nice or nasty, rich or poor. They were all the same underneath. Regardless of Father's words, I didn't see why I couldn't choose who I met. Kayden was bright and intelligent and wanted to be a Healer. Healing was an excellent path to choose and far better than Legal. I couldn't wait 'til I could escape from Thena and live my own life. I still needed to work out the details, but I'd find a way.

To my absolute amazement, a month or so later, one of my school friends from Delphiope invited me to a party. Thena children were often excluded from party invitations. (Apparently, it avoided embarrassment when their family prevented them from attending). So, you see, I couldn't believe it when the invitation arrived, and I was even more surprised when Father said I could go. I suppose the party being held in honour of a girl whose father was a member of the High Council helped. It took me ages to decide what to wear. I also had to work out how much makeup I could get away with before I left home. Then there was what I would change into when I arrived at Gia's house and the makeup I would need to take with me to finish my look. Eventually, I settled on a greeny gold dress of water silk that brushed my knees, swirling like water as I walked. It had a fitted top showing a little cleavage with the proper undergarments. Of course, I had the right undergarments, secretly obtained when shopping with Mother. The precious package had been hidden under a loose board in my wardrobe for weeks. It was the only place I didn't think my parents knew about. The bonus was that the dress could fold into a tiny package without creasing, making it easy to hide. I dressed in a modest pink satin dress with my favourite gold drawstring bag as I left for the party in the family conveyance. My precious makeup and gold dress were tucked at the bottom of my bag underneath my wallet. On top of that, I had the permitted makeup and some handkerchiefs in case Mother checked before I went out.

When I arrived, Gia's father welcomed me and directed me to the Garden room, where Gia was greeting her guests. When I met Gia, she showed me where I could change and touch up my makeup. We'd planned everything, of course, and she'd directed me to a bathroom away from the main party area. I excused myself and headed off to change. After changing my dress, I applied the gorgeous gilded rose lip highlighter. Finally, I sprayed myself liberally with the delicious 'Heavenly!' fragrance. Folding my pink dress, I put it into my bag to put back on later before I returned home. I was pleased with the result as I caught sight of my reflection as I walked past a looking glass in the hallway. I strolled through rooms, chatting and laughing with my friends all the time, looking for Kayden.

As I walked towards the garden door, I caught sight of Kayden. He stood with two other boys near the fountain, laughing and chatting. My heart flipped, and my breath caught as I stood rooted to the spot.

"Chin up," Gia said as she passed me, breezing her hand against my chin to close my open mouth. She had a twinkle in her eye as she glanced at Kayden. It was no secret I was crazy about him, and the rumours were that he wasn't with a girl at the moment so that I might be in with a chance. Passing the drinks table, I reached out and took a drink, then hurried outside, hoping to find an empty bench. Perhaps if I sat alone, he might join me, but my heart sank as I looked around. Couples engaged in tight embraces now occupied all the benches, and Kayden was nowhere in sight. Sighing, I walked back inside and perched on a stool near the door where I could watch for him. I'm not surprised, though; I wasn't the greatest beauty, and my father, being who he was, didn't help. I suppose it would've been too good to be true for Kayden to be waiting for me. He had probably disappeared to a remote corner of the garden with some beauty. Everyone I knew was paired up or in deep conversation as I looked around. It made my disappointment even greater.

I suddenly felt very alone. I picked up my drink and looked at the goldy blue liquid swirling around the beautiful squat glass. It was very exotic. I had no idea what it was. I didn't look when I picked it up, but now, I hoped it was very strong and very alcoholic. Raising the glass to my nose, I inhaled. It was fruity, tangy, and minty all at the same time. Taking a big gulp, I screwed up my eyes as the sour liquid scorched my mouth. Forcing it down, I felt it burn its way to my stomach. I hoped the effect was worth it. Lifting the glass again, I risked another smaller sip. The boiling fire in my gut told me that would be the last one. Rising from my perch, I walked outside, pausing near a beautiful rose bed and looked around. Seeing no one nearby, I took a few steps closer to admire a beautiful red rose. Glancing around again, I tipped the foul cocktail into the flowerbed. I let a silent 'sorry' escape from my lips as I thought of the poor roses whose roots were about to be assaulted by the putrid stuff.

On my way back, I couldn't believe my luck when I saw Kayden by the drinks table talking to Gia. Trying to look relaxed and sophisticated, I walked up to them, nodding and smiling. I was about to take a soft drink when Kayden looked over with a twinkle in his eye and asked if I would prefer the Puce Punch. Diplomatically, I said it didn't agree with me. As Gia moved to welcome another guest, Kayden leaned forward and whispered.

"Gia's parents always serve that brew. It's notorious for its putrid taste." He offered me a glass of soft fruit punch instead. It was a pretty peachy colour with rainbows swirling through it. With a conspiratorial grin, he picked up a bottle of ale, flipped the lid off and took a quick sip.

"I prefer the bottled ales." he winked as we walked into the garden. "Why don't we stroll through the rose garden? It's quite famous, you know." I agreed, my heart almost bursting as I grinned back. When we moved away from the little clusters of guests, I leaned in conspiratorially.

"I'm feeling a little guilty. I dumped the punch on those poor red roses. I hope I haven't poisoned them." He chuckled.

"I think they're used to it being so close to the Garden room. It could even be the secret of their success. Many people have been after that secret." I giggled, and soon, we were both laughing. The more we laughed, the funnier it became. Our sides ached, and tears ran down our cheeks as we turned into a small open area. There, beside a beautiful pink rose, was an unoccupied bench. We collapsed breathlessly onto it. I wasn't sure whether we were intoxicated by the rose's fragrance or something else, but time stopped as our eyes met. We gazed deep into each other's eyes, hearing the song as our souls entwined. I don't know how long that moment lasted, but he took my hand and slid an arm around my back at some point. In such a romantic setting with the heady scent of the roses, how could we not fall in love as his lips softly met mine?

The most perfect moments of my life began after that party. Kayden was a few months my senior and came from a large, well-respected family who lived in Central Caws, the primary town of Cawsal district. I had several friends who lived nearby, so it was an area I was familiar with. Kayden and I usually met after school and walked together to the crossroads. Here, the road to Cawsal went North and South to Central Thena. We spent as much time together as we could that summer. After a time, we lay together, enjoying the closeness of our skin without fabric between us. I was so happy; nothing could separate our entwined hearts; it felt so right. How little did I know, I'd almost forgotten about that talk with Father, well almost. It seemed so old-fashioned anyway. I couldn't believe it really applied to me.

11

Rush

As the oldest, I was expected to set an example for my siblings. I was also the first to be disciplined when things went wrong. I tried to keep my four brothers out of Father's way as much as possible. My sister, Amelie, found it more challenging to follow Father's rules. She had a rebellious, free spirit that Father wanted to crush. It wasn't fitting for someone of her status. I tried my best to help her and hated hearing her screams when she was punished. She used to creep into my room at night, and we talked for hours about her latest trouble. Father was often away from home, and the whole household relaxed a little on those days. Mother saw us every morning; if Father was away, she returned in the afternoon, too.

We had lessons in Thenan culture and responsibilities with our grandparents. Our tutor, Professor Hog, covered the academic subjects. I must have been about five when he arrived. Professor Hog was a round, warty little man with grey, wiry hair that I don't think ever saw a comb. Prof Hog always wore the same suit of fine green wool with a dark brown thread running through it. It had probably been a very good suit when it was new, but now it had leather patches on the elbows, and the seat had been worn to a shine. We laughed behind his back that he even smelled like a hog. Certainly, he had an odour that didn't come from any bottle of cologne. He sat at the front of the room we used as our school room beside a board on which he made spidery squiggles that were almost impossible to read. We liked it best when he drew pictures, he was quite an accomplished artist and his pictures were usually funny.

I wanted to learn and achieve the best possible scores so Father would be pleased with me. Father's face rarely smiled, but he did his whole face changed. How we longed to be the one that brought that smile, to bathe in its radiance. Everything else faded in that moment. I was an ambitious young man with a head full of dreams. I'd set my sights on the top of the Legal Octon and worked hard to ensure I got there. I'd never considered whether it was my calling. It was expected. I was to be the next Thena Legal Councillor. When Father retired, he expected me to replace him as Legal Councillor and Head of the High Council. My two high-born friends and I swept through school, leaving everyone in our wake. We were high achievers, and our fathers had similar expectations for us. Jak, like me, was expected to become a Legal Councillor. We had a friendly rivalry as we strove to outdo each other in our achievements. Jak's father was Stratagon Wiklon, Militaria Councillor to the High Council (Stratagon – a military rank similar to General). He had wanted Jak to pursue the military path, but it became clear Jak's talents lay elsewhere. Wiklon was satisfied that the Legal Octon would give his son the same opportunity to play a prominent role on the High Council.

Elon was also expected to follow the Legal path but was called to Faith. I often wondered why he stayed with us when his calling was so different. Elon's father, Marc, was the Legal Councillor for Pollo, so he understood the Legal world quite well. This made his calling all the more bizarre. Elon faced fierce opposition from his father when he finally told him he would change from Legal to Faith. Although Elon considered all faiths, his calling was to follow the teachings of Singularity and become Senior Steward. Of course, like Jak and I, he was aiming for the top, so it had to be Senior Steward, Thena Faith Councillor, and Faith Councillor to the High Council. Father, of course, disapproved of my association with Elon after he left the Legal College. It was a benefit and a curse that our fathers were well-connected on the High Council. We were constantly scrutinised for our actions, and any slips were reported to our parents. We flew to the top of our classes each year until our sixteenth anniversary. This was when Elon made his significant announcement. I would have given much to have been a spider on the study wall when Elon told his father. What an explosion that must have been, but I would rather stand before his father than mine any day of the year. After Elon had proved his calling and still studied at the highest level, his father began to acknowledge his calling.

When friends began to talk about Promisary Agreements and Introductions, I began to feel something was wrong. My parents had spoken to me about it, but I was never told they had made an arrangement for me. It was one of the things we were not allowed to speak about at home unless my parents started the conversation. The day I met Thea at the National Introductions Agency has always stuck in my mind. She was so beautiful, standing there with her head held high. Midnight black hair caressed her shoulders and flowed down her back. Those piercing green eyes met mine, and I knew I wanted to be with her, but I also sensed she didn't feel the same. Guarded hostility oozed like a smoky cloud surrounding her. Thea was almost a year younger than I was, so our introduction had been delayed until she reached her sixteenth, and I was approaching my seventeenth. We made the formal greetings and went through the official introductions as expected. Each of us word perfect, performing our roles as we had been taught. I wanted a girl who would fulfil her duties and responsibilities without question, but

I also wanted someone who could match my enthusiasm for life. Thea performed her tasks and responsibilities flawlessly, but I struggled to discover who she was behind the smoke screen. It had never occurred to me that she wouldn't feel the same as I did or might resent our match. Thea was the beautiful, elegant woman I'd always imagined, and I really tried to make her like me. I knew love would take longer, but I never knew what went on behind those eyes. She was closed to me. She would smile and nod but gave the impression that she didn't like to talk too much. I hoped it would change over time. As we got to know each other better, I discovered she was intelligent, and I worried that perhaps she might be too capable for the role expected of her. She had wanted to study Healing, but it wouldn't be possible when we were married. Her father encouraged her to study childcare, home management and garden care subjects instead. I suggested she should study accountancy as well. Although she wasn't very enthusiastic, she agreed and was more than capable in this subject.

We married in the summer after my twentieth, when I'd completed my studies and could finally support a wife. It was on the third anniversary of our meeting and Thea's twentieth anniversary. I thought it might be romantic, but she merely gave a curt nod of agreement when I proposed the date. I suppose I should've known then our marriage wouldn't be the one I'd dreamt of. We had a traditional Thenan wedding—a private ceremony followed by a celebration with many guests. Senior Steward Mica conducted the ceremony on a bright sunny morning on the eighth day of the spirit in the fifth month of Singularity. We stood before the Great Pillar of Singularity. Our hands were placed on the smooth surface as we gave our promises before turning to Mica for the formal blessing. Thea was so beautiful in her sky-blue dress flowing from her shoulders over her shape like water. She wore a sparkling floral bridal pin in her hair of the most dazzling blue, matching her dress perfectly. I learned later it was a water sapphire from one of the great lakes in Delphiope. The bridal chain was of gleaming silver gold. I was so nervous my hands shook as I tried to fasten it around her neck. I nearly dropped the necklace, which would've been a bad omen. Fortunately, I managed to secure it and saw Thea's slight smile of relief. After the ceremony, we moved to the Thena Council chambers for our wedding celebration. All our friends and family were there, along with political guests befitting a marriage of status.

The receiving of guests took a long time, and both Thea and I were becoming tongue-tied by the end. Remembering names, responsibilities, relationships, and friendships between our two families was difficult. As for the other guests, it was impossible, especially the guests neither of us knew. These were the political ones our parents had requested us to invite. The feast was sumptuous, with many types of meat, fish, plates of salads and vegetables. Then, traditional dragon fruit tarts, rich, creamy and sweet. Dragon fruits were supposed to be an aphrodisiac and were traditionally used in desserts at weddings. I wasn't very fond of them, but I took my dessert, as did Thea. Our families all watched with suggestive eyes as we ate. Couples with Anlan Bloodline matches were expected to give birth to children early and have large families. The wedding night would be an important start to our marriage and, with luck, our family. Glancing at Thea, I saw she was uncomfortable with all the attention and only took one or two bites of the dessert. I might have worried about bad luck if I were superstitious, but I never concerned myself with such things. Sadly, the anticipated child did not come as soon as we had hoped. I couldn't help thinking back to the Dragon fruit tart and wonder if things might have been different had Thea eaten more.

12

Amelie

A few months before my sixteenth anniversary, Mother, always observant, caught me after breakfast. She said I was getting fat and my clothes were becoming tight. She made me stand before her in the kitchen while she felt my shape in front of everyone. It was humiliating, her unfamiliar touch on my body and the embarrassing questions, even when I had my monthly course! Then, she turned and walked away with her face as black as thunder. I'd never seen her look like that, and suddenly, I was afraid. I had missed my monthly courses a few times, but that didn't mean anything. I knew I'd gained a little around my waist, but I'd lose it. Amber and I were planning to exercise together. I went to my room and waited.

There followed the most terrible row; my parents' voices echoed through the house. From what I could hear, it was about me, and I was terrified. What had I done? I huddled on my bed, clutching my pillow. I didn't know what to do. I wished Rush was here. Then, it went quiet, and my heart began to pound. I didn't have to wait long. Mother's voice came up the stairs; she demanded I come down. She stood at the bottom of the stairs, arms folded, watching as I descended. Without a word, she directed me to the study, where Father sat behind his desk. He looked like thunder, his face dark and terrifying. The vein in his forehead throbbed as he watched me come in. I had never been so scared in my life. But still, I had no idea what I'd done wrong.

He said Mother had informed him I was with child. I was shocked. *Why would she say that? It wasn't true.* He demanded to know who I'd lain with. Stupidly, I suppose, I said nobody. He kept asking, and eventually, I admitted I'd met a boy from Cawsal. Mother flew into such a rage, her face demonic, as she took a poker from the fire. She began to beat me. The hot metal hissed as it touched my clothes, burning into my flesh. The searing pain was indescribable. I begged her to stop, tears rolling down my face. With every stroke, she said how much I'd disgraced my family and broken the Law. On and on until I thought I would die. Later, bruised and in pain, I was taken to the attic room at the top of the house, and the key was turned in the lock. Mother stood outside the door and spoke in a cold, alien voice. She said I would stay in that room until the birth. From that day forward, my family would deny my existence. *I was in shock! Why had I been beaten and locked up here? Would they really throw me out? Was I really with child?* I didn't understand. I was so confused and wished Rush would come and explain it all to me.

Later that day, Father gently asked who the boy was. He sounded so kind and understanding, and I was so desperate to improve things that I told him. He said I would never see him again because Kayden wasn't Thenan or of the Bloodline. His following words were spoken in a voice so icy cold it chilled me to the core. He said I was ruined, and he could no longer bear to lay eyes on me. He would ensure we were both punished as severely as the law allowed. My heart broke at the cruelty of it. I couldn't imagine life without Kayden. As Father's footsteps retreated along the hallway, I curled up on the bed. Tears poured down my face, and pain grew in my chest where my broken heart lay. Later, when it was opened, I discovered a small flap at the bottom of the door, and food and water were pushed through. There was a note from the maid and a bowl of water, cloths to clean my wounds and salve for the burns. I tended to my battered body as best I could, although reaching all the places on my back was difficult. The note said the maid would take the soil pot from the commode when she brought my meal. One hour later, she would return with it and collect the dishes from my meal. Once a week, I could push soiled clothes and linen through for laundry, and they would be returned in the same way.

The feelings of misery and pain were so profound in those early days that I cared little about anything. I couldn't eat and only sipped from the bottles of water, which arrived three times daily. The rest of the time, I lay on the bed, overwhelmed by events and the unfairness of it all. I became angry and raged, crying and screaming until I was hoarse. Other times, I hammered on the door, but no one came. Then, with my hands raw and bruised, I sank back on the bed, and tears flowed down my cheeks. I let them soak my pillow. The flow from my nose joined the tears as I wallowed in misery. I was completely cut off; not even the maid spoke to me. After a while, when the anger subsided, I paced the small room like a caged animal. I was restless, frustrated and uncomfortable as the child grew, for I realised that Mother must have been right. I could feel the movement growing as my belly grew. All through the cold depths of winter, my anger burned inside, keeping me warm as I'd never felt before.

I was given a book to write daily appeals to the Singular God to forgive my wickedness. At first, I tried, but then I gave up. It didn't feel like I'd done anything wrong, whatever my parents said. When I tried again, the words flowing from my pen were the most heartfelt song lyrics I'd ever written. Music followed, and I tried to note it down so I could play it if I was ever let out. When I wasn't writing, I stalked my room, longing to feel the sun on my skin and the breeze in my hair. The only window in the room was so high I couldn't reach it, and even if I could, it was barred.

I was lonely and longed to share the moments when I felt him move (I was sure it was a boy). To share those moments when my stomach churned and lurched as he turned over. I didn't hear my parent's voices for quite some time until one day, I heard another terrible row downstairs. Two male voices rage through the house this time, like angry bears roaring and growling. I guessed it was Father and Rush. The deep ache began again in my chest as I thought of Rush. We'd been close until these events separated us. It hurt that he hadn't tried to sneak up to talk to me. I felt sure he would have found a way if he had cared for me. My sixteenth anniversary was forgotten entirely, with no good wishes or special food. Not even the silent maid acknowledged my coming of age. I'd lost everybody. They'd stolen my life and destroyed the only good things I had. Through all this, the only thing that was blameless was the child growing inside. He hadn't learned to hate me. Not yet, at least.

My whole world had become these four walls. I was a prisoner, denied all things that gave comfort. The tiny window only let in a pale light, but more than enough to see how far I'd fallen. I even had the indignity of using a commode with just a bowl of tepid water to wash in. It wasn't enough for a proper wash or to wash my hair thoroughly. Time passed in a haze, and I lost track of the days and hours. One day, a Healer came to examine me. I didn't know how much time had passed, but my belly had grown. He said I should ask for a wisewoman when birthing pains started, whatever that meant. He was the only person to set foot inside my room all this time. He had stayed long enough to complete the examination and ask what he needed to assess my health. There was no chat or conversation, and he left me as soon as he was finished.

Early one morning, as the sun was rising from its slumbers, I was woken by a nagging pain low in my belly and back. At first, I ignored it, assuming I'd slept in a funny position or something. It seemed to go, and I turned over and went back to sleep. A little while later, the pain was back. Was I ill? I felt as if anything could happen as if the worst gastric parasite had struck. I panicked. I was sure something awful was happening. Then again, it went away, but as soon as I relaxed, it returned, and I cried out. It hurt, and I didn't know what to do. When my food arrived, I couldn't bear to eat and only drank warm tea. The maid who collected the tray must have told Mother because she arrived at the door. She demanded to know why I hadn't eaten. I didn't know what to say. I was afraid I didn't want to tell her about the pain, but my body had developed a mind of its own. The pain came again, and unbidden, a groan escaped from my lips. Mother said nothing.

Later, a woman bustled in with a basket over her arm. She had a ruddy face with a white cap covering her hair and a smooth white apron over the red dress of a wisewoman. She was short and dumpy with a kindly expression. She introduced herself as Mother Pod and said she'd stay until the baby arrived. It was clear she knew of my fallen circumstance, and I knew I couldn't have a conversation with her. Conversation, though, was far from my mind. My body strained at its very seams to expel the intruder from my belly. Mother Pod stripped my bed and remade it with padded bedding. Then she looked at me, running her eye over my swollen belly before she reached out and put her coarse red hands on my body. She felt me like she would a prize cow and told me my body was getting ready to push out the babe. I asked how long it would take. She shook her head but didn't reply.

As the sun prepared for its slumber, pinky gold blankets drifted down, hiding it from view. From that moment, things began to get worse. The most dreadful pain started deep in the pit of my belly. It came in waves, each stronger than the one before, until I didn't think I could go on any longer. Finally, it ended, and Mother Pod swiftly took the babe, wrapping it in a towel. She turned and handed it to my mother. I didn't know she was there and she left without saying a word. I didn't understand what had happened. I hadn't been told anything. I was alone and in pain, engulfed in the deepest misery. Soon, completely exhausted, I fell into a deep sleep. When I woke the following morning, I felt my empty belly, now flabby and uncomfortable. At that moment, I wanted to die. More than anything else, I wanted to stop living this life that was so cold and cruel. Mother Pod came in several times to check me over. I no longer cared about her probing hands that manhandled me each time. I was in a distant place far beyond caring.

It wasn't until the following day that my parents came to see me. I was then told of my fate and that of the child. They said I must go with Mother Pod. My baby girl, for that is what it was, had been given to my brother Rush and his wife. They would bring her up as their daughter until her sixteenth anniversary. Until then, I must not contact them or try to see the child. I was banished from the only family and home I knew. I had disgraced them and my Anlan heritage, which carried the harshest penalty. I must not contact anyone in my family or try to see them. At that moment, I never wanted to see my parents again. Yet, still, I hadn't grasped the depth of my disgrace. I was sure it would only last a few weeks, and then I will be forgiven and welcomed back. I was sure I'd be forgiven.

13

Amelie

Mother Pod arrived early the following day to wake me. It was still dark, and the house was silent. She had clothes in her hands and asked me to put them on. *I didn't understand why she had brought me clothes.* Then I remembered I was leaving today. Father's cold words rang in my ears, 'You will be banished, cut out of the family like a poisonous canker'. I hadn't believed it would happen. My eyes filled with tears as I sat on the bed. *Where would I go? Would I see my brothers again? Could I say goodbye to Rush?* I felt so alone, and nothing felt right anymore. My body felt odd, and I was nauseous. Mother Pod helped me dress, then picked up a small travel case I hadn't noticed. We left the house by the side door. None of my family saw me go, not even Rush. We followed the drive to the road in the cool morning air. The new day was dawning, and the streets were quiet as we walked away. Away from the only home I'd ever known. I was scared. *How will I cope? Who will look after me?* My mind was full of questions without answers. We walked silently for a few minutes, and then Mother Pod began to tell me about the house I was going to. She said I could stay there while I healed, then I must leave and find my way using the skills the Gods gave me. I couldn't concentrate on her words, and nothing made sense. *I was in a waking nightmare. My life was shattered. I was cast aside from a world that no longer wanted me*. Walking briskly, Mother Pod led me away from Central Thena. I struggled to keep up, still weak and uncomfortable from the birth and months of incarceration. She paused every so often as we made our way towards Delphiope. At the outskirts of Central Thena, we waited for an interdistrict transport to take us to Delphiope.

It was an uncomfortable journey on hard bench seats. My battered body ached so much that I barely noticed the changing scenery. When we left the transport in Delph, it was a short walk to a small dwelling. On entering, I could see it was much larger than it looked. A long corridor stretched as far as I could see, with doors and open areas branching off at intervals. Mother Pod showed me to a room where I would sleep for the first night. The room was white: white walls, window covers, white covers on the bed, everything was white. It felt too white for me to touch. I stood for a while before sitting on the spotless bed in my travel-worn dress, looking down at my dusty shoes. I longed for a bath to wash away the past months, but it wouldn't make any difference. What I felt wouldn't wash away.

I was still sitting there when Mother Pod returned with a pile of towels.

"Here you go, Amelie. Your mother packed some of your clothes for you, and I've brought towels and other things I thought you might need. The bathing room is two doors down on the left, where you can wash. If the door is open, feel free to go in. Make sure you lock the door so you aren't disturbed. On this card are the times when meals are served. We eat together in the dining room at the end of the corridor. You'll be expected to take your turn in the kitchen, preparing food and clearing away afterwards while you are here. I've marked your shift on the card for you. The kitchen is next to the dining room, so it's easy to find. The garden room is on the left of the dining room with doors out to the garden, which you are welcome to use. Now, do you have any questions?" I shook my head dumbly.

She smiled kindly before she came over and sat beside me on the bed. Her red dress was stark against the white bedclothes. The bed sank, tilting me towards her, and she put her arm around me as a mother would, except mine rarely did.

"Come now, Amelie, you've passed the worst. It's up to you to make your own way in the world now. I know it's a lot to take in, but you'll get used to it. I've helped many young girls like you from Thena who have fallen foul of those silly Bloodline Laws. They all settle and make new lives for themselves, some here in Delphiope and others in Pollo or Cawsal. None have returned to the lives they left behind, not once they've tasted freedom. When you go to Ascension House tomorrow, you'll meet some of them, and they'll help you find your feet." Tears began to roll down my face, and I leaned into her as they fell.

"There now, let it all out." she crooned as she rubbed my arm. She was comforting and reassuring, quite different from the woman I met in that horrible attic room. It was as if she'd shaken off an old cloak and replaced it with a motherly apron and the smell of freshly baked bread.

After a while, as my tears dried, she pulled away to look at my face.

"Now, there is one thing you must do for the babe. Do you remember anything of the Bloodline Laws? I'm guessing your father has told you of them by now?" I shook my head. I had no idea what she meant.

"As the birth mother, you have the right to make a Promisary Agreement for your daughter. That means you look for a boy child of a similar age and a good family whose parents agree to the match. Together, Mothers go to the National Introductions Agency to register the Promisary Agreement. Many good families in Delphiope and Pollo look for matches with a child of Thena. Even those born in disgrace."

"I can't go back to Thena," My eyes began to fill with tears again.

"Oh no, you don't need to go back to Thena. There's a Registration Agency in Delph where you can register your Promisary Agreement. They submit the registration to the National Introductions Agency of Central Thena." Then she said, with a twinkle in her eye, "Of course, when you register in Delph, it makes it more difficult for anyone looking to find it. There have been challenges from Thenan families in the past, but you should be OK registering here in Delph."

"OK." I managed gulping back my tears. "Thank you."

"Why don't you wash and change your clothes before dinner? You'll feel much better when you're all clean. At dinner, you'll meet the other girls; they're a friendly bunch, and it's quite informal here. If you need anything, go to the office near the entrance. There'll always be someone to help you." She stood and walked to the doorway, then turned.

"It will get better, Amelie, truly it will," she said gently before she closed the door behind her. It felt like she'd taken all the air with her, leaving me in a silent vacuum. It was a few minutes before I could breathe again. I felt gritty dust on my face as I wiped away the last of my tears. That was the push I needed. I've always hated dirt, and to feel it on my face was too much on top of everything else. I gathered clean clothes, a towel, and the wash bag, then cautiously opened the door. The corridor was a soft cream colour with warm brown doors. I could see the bathroom door standing open and sighed with relief. Looking back at my door, I saw the letter A on it. Easy to remember, I thought as I shut the door behind me.

Later, after breakfast, I took my turn in the kitchen. I was unfamiliar with the routine, but the other girls showed me what to do—the day passed in a blur of meals, sleep and faces. I was exhausted and overwhelmed. I felt like I had been cast into the deep ocean without a float. I was drowning and couldn't see how I would ever survive. Later, after dinner, I returned to my room and tumbled into bed. I fell into a troubled sleep full of pain and heartache. The following day, it all began again. There was a knock at the door, and a wisewoman smiled at me and said that breakfast would be in an hour. I looked blankly at her before thanking her. I dressed like an automaton, pulling garments on, tidying my hair and putting on my shoes. The long table had faces that blurred together. I heard greetings, and I thought I was smiling. My head nodded, but I couldn't find any words. *What do I say to these girls?* I took my turn in the kitchen before I returned to my room and waited. *I didn't know what to do. I wanted to find Kayden to tell him what had happened, and perhaps I could stay with his family*. Mother Pod only told me about yesterday. Should I be somewhere or go somewhere? I didn't know. I didn't have to wait long to find out.

There was another knock at the door, and Mother Pod came in. She helped me pack my bag and told me I must find my way to another house, Ascension House, where I could stay until I was healed. I didn't understand. I thought I would stay here. I was being turned away yet again, and despite the kindness, I felt rejection yet again. She gave me directions and a letter of introduction. I thanked her for her kindness. It felt emotional to leave this gentle woman after all that had happened in the past few days. She was the only person who had offered kindness to me. I couldn't remember when I last felt that from anyone. She led me to the door, gently encouraging me and said it would be OK. I felt her eyes on me as I walked away towards the main road into Delph.

As I walked, I began to think, realising, for the first time, that I was free to make my own decisions and nobody would be there to judge. I knew exactly where I was going, and it wasn't to

Ascension house, at least not right now. First, I wanted to find Kayden. I had to know if he was OK. I wanted to tell him we had a baby daughter. Taking an Interdistrict transport, I headed to Central Caws in the Cawsal district. Kayden described where to find his house many times; following the directions I'd memorised wasn't difficult. When I reached where the house should be, I stood in shock. Where once there had been a house, there was just a mound of rubble. Broken timbers, stones, bricks and bits of furniture were strewn around. It was a few moments before I understood what I was seeing. Then my heart began to thud, and I looked for someone who could tell me what had happened. *There must have been some terrible accident. Where were Kayden and his family?* I couldn't bear to think of the alternative.

I tried talking to people, but as soon as they heard my voice with its Thenan tone, they turned away with fear in their eyes. Central Caws suddenly began to feel hostile, and I was afraid. I didn't know what to do. The only thing I could do was to make my back to Delphiope. But before I could take a step, I felt someone's eyes on me. As I looked around, I caught sight of someone in the shadows of a building across the road. A small figure with a dark shawl pulled over their head was gazing intently in my direction. I heard a voice telling me to go over to the person, a voice inside my head. The person beckoned, and I was compelled to walk towards the person.

When I reached the person, I realised it was a young girl. Opening my mouth to speak, she covered it with her hand and shook her head. Beckoning, she walked down a narrow alley, and I was compelled to follow her. I didn't feel threatened, and honestly, what else was there to lose? We entered a small accommodation at the end of the alley. The door closed behind us, and I heard bolts slide into place, sending a chill down my spine. Without windows, the room was plunged into a deep, inky blackness. The smell of stale food, stale bodies and all manner of odours assaulted my nose, and I pulled my shawl to my face. Then I heard a strike and saw the soft glow of a candle and a shadowy face looking at me. She lit a lamp, and I could finally see her. She was very pale; thin wisps of lilac-white curls sprung from the scarf that covered her head. Her pale, icy blue eyes seemed oddly large for her face. She offered a stool, and I gratefully sat, still weak after childbirth. She sat beside me, looking down at her hands clasped in her lap and then up and across the room. She had a dreamlike look on her face, and I began to wonder if she was a dreamer. Dreamers had one foot in today and one foot in their dreams, so I'd heard, but I'd never met one. They were always children, never reaching their sixteenth anniversary.

Looking at the girl beside me, I guessed she must be close to that anniversary, a similar age to me. Her eyes, of the palest icy blue, were mesmerising and drew my attention as she turned to me,

"You're Amelie? You're looking for Kayden?" her voice was light, little more than a whisper.

"Yes, do you know where he is? Nobody will tell me." I heard the tremble in my voice as the words spilt from my lips, and I felt tears in my eyes.

"They're afraid, afraid it's a trap. Nobody wants their home to be next."

"But why?"

"Months ago, the guards arrested Kayden. He was sentenced to sixteen years in the mines. They said he had lain with a girl from Thena," she looked at me accusingly. Dropping my head, I felt sick.

"I didn't know," I whispered, tears spilling down my cheeks.

"A week after he was sentenced, the guards returned. They were seen entering the district heading towards Central Caws, and word was sent to Kayden's family. They fled, fearing for their lives. The guards brought a great machine and crushed the house. They didn't stop until there was nothing to be salvaged from the rubble. No one knows where the family went. When they couldn't be found, other family members were arrested, including one of Kayden's brothers. All followed him to the mines." Her voice drifted into silence. I was horrified, and I didn't know what to say. I knew it must be my father's doing and all my fault. The tears fell silently for all the pain I'd caused Kayden and his family. She looked up, cold eyes bore into me as she spoke, and I heard the truth of her words.

"Amelie, you must leave here. It's not safe for you to be in Cawsal. You've been seen; I don't know what they will do if you're found. They hold you responsible for what happened to Kayden and his family."

"I, I don't know where to go."

"I can take you back to the crossroads a safe way." She stood and indicated I should follow her.

"Cover your head with your scarf to hide your hair," she said. I did as she asked, pulling my scarf over my head and around my face.

"We go now." She extinguished the lamp and candle, plunging the room into the thick, velvety darkness once more.

"Please tell me your name." but there was no time. The door opened as her hand covered my mouth. Silently, we left and walked briskly through a series of alleys until we reached a crossroads on the outskirts of Central Caws.

"Thank you for your kindness. May I know your name?"

"It doesn't matter now. In time, you may know it," she said cryptically.

"Will I see you again?" she was the only link I had with Kayden. She looked at me sadly.

"We will not meet again, but you'll be reunited with your daughter when your name is in lights."

"Really? I'll see my daughter?" *Can it be true?* I had so many questions, but there was no time.

"Go now," she said before she turned and hurried away.

14

Amelie

I returned to Delphiope. It was the district where most artisans and skilled workers of all trades lived. I'd researched it many times, dreaming of the college I'd attend and how I'd follow my dream to perform. But it had only been dreams back then. Now I'm on my way, and I realise I didn't know where to go or how to find lodgings. I hoped someone would take pity on me. It didn't occur to me to go to Ascension House as I'd been instructed. I'm not sure why. I was free now, though, and I felt the wrappings of my old life beginning to crack and fall away. A fluttering excitant grew with my worries for all the unknowns. I'd heard Delphiope was a proud district without the starchy formality of Thena. It might be a place where I could find work and somewhere to live. Perhaps even a good match for my daughter. A watcher met me as I entered Delph, the primary town of Delphiope, and directed me to a house where I could stay for a few days until I found permanent accommodation. I met Rosa there; she was slightly older than me, but her story was painfully similar. She arrived from Thena when her family disowned her and her newborn child, casting them out. Now, she was training as a weaver and hoped to qualify so she could apply for accommodation. She hadn't been able to gain enough credit to make the application yet. We decided to apply for joint accommodation when I had training and work.

I had few skills to offer. I wasn't artistically inclined and didn't tell tales. My only skill was my voice, and I realised that I could finally follow my dreams to perform. It took time, but I found the right academie, The Academia Choral. Although I didn't have certificates, my voice had enough in its tone to persuade them to accept me. Surprisingly, I received a bursary, which meant Rosa and I could apply for accommodation. My father would have been horrified. He considered performing arts a passing phase in childhood or one which a much lower class might do. It wasn't regarded as suitable for someone of my status. I suppose I've already shown I wasn't worthy of that status anyway. It made me sad to think of my family. I missed my brothers every day, each time I had to make decisions. I would have been glad of their counsel, especially Rush. He'd been my confidant in almost all things. Now, I have to make big decisions independently for the first time.

Everything was challenging, from allocating coins for food and everyday clothes to cooking and cleaning. So much was new to me. I'd never bought food or simple clothing before. Such things were the realm of maids and lower classes, not children of high-born Thena families. Then, there were the gowns I needed for performing. I'd never had to choose between food and frivolous things. Sweet treats and pretty gowns now weighed against the hunger in my belly and the four walls around us. I grew up very fast in those months. Rosa helped me learn how to allocate coins for the essential things while keeping a little back. Over time, I used what I'd put aside for the less critical, frivolous things. We ate simply a little meat, with vegetables from the market. We went into the forest and foraged for fungi, nuts, berries and herbs that grew wild to make our food more enjoyable. Rosa taught me how to cook poor-quality meat, so it became tender. She showed me the herbs and vegetables that could be added to make delicious meals go further. We sat around our little table at night with a bowl of stewed meat and vegetables, sharing the fresh rolls we'd baked that morning. Our first lodgings were meagre, just two rooms, one to sleep in and the other where we ate, cooked, and entertained friends. We shared an outhouse with our neighbours, which was another new experience. We'd both grown up with a bathroom inside the house where we washed ourselves and did our personal business. Here, we shared responsibility for cleaning the outhouse and how I missed the maids from home. I'd grown up with them in the background, never knowing what they did. Now, I know only too well and regret not thanking them.

Dorcana and I first met when Rosa took me to have a gown made. Dorcana was a weaver and dressmaker and very skilled at both. She grew up in Delph, learning her trade very early. She had a son who was almost six months old and didn't have a Promisary Agreement. Although having a Promisary Agreement in Delphiope wasn't law, it was still a widespread practice. Almost as soon as we met, I knew her son was the one I wanted for my daughter, and she agreed. We went to the Delphiope District Introductions Agency and registered the Promisary Agreement. It pleased me that my family would be unlikely to look for a Promisary Agreement registered outside Thena. I named my daughter Tilda. I didn't know what name she had been given, but her birth name would be Tilda, with Kayden and I as her parents. The boy was called Orlan, with Dorcana, his mother, and Ando, his father. Until she was sixteen, I had to bear the overwhelming pain of Tilda's loss, not seeing her grow up or hearing her voice and not knowing the colour of her eyes or the smile on her face. I couldn't see or write to her; my father made that very clear. Nor would I receive any pictures of her likeness. I tried writing to my mother, but my letters were returned unopened. I have shed so many tears. The pain never left me and was most acute on each anniversary.

My life became full of rehearsals, singing lessons, meditations and performances. It left little time to dwell on the past, which was a blessing. Life in Delphiope was very different to life in Thena. For the first time, I was truly free. Even in the residential areas where the most senior Councillors for Delphiope lived, it felt different. There were no high walls or locked gates around accommodations as there were in Thena. Although there were walls to mark boundaries, they were lower and more welcoming. Formal areas often had no gate and a welcoming path to the door. People sat in the evening talking and singing folk songs with neighbours. Rosa and I worked hard, but at night, we relaxed and visited the many social areas. Of course, there were theatres and music venues, but even in the cafes and bars along the streets, you could always hear voices singing and music playing. It was so full of life, the creative atmosphere so thick you could touch it. As we inhaled, we breathed it in, fizzing and popping around us as if it had a life of its own. There was so much colour in the decorated walls of the houses and the bright clothes everyone wore. It was as if I'd lived my whole life in the dark until now. No one wore dark, serious colours, not even the most serious of people. Such suits were only needed when visiting Thena on official business. Then, the 'Thena suit' came from the darkest depth of the closet. I loved living in Delphiope; it felt like home from the moment I arrived. At last, I was welcomed and accepted without judgment. As I walked down the street, the heart-warming greetings were so different from the severe streets of Thena, where friends passed in silence, barely a nod of acknowledgement. From being the outsider, I soon became part of Delph society.

I wrote to Kayden as often as possible, but writing materials and carriage took coin that I couldn't always spare. The first letter I received from him was so sad and full of regrets. He described the brutal regime of the prison mine, living conditions and food.

Conditions in the prison mine were severe, and my blood ran cold at the thought of him there. He worked all the daylight hours and had food at night if his prison house had earned enough credit. Credits were not easy to earn and were easily lost, it seemed. A little slow starting work, not enough carts of ore mined, too much time taking air, more than a day with injury. It all cost credits. The guards were cruel and often beat prisoners without cause. When his second letter arrived six months later, I could tell his spirit had been broken beyond measure, and he feared for his life. Accidents were common, he said. Several others had taken their lives or been involved in suspicious accidents, yet nobody cared. One worthless prisoner's life didn't merit investigation. It was one less to guard and feed. Prisoners even had to dig graves and bury the emaciated bodies of those who escaped mortality for a better place. There was no ceremony, although sometimes one of the prisoners versed in such things said a few words. The cruelty of the guards and increasing attacks were making his life unbearable, he said. It was the last letter I received.

My heart broke as I read and reread these two treasured letters. Their pages became marked with the stain of my tears as I wept over them. The paper became fragile as time passed, and I no longer dared take them from their envelopes. I never heard from Kayden again, but it wasn't until Rosa and I went to the courthouse in Delph and asked for word of him that I learned of his fate. He died in a mining accident. His death had been on the first anniversary of Tilda's birth. My heart broke again, and Rosa had to help me return to our accommodation. I grieved for days, not going out until I had to return, or we would be in danger of losing our accommodation. My voice sounded strangled and harsh at first, but gradually, it regained the fullness it had. There was an understanding among vocal performers that events affected the voice, and by using it again slowly, the pain became soothed. I knew in those dark days that I'd never find another love to replace Kayden as long as I lived. Part of my heart had died, and no one could ever fill that deep, dark void.

From that day forward, I threw myself into perfecting my trade. I progressed from being part of the chorus supporting the performer to being the performer with a supporting chorus. The first time I performed alone, I stood on the stage looking at the sea of faces waiting in anticipation to hear my voice. I was full of nerves. I must have looked so timid standing frozen in the bright lights. My hands shook so much I had to hold them together in front of me. But when the music started, it was as if the notes filled my soul, leaving no room for fear. My voice rang clear from the very first note to the last. When the echoes of my voice faded, there was a momentary silence before the most beautiful noise erupted. The audience rose to their feet, hands clapping with bright smiles, and I knew I'd arrived. The Academie helped me grow in confidence, and I began to write more words and music. I included my work alongside those of other artists and composers. My aching heart was soothed as I poured out my pain into the lyrics and music I wrote, and it resonated with many of my followers.

Invitations began to arrive for me to perform at venues throughout Delphiope. I developed a punishing regimen of writing, rehearsals, meditations, fitness and performance. I had to prove that I could succeed and reach the top of my profession. I hoped that if I did so, it would prove to my family that I could succeed without them. I never forgot my daughter; each year, I marked her anniversary with a visit to the temple. My family in Thena were raised in the Singularity faith, but after meeting the dreamer in Cawsal, I became interested in Fatalism. Putting faith in the fates seems far better than in some spiritual nonsense. After that first one, I met other child dreamers and one or two of the most revered dreamers who had reached adulthood, but I never again saw the girl I met that day in Cawsal.

As the years went by, I spent more time socialising and building my network of friends, some of whom became the family I'd lost. I could always rely on these friends to be there as I was for them. Although a few men would like to have become more than friends, I never allowed any relationship to develop. I was joined to my performance, and there was no room for a relationship in my life. It was a proud day when I received my first invitation from a theatre in Pollo. Until then, I had only performed in Delphiope. This was only the first of many invitations to perform across Pollo; then came the first invitation to perform in Thena. My hands shook as I read the words. I was terrified my family would find out, and yet, in a small way, I hoped they would. Standing on that stage in the Esternia Theatre of Central Thena was the most terrifying place I have ever stood. I heard the waver in my voice as I sang the first note before I closed my eyes. Shutting out the audience and focusing on the words and music, I allowed them to swell and fill me before flowing from my mouth. The response as the last note faded took my breath away. I'd arrived. I'd been received and accepted for who I was. From that moment, there was no venue I wouldn't go to and no event I turned down. I fed off the exhilaration from each performance, which drove my writing and musicality even further.

I rode that wave right to the top, where I was privileged to remain. As I travelled across Anacadair to venues of all sizes, I was still overwhelmed by the generosity of audiences. Their response to my performance and coin towards the charitable causes I supported was terrific. One of the charities I set up was to help girls like myself who fell foul of the Bloodline Laws.

The coin I provided supported accommodation for girls and their children, enabling them to train and become self-sufficient. I quietly campaigned for the Abolition and Modernisation of Bloodline Laws (AMBL) to help protect these vulnerable girls. The change was most needed in Thena, where this had the most severe impact. However, families from Pollo and Delphiope were also impacted. This was a mission I had given to myself, and I would not rest until these practices were pushed out into the archives where they belonged. I longed for a time where greater tolerance and understanding could begin. Unfortunately, this was also a political issue and must be handled cautiously.

Part 5 – One week earlier

15

Amelie

Tilda's sixteenth anniversary was approaching, along with the anniversary of Kayden's death. It was always a bittersweet time, even more so this year. I was preparing to send Tilda's formal Invitation to the National Introductions Agency in Thena, according to Thena Anlan tradition. On that day, she will meet Orlan, the boy named on her Promisary Agreement. Dorcana's son, Orlan, has grown into a tall, handsome young man I was very fond of. I didn't know how Tilda would feel about a Promisary Agreement made by someone she hadn't met. I would be far from pleased were I to stand in her shoes. After their formal Introduction, the two young people would begin their required sessions at the National Introductions Agency. They would receive guidance on managing their household, finances, along with Delphiope and Anacadair law. Instruction will take several weeks, allowing the couple to get to know each other. Guidance also covers raising a family, educating children and finding suitable matches. The couple will be expected to marry, but the agreement may be broken if they find they aren't compatible. When I heard what they would be taught, I looked back on my life and realised how much I'd given up by taking the path I did.

Rosa left several years ago to live with a man who had offered her the security and love she craved. I'd never met anyone who could fill the void left behind by Kayden, and so I remain alone. But, at thirty-two, I can honestly say I'm happy. Everything I possess I have earned through writing and performing my work. I owe nothing, financially or otherwise, which gave me great pride and satisfaction. When I chose the Invitation for Tilda, I used the Anlan Seal on the front. It was who she was, after all. I chose the best quality paper and an elegant and simple cover design in black and white. Inside, the formal wording was printed with no amendment. I enclosed a letter on good quality pink writing paper. It took several attempts before I found the right words, which I knew would be read by Rush and Thea. I wanted them to know a little about the boy in the Promisary Agreement and his background. I added a little about myself too, guessing Tilda wouldn't know anything of my life if my father had carried out his threat.

According to tradition, we should meet on her sixteenth anniversary at the National Introductions Agency in Thena. When the letter was sent, all I could do was stand at the gates on the day alongside Dorcana and Orlan. *I hope Rush honours my right and delivers her to me*. I'd no idea what she looked like. I didn't even see her at birth, but I knew she would be beautiful. It had pained me every day that I couldn't see her and marvel at her achievements or comfort her when she stumbled. The dreamer, Silph, whom I met all those years ago in Cawsal, told me I would meet Tilda again. I had to put my trust in the fates that she was right.

So here we were on a grey day, sixteen years after I gave birth. Orlan stood between Dorcana and I, tall in his green tunic, matching his rich green eyes. His golden-brown hair was neatly trimmed to his shoulders, as was the fashion for young men. He was clean-shaven and pleasing to look at. I've seen his smile as he looked at Dorcana; the warmth and kindness radiating from it warmed my heart. The poor boy was nervous, rubbing his hands down his legs as he moved from one foot to another. Today was also important for him, his first step towards manhood. Beside him, Dorcana stood motionless. She was a small, motherly woman of generous proportions. Her tailoring skills had created a flattering deep blue dress and jacket that drew the eye to her neat legs and tiny feet. She wore a hat with a wide lace brim to shelter her face from the sun's intense rays. Today, there was little need to worry about the sun. I had taken special care with my appearance to make the right impression. I wanted Rush to see I was successful. My peacock green suit, wide trousers, and fitted jacket showed my neat figure. The cream blouse showed the healthy glow of my skin from time in the sun. I'd used little makeup, just the lightest of pink swept across my lips. My wide-brimmed cream hat, the height of fashion, sat on my curly, dark copper hair, tipped down to one side. We were standing near the gates, allowing us to see those who arrived throughout the day. Many others like us gathered by the gates throughout the morning, and there was quite a crowd by midday. Dorcana slipped away to bring refreshments, and although I couldn't face much, I had to maintain my strength and accepted graciously. Gradually, through the afternoon, the crowd began to thin, yet still we waited.

There had been no reply to the Invitation, but I suspected Rush and even Father would not be able to deny me this one thing. I was sure he would come, but as the hours slipped by and the pale shadows lengthened, there was still no sign of him. I was increasingly afraid that they wouldn't come and equally terrified that they would. *How could I face Tilda? What would she think of me? How much did she know?* I hadn't seen Rush since I was sent to the attic. We'd been such friends as children. He must hate me for causing so much pain, disgracing myself and shaming the family. He must, because if he didn't, surely, he would have written to me and answered my letters. Time crawled by as I tortured myself with such thoughts. I was only brought back to the present when Dorcana began chatting about a forthcoming celebration and the displays that would be set up. I was singing as part of the celebration with a group of schoolchildren, which had been so much fun. I was grateful Dorcana was here with me. I don't think I could have done this alone.

It was late in the day as we stood alone at the gate when a conveyance drew up. I watched my brother step from it. I would know him anywhere. That angular face was so like Father's. He had more lines now than the last time I saw him. When I saw he was dressed in funeral black, my face burned with shame. *How could he?* Thea's tall, willowy shape stepped from the conveyance, and I saw she was heavy with child. Beside her stood a slight young woman in a cream dress that flowed over her shape. It didn't cling to her curves in a vulgar sense but elegantly defined her youth. Her hair was a mass of dark copper curls like mine, with a cream flower pinned on one side. She was so pretty. My heart swelled with the love I'd stored for the past sixteen years. It was all I could do not to rush over and throw my arms around her. I felt the pressure of Dorcana's hand on my arm and knew she must have read my thoughts. Dorcana and I had talked for hours about this moment. She cautioned me to curb my desire to be reunited, warning me that Tilda might not want to meet me or have this match. She reminded me of my reaction when Father told me about this event. I knew she was right. I remembered how rebellious and resentful I was at her age.

As they drew closer, I saw Dorcana had been right to warn me. My beautiful daughter was not full of smiles. She walked as if each step was almost too painful. It was as if she was being dragged towards a terrible fate. I hadn't wanted to believe Dorcana. I had wanted the dream reunion. Yet, here was my daughter beside another woman whose arm was around her shoulders, and she leaned into her. My dreams crumbled. Dorcana was beside me, and I drew strength from her calming presence. I could not show weakness now, so I drew myself up to my full height, took a deep breath and stepped forward as if stepping out on stage. This would be, without doubt, my greatest performance without singing a single note.

"Amelie of Delphiope, formerly of Thena and daughter of Anlan. I bring your daughter to you as requested by Invitation. Is the family from the Promisary Agreement here?" I heard Rush speak, and the years fell away. His voice was more mature but still his. He was saying the stuffy formal Thenan words, his tone cold and neutral, devoid of emotion. I was desperate to hear something of the brother I once knew, but perhaps it was too much to ask how he must have hated the Invitation's arrival after all this time. Meeting me would bring back everything that occurred. I took a deep breath, held my head high and looked him in the eye. I was proud of who I am. I didn't need his approval or recognition.

"Rush of Thena and son of Anlan, I welcome my daughter's return on her sixteenth anniversary. I bring Orlan named on the Promisary Agreement and his mother Dorcana, both of Delphiope." The hours of careful rehearsal with Dorcana ensured I was word-perfect. My voice was confident and clear in my Thenan dialect, reflecting my heritage. Our eyes locked for the first time in sixteen years, and for a moment, a tiny moment, I saw the boy my brother had been. Then, in a blink of his eyes and a nod of his head, he turned and beckoned to Thea and Tilda. Slowly, they made their way towards us across the void between the world she had known and the world she would meet. Rush stood straight as a poker as he observed their progress. His index finger tapped his trouser leg, the childhood sign of irritation. Was it their slow pace or just being here? I wondered. Like father, like son perhaps? Father was not patient and didn't like to be kept waiting. Turning my eyes to them as they approached, I wondered who supported whom. The mother supported the child or the child the mother. When they drew alongside Rush, Thea looked at me, pain etched in her face. She gave a small smile before Rush spoke again.

"Amelie of Delphiope, I present Millie, your daughter placed in our keeping for these past sixteen years and now returned to you." as he spoke, I watched Thea and the girl beside her. I saw them wince as the words struck home. She was leaving the only home she had known. I wished with all my heart I could make it easier. Watching her cling to Thea, I wondered, for the first time, if I had been right to issue the invitation. I felt the first pang of doubt rise. I hadn't wanted to believe how much this might affect her until I saw the pain written across her face, but it was too late. I had to say the words expected of me, so I continued.

"Rush of Thena, I thank you for your care of my daughter and her return to me. All obligations towards her are now complete. Until her marriage, I will keep her safe and provide for her as expected, according to Anlan tradition. Thea of Thena and daughter of Anlan, I thank you for nurturing and mothering my daughter for the past sixteen years. Today, your obligations are also now complete." The formal words couldn't convey my feelings at this moment. I was glad of the ceremonial language as I turned towards Dorcana and Orlan, who, at my signal, joined me.

"Millie of Thena and daughter of Anlan, I welcome your return. You were given the name Tilda when you were born, so your formal name from this day forward will be Tilda Millie. Informally, of course, you can choose which name to be known by." *Those eyes, like mine, burned with pain. It wasn't easy to see them and hold her gaze*. I turned to Orlan and began the formal words.

"Orlan of Delphiope and son of Ando, may I present my daughter Tilda Millie. According to Anlan custom in Thena, you and Tilda Millie were cited in a Promisary Agreement, which is now fulfilled. Your Introductions will begin here at the National Introductions Agency." Orlan looked shyly at Millie, but she didn't look up. Tears ran down her face, affecting him as he looked away. I felt sorry for him. He was a kind and sensitive boy. Millie had gone to a place where she was lost to what was happening around her. A stab of pain hit me as I remembered being in that place when my life was taken from me and they took her away, banishing me.

"Tilda Millie of Thena and daughter of Anlan, I greet you. Today is a great day and is a new beginning for us." his voice was soft and hesitant. He might expect his words to bring joy in other circumstances, but these were far from usual. I felt sorry for him. He was so nervous and keen to make the right impression. Dorcana and I had done our best to prepare him and explain Tilda's circumstances. Thea leant down to whisper in Tilda's ear. I couldn't hear what was said. Usually, it would be considered poor manners, but I forgave them today. I could see Millie was unable to give the ceremonial greeting expected. If I stood in her shoes, those words would have stuck in my throat, too. For the first time, I wondered how Rush and Thea had prepared her for today. Thea uncurled as I considered this question, replacing her arm around Tilda and drawing her close.

"Orlan of Delphiope, I greet you on this day on behalf of Millie. Today will indeed mark a new beginning for you both." I saw Rush's temper rise. The deep hue on his cheeks and the cough were all the reminders she needed as she stopped speaking. She held out her hand graciously towards Orlan, who took it and lightly kissed the back of it. It should have been Millie's hand, but I could see how impossible that was.

The formalities were concluded, and suddenly, I wanted to contact Rush to reconnect with him again. I blurted out.

"Rush, thank you. I know this is not the time, but perhaps we could..." but he had already turned away and was walking back to the conveyance, my words hung in the void. While his back was turned, Thea quickly took a step closer.

"We must talk. I will visit you in one week if you will permit. There are things you should know." I nodded briefly as she turned and walked back towards the conveyance as if she had never spoken. Dorcana met my eye and shrugged. It was odd, and I couldn't help wondering what she wanted to talk about. After all, there had been sixteen years to speak or write to me. Now, though, I had to take Tilda Millie to her new home and find a way to reach her. Turning to the young woman before me, I stretched out my hand, but she didn't take it. Gently, I placed an arm on her shoulder and guided her towards my conveyance. We travelled together to Delphiope, arriving in Delph just as nightfall descended. It was just a short walk from the conveyance to my door. Millie stood motionless in the cool hall, I wished I knew how to reach her. We were both lost in the moment. We would have to find some sort of balance, but for now, I would take the lead. I knew how it felt to lose everything and everyone.

"Why don't we go through into the garden room? It's comfortable, and we can talk a little and get to know each other. This must be very frightening for you." Millie allowed me to lead her into the light, airy garden room with its floral chairs and pastel walls. Lola popped in and asked if we would like something light to eat and drink. I nodded, and she disappeared again. Millie perched rigidly on the edge of the seat. Hostility oozed from her in every breath and every pore of her skin. Sitting on the settee near her, I looked over.

"What name would you like to use?"

"My name is Millie," she snapped.

"I guessed as much, so Millie it is. You should call me Amelie," she said nothing and stared down at her feet in their pretty cream shoes. I wondered if they were comfortable, they looked new.

"Would you like to change or slip off your shoes? I always find new shoes are a little uncomfortable when I first wear them." She said nothing, but I saw an involuntary easing of her feet. I slipped off my shoes and wiggled my toes before tucking them underneath me. I remembered I was still wearing my hat and deftly removed it and began to unpin my hair so it fell over my shoulders. I shook my head and ran my hands through my hair, relieving the pressure around my temples. Millie watched, her eyes dark and unreadable. I moved over and knelt before her. Gently, I slipped off her shoes and placed them beside the chair. Then, taking each foot in turn, I massaged it before placing it back on the floor.

"Does that feel better?"

"A bit," she muttered. "Thank you."

"What about that pretty hair clip? It must be pulling by now. Would you like to remove it?" I returned to my chair across from her and waited to see what she did. A moment later, she raised a hand and removed the hairclip, giving her head a rub.

"There, that must feel better." I said, "Millie, I can't replace Thea as your mother, and I don't have the right to. She will always be your mother, but I'd like to be your friend. We are both in a situation that neither of us would have wished. Over the coming week, I will tell you about myself, and perhaps you can tell me a little about yourself, too. There will be time to meet with Orlan and Dorcana in a more comfortable setting with no formal language or expectations. You should know that in Delphiope, although we respect the Bloodline Laws, breaking a Promisary Agreement is possible. It can happen if you both agree. Marriage should be something you wish to do, not something you are expected to do for your parents. I believe love should drive our choices and not laws." As I said that, she looked up for the first time, and I realised this might be what troubled her most.

"Is there someone you have left behind that you care about?" she looked down for a moment, but I saw her soften.

"Yes," a tear ran down her face.

"Oh, Millie, I'm so sorry. Tell me about him," and she did. We talked long into the night on that first day, covering her early life and mine. Over the week that followed, we finally got to know each other.

16

Rush

As the front door closed, Thea turned, her face white with rage. Her green eyes were bright with an unnatural glow. She was no longer my mild, reassuring wife but some unnatural witch. I wanted to take an involuntary step, but I was frozen to the spot, unable to move, and I felt a surge of panic.

"How dare you stand in your funeral suit? You disgrace her and our family." She growled in a deep, low voice that echoed through the hall. Spital flew with each word like venom from a snake, and some landed on my jacket in frothy green globules. I've never seen such fury from her. I felt my own rage rise, but it stopped as if blocked, boiling painfully in my throat. My eyes widened. How could I respond to the fury standing before me?

"It was no celebration…" I began. At least I still had my voice.

"…and whose fault is it that?" Her voice, deep and primal, silenced me. Green venom burned my face like acid, and I wanted to wipe it away, but my hand remained obstinately at my side.

"We knew this day would come…" I tried, but she interrupted.

"That child was ripped from her mother as a babe and is now ripped from her second family." she punctuated every word with a stab to my chest. Her finger pierced my shirt like a blade, and pain seared through me where it touched my skin. Blazing green eyes held mine, and I couldn't look away. I was trapped like prey to a cobra.

"You knew how it would be when we took her. You knew…" My words dried up in my throat, and I fell silent, unable to speak. I tried to look away, but still, she held my eyes. My fear was plain to see, and I was ashamed of my weakness.

"I did not agree," she hissed. Her fists clasped, bringing them down to her sides, knuckles white. My arms tightened at my sides. "I accepted her with compassion for her mother, whoever she was. I loved her as my own. I even accepted your parents in my house. YOU agreed to all these things, not me." I was lost for words. The pain inside me was overwhelming, and I realised it was her pain I felt. *How could I feel her pain?* I'd never experienced such intense pain, and it took my breath away. I tried to find words to soothe her pain.

"She was Amelie's daughter. She belonged with family, not strangers. It was the only way…" My voice was silenced again, cut off mid-sentence.

"You never told me who she was." her voice was low and intense. A fresh wave of pain swept through me, so fierce it took my breath away. I tried to speak but only managed to gulp.

"You NEVER showed kindness to her." she hissed, and the barb struck home. Another hot spear of pain drove deep into my heart, my pain mixed with hers. It was overwhelming, and to my increasing shame, I felt tears in my eyes. The humiliation rose as I blinked back the tears. I hoped she wouldn't see. I tried to find the right words again.

"I could not…" I began. A tear rolled down my cheek, followed by another, but my hands wouldn't let me wipe them away. More followed, the raw emotion bleeding tears I never wanted to shed, stored up over the decades. "Promises were made. Consequences…" The words tumbled from my lips unbidden.

"I was hard on the child because I was angry with Amelie. She was so like her, and it hurt every time I saw her. I couldn't bear to look at her." my voice trembled. She looked at me, and I saw the Thea I knew return. The hurt in her eyes told me she knew all too well the reality of my words. Wordlessly, she turned towards the garden room.

Automatically, my hand tried to go to my pocket, and I found I could move. My fingers felt for the key and encircled it. As I reached the study door, the key moved to the lock. Closing the door, I locked it behind me and stood with my forehead resting against the cool wood. *What had just happened? I'd never seen Thea like that before. I've never felt such raw emotion and pain, and why did it feel like her pain? Why did my eyes brim with tears? I haven't shed tears since I was a baby. How did she fix me to the spot so I couldn't move or speak?* I'd always been the strong one. For the first time, I felt powerless and could do nothing. Thea had become a different person with such powerful emotions they could transfer to me. I'd never seen or felt anything like it before. I looked down at my shirt and saw the tiny perforations where her finger had stabbed me. Each perforation was now edged with a red bloom. How did that happen? Her manicured nails were always carefully shaped to protect even the most delicate skin. They could never cause such damage to a shirt or me. Yet somehow, they had. How could I let this happen when she was so close to her time? Suddenly, I couldn't bear to travel this road any longer. I'd tried to be like my father all my life. Tried to become the man he wanted me to be, desperate to gain his approval. Suddenly, I wanted to claim back my life before it was too late. To be the man I was born to be.

I sat in my armchair, gazing at the cold fireplace. Everything about today had been wrong. *Why should Millie suffer for her mother's disgrace? What kind of Father takes his revenge on his daughter and granddaughter?* Revenge for a shame that would cause him embarrassment. He was only protecting his pride, nothing more. I could see it now. The Bloodline Laws were ridiculous. If our experience was mirrored in other families, then the laws were a mockery. *What about the child's wishes?* Who would listen to the child if their parents were never listened to as children? How could families learn respect? At the root of all this were the Bloodline Laws. It always came down to them. In today's society, why do we expect women to raise children and not have a career? Thea had wanted to become a Healer. She would have been good, too, but she didn't have the chance because she was a woman.

How could the laws change while Father was Head of the High Council and believed in the old ways? He had so much influence there was no way to challenge him. My mind ran over all the scenarios I could think of, finding none remotely feasible. Eventually, my eyelids drooping, I left the study and climbed the stairs, creeping along the hallway to our bedroom. Pushing open the door, I saw Thea lying peacefully on the bed. Her black hair, released from its usual pins and clips, softly surrounded her serene face like a dark halo. Under her eyelids, with their sweep of coffee colour, I saw movement betraying her dreams. After the trauma of the day, I was drained. I slipped off my jacket and shoes, loosened my tie, and carefully climbed onto the bed beside her. I longed to take her in my arms, but I resisted. It was enough to lie beside her and watch her sleep, inhaling her sweet perfume. As I did so, I felt my own eyes begin to close. *Why not? Why not let them close for a few minutes, just this once?*

Sometime later, I stretched and opened my eyes. It took me a moment to remember how I came to be lying on the bed, fully clothed. I was cold and looked over to the crumpled bedclothes where Thea had been lying, but she had gone. I felt for any warmth but was met with the coolness that only hours could bring. A single long black hair lay on the pillow, proof, if I needed it, that she had been there. I sat up with a sigh and swung my legs over the side of the bed. Listening, I heard no noise to suggest where she might be. Perhaps she'd gone out, although where she'd go, I couldn't imagine. Taking a deep breath, I slid my feet into my shoes, put on my house jacket, and tightened my tie. Even though I had taken leave to attend to family affairs today, I had work to do. There was always work to do, but it could wait until I'd made a pot of coffee.

Thea sat in her favourite chair near the window in the garden room. Her face bore the streaks of tears shed silently, and they continued to slide down her face. She sat in dignified silence; her body gently shook with emotion. I walked over to her and touched her shoulder as a swell of emotion filled me. It was always the same. I was supposed to uphold the laws and have a model family. I was supposed to be in control of myself and those around me. There was so much pressure to be the perfect family. My responsibilities were deeply ingrained through years of instruction. Father ensured that he beat them into me until they could never be forgotten. Yet deep inside, a different person longed to show tenderness and compassion. A man who longed to stand up to injustice and prejudice, to defend those unable to protect themselves. I wanted to put my arms around Thea and wipe away her tears, but would she accept my comfort? Gently, I lowered myself to my knees, sliding my arms around her. I expected to be rejected and pushed away, but it didn't happen.

"I'm sorry" I whispered. Laying my head on her shoulder. I breathed in her scent, "I'm so sorry for everything." She didn't say anything, but her hand moved to my arm. I waited for her to push me away, but she rested her hand on my arm and caressed me as she softened into my embrace.

"We need to talk," I said, and we turned to face each other. Briefly, our lips met before pulling apart, self-conscious, unused to the spontaneity.

"Rush, there is so much I want to say..." she began.

"The future..." I said.

"About Amelie..." she said.

"...and Millie." I added.

"Both." she agreed.

It was the beginning of a very long conversation. For the first time in eighteen years of marriage, we allowed ourselves to voice truths and fears held deep inside. Something had changed as if a switch had been flipped. In our private bubble, we were free from the constraints of Thena and Anlan. We talked deep into the night, pausing when the children returned home before continuing after dinner. Although it was unusual for us to dine as a family, none of the children remarked on their father's presence at the table. It was as if they could feel an undercurrent of change that must run its course. At the table, we ate, chatting lightly. Thea asked about the children's school day, homework assignments, and the usual topics. She reminded them to revise for upcoming end-of-term evaluations. The twins talked animatedly about Prof Hog. How old he was, how boring the lessons were, and how he snorted when they said something silly or wrong. Later, after the children had gone to their rooms, Thea and I retired to our private parlour. Thea was surprised at how things had gone, but the most challenging part was yet to come. She wanted to discuss a far more significant change. I'd given up a little of myself as I acknowledged the need for change. We agreed to allow Amelie back into our lives. I held back my part in those events, but perhaps a time would come when I could tell Thea and eventually even Amelie.

17

Thea

The day dawned bright and warm as I prepared to see Millie. I was worried; Millie was such a fiery girl, but last week, I watched her retreat, deep inside herself, to a place I couldn't reach. *Would she hear me today?* I brushed my midnight black hair thoughtfully before pulling it back and securing it in a chignon. I would have left it loose, but Rush disapproved of that, and I wanted to go out without raising questions. Thank goodness his parents are finally gone, and the house is mine again. It hadn't been easy for Rush to raise the subject with them, but they had no reason to stay once Millie had left. Rush had never told me they came as part of the agreement for Millie, although I guessed as much. He told me they would 'help' bring her up. As a new mother, I was initially grateful. Later, as time passed, I became aware there was more to their presence in our family home than just helping a new mother. I had felt patronised and insulted that my mothering skills were presumed to be so inadequate. Zillah never failed to point out every fault. I resented their intrusion and the way Thenan politics reached so far into the home.

I took a last glance in the looking glass at my reflection. The pale green water silk dress with meadow flowers flowed comfortably over my curves and swollen belly. My white-heeled shoes gave the formality expected of me. Simple house shoes would have been more comfortable this late in pregnancy when my feet swelled during the day and were uncomfortable. But if Rush were to see them, it would raise questions. A Thenan woman of my status was expected to maintain high standards at all times. With a sigh, I picked up my green wrap and the bag I usually took when shopping. It was the one time I could go out unchallenged and unaccompanied. Shopping was an approved activity for a Thenan woman. Women of Thena were expected to care for their appearance and follow the latest fashions. I slipped a few of Millie's smaller treasures into my bag and covered them with the wrap. The study door opened as I descended the stairs, and Rush stood waiting to greet me.

"You look lovely, Thea. Where are you going this afternoon?" his tone was light, but there was a steely undercurrent. He wore a light grey suit, pale shirt and a grey patterned tie. As usual, he was immaculately groomed, his black shoes gleaming in the light from the hall window. I knew he was trying to be agreeable, but the past week had opened such a gulf between us it would take time to heal. We'd reached a fragile understanding after that day when we finally spoke, but the undercurrent of what had happened wasn't far from the surface.

"I'm going to look for a new dress. I have so few I can wear now, and you want me to accompany you to the Legal Octon dinner next week." that was true, although I had a dress I could wear, but I didn't think Rush would know that.

"An outing will do you good after... after everything. A new dress will make you feel better." a pained expression crossed his face.

Only I knew how much this whole business had affected him. Seeing Amelie would have brought back all manner of painful memories exacerbated by fiery arguments with his parents before they left. I'm sure the echoes of those arguments were still ringing in his ears. Leaving Millie with Amelie was the final, most painful act, and his rage had been terrible. All the hurt and pain boiled over, and he raged at his parents in a way he had never done before. His parents met his rage with their own, and what was said and done could never be undone.

"Thank you," I said, mirroring his agreeable tone.

"Have you called for a conveyance?"

"Yes, it will be here shortly. I wanted to walk down the drive to the road as it was a nice day. I asked for it to wait at the end of the drive." I said, stepping through the door and closing it behind me without a backward glance. I knew it was petty. He would have expected the usual kiss and reassurance I would take a conveyance home, etc., but I couldn't bring myself to say anything else. I've borne the brunt of his rage since his parents left and ached from its outpouring until it burned out. I hope giving him some time alone might help dampen the embers and bring him back to himself again.

Everyone knew it happened in families. It was accepted as part of life in Thena. Thena Anlan society demanded high discipline and self-control for all family members. Some found it difficult to achieve and maintain the required level, and responsibility for discipline fell to the head of the house. It was his task to enforce compliance with laws and social expectations. Measures for enforcement within families were typically handed down from parent to child. In Thena, there was no sign of the progress and freedoms beginning to take shape in Delphiope and even Pollo. In Cawsal, of course, there had always been a more relaxed way of life. Cawsal culture is almost the opposite of Thenan culture, you might say.

At the end of the drive, I slipped through the small side gate and locked it behind me. As expected, the conveyance was waiting for me; its sleek lines glistened in the sunlight. The driver opened the door for me to enter. It rocked gently as he took his seat, and we pulled away. I watched as neatly organised streets with high fences and locked gates became more open as we moved into Anthara. This was the area of Thena where the great fashion houses were found. My favourite was Silk, with its rows of beautiful water silk dresses and fine linen suits. Great bolts of water silk lay in vats of lake water, their colours every hue imaginable. We entered Delphiope and the town of Pera. Then beautiful mountains rose on the right before we reached Delph, the primary city of Delphiope.

The conveyance pulled away, leaving me on a pretty tree-lined road. Branches laden with pink blossom gave a delicate fragrance to the air. I'd memorised the short walk from where the conveyance would stop all the way to Amelie's house. It took me along a small road before winding up a gentle slope. I passed large houses with welcoming gardens full of colour. It was so different from Thenan residential roads with high fences and locked gates. Here, gates of wrought metal work in intricate swirls allowed guests to pass through without locks or security. The gardens I saw through the gates were beautiful, full of colour and structure. As I turned the last bend in the road, I saw the most beautiful gates. Each gate had a large letter A surrounded by scrolls and swirls painted gold. This was Amelie's house. I would recognise her style anywhere.

I pulled the latch, and the gate swung easily back, allowing me to pass through. I found myself in a landscape of colours blending and swirling in the most beautiful patterns. Elegant flowerbeds surrounded by manicured lawns escorted me to the house. I was relieved my walk was almost over. The slope up to the house had been steeper than I had anticipated. I felt beads of sweat run down my face and back. The weight of my belly seemed to increase with each step, and my feet were tight in my shoes. I regretted not risking the comfortable house shoes. To arrive hot, sweating and flushed wasn't how I wished to greet Amelie and Millie. It wasn't polite in Thena, but perhaps I might be forgiven as I was with child. The house was a delicate shade of grey accented with pale, creamy yellow frames. Floating beneath each window were planters with garlands of colour. The main door opened as I approached, and I saw Amelie, her dark, coppery hair flowing loose around her shoulders. She wore a simple blouse with flowing navy trousers that oozed elegance and style. I felt dowdy as I approached, my breath coming in deep, ragged gasps as I fought for space to breathe with the baby I carried. I was unsure how Amelie expected me to greet her, but I needn't have worried. She came forward and embraced me, kissing each cheek lightly. Such informality usually made me feel awkward, it never happened in Thena. Here and now, it felt completely natural to return to her embrace.

"Thea, welcome to my home. Did you walk far?" her voice was full of concern as she stood aside to let me enter the cool hallway.

"Thank you, Amelie. I walked up from the main road but didn't realise how steep it was. I need a moment to catch my breath." The entrance hall was beautiful in shades of cream and brown. A glass-topped table with a vase of exotic flowers stood to the left beside a large mirror. Standing by the table was Millie. My breath caught as I looked at her. She was so beautiful and so like Amelie. Why I hadn't realised before? I suppose I'd had no reason to make that connection.

"Millie, I..." *What could I say?* "I've missed you," I finished as I stepped forward, putting my arm out to embrace her. She resisted my touch, and I stepped back as pain shot through my heart. I struggled to hide my emotions.

"Why don't we go through to the garden room?" Amelie said, "We've laid out some fruit juice and refreshments." Her voice had an energy and friendliness that drew me in.

We enter a cool room with glass walls, looking out across beautiful gardens. There was an array of chairs in soft pastel colours and a small sofa, which I gratefully sank into. The room felt as if it was part of the garden. The clear glass was invisible as I looked out.

"Amelie, this is truly lovely. "I managed after a few moments. She took a chair opposite me, and Millie sat between us around a small table. The table had a lacy cover, elegant white plates, tall glasses, and a jug of fruit juice. On a tiered stand were cakes, pastries, shortbreads and other delicacies. Gratefully, I accepted a glass of fruit juice and sipped it slowly.

"How are you?" it was Millie, her voice small and tentative. My heart swelled with love at her voice.

"Oh, Millie..." I swallowed and tried again, "I'm well, thank you. How are you?" I tried to keep to the formal conversation style, but it seemed stuffy and unnecessary here.

"Amelie showed me around Delph, and we did some shopping, but mostly we talked. What happened when you went home after, after...?" her voice broke, and she looked down at her hands.

"It was complicated with your... with Rush. He was very upset, we both were. "I looked at her tiny frame, rigid with tension. I wanted to reassure her it would be OK, but I couldn't.

"Were you OK with the baby… he didn't..." She looked at me, and I saw tears flood her eyes. In that moment, I realised she knew. I'd always tried to conceal things from the children, yet she'd seen the truth. My heart ached with shame.

"The baby is fine; it won't be long now. I'll be glad when she finally arrives." Millie looked up as I said that.

"She?"

"Yes, I decided I wanted to know this time. You will have a sister in a few weeks, Millie." Her face fell.

"But she won't be my sister, will she..." Her voice was brittle and spiked with pain that radiated like shards of glass that struck deep into my heart.

"Millie," it was Amelie, her voice soft and gentle. "Thea will always be your mother in the ways that matter most. I hope, perhaps, in time, we may become good friends. I can never be the mother to you that Thea is." Millie doesn't reply.

"Thank you, Amelie. Millie, I am and always will be proud to be your mother. I know this has been tough for you, but I hope we can all become friends." I looked at Amelie, "You have lived with this secret for the past sixteen years and in a different way, so I have. We have both known this time would come, the time for truth. Your story is now known, but it's time for me to tell you mine. After that, we need to decide where we go from here. Our lives are intertwined and have been ever since you were born, Millie. My story has never been told. To my knowledge, only my immediate family know the truth. After the baby arrives, I plan to correct that. No more secrets." Amelie nodded and uttered quiet agreement. Millie looked as if she might speak, but I raised a hand. It was time for my tale to be told.

18

Thea

"I was born in Cawsal. I know that will shock you, but it's true. I can't believe I'm finally telling the story of my early life and how it was stolen from me. My father was a wealthy farmer in Central Caws, owning quite a large farm. He also had several distributions that supplied Delphiope, Pollo, and occasionally Thena. I was educated alongside the best students from across Ancadair. I expected to gain my certificate to study Healing in Pollo. My father was so proud of me. From a young age, he wanted me to have the best opportunities. When I was twelve, my mother was killed in a farming accident. It was a terrible time. Father mourned her dreadfully and was unable to look after me. It was decided to send me to live with relatives in Pollo. They were Healers and well respected because their bloodline linked them to Thena. I don't know when or why the Promisary Agreement was made, but it was probably quite late after my move to Pollo. You may know that in Cawsal, we don't go in for such things, preferring nature to find the best match."

I stopped momentarily and picked up my glass with a shaking hand. Taking a few sips, I set it down again. I needed a moment to find the right words. I hadn't put words to my story for almost twenty years, and they didn't come easily. Shifting my weight a little, I eased the pressure on my legs before I continued.

"When I moved to Pollo, I didn't know it would be forever. I thought it would be while my father was grieving. It was only later I found out that I wouldn't return and couldn't see my family. I knew, even then, how much my father had given up for me, but I missed him desperately and grieved in private for my mother. Children weren't considered capable of experiencing grief. It isn't too different even now, for that matter. But I can tell you that wasn't true for me. The aching hollow inside almost consumed me, but my aunt and uncle were kind. They helped me accept her death and come to terms with my new life in Pollo.

It was soon accepted that Mother Lib and Father Jonca were now my parents. Although not typical, it wasn't unheard of for children to live with extended family members. Moving children to extended family members can offer the opportunity for a better future. Pollo treads a fine line between Thena on one side and Delphiope on the other, looking for the best advantage of each. Only in Thena are bloodlines carefully considered for a good match. I'm sure I wasn't the only child whose true heritage has been concealed. Father Jonca was Thena/Pollo (Father from Thena, Mother from Pollo). Mother Lib is Delphiope/Thena. This was important and gave me a good bloodline for a match with a boy from Thena. For a long time, I was unhappy. I wasn't allowed to see my father, and nobody told me why. I concluded it must be because something terrible had happened to my father. I resented calling my relatives, Mother and Father because I knew they weren't.

You should know they weren't unkind to me, and I did come to love them, but they weren't my birth parents. They could never hold that place in my heart. After some time, we agreed I could call them Father Jonca and Mother Lib. It was an accepted way to acknowledge parents in Pollo, and my birth parents remained Mother and Father. This turning point enabled us to find a middle ground to build my future. The school I attended was good, and I enjoyed learning about healing in particular. It was the only thing I lived for. Father Jonca took me aside at fourteen and told me about Bloodlines and my Promisary Agreement. The boy was older than I was and studying law. I reacted much as you did, Millie. My whole life had been taken over, and I could do nothing about it.

There was a boy from Delphiope I had become very friendly with, who was also hoping to become a Healer. When I was told about the Promisary Agreement, Dylen and I decided to run away before my sixteenth anniversary. By then, we would have certificates to continue our studies in Healing at an Academie in another district. We made our plans and thought we were being so clever and discrete. But we were very wrong; I was watched from the moment Father Jonca told me of the Promisary Agreement. Looking back, I had probably told Mother Lib all about Dylen, and they must have guessed the rest. Dylen was warned off by Father Jonca, who also told me to stop seeing him. Young and naive that we were, it only made us more determined to escape. In fact, on the last day we met, we decided to run there and then. Of course, we were followed and trapped. It was terrible. Dylen was captured and beaten while I was put into a locked conveyance and taken away. For many months, I'd had nightmares of being trapped somewhere, unable to escape, waking in a cold sweat each time. Now, here I was, in a locked conveyance, the place of my nightmares. The panic rose as I screamed to be let out. It wasn't until we were home that I was released and escorted to my room. I thought my life was over, not worth living without Dylen, but I couldn't even control whether I lived or died. I cried so much until there were no tears left. It was a very dark time." I had to stop, gulping back tears that threatened to overwhelm me. I hadn't thought of those days for a long time, but the pain was still as intense as it was then.

Reaching down, I slipped my hand into my bag, feeling for my handkerchief. Carefully, I dabbed at my face, wet from tears.

It was a moment before I reached for my glass and drank deeply, draining the contents before placing it back on the table. It helped, and I was in control again and able to continue.

"Father Jonca and Mother Lib spent a long time trying to talk to me that day and the next, but I didn't want to hear from them. I stayed in my room, curled up in my bed. I was so angry and heartbroken. I felt betrayed and so many more emotions I couldn't and still can't find the words for. Even after those few early days, the deep feelings have never healed, but eventually, I resigned myself to my fate. I promised that one day, when the opportunity arose, I would take back my life." I paused.

"Rush and I married on my twentieth anniversary in a big ceremony arranged by our families. My true father, of course, was not invited, and I was told never to mention my original parents to Rush or his family. It was another stab through my heart denying them to my husband. This was someone with whom I would build a new life based on trust and honesty. I missed my mother and father and hated that I had to hide their names to achieve the better life they wished for me. I suppose wealth alone might seem the key to a better life when you have little, but as we all know, that is far from the truth." I reached out again and took several long sips from the glass Amelie had refilled. I was grateful to have the settee to myself and rose slightly to settle more comfortably before I continued.

"You must understand Rush was a good man at heart. We have much in common, which made it easier. He was very fond of you, Amelie. You were the favourite of all his siblings, perhaps because you were the only sister. He was distraught when he learned you were with child and terrified of the consequences.

However, he couldn't tell me of your situation. We were told you had gone to study in another district.

Your parents were furious and wanted you and the boy to receive the maximum punishment possible. There were so many heated arguments between Rush and your parents. I don't know what happened during these arguments, but he would return to me full of frustration, unable to tell me why they had argued. I've learned since he was trying to protect you, to save your life and that of your child. We thanked God and all the Fates when you were delivered to us, Millie. We had longed for a child, but it hadn't happened. That day, the fates and the Singular God smiled on us. We loved you from the moment we saw you, although my heart ached for your mother, forced to give you up. I didn't know then that you were the baby's mother, Amelie."

There was a stunned silence, then Amelie's sobs began, and tears flowed down her cheeks. She drew her knees up and hugged them, rocking as she wept. Millie looked between us, not daring to speak. She had thought after the revelations of the past week, nothing could shock her again, yet here she was, shaken to her core again. Slowly, I rose, burdened by my bulk. I put my arms around Amelie and hugged her tightly as she cried. Millie joined us, and we let our tears flow for a while. We were each lost in our memories and shared pain. Eventually, I pulled back, dabbing at my cheeks and eyes with my handkerchief, and blew my nose. Amelie and Millie did the same. Millie pulled up two chairs on either side of Amelie and indicated I should take one while she took the other. We reached into the space between us, and our hands clasped together. It was Millie who spoke first.

"I wish I'd known this before. I wish you'd told me, Mother." she looked at me sadly. "I understand it wasn't possible." Then she turned to Amelie.

“I was so angry that you’d given me up and I’d been lied to all my life. I keep hearing that we live in progressive times, but it’s bullshit. These aren’t progressive times at all. Women are pushed around, hurt and intimidated behind closed doors. I know I’m not supposed to know, but I have eyes and ears. Why can’t I live my life as I want and make my own mistakes? I want to choose my husband and not have to go with the one chosen for me. Why, after all you have suffered, are you letting it happen to me? Why can’t it change?” her voice grew in volume as her words became more emotionally charged, and tears ran down her cheeks, now flushed deep red.

“I agree with you, and I believe now is the time for change, but it won’t be easy. Rush is Thena Legal Councillor, as you know and as a family, we do have some influence. That, sadly, isn’t enough to make such changes. Alone, he would be overruled and, worse, disgraced. Despite that, I’ve asked him to begin exerting pressure for change. After much discussion, he has agreed. It seemed he had long felt the Bloodline Laws were unfair and outdated. With his father’s position and influence, he hadn’t dared to express such controversial views. Even now, it would be suicide to raise a challenge without a majority support behind him. With the current unrest in several districts, there might be a chance. It will need all the influence we can find to support his challenge.” I turned and looked at Amelie. She remained motionless for a moment before looking up. Her cheeks were tear-stained, and her eyes red.

“Thea, I’m sorry my father has caused so much pain in your life. I’m sure he was behind my parents’ intrusion in your home for so long. Father was punishing me through you and Millie. I’m ashamed to be part of such a family. I wonder if he might have discovered your true heritage. He’s a very powerful and manipulative man with a network of like-minded men across Anacadair.”

"I think you could be right, Amelie. It would make sense of their increasing scrutiny of me over the years," I said, and she agreed.

"So, the question is, what are we going to do? Millie is quite right; things must change, but we must find influencers who can support Rush. Ones who have the power to challenge your father and his allies. Amelie, do you have any contacts who might offer their support?" I had to ask, but my heart was in my mouth as I waited for her reply.

"Yes, there are some who I think would be willing to help. Here in Delphiope, we have some influencers on the Council, but it would be from Pollo that the strongest influence should come. I'm not sure I know anyone from Pollo who can help, and certainly not in Thena." she shook her head sadly. We sat together, lost in thought.

Then Millie looked up and, with a nod of encouragement from Amelie, began, "I have a friend who lives in Pollo whose father might be able to help."

"Millie dear..." I began, interrupting her, but Amelie gently squeezed my hand. Millie's face clouded with uncertainty until Amelie nodded again.

"Millie, tell us about your friend in Pollo," she said.

"Well, Yan is a friend from school. I may have mentioned him before. I… we've been seeing each other before... before all this. His father is a senior Healer and often travels to Thena for meetings with the Council for Healing. I think he is on the High Council, but I'm not sure."

"Oh, I see..." I was at a loss for words. I had no idea Yan's father could be on the High Council.

"Yes, well, his father disagrees with the Bloodline Laws. He says they damage the health of girls. Yan says his father has had to treat girls forced to undergo terrible things to stop a child growing. Some can never carry a child again; the damage is so bad. He says senior wisewomen have raised concerns in Thena and Pollo for many years. Girls like me are suffering, and some are so damaged in the mind that they can never recover." she paused, tears spilling down her cheeks. Amelie and I took her hands, holding tight in shared understanding.

"Millie, could you arrange for your friend's father to meet with us?" Amelie had regained some of her former energy and now spoke in an efficient, business-like tone. Millie looked between us as she wiped the tears from her face and blew her nose again.

"Err... yes, I mean, I'd have to meet Yan again. I can do that, right?" her eyes flashed the challenge directly at me.

"Thea, if this is going to work, I think she should meet Yan, don't you agree?" Amelie looked at me.

"Yes, I do." I said, turning to Millie, "Today is the beginning of a new way of doing things." I turn to Amelie.

"Do you think Dorcana and Orlan would support this action? Would they object to Millie meeting Yan under these circumstances?"

"Dorcana understands our situation, at least most of it anyway. We agreed to go through the formalities and see how things turned out. Neither of us wants to force a match that isn't wanted. She disagrees with the Bloodline Laws as much as we do. Delphiope prefers to allow nature to take its course with guidance from family and close friends."

"I see." my mind spun at everything I'd heard. "I'd no idea there was so much difference between the districts or that there was already a desire for change in other districts."

"I also know there is a girl Orlan is sweet on, so perhaps this might be a favourable path for him as well," added Amelie with a smile as she looked at the young girl between us.

"Err... great, I mean... really? So, I can really see Yan, and it's OK?" her eyes sparkled in a way they hadn't since everything went wrong that day in the study last week, and she filled with an energy that had been missing.

"Yes, really, and then when you've spoken with him, why don't you invite Yan and his father to coffee at the end of the week? It would allow us to meet him and hear what he has to say. In fact, why don't we invite Yan and his parents here for dinner?" Amelie smiled over at her.

"Oh, Wow, I never... I thought... oh this is amazing. Can I go and write to him now? We can take the letter today, can't we?" she looked eagerly at us, and we smiled back.

"Yes," we said together before looking at each other and laughing.

"Off you go now, Millie. Amelie and I have much to discuss," I said as Millie darted through the door, and we heard footsteps running up the stairs.

"Well, that went better than I thought it might," I said.

"I wish I'd understood how much Rush did for me back then. I hated him so much for going along with my parents," Amelie said sadly, "I'll never forgive my parents, never." There was so much pain in her last few words I couldn't speak for a moment.

"Amelie, I understand, but we will need Rush now if we want to take away the power of these awful Bloodline Laws. I have no Thena blood, yet I have been presented as Thena/Pollo all my life. A line must be drawn. The secrets and lies hidden behind our doors make a mockery of everything. When this is over, I think I would like to meet my birth father again. I've not heard from him since I was taken back to Pollo after I tried to run away." my voice trailed away, and silence fell between us as we sank deep into the past.

19

Thea

Rush was waiting for me when I arrived home, his face dark like thunder in the sky. He guided me straight into the study. I was hot and uncomfortable after my day out and longed for a cool drink and a rest before dinner. Neither seemed likely now.

"Where have you been?" he demanded before I had time to sit.

"I told you this morning, I went..." I began, but he cut in.

"You went to see Amelie. You should have told me where you were going," he growled, fists clenched on the desk before him as he glowered at me.

"I wanted to take some things for Millie. It was a spur-of-the-moment decision." His fist thumped on the desk, and I shrank back at the force of the blow.

"Rush, what's happened?"

"You were seen entering Delphiope, and it was reported to my father. Don't you remember the conditions?"

"But that's ridiculous now Millie's back with Amelie. What harm can it do for me to visit Millie?" *why was Rush so angry*? Then he explained that his father could enforce the full punishment on Amelie and Millie at any time for the rest of her life. The threat would never be lifted. I couldn't believe what I was hearing.

"Thea, you don't know my father. The more I learn about him and the Legal Octon, the more I realise I don't want to be like him at all. His type of power is not the power I wish to have. We must stick closely to our agreements if we are to protect Amelie. Even more so now that Millie is with her. Millie is more at risk now than she was with us."

"I had no idea!" I gasped in horror.

"If you must communicate with them, we must do it together. I have safer ways to communicate outside my father's view."

"We must warn Amelie they are not safe."

"That will be difficult, but she should know Father has forbidden contact with them." I sat in shock. I couldn't believe we were still in this awful place, even after *they'd* moved out.

"They won't come back when the baby comes, will they? I couldn't bear to have them back in the house." my eyes filled with tears.

"I don't think so. Now Millie has left, there's no justification." Rush was calmer now, and there was a softness in his voice.

"You're sure? really sure?" I swiped at the tears on my cheeks.

"No, but I don't think they will. You have Elia and Cam, who can help you with the twins." He stood and came round to face me, extending his hand. "Come now, you look tired. You should rest. I'll ask Suzi to bring refreshments to you." gratefully, I took his hand and rose from the chair. We walk together into the hall, and I turn to the stairs and begin my climb to the first floor.

20

Thea

The following day, I woke early with the pale light of dawn. I was restless and uncomfortable. As I began the long manoeuvre to heave my pregnant body into a sitting position, I suddenly felt an aching pain growing deep in my belly. After four children, I knew what it meant. I reached behind me to give a firm prod to whatever part of Rush my hand found.

"Rush…" then a little louder, "Rush, wake up," I felt movement as he stirred, grumbled and rolled over.

"Rush, I need you to fetch Mother Plumb." I gave him another sharper prod to emphasise the point, but he still didn't stir.

"Now, Rush, the pains have started." That got his attention, and I heard him get up and come around to my side of the bed, the morning stubble rasping as he rubbed his hands on his face. His night clothes were uncomfortably twisted around his body as he stood beside me, now rubbing his hands through his hair. He rested a hand on my shoulder.

"Give me a few minutes to get ready. Do you have the package Mother Plumb left for you?" (Pregnant ladies were given a package to keep at home ready for the birth. It meant the birthing room could be prepared while the wisewoman was called).

"The pack is on the chair, and I prepared the bed a few days ago. Please ask Elia to come and help, then ask Cam to be ready when the twins wake. Now go." Used to being in charge, Rush was unaccustomed to the change of role, but he dressed quickly and left the room.

I heard him rouse Cam and Elia for their assigned tasks before collecting Mother Plumb. Unlucky never to have children of her own, Mother Plumb has been delivering babies for over twenty years. She's among the few wisewomen considered skilled enough to deliver Thena Anlan babies. Mother Plumb was small and easily underestimated, gifted with the face of one much younger. Once she begins to talk, it soon becomes clear she is more than capable. Like all wisewomen, Mother Plumb was recognised by her red gown, crisp white apron, and scarf over her hair, identifying her trade. She carried a large black bag holding all the essential equipment she might need. When she arrived, Rush brought her to my room. Twelve-year-old Elia had made everything ready, as I'd asked, and now stood at the foot of the bed, her blue-green eyes sparkling excitedly. She'd been too young to help when the twins were born, but now, she was here and determined to stay.

Rush retired after he had brought Mother Plumb to me, closing the door behind him. I hoped he might check on Cam and the twins, but I suspected he would go straight to the study. Either way, I had more pressing things to focus on now as my abdomen contracted sharply, causing me to lean over. Elia looked alarmed, but Mother Plumb took charge. She asked Elia to sit beside me and hold my hand, offering encouragement each time the pain came. Mother Plumb told Elia what was happening and how the pain would help the baby come. The natural process of birth was vital for girls to understand so they could support their mother without fear. The toil of labour was short, and I thanked the Singular God for safely delivering my baby daughter. When Rush came in, Elia sat proudly, holding her little sister. Tradition dictated that a husband should acknowledge his wife's labours and greet his new child. A task Rush was delighted to do. He took her in his arms and looked down at the tiny bundle. For the first time, his face was full of pure joy. A joy not constrained by his father's expectation and formality. She was a beautiful baby with fine, downy black hair across her head and long, curly lashes. Her fingers closed around his finger, and he felt her strength. He knew she would bring new energy and life to the family after all that had happened. The Singular God has, indeed, blessed us, he thought.

I sat propped up in the bed and watched him curiously, observing the naked love in his eyes. As our eyes met, there was a spark of something I hadn't felt since Millie arrived.

"Thea, thank you for bearing our daughter through the months of development and bringing her safely into the world. I name her Amillia, Am for Amelie, il for Millie and lia for Elia. Three of the strongest female members of our family in the new generation. Amillia has a lot to live up to, but already I feel her strength and know she will be more than a match." Carefully, he laid Amillia in my arms and kissed her head, then mine.

"We should send word to Millie and Amelie," I said softly as I smiled at the child in my arms. She seemed to glow as the morning sun touched her. Elia crept up beside me to peep at Amillia. She was beaming with pride that Amillia had part of her name. She didn't know the origin of her own name and had never asked. Rush had kept that secret even from me until recently and would continue to do so until he felt the time was right, if it ever was, for her to know.

The door flew open at that moment, and two excited five-year-olds burst in, followed by an apologetic Cam. They bounded onto the bed, scrambling towards me and the precious bundle I held. Their squeals of excitement were infectious as Rush and I looked on.

"I'm sorry, sir," Cam looked cautiously at his father. "They were desperate to come in. They were supposed to wait at the door for permission to enter. Please don't be too cross with them." Rush felt the colour rise in his cheeks as he realised he had always expected his children to behave like adults. When they didn't, he gave punishments just as his father had done. While his parents lived here, they had expected him to be as strict with his children as they had been with him. Cam was waiting to be reprimanded, he thought sadly. Looking at his young family, he knew things would have to change. Smiling, he ruffled the heads of his two younger sons, nestled beside their mother on the bed.

"I think we can overlook their eagerness," he said as he looked at his oldest son and saw the relief followed by a shy smile.

"Come, Cam, greet your new sister Amillia." Cam cautiously drew closer to peer over at the tiny bundle in my arms.

Later that day, Amelie and Millie arrived and, after a slightly awkward greeting with Rush, hurried up to meet Amillia. Both were thrilled when they heard her name, and Elia proudly told them why she had been named Amillia. I saw tears in Amelie's eyes, matched by Millie's and my own. It was the first step towards rebuilding our family, giving both women their place in our lives. I knew it wouldn't be easy, but it was long overdue. I sighed with contentment as Millie and Amelie took turns to hold Amillia. They felt her soft, tiny hands and feet and inhaled that delicious smell only a new baby had. Still in charge, Mother Plumb returned to the room when she thought we needed privacy and rest. She would remain at the house until she felt her duties were complete. Amelie and Millie didn't stay long, aware of my need to rest. They briefly looked in on Rush, but it wasn't an easy meeting. There was much to be said, but this wasn't the time, and I would need to be part of the conversation.

21

Rush

Was it really possible? Could it finally be the right time? I already had the beginnings of a plan, but how could I achieve everything Thea has demanded? It wouldn't be possible without High Council allies. If I approached the wrong person, the consequences would be enormous. There was a genuine risk Father would punish those who supported me and the Abolition and Modernisation of Bloodline Laws (AMBL). I would be risking Amelie and my family's safety if I got it wrong.

My mind was still full of such thoughts a week later. I was at the temple to give thanks for Amillia's safe arrival and arrange for her naming ceremony. The peaceful temple sanctuary was ideal for contemplation and asking the Singular God for advice. Singularity was the predominant faith in Thena with the belief in a single God, The Great Singularity. Temples were simple minimalist buildings unadorned by images or elaborate decoration. However, they were no less impressive than those of the Quartative or Fatalist faiths. They made up for their lack of elaborate decoration with elegance and sophistication. The Temples had the best stone and marble, adding richness to their simplicity. The single pillar in the centre of the sanctuary signifies the Singular God of earth, sky and all between. The circular sanctuary around the pillar symbolises the all-seeing nature of the Singular God. The Temple of Singularity in Central Thena was almost as impressive as the Grand Temple in

Sorcia, Pollo District. The Grand Temple in Sorcia was where High Stewards of the Singularity were trained.

As I slipped quietly into the sanctuary, I stood momentarily gazing at Singularity's smooth, creamy pillar. Bowing my head, I walked up to it and placed my hands on the smooth surface, drawing strength from its firm foundations. The pillar was cool to my touch as it always was, worn smooth by many hands performing the same action. I took my seat on a stool facing the pillar. Raising my hands towards it in reverence, I offered my thanks for Amillia's safe arrival. Drawing my arms back to cross my chest in prayer, I sat quietly, my eyes closed. I was lost in prayer until I became aware of a presence nearby. I raised my head, opened my eyes and saw the green robe of a steward. It was Senior Steward Mica, responsible for Singularity in Thena. My arms dropped to my knees, and I smiled at the Steward. Senior Steward Mica was an elderly man with silvery white hair thinly covering a head that seemed polished to a shine. He was dressed in the customary long, dark green flowing robe. A single cream panel down the centre of his back stretched to a point finishing just above the top of his head. He was smaller than me, and I could look straight into his face even while seated.

"Rush, what brings you to Temple today? Is there something I can help you with?" I was pleased Mica was officiating this evening.

"Most Senior Steward Mica of the Singularity, I have some joyous news. This morning, Thea gave birth to a daughter. She's a beautiful child, just like her mother. I would like to arrange her formal Naming Ceremony. I've named her Amillia." I couldn't help smiling with pride.

"What wonderful news, Rush. Please carry my congratulations to Thea. I presume Mother Plumb was in attendance?" his eyes shone as he spoke with the clarity of one who was at peace and could genuinely bask in the glory of Singularity.

"Mother Plumb is with us as usual, and Elia supported Thea this time. She's leaving childhood behind."

"Ah, Elia, it seems only a few years ago that you were announcing her arrival, but I suppose she's almost grown now?"

"Indeed. Our twins are now five, so quite a family."

"And what of Millie?"

"Kind sir, I need your counsel on a delicate matter which relates in part to Millie and in part to Amelie, my sister, and also Thea." I paused, looking down. I was unsure how to continue and whether I could trust Mica with the sensitive matters on my mind.

"Rush, you know I can only be a vessel for you to talk to and receive counsel from the Singularity. My own humble opinions are of little consequence. How can I assist you?" After looking around to confirm we were alone, I told Mica. I felt elated and unburdened by the conversation when I left sometime later. Mica's final words echoed in my mind as I travelled home.

"Rush, you've been given a wonderful opportunity, but it comes with great responsibility. Not everyone will welcome change. They may be afraid and resist attempts to change the familiar. Take time to listen and be open to those who wish to support you and, more importantly, those who oppose you. You can find the path forward only by listening for the single voice." I knew the truth in Mica's words and was grateful for what appeared to be support from the kindly old Steward.

22

Thea

We sat in the drawing room after dinner the day before my anniversary and our wedding anniversary. Amillia was with Mother Plumb for a bath before settling down for the night. Cam and Elia were looking after the twins and would prepare them for bed soon. This left the rest of the evening for Rush and I to talk. I'd decided not to warn Rush. I wanted us to enjoy our first dinner alone since Amillia's arrival first. Now, with an after-dinner sweet wine beside us, I turned to him.

“Before Amillia arrived, we began to talk about things that arose after Millie went to Amelie.” I paused and sipped my wine, “I'd like to finish the discussion about change...” I hesitated, not quite sure how to continue.

“You're right. We should continue that discussion. There are some modifications I can make now, but the rest, I'm not so sure.” He sounded agreeable and relaxed, which was a good start.

“Did I tell you Amelie and Millie had suggestions for possible allies to approach?”

“No...” his voice was quiet.

“Amelie has some contacts, but an interesting one is through a friend of Millie's. A friend whose father is Pollo Healing Councillor.”

“How does she know this person is in favour of Modernisation? Has she already been talking, telling people I want change? It must be handled with care. If it gets out, the consequences for us would be unimaginable." I heard the steely tone creeping into his words. His hand gripped the goblet so tightly that I feared he might shatter the dainty vessel.

"No, of course not. But this friend knows her circumstances. There has been no open discussion with him, but he could prove a valuable ally."

"How do you know he would support Modernisation?" He shot the words at me like daggers. I needed to diffuse things before I destroyed my chances of his support.

"It was a topic at school in the debating hour. Students were encouraged to see the benefits and disadvantages of laws that affect them. Some students wanted to debate the Laws around Bloodlines and Promisary Agreements. I confirmed this with the Senior Secretary for Education at the school. I wasn't aware laws would be debated before, were you?" This was true, and I was pleased when I remembered.

"No, I didn't. It's irresponsible for the school to talk with students about such topics. There should have been parental agreement and proper guidance from the Council. I'll talk to the Thena Education Councillor, Professor Ben, about it."

"I know that's important, but can we look at the matter in hand." He was in danger of exploding into an angry tirade against school practices, and I didn't want any distractions. "Despite the way she found out, the fact remains that Millie may have a valuable contact who supports Modernisation." *There, I'd said it. Now let's see what happens.* I held my breath, and the silence stretched for several minutes until he looked up from his goblet.

"That does present an interesting situation..." he hesitated. He hated to admit weakness or ask for support. His father had beaten it into him as he grew up. He was responsible for making decisions and taking the lead. Accepting the help offered was simply another way of showing weakness.

“I think we should invite Amelie and Millie to join us after dinner tomorrow.” he continued, “Mother Plumb will still be here. Cam and Elia can look after the twins. Millie can tell us more about her friend and what her father knows about the situation.” I didn't correct Rush's assumption that the friend was female. It wasn’t the right time and could cause his temper to flare. If that happened, I would lose this fragile step forward.

“Thank you.”

“You can send word tomorrow morning. Mother Plumb will stay with us for the rest of the week. You still have some time before you become occupied with Amillia. On this occasion, it would be acceptable for them to visit and meet the new baby one last time. I will write the communication, Father will likely see it, and it must present no cause for him to challenge.”

“I wish we didn't have such restrictions. It makes life so difficult. Why shouldn't we see a child who was our daughter for sixteen years?” I sighed.

“I know, but it’s the way things are. It will change one day, but we must be patient for a while.”

“You're right, and now it's getting rather late. “I disguised a yawn as a sigh of relief that it had gone better than expected. “Thank you. I know this is your area of expertise. We need your knowledge to find the way forward.”

“As I've said, AMBL, including Promisary Agreements, is very sensitive. It won’t be easy.” He drained his goblet before placing it on the small table beside him. He rose and turned to me, offering me his hand.

“Shall we retire?” I winced at the implication.

“I'll need to check on the twins to ensure they're asleep and look in on the other two. They should be in bed as well now. Mother Plumb asked me to sit with her tonight and feed Amillia before I turn in.” A shadow passed across his face before he smiled softly at me.

"Of course, I remember now. You must feed Amillia and ensure she is clean and ready to sleep." I took his hand and rose. My body was still not entirely my own and bore the effects of my labours. We walked upstairs in companionable silence before I left him at the door to our room.

23

Thea

Amelie and Millie joined us for dinner this evening, and we were retiring to our private parlour for coffee. There was a frizzle of anticipation in the air. Amelie and Millie exchanged nervous glances as Rush sat erect and businesslike. I took my seat between Amelie and Rush, opposite Millie.

"Amelie, it is good to see you this evening. I'm glad you could come; thank you for bringing Millie with you." began Rush.

"It's my privilege to bring Millie to see you, and to be honest, I'm curious to hear why we were invited at such short notice. The message was rather brief," Amelie replied. She was dressed immaculately in a bronze silk trouser suit with a cream blouse. A waft of floral fragrance filled the air as she moved. It seemed familiar to me, although I couldn't quite place it. She had a beautiful sparkling broach shaped like an exotic flower on her left lapel, and her slim fingers were tipped with matching bronze nails. Amelie had taken Millie shopping, and I saw approvingly she was wearing a pretty floral blouse in pink and green with a dark green skirt and jacket. It's lovely and makes her look quite the young lady. Knowing how sensitive Rush could be, I wondered privately if this was wise.

"Millie, you look lovely." I smiled fondly at the young woman I would always consider to be my daughter. "I suspect Amelie has been shopping with you." Millie blushed and looked down before smiling.

"Thank you, we went shopping yesterday in Midelphi and then Delph. There are so many lovely shops,"

"Millie, it is good to see you looking so well," Rush said. The colour of Millie's cheeks deepened even further, and she looked down at her hands.

"Rush, would you tell Amelie and Millie what we discussed yesterday?" I was keen to move the discussion away from Millie, who was clearly uncomfortable with the attention.

Rush outlined a summary of our discussion, what he felt could be addressed first and the more complex topics that he said would be unlikely to succeed. He stressed that we should focus on what was feasible and saw me stiffen as he said this last piece. *I don't want to compromise.*

"Thank you, Rush," I began formally. "For the most part, I agree with your summary. However, I do not agree to compromise." I looked at Amelie and Millie as I spoke. "Even with the experiences of just the three of us here, the damage caused by such archaic laws is apparent. Why should we continue to suffer just because it is inconvenient or difficult? The High Council cannot imagine how it feels to be trapped in such a way, our lives governed and not our own. These laws don't impact them because they're men. After all, they are responsible for government and law, and there is no incentive for them to modernise." I was warming to my theme and saw discomfort flush on Rush's face.

"Perhaps we should look at this as a wedge to drive the bigger changes we want," Amelie said in a conciliatory tone.

"I'm tired of compromise and empty promises," I burst out, but Amelie held up a hand as she continued to speak.

"Thea, I understand. I, too, am tired of compromises, but we must play a strategic game. We have to meet their opposition head-on. We need to gain as much support as possible before challenging openly."

“I don't think you realise how futile it is to imagine the High Council will allow such changes. These matters are the realm of men and those tasked with ruling and sustaining the Anlan Bloodline Laws.” Rush spoke calmly, but his face showed the tell-tale warning of a dangerous outburst.

“We may be brother and sister, but you don't know me. I’ve lived outside the blinkered society in Thena, where it’s possible to see more clearly. I’ve had the privilege to stand beside people from all districts and responsibilities. You're not the only person with contacts and connections.” She spoke softly, but the steely hardness so often in her brother's tone was there in her voice, too.

“I know you mean well, Amelie, but the world of the High Council is not something you can comprehend...”

“How dare you?” Amelie's eyes flashed; her hands gripped the arms of the chair as if she was about to leap from it.

“May I say something?” Millie's small but clear voice cut in. She looked out of her depth as the adults around her seemed ready to fight.

“Millie, stay out of this.” Rush snapped. It was enough to bring Amelie back to the objective of their visit and away from the fight for a moment.

“I think you need to hear what Millie has to say. This concerns her too,” she said, “Millie, go ahead and tell Rush.”

“Father, my friend Yan lives in Pollo. His father is a Healer at Sorcia Quintarea Hospital in Pollo. Yan says he is the Pollo Healing Councillor as well. Maybe he could help?” she felt so childish among these three, who were all parents to her now.

“Millie, I know you are trying to help, but a friend from school with a nice dad doesn't mean he will take this seriously.” He was dismissive and condescending. His tone was designed to stop further discussion. But today, here and now, Millie suddenly felt empowered to give voice to her feelings.

“Father, why won't you listen to what I'm saying?” she cried, her frustration at being dismissed was painfully clear.

“Millie,” both Amelie and I spoke at the same time. I inclined to Amelie.

“Rush, you have not even asked who this Councillor is, yet you dismiss it out of hand. I, however, do know. His name is Kiron, the most senior Healer at the Sorcia Quintarea in Pollo, and he was the Pollo Healing Councillor for many years before recently becoming Healing Coun7cillor. You know who he is. He is well aware of the oppressive Bloodline Laws in Thena.”

“I know you both mean well, but the kind of influence we need is scarce.” His face was dark now, and we all saw the warning signs, but we couldn’t stop now.

“Kiron has many connections on the High Council, Rush. Don't dismiss him lightly. You should talk to him and hear what he has to say.” Amelie's voice was calm, yet I could see her own emotions boiling.

“That would be a good idea, Rush. Why don't you meet with Kiron and talk things through?” I agreed.

“By the Singular God, to talk openly? If I, we are associated with dissenters, the consequences could be catastrophic.” He stood and took a menacing step forward before he stopped, seemingly unsure which of the three women in front of him to approach.

“Sit down, Rush. Of course, you're right, and I agree. How terrible it would be that our worthy name be associated with progress.” Amelie's voice dripped with sarcasm, and Rush moved back. She continued drowning out the words that silently fell from his moving lips.

“Kiron happens to be a good friend. I was at school with his youngest sister, Anke. After I left Thena, his family was one of the few that were kind to me and understood my situation.” Millie looked up in surprise.

“You know Yan's father?” she said incredulously.

“Yes, I'm sorry, I hadn't realised when you first mentioned Yan. As we spoke today, I realised Yan had to be Kiron's son, whom he had spoken often.” Amelie smiled at Millie.

“I can't believe that someone of Kiron's standing would discuss such controversial matters outside the official channels. It's bordering on treason.” Rush almost shouted as he slammed his fist onto the glass table beside him. It shattered into glittering shards sprinkled across the floor, and we fell silent. I was visibly shaken at the crash but settled in my seat as Amelie spoke.

“Rush, I am Thena Anlan, remember?” came Amelie's immediate sharp response. At the same time, I said firmly.

“Enough!”

“Thea, this has gone far enough. I have given the steps I'm prepared to take, but enough is enough.” He stormed from the room, slamming the door behind him. His footsteps thundered through the house until we heard his study door close with a loud thud.

“Well, I think that went better than expected,” I said into the vacuum he’d left behind.

“Give him time. He'll think it through. He was always frustrated when Father tried to push him in a direction he didn't want to go or would be difficult. Maybe he’ll see the sense of what we’ve said tonight.” She looked thoughtful. This brother was the Rush she remembered from childhood, but it had always been the two of them against the world back then. They seemed to be on different sides now, and it didn't feel right. So much had happened in their lives since they’d last spoken.

“Amelie, how well do you know Kiron? Does he know how you feel about the Bloodline Laws?” I wondered how much of what she had said was bravado and how much was true. *I hoped it wasn’t just words. I couldn’t bear it.*

“I know the family well. Anka, his youngest sister, was at school with me. When I was thrown out, it was one of the few families that offered me shelter when I needed it. Although Kiron is somewhat older than I, we’ve spoken frankly about my experiences, and he has long been waiting for the right opportunity to propose change.”

“I still can't believe you knew Yan's father all along.” Millie's eyes were shining.

“I'm sure we can engineer an opportunity for Kiron and Rush to meet. He would probably be willing to raise the issue with Rush and, because he's male, would get a better hearing without the dramatics.” Amelie looked over at the shattered remains of the table.

“We've made a good start. We must keep the water flowing where we want it to go,” I agreed.

“I have something that may be helpful for us all to know.” Amelie opened the document wallet she had brought, slipping out several sheets of paper.

“Here are the Councillors by Octon and by district. I've marked those I know to be supportive of our cause and those I know to be definitely against. The others are undecided. Of course, I don't know all the Councillors, so there is still work to determine how much support there truly is. I believe Kiron and Rush could be major allies and make a difference.” She passed the pages to Millie and I. We studied them carefully before looking up with smiles.

“So, there is already more support than I had thought,” I said, “but I still have to talk with Rush so he knows my reasons for demanding change. It'll be a difficult conversation, but now is the time for him to know.”

“Oh, Thea, I know it'll be difficult. I can be here too if it would help?” Amelie says with concern in her eyes.

"It'll be OK. Rush is changing; I can feel a difference, but I'm unsure why. I'll talk with him later while all this is still fresh in his mind. I'll share this detail with him if I have the opportunity."

"It'll be interesting to find out if Rush agrees with my findings, won't it? So please go ahead, "Amelie said with a smile.

24

Thea

Later that evening, Rush and I met in our private parlour for coffee. I wondered if he'd had time to consider what we discussed earlier with Amelie. All traces of the broken table had disappeared, replaced by a different coffee table. As we sat in our armchairs, Suzi poured coffee before closing the door behind her. The silence grew thick and heavy around us. It was as if we were waiting for a signal to speak. I sipped my coffee before putting it on the table beside me. Rush did the same.

"Thea, we have much to discuss," I was curious to hear what he had to say, but if I didn't tell him now, I'm not sure I'd find the courage to try again.

"Rush, there is something important I must tell you first." words tumbled from my lips. I couldn't look at him.

"Thea, it is about you. It could change many things..." he began, but I had to speak; it couldn't wait.

"Rush, I need to tell you something. It's about my parents." he looked up, and I saw I had his attention.

"Go on," he said. I couldn't read his expression, but it didn't matter.

"First, you must know I have carried this secret to protect my family. It hasn't been my choice, but I understand its importance. You know my parents as Father Jonca and Mother Lib, but they aren't my birth parents. They are from my father's family. My true mother and father are Cawsal." I paused, waiting for the explosion, but it didn't come. Instead, Rush met my eyes, and I saw he already knew. *I've agonised over telling him for so long, and he already knew. I was lost for words.*

"I heard today from Father that your cousin Bogdo was elected Cawsal Militaria Councillor. He saw you at the Council dinner last week and recognised you. He mentioned your relationship to Stratagon Wiklon, Militaria Councillor, who, as you may know, is a friend of Fathers. Father was furious to have been deceived by your family. This is a very dangerous situation."

"Rush, I had no idea. I don't remember Bogdo. He must be on my mother's side of the family. My mother died when I was twelve, and I went to live with Father Jonca and Mother Lib. Since then, I have had no contact with anyone from Cawsal."

"You should also know that your father has done very well for himself. He's now the Cawsal Industry Councillor."

"I discovered that recently, although I haven't seen him as far as I know." I couldn't bear the thought of my father being in the same room as me and not knowing who he was. *Would I recognise him?*

"He was only elected recently and hasn't been at any of the Council dinners where you have been present."

"What am I to do? What are we going to do?" fear surged through me. These were my worst fears all rolled together. My hands rose and covered my face, fingertips resting on my forehead. So many emotions raced through me: fear, relief, anxiety. Adrenalin coursed through my veins and sent my heart racing.

"I don't know yet. There's a Council meeting tomorrow to discuss the situation. I don't need to tell you how serious this is. It would be best if you prepared to visit your family in Sorcia, Pollo; it would be a good time to introduce Amillia to them. It's a valid reason for travel. I will get your travel confirmed today. It shouldn't raise any questions."

"Rush, I'm scared. What of the children? Are they safe at school? And the twins, what about them?" My mind raced through possibilities so fast I couldn't keep up.

"Hush, the children should be OK at school, but perhaps they can help you prepare to travel? They can study at home for a few days. I'll arrange that. Perhaps they have an infectious virus and must be confined."

"How much can we tell Cam and Elia? They should know what's happening."

"You can tell Cam and Elia before school when Suzi takes the three younger children for their morning walk tomorrow."

Sitting back, I took my cup and sipped the bitter coffee, relishing the sharp tang in my mouth.

"These secrets and lies have been the cause of so much pain in our lives."

"I wonder how much my parents knew about your family when the Promisary Agreement was registered until we were married. I never had the feeling there was this kind of secret hiding in the sand."

"Things seemed to change as we approached Millie's sixteenth anniversary. I could feel something change in the way they spoke to me. I thought yet again I had crossed a line that I didn't know was there."

"That could be the case. I wish you'd mentioned it to me. Perhaps we might have learned of this complication sooner."

"How could I when there was nothing to tell you other than your parents were being more unreasonable and difficult than usual." We sat drinking our coffee, all words exhausted.

Putting down his cup, he looked at me, his face grave.

"I'll prepare the ground for you to travel. I think you should all go. The older two can help with the younger ones. Talk to the children in the morning after breakfast. Then, prepare for an extended visit, but only use the bag you would take for a short trip. I know it won't be easy, but there must be no indication you may stay longer. We can have the conveyance come for you mid-morning. Well before the Council will have reached any decisions."

"I understand." I stood. There was nothing further to say. I'd been sitting on a knife edge, waiting for the explosion, ready to dodge a blow that never came. Now, I was exhausted. Rush stood with me, and we left the parlour in amicable silence.

25

Thea

The following morning, Suzi took the twins and Amillia for a walk after breakfast. It was a bright, sunny morning, perfect for a stroll to the woodland and stream nearby. I went to find Cam and Elia and invited them to join me in the private parlour for coffee as a treat. We sat in the parlour an hour later with coffee and a plate of sweet treats. Cam was wide awake, enjoying the opportunity to be here. His gaze roamed the shelves and desk. He was keen to walk around but remained seated for now. Elia sat hunched over, clutching her cup of coffee. It usually took several cups of coffee before she was fully awake.

"Thank you both for joining me. I know it's an unusual request." I said as I paused to sip my coffee. "I have much to tell you, but first, I must have your promise that what's said here won't be discussed with anyone else. Will you make this promise?" I looked over at my children sitting together on the small settee.

Cam spoke first, his face full of curiosity, "Sure, but how can we promise without knowing what we are promising?"

"You'll have to trust me. What I have to say requires absolute secrecy." I looked intently at each child.

"OK, well, for what it's worth, you have my promise for now," he said, then looked at Elia, who was staring into her coffee cup.

"Elia?" I looked at her long, dark lilac hair hanging loose, draping like curtains on either side of her face.

"If Cam agrees, then I suppose I can, too," she looked up at me, her pale face drawn. Elia was the worrier of the two.

"As you know, we discovered the other day that Millie's birth mother is your father's sister, your Aunt Amelie. It was quite a shock for us all, including Millie herself. You must understand there were reasons for the decision to keep it secret."

"But you..." began Cam, but I interrupted.

"This is not why I want to talk to you, at least not the most important reason. Let me tell you first, then we can talk, and I'll try to answer your questions," he nodded.

"The Anlan heritage and Bloodline have always been important in Thena, as you know. Unfortunately, it has also meant that sometimes families hide a child's heritage. The prestige and power a child with Anlan Bloodline can achieve cannot be overstated. It is far greater than even a highborn child of Thena or Pollo." I paused to sip my coffee. "My own heritage was concealed from your father's family." Cam looked over, his eyes wide.

"That can't be true? What would you have to hide?"

"My real heritage is Cawsal..."

"I don't believe you," he said in disbelief.

"I'm sorry, but it's true. I was born in Cawsal and lived there for my early childhood. When I was 12, my mother died in an accident, and my father was completely heartbroken; he couldn't look after me, so I went to live with Father Jonca and Mother Lib in Pollo. They are an aunt and uncle from my father's family." I stopped momentarily; it wasn't easy telling my children such things and watching the shock register on their faces. I've tried to protect them, but now I realise they have the right to know the harsh reality of the world around them. I took a deep breath and continued with my story. I tried not to shock them too much when I told them of the last time I saw Dylen. There was a stunned silence when I finally reached the end.

"I promised myself that one day I would throw off the coverings that have hidden my heritage and retake my life. That time is here and now. You, my children, including Millie, know the truth, as does your father and Amelie. The twins are too young, but this will affect you all. I don't know what will happen, but I can make this promise to you. As I have breath, I will fight for you to have the freedom to choose your match and the direction of your lives." I stopped and sat back in my armchair.

Both children looked at me and then at each other silently for a moment. Then Cam spoke.

"Why have we never heard about this before? Why has it been such a secret? I don't understand."

"Neither do I. Have I got a Promisary Agreement, has Cam?" Elia's voice was small, growing as she spoke.

"I was forbidden to tell anyone about my heritage, including your father and his family. I'm sure the Promisary Agreement would have been dissolved immediately if the truth had been discovered before we were married. Grandma and Gramps would not have considered a match with someone from Cawsal. You may not know, but your grandfather, Maxim, is a powerful voice in the High Council. As a highborn family, your father had to marry someone with a good bloodline. My Bloodline was considered Pollo/Thena/Anlan, which was an appropriate match. Your father is expected to rise to Legal Councillor and Head of the High Council when Gramps retires.

As is our custom, I have made Promisary Agreements for you all. Cam, you are aware of this. Elia, it will be discussed with you formally in a year or so. With the recent events, I think you both need to know that they exist. The details will be explained to you at the appropriate time, Elia."

"So, what happens now?" Cam asked.

"When Amelie was disgraced, her father was outraged. He wanted the full force of the legally permitted punishment to be levelled at Amelie and Millie's father. Your father negotiated for Amelie to have a lighter punishment and, by default, Millie when she was born. It was reluctantly agreed, but Gramps can still apply the rest of the punishment if he wants to. Your father and I now feel that this time is coming, and we must take action to protect Amelie, Millie, and ourselves."

"I don't understand. What else can Gramps do to Amelie? He's already taken away her life and Millie. From what you said, it sounds as if he might have been behind her boyfriend's death. So, what else is there? and how does that affect us?" Elia looked worried.

"The full penalty for a disgraced daughter is to be bound to the flogging post at the crossroads and flogged almost to death. She's then left bound to the flogging post to die as an example to others." both children were horrified as they took in my words.

"But how can that be? It's horrible!" cried Elia.

"It's barbaric in this age." Cam jumped up, his fists balled, and I saw Rush in his stance. he was getting so tall now, almost as tall as his father. I shrank back into my chair. He sat back and perched on the edge of his seat. I took a deep breath.

"I agree with you both, and it's horrible and brutal. Unfortunately, the law still allows such things to occur to protect the Anlan Bloodline. At the same time, families are concealing their children's true heritage to try and gain better futures for them. It's time for modernisation, but such changes bring danger as well. I believe that Gramps has learned of my heritage. My family and I have broken the laws prohibiting falsely claiming to be Thena Anlan. By default, all my children now falsely claim to be Thena Anlan. Your father feels it might be safer for us to go away for a while. He will stay and try to make amendments to the laws."

“You mean leave Thena?” Cam was on his feet again, pacing around the chairs. “But surely that’s overreacting. I can’t believe there’s a threat to us. To Elia and me, the twins and Amillia,” his voice rose. The pacing was making me nervous. His temper seemed so like his father’s it was worrying. *Why had I not seen that before?* Even the dark colour creeping up his neck was like Rush. I must tread carefully.

“Cam, sit down. There is much you don’t know, and this is a very dangerous time. Gramps has a strong network and a powerful reach across the country. Although your father is not without influence, he is nowhere near as powerful as Gramps. He feels there is a real threat to our safety now and wants us to leave before a direct attempt is made on our lives. This is no empty threat. This is very real, I’m afraid.”

Cam perched once more, clenching and unclenching his fists, but it was Elia who spoke.

“So, we’re at risk because we’re not really of the Anlan Bloodline but Thena/Cawsal, right?”

“Yes.”

“Why has this only just become known?”

“A cousin of mine is now Cawsal Militaria Councillor. He recognised me at a recent council dinner. I believe that is where the first rumours began. I’ve since discovered my father has become the Cawsal Industrial Councillor. It would bring further risk to us should our relationship be discovered.”

“I see,” Elia said thoughtfully, then, glancing at Cam, continued, “so we must leave then. When will we leave, and where will we go?”

“Today. Your father is preparing a travel pass to visit Father Jonca and Mother Lib in Sorcia. We’ll take a small bag each, as we would for a short visit, but please fill it with everything you will need for a longer trip. Remember, though, the bag must be no bigger than what you might take for a short visit so we don't raise suspicion."

"What about school?" Cam and Elia both spoke together.

"I'm sorry, but you will not return to school for a while. You can study at home once we reach Father Jonca and Mother Lib."

"What about the little ones?" Cam was now thinking through the practicalities, and I was relieved.

"Suzi will travel with us to help with the little ones. I'll talk to her when she returns. It would look odd for us to visit my parents without you all. Suzi accompanying us on the journey would not be unusual with Amillia so young. After all, one of the main reasons we are going is to introduce Amillia to my parents. They would love to see her, and it's been a while since they saw the rest of you."

"So, we go to school today to say goodbye to our friends, right?" Elia looked anxiously at me.

"No, I'm sorry, you can write to your friends after you are packed and ready if there is time. You may only tell them you're visiting grandparents and will be back soon, nothing else. I know this isn't easy. There is a lot to do, and much we must keep secret. You're both old enough to hear what I've told you and understand the risks involved. For example, we must learn to be aware of our surroundings and the people around us. Your father and I will talk more about that with you later."

"There really is no other way?" Cam asked.

"No, our safety is no longer guaranteed. Your father wants us to be safe while he proposes the changes. If it becomes unsafe for him to remain here, he'll join us." I stood. It was time for us to begin our preparations. The children stood with me, and I awkwardly pulled them in and held them tight. It wasn't going to be easy. They were so young and should have remained innocent of the world's cruelty for a while longer, but it wasn't to be.

26

Rush

Now the family were on their way to Sorcia, I planned to meet Kiron, Healing Councillor. Amelie said she'd prepare the way and let Kiron know I'd contact him. With everything that had happened, I still planned to use caution. Mother Plumb was a candidate for the Pollo Healing Councillor vacancy. It was the perfect excuse to meet Kiron and discuss her candidacy along with the other candidates. There would be concern because she was a woman. Some Councillors felt the law prevented a woman from standing as a District Councillor, even questioning whether a woman could carry out such a role. I did a legal assessment, and there was no law to prevent a woman from becoming a Councillor. As for not being capable, from our own experience with Mother Plumb, I couldn't think of anyone more competent.

Father had supported my meeting with Kiron, strongly recommending that Mother Plumb's candidacy be considered illegal and thrown out. I was going to meet Kiron at the Council rooms in Pollo. The journey gave me time to think and prepare for our meeting. It was a relief Kiron was in Pollo and not the High Council Rooms of Thena. I was sure our conversation would be overheard and reported to Father if we met in Thena. I hoped Pollo was less closely observed.

The Council rooms in Pollo were in a smart new building close to the Sorcia Quintarea Hospital. Kiron continued to be the Most Senior Healer at the hospital, making this a convenient arrangement. As the conveyance drew up, I could see the imposing doors of the hospital on the right. On the left was the newer building where the Council rooms were. As I approached, the arched glass doors swung open, and a door attendant in a grey uniform came forward to greet me. I was expected, and he ushered me into the atrium and towards a glass elevator. I travelled up to the first floor, trying not to look at the ground dropping away from me on either side.

Kiron's tall, elegant frame was waiting for me when the doors opened. He was an impressive figure, tall with dark hair that wrapped around his chin in a neat beard. He wore the traditional clothes of a Healer: a long dark grey jacket over maroon trousers. His dark eyes twinkled as he smiled at me.

"Welcome, Rush. I hope your journey was uneventful." He extended his arm to me. We touched hand to elbow in the traditional formal greeting before he led me along a bright corridor.

"These are very impressive rooms. I've not had the privilege of visiting them until now."

"They were built ten years ago when Councillor roles were finally permitted to reside locally rather than in Thena. It meant we could continue to practice our professions at the same time as serving the High Council."

"I was a junior then, but I remember the debates. There were objections because power could be moving from Thena. I believe it strengthens the High Council, giving it more credibility in the district." I shook my head as I remembered the ridiculous arguments presented back then. Thank goodness the Singular God had guided the Council to the best decision. We entered Kiron's light, airy office, and I was directed to a seating area on the left with a low coffee table and coffee set out.

"Please sit and be comfortable. I thought you might like some coffee. We can talk about Mother Plumb and her candidacy, then move on to any other current concerns I can help with," Kiron cocked his head quizzically as he spoke, "Yan and Millie visited me a few days ago with Amelie. We talked a little, but they said you would tell me the rest. It's quite safe to talk here, I assure you." he passed me a cup of coffee. I took a sip, savouring the rich, intense tang just as I liked.

"Thank you," I said, sitting back in the comfortable armchair. I had been considering how to begin this conversation, but Kiron has given me the best opening I could have wished for. "These are indeed unusual times, Kiron. The past few weeks have led me to challenge many of my long-held assumptions. I used to dream of change as a young and foolish student. Over time, I have realised how impossible it is without supporting influence. Recent events have allowed a window of opportunity that I cannot ignore." I sipped my coffee. *I wonder which blend it is?* I took another few sips before placing the cup on the coffee table.

"Perhaps I should start where it all began. Millie received an Invitation to the NIA from her birth mother, my sister Amelie, the day before her sixteenth. Until then, she had been unaware of her true parentage. I suspect you already know the circumstances from your meeting with Amelie and Millie." Kiron nodded, "Well, it seems that this event was the trigger to discover another long-held secret. I tell you this in confidence. I know you will understand the significance of it and the damage it could cause when I tell you." I reached for my coffee and drained the cup as Kiron began to speak.

"As I said, what we say here is in confidence. Allow me to tell you my story, which may reassure you." I nodded. Learning more about this man who sat confidently before me would be good. He was quite unlike any Healing Councillor I'd met before. Previous Healing Councillors had been small, bookish men who were so old it was surprising they still breathed. They would hunch over sticks as they shuffled along. Their speeches were long and ponderous, delivered in thin, wavering voices. Kiron spoke with a confidence I'd not expected, and he was much younger than the relics of the past. I'd heard him speak in the High Council once or twice, but the formal language we must use makes even the most animated person appear dry and dull.

When I began training as a Healer here in Pollo, I never thought of the Council other than something that happened in Thena, which was true then. The Healing Councillor would rarely be seen in Pollo because they had to be in Thena. Nominees were usually those who were retiring from practice. It was with reluctance that I accepted the nomination for Pollo Healing Councillor. I wanted to remain here and continue my work as a Healer alongside my High Council responsibilities. It was the only way I could effectively represent current Healing practices. I found allegiance in an unexpected quarter when Father Anberto took up his role as Faith Councillor. He wanted to have his Council office in Cawsal, which, as you can imagine, caused quite a stir. He was still active in the Quartive faith of Cawsal. He didn't want to leave his people without their faith leader, and it was too far to travel each day. Max and Hog (Education High Councillor) were very against it. Norbarto, Industry Councillor, was also Cawsal and saw an opportunity to see more of his family. Wiklon (Militaria High Councillor) went against it, but Otto, Healing Councillor, went in favour. Otto was from Delphiope and wanted to spend more time with his patients.

Deliberations went on for a long time, but eventually, it was agreed Councillors could have rooms in their districts. The rooms must be solely for the High Council and no other purpose. I think it was to be a deterrent, but we were determined, and so it was finally agreed. We built a dedicated set of rooms in Pollo next to the Sorcia Quintarea Hospital. It's practical for senior Healers likely to stand as future candidates on the High Council. Councillors from other Octons also have their offices in this building now. It was my first introduction to the way the High Council worked. I also gained insight into the network Max had spread like a web throughout the High Council and further afield. I know he's your father, and please know that I mean no disrespect, only to speak the truth as I have seen it." he paused.

"I know my father and have experienced how he works first-hand. You will not cause any offence to me with the truth," I said.

"I'm grateful for your reassuring words. As I rose in seniority, I became responsible for reviewing the integrity of the Anlan Bloodline and supporting its purity with the Legal Octon. As you know, it's a joint responsibility between the two Octons. Maintaining the best blending possible for each generation is dependent on good marriages. I cannot speak to the previous methods, only those I have used and my findings. I took samples from all the new babes and compared them to the purity sample. The results were unexpected, so I checked the purity samples from Delph, Pollo and Cawsal. They only served to make matters even more confusing. I feared to share my findings until I had conclusive proof the data was correct. Using different methods, I validated my conclusions many times. I even asked other colleagues to repeat my methods, but the results remained the same. The Anlan blood purity was declining. It was 50-75% compared to the previously reported 95-100% purity.

Eventually, I prepared my report, including all the validation I had done and submitted it to the High Council. Max reviewed the report as Legal Councillor, head of the High Council and

Guardian of the Anlan Bloodline Purity. He dismissed my findings, and recommended I spoke with Otto to request his method. He implied my methods were the root of the discrepancies. When I spoke with Otto, he confirmed his reported data and methods. He was reluctant to discuss the matter unless we met informally in Delph. He confided in me that he had continued to report the data as it always had been reported because his predecessor had warned that it would be dangerous to report anything else. Otto was very afraid of Max and didn't dare raise anything so inflammatory as the decline of the bloodline purity."

"I'm not surprised Otto's afraid of Father. I've become aware of the real and implied threats used to gain agreement with a certain way of doing things." Kiron's words deepened my fear of a dark rot in the High Council.

"Max said if I found a change in bloodline purity, I must reverse it. Of course, that would have been impossible at the levels I saw, and even at higher levels of purity, it wouldn't have been feasible. I was forbidden to discuss the report with anyone other than that initial consultation with Otto. I realised that if the bloodline purity declined, the strength of Anlan influence in Thena would decrease. There would be a dramatic impact on the balance of power, perhaps even another war. The threat to the High Council and Anacadair itself was unimaginable.

Shortly after I shared my findings with Max, there was a request from an unknown origin to replace me as the Pollo Healing Councillor. It seemed there were inconsistencies in my practice at the hospital. I was furious. I've always made sure my conscience was clear. Unfortunately for Max, Otto chose that time to retire, and I still wonder if he was under pressure to do so or whether it was an attempt to force Max to retain me. It was by overwhelming vote that I became Healing Councillor, much to Max's disgust. He hoped to have a replacement to help tighten the Bloodline Laws. Someone malleable who could be persuaded to continue concealing the true purity of the bloodline. Not someone independent-minded like me. I always knew Max was no supporter of mine."

"I remember those discussions. Father never discussed Council matters at home despite us both being of the Legal Octon, but he began to discuss matters in the conveyance around that time. I knew he was very worried but had no idea of the source. Now it all makes sense."

"Amelie and I have spoken openly about her experiences with the Bloodline Laws. She was at school with my sister Anka. I am not sure if you know that."

"Amelie mentioned her to me when we spoke recently. I do remember your sister. She was a beautiful girl and very popular at school with the boys," I remembered with a smile.

"She had quite a following of suitors." Kiron grinned. "Amelie also told me of Millie's most recent experience and how she heard of her Promisary Agreement. I must admit I was more than a little surprised at the brutality of it." he looked at me enquiringly.

"Circumstances prevented me from informing Millie of her Promisary Agreement until the day before her sixteenth. That was the day when the Invitation from Amelie arrived by post in the morning before we'd had time to speak to her."

"That seems cruel if you will excuse me for speaking plainly. May I ask if there was a reason behind such decisions?" I closed my eyes. I didn't want to admit my part in this. I was ashamed even though I didn't have a choice.

"I was protecting others with my actions. Father was humiliated at Amelie's disgrace. He wanted her to be flogged at the crossroads and left to die while she was still with child. I couldn't let that happen." I paused for a moment as the truth of my words sunk in. They sounded far worse out loud than in my head. Kiron's face reflected my horror.

"Those punishments still happen? I thought they were something of the past. It's barbaric!" My humiliation rose on my face, hot and uncomfortable. I'd dreaded this moment when the truth would be told. I told Kiron of Amelie's disgrace and my attempts to reduce her punishment. Telling Kiron of the difficulties Thea and I had in beginning our family was embarrassing, but as a Healer, I was sure he would not judge us. When I admitted we had taken Millie to protect her, I saw him nod and recognised his understanding.

"This brings more clarity to the situation. I had no idea." Kiron remarked. He had recovered his composure and was now regarding me intensely.

"Thena conducts most of its business behind closed doors, especially in Anlan families. He made it clear that if I spoke of my part or went against his demands, he would review penalties for Amelie and Millie as was his right according to the law. I couldn't face that possibility. It brought a wedge into my relationship with Thea that I'm not sure will ever recover." To my shame, I felt a lump of emotion rise in my throat and paused. Pouring myself another cup of coffee, I blinked back the threat of tears, hoping Kiron didn't notice.

"Reinstated? But that's..." Kiron seemed lost for words.

"My father fears loss of power more than he fears criticism. He sees it as exercising his authority, which I suppose it is."

"It's barbaric in these times to sentence your own daughter to death just for conceiving outside marriage." I understood how he felt.

"I can't imagine suggesting such a thing for my daughters, whatever disgrace they might bring. It brings me to another matter I recently became aware of that may further explain the decline in purity. It must remain between us for now. Can you assure me that it will remain in this room?"

"Again, you have my word, Rush,"

"Thank you for this matter, concerns my wife, Thea. It would be unwise for anything to cause Max to take further undesirable actions."

"I understand." Kiron nodded, his face full of concern. I leaned forward to sip my coffee, wincing as the cold liquid filled my mouth.

"When I married Thea, I knew she came from Pollo and had Thena in her father's bloodline. It was quite a good match, although not the one I had hoped for, but I guess it rarely happens that way. Thea looked every inch the Thena Anlan woman, and I've been proud to have her take my arm." Kiron smiled and nodded his agreement. "I'd never had cause to doubt her heritage. The discovery of Millie's true heritage and Amelie's treatment greatly shocked her. It seems to have sparked something she had buried deep inside. She told me recently of her true heritage and the deep sadness in her past." I told Kiron Thea's story as she had told me.

"It may never have been questioned had there not been a new Cawsal Militaria Councillor who recently recognised Thea as his cousin at a dinner." I paused.

"That must have been quite a burden for Thea to carry all this time and a shock for you, too. It certainly gives further insight into the declining bloodline purity. I've long suspected something like this must have been happening. Is your father aware of her true heritage?" I could see the alarm on his face.

"That's something I don't know for certain, but it will only be a matter of time if he doesn't. I've arranged for Thea and the children to visit her adoptive parents here in Sorcia. They could go on to Cawsal if it became necessary. We haven't introduced our latest addition to her family yet, so it was a good reason to make the trip without raising suspicion."

"You're wise to do that. If I can help in any way, you only have to ask. I have no loyalty to Max, as you must be aware by now."

"Your offer is appreciated. These are very uncertain times, and it's good to know we have friends we can trust."

"I'd also like to request a formal review of the Bloodline Laws in light of my findings. I don't want to bury them, as has been the case before. These examples further highlight that the Bloodline purity is no longer what it was. Would you support this proposal?"

"I was going to make a request to you too. I want to assess how much support we have against my father. There will be powerful opposition from my father and his supporters." I wondered how much support Kiron was aware of already.

"That opposition cannot be underestimated. Neither can the pressure Max exerts on those who might go against him."

"We have several elections coming up. A few new Councillors would be to our advantage if they were favourable to AMBL. We should canvas each candidate carefully to assess which side they favour," I finished.

"There is one additional matter I should mention. Max offered to support Yan's college place at the Sorcia Quintarea Academie. Places are highly sought after, as you probably know. At first, I didn't want to accept because Yan is a good student, but it was explained that the hospital's status and link to funding would be at risk if I didn't accept. If Yan applied without support, his application would fail. I very reluctantly agreed, but I must admit I don't feel comfortable about it." Kiron looked down at his empty coffee cup but didn't reach to refill it.

"I'm sorry you have been put in such a position. I'd suspected Father of blackmail but had no proof of corruption until recently. It confirms my feeling there is a real risk to my family. I've lived under the veil of threats for so long, but it must stop. Driving out such deep-rooted corruption won't be easy and carries great risk. If you wish Yan to join my family, I will understand. Although I cannot guarantee his safety any more than I can guarantee that of my own family." Talking with Kiron openly about such difficult matters was a relief.

"I know you're not responsible for your father's actions. As there hasn't been a direct threat to Yan, I will keep him at college for now. It may help if I appear to distance him from Millie. I know it'll be difficult for them to be apart. They've formed a close bond."

"Millie will be free to choose her partner when it's safe for her to do so. Amelie has declared that she is free from the Promisary Agreement. Millie has met the boy Amelie chose a few times. He also has a sweetheart, so it would be convenient if he were free to choose his partner."

"In the meantime, I will begin to assess support in the Healing Octon and the Pollo Councillors from other Octons. I can talk with our Faith Councillor Elon and Professor Ankharl, Education Councillor, who I know well. Would you be willing to focus on Militaria and Industry besides the Legal Octon?" Kiron had an enthusiasm and energy as he spoke that I hadn't expected.

"It makes sense to divide the Octons. Legal, of course, I can do, and I also have contacts in the Faith Octon. I was at school with Elon, but I know Mica and Father Garten. Militaria will be more challenging. My father's support is quite strong there, but I'll see what I can find out. Thea's cousin is Bogdo, Cawsal Militaria Councillor, although I don't know his loyalties. Industry is the Octon I've had the least contact with, but I'm sure I can glean some information there, too. Interestingly, Cawsal may be helpful here. Toba, Cawsal Industrial Councillor, is Thea's father, and I plan to approach him first and see if his relationship with Thea has remained strong enough to support us." I had no idea how Toba would react.

"Good, so we should agree to meet again soon to assess our progress. I'd recommend we continue to cover our meetings with the bloodline research for now. I'd like there to be a minimal risk that Max discovers our intention until we have had time to assess support." Kiron sounded confident wearing the mantle of his High Councillor role. More confident than I felt in that moment.

"There is one more thing that could help. Amelie passed on this list of Councillors and their potential support. It could help narrow down our discussions." I passed the page that Amelie had given to me to Kiron.

"Typical of Amelie to be organised with a good network of governing officials. She's always had one cause or another for which she's needed support."

"Now, I should take my leave and return to Thena. If all's gone well, the family should have arrived at Thea's parents here in Sorcia." I took a deep breath as I stood. I don't want Kiron to see how much it affected me to know my family wouldn't be at home and might be in danger. We returned to the main entrance, where my conveyance was waiting. My head was full of swirling thoughts after our meeting. It had gone far better than I could've hoped. Now, we would have to see where it took us.

27

Rush

The house was in darkness when I arrived home, except for the hall light. I shook rain droplets from my coat and watched them fall to the hall floor. Dark glistening marks grew around me, but Thea wasn't here to fuss, so I left them. They would dry on their own, or Luzi would take care of them. When I looked up, I noticed a faint glow at the end of the hall. My heart began to pound as I walked towards the drawing room, where light flowed from under the door. When I entered, it wasn't Thea waiting for me but Father. He stood and greeted me warmly, and I was immediately on my guard; Father wasn't known for his warmth. *Why was he here? Had he found Amelie? Am I to be taken now*? My mind was racing.

"Father, it's good to see you. Had I known of your visit, I would've ensured I was here to greet you. May I offer you some fresh coffee?" I need the mundane things to lock away the recent discussions with Kiron.

"Thank you. A fresh pot of coffee would be nice. I'd hoped to catch you and Thea, but I was unlucky in my choice of time." he said.

"As you know from the travel notice, Thea has gone to her parents with the children. She wanted to introduce our latest addition to her family. She'll be back in a few days." I rang the bell for Luzi, our housekeeper. A few minutes later, the door opened, and her stern face appeared.

"Luzi, could we have another pot of coffee and something to eat?" she nodded.

"I have some afternoon cake or meat rolls, or I could bring a light afternoon platter." Her face, schooled to show no expression, remained neutral.

"A light platter would be a good idea. Thank you, Luzi." I said. With a nod, she disappeared, closing the door behind her.

"She is a disagreeable woman, Rush. I don't know why you keep her on," Father said.

"Thea likes her, and they manage the household well together," I said.

Father huffed and settled back in his chair. He's still wearing his formal suit, I noticed. Perhaps he came straight from the Council offices. *Was it significant if he had?*

"To what do I owe the pleasure of your visit, Father?"

"May I not visit my son and his family at any time?" he said amicably. Father never visited unexpectedly; my suspicion rose even further.

"Of course, you may, Father, and we are delighted to welcome you at any time. Although, if you had advised me of your intention, I would have mentioned that Thea was away." I pushed my mouth into a smile. The door opened, and Luzi brought in coffee and a platter of assorted sweet and savoury foods. She left quickly, shutting the door behind her. My mouth watered as I smelled the delicious aroma of the warm meat rolls. My stomach growled, reminding me I'd missed lunch.

"Father, take a plate and try the meat rolls. They're excellent. Luzi is an exceptional cook." Taking a plate, I offered one to Father, who accepted it but remained seated. I took some meat rolls and other savouries, which smelled delicious. Pouring coffee for us both, I sat back and bit into the meat roll. The herbed meat was juicy and well-seasoned, and the pastry surrounding it was crisp and light. I couldn't speak momentarily as I let myself enjoy the sensations. Then, after licking my lips and fingers, I took a napkin and wiped my hands before I picked up my coffee. Father had only taken a small sweet tart, and I guessed he had taken his usual lunch at the Council offices.

"Have you seen anything of Millie since she went to her mother?" he asked, *here it comes...*

"We've seen them once to deliver the rest of her belongings. Thea wanted to see she'd settled in. She was worried, pregnancy hormones, you know. We also saw them briefly when Amillia was born. Amelie brought Millie to meet her sister."

"Was her Promisary Agreement legal? When did you learn of it?"

"It was legal. I confirmed it was registered correctly in Delphiope. I knew nothing of it until it arrived." *I'm glad I got that checked so quickly.*

"That is unfortunate. The match we made for Millie is a very good one. If she were to make the wrong choice, that would be most unfortunate." *He couldn't say her name.* I felt saddened and angry.

"Amelie will not change the match. She feels her match is the right one for Millie. The final decision in law is hers, as you know."

"Of course, I know the laws." He snapped, "You need to tell her mother that my match has the greatest merit?" his voice hardened, and I saw the father I knew appear.

He straightened in his chair, somehow growing taller. His arms rested on the chair's arms, a confident and powerful pose designed to intimidate. It was reassuring nothing had changed. He still bullied and threatened to get his way. But those days are over.

"Father, Amelie is well aware of her position. She intends to support Millie and help her adjust to life in Delphiope and in time to her life as a married woman." I took a deep breath and reached for my coffee. *Let him think he's pushed me over the limit as he used to. I had control now, and I knew his tricks.*

"It isn't wise for her to draw so much attention to herself. It could be unhealthy for her and the girl," he said, and a chill went down my spine. We sat in silence, sipping our coffee. The void between us grew dark and menacing. I dared not speak. *What else had brought him here? I was sure there was more than just Millie and Amelie.* I held my breath.

"How well do you know Thea's family? She is becoming quite outspoken, which is unwise in her circumstances." his voice was quiet, but there was an underlying threat now. Challenging barbs flashed from his eyes. This must be why he was here.

"Thea is a modern woman of Thena, Father. I enjoy her intelligent dialogue and gentle questioning of our laws. It enables me to explain them to her, giving her a greater appreciation of their value." in part, that was true.

"Thea should take care. Her bloodline is thinner than her parents declared, as we recently discovered. In fact, it is non-existent, isn't it?" He rose and stood over me as I rose from my chair. We were of similar height in truth, but this evening, he seemed to look down on me as he had when I was a child. I stepped sideways, so we looked eye to eye.

"I did not know of this until you told me," I said, "Why was this not discovered before we were married?"

"That is another matter I will address shortly. As for your marriage, it was based on a lie. Now you have half-breed children that don't belong in Thena or anywhere. What are you going to do about them?"

"My children are innocent in this, as Millie is. None of this is their making. They have my blood in their veins as Millie has yours." I stepped back to put a little space between us, but he came towards me again, his face the darkest red I had ever seen.

"Those half-breeds should not exist, you must see that. They must not be allowed to breed," He snarled as his arm swung back. I ducked, and the blow missed, but his other hand caught my upper arm in a vice-like grip.

"If you can't see that, I fear for you. I will not protect traitors. Show you are worthy of the Anlan blood that flows in your veins," he growled in a low voice before releasing my arm and walking out of the room. He put on his coat and hat before opening the front door and walking to the side of the house, where I now saw a dark conveyance waiting. I watched him leave before closing the door, bolting it behind me. I returned to the drawing room. The food on the platter now held no appeal; my stomach was churning. The memory of his words soured everything. His bitter, twisted presence remained strong here. The room had been his domain when he lived with us, doubling as his study. *How can we ever remove his stain from this room*? I wondered. His poison had permeated the walls and every corner, and no decorator could ever cover that. I'd have to talk with Thea; she might know how to make it ours again, but now there were more pressing matters to take care of.

My encounter with Father left me deeply concerned for my family and Amelie. His cruel mind was even more bitter and twisted, and I knew now that my family was in danger. I was glad I had sent them away, but Father knew where they were from the travel advice. It was like a blade of ice to my heart. I paced the drawing room, and my hands grasped handfuls of hair as I tried to think. How could I move my family far enough from his reach and keep them safe while they travelled? It would be easy for him to arrange an accident while they were travelling. *'Such things are so tragic', I could hear him say*. There were so few I could turn to, and even fewer had no known alliance with

Father. With a sigh, I decided on the Temple. If I go now, I should be in time for Evening Thanksgiving. With luck, I could catch Mica afterwards. He might pass word to Elon in Pollo. I pulled on my damp coat and hat and set out again. This time, I took the conveyance from the front of the house and drove myself. It was something I rarely did these days, but I enjoyed the freedom it gave me. I could travel unobserved in the privacy of this vehicle with its one-way glass.

28

Rush

I reached the Temple in good time and filed in alongside other supplicants. I took my place in front of the Symbol of Singularity. The calming words of Thanksgiving and familiar responses soothed my mind. As Thanksgiving drew to a close, I began to think about what I would say to Mica, and my anxiety returned. It was a Singular blessing that Mica was officiating today and was now standing beside the Pillar to give blessings. Joining the orderly line, we slowly shuffled forward. I watched as the people in front of me were blessed one by one. Then they turned and reached out to touch the smooth surface of the pillar, sending private thoughts upwards. I smiled and nodded to people I knew as they passed on their way home.

The line was short this evening, another thing I must give thanks for. Mica wasn't the most popular Steward; he often spoke his mind even when it wasn't kind. He had offended many people over the years, and there were far fewer in the Sanctuary when he was in attendance. I rather liked his straight speaking. He was like my father in a way, without the cruel streak. We'd never talked politics in the past. It wasn't an appropriate conversation for the Temple, so I was unsure of his inclination. I had to hope my instincts were correct. Unfortunately, I would get close to politics if he had time for me to take counsel tonight. I hoped Father hadn't already visited him. After Father's visit earlier, I doubt it would be long before Mica received a visit to request his support.

Finally, I reached the front of the queue, relieved I was the last person remaining.

"Mica, thank you for your words this evening. May I trouble you for a little more of your time? I have great need of your guidance." The elderly Steward held out his arm, and we greeted each other hand to elbow before we sat in the chairs nearby.

"Rush, how can a poor steward help you this evening?" he said, his green eyes glinting in the candlelight.

"I wondered if you had news of my father?" a small untruth, but at least it would confirm if he had heard anything. A smile crossed the old man's wizened face.

"Sadly, I have not seen Maxim this week, although Zillah came to the Sunrise Welcome two days ago. She seemed troubled but didn't say why." I wondered at that. I'd always assumed Mother supported Father without question, but perhaps it wasn't that simple.

"I have deep troubles on my mind. May I speak in complete confidence?" I could see the Temple had emptied, but I was still worried we might be overheard.

"We're alone here, son, but if you're concerned, we could take a cup of tea in my sitting room." He rose and led the way through a small door at the side of the Temple. I followed him down a narrow corridor, his green gown swishing as he walked. The stiff cream point extended from his shoulders to the top of his head, nodding in time with his steps. *I wondered idly if it tapped on his head as he walked.*

Mica stopped by a recess on the left, unlocked a door, and led me inside. The room had two distinct parts: a small sitting room with two armchairs beside a fire on the left and, to the right, a small kitchen where Mica began heating water for tea. I wasn't very keen on tea, but I knew coffee was frowned upon at the Temple. It stimulated the mind rather than allowing thoughts to proceed naturally.

When we were seated with our tea, Mica looked at me.

"What troubles you, Rush?"

"How much do you remember of my sister Amelie?" I took a tentative sip of the tea. It was hot and intense. I savoured the taste, welcoming the sharpness that made it palatable.

"I suppose it's Millie's sixteenth anniversary this year, and it has raked up old troubles?" he looked at me, his expression unreadable.

"Yes. Old troubles are indeed rising along with some new ones."

"I can see how that might trouble you. Have you spoken with your father?"

"He visited this evening."

"I see, and how did that go?"

"Not well,"

"Tell me what happened," and so I did. I tried to make my retelling as concise as I could while expressing my fears for my family. He didn't interrupt while I spoke but sat sipping his tea, nodding. When I stopped talking, he waited and allowed the comfortable silence to fill the room. Then he put down his cup and clasped his hands together.

"I long feared this day would come. I watched Maxim grow up and could see from a very young age that he had a darkness inside. The match with Zillah was an interesting one. I had always suspected there was more than a little tainted blood in the mix. I presume you know Zillah and Libertine, Thea's aunt, are sisters?" I nodded.

"I only recently became aware of their relationship. Thea had never mentioned it before."

"Zillah and Libertine were quite close as little girls. As they grew up, it became clear that Zillah's future would be in Thena and Libertine's in Pollo. It created a rift between the two girls, particularly when Zillah married Maxim. He didn't like Libertine and persuaded Zillah to cut off all connections with her. It was a sorrowful time. I don't know how the match between you and Thea came about. Maxim couldn't have known about Thea's Cawsal background, or he would never have agreed to the match. I can only think he believed Thea was the daughter of Jonca and Libertine and didn't discover the truth until now." he paused.

"I believe you're right. Father hadn't spoken of Thea in such a way before tonight."

"Your kindness and compassion for Amelie was foolish but merit-worthy. Neither of which earns you many friends. I saw her need for freedom growing and feared for her if she were confined to Thena. You did her kindness and permitted her to build the life she wanted, albeit without the young man, Millie's father. I see her occasionally when she performs in Thena."

"Mica, what am I to do? I sent Thea and the children to her parents, Jonca and Lib, thinking they would be safe. Now, realising the connection between Lib and Zillah, are they still safe? How can I warn them without raising Father's suspicions?" I placed my cup on the table between us and dropped my head into my hands.

"All is not lost. I'm in contact with Elon in Pollo. You were friends with Elon, weren't you?" he looked at me, his face troubled.

"Yes, we're still friends, but we don't see each other as often as we would like," I admitted.

"Well, I can contact Elon this evening and ask him to visit Jonca and Lib to bless your daughter. It's a reasonable request and innocent enough for him to call. Does he know of these troubles?"

"No, he has no idea. He only knows Amelie was sent to college in another district. He knows nothing of Millie." I sighed, dropping my head against the back of the chair and raising my eyes to the ceiling.

"I'll bring these things to Elon's attention discretely. It may help when he sees your family. Elon is a bright Steward and will know if there is something amiss. He's sensitive to such things."

"Please do as you feel is best. I wish my family to be safe. Everything is happening so fast, and knowing who's a friend isn't easy. I'm grateful for your advice." I sat back. I was exhausted and alone, but at least Mica could offer a way to contact my family.

"Perhaps we should place our hands to the Pillar and raise our words in supplication." Mica stood. I followed him back to the Sanctuary.

"Thank you, Mica. It will be good to petition the Singular God in these difficult times." I moved my leaden body forward with effort. Together, we put our hands on the smooth marble. I looked up, following the white column as it rose to the heaven above. Lifting my fears and hopes, I petitioned as I had never done before. The words flowed through my hands to the warmth beneath and into the column, where they travelled up to the Singular God. With all my heart, I hoped my words were received and considered favourably. Finally, I removed my hands and turned to Mica, offering my arm to him. He took it, and we embraced.

"Mica, you are a good and kindly Steward. One day, you would be a great addition to the High Council." he really would be, and I was sure there would be an opportunity at some point. I hoped I would be able to persuade him before then. The old Steward smiled, and his wrinkled face lit up. In his sparkling eyes, I saw his faith shining in that moment.

"Rush, my son, you are kind and thoughtful. Go home now and rest. Trust in the Singular God. The Council is not my choice, but if it pleases the one above, I will serve." he raised his head as he spoke. Turning, I went to the door and out into the world again. The peace in the Sanctuary tonight had been precious and renewing.

29

Rush

The High Council was in disarray after the sudden death of Father Anberto (Quartive faith). Father Anberto was very popular and known for his calm and honest manner. He always had a clear perspective regardless of belief or persuasion. According to tradition, elections must be held within a week of his death. After an urgent search for candidates, there were just three nominations:

1) Father Garten (Quartive), Cawsal Faith Councillor. A strong candidate, popular in Cawsal and Delphiope. He was softly spoken but had gained tremendous credibility for his open and wise counsel to those who sought his advice.

2) High Steward Mica (Singularity), Thena Faith Councillor and another strong candidate. He was a quiet man, which was the most compelling argument against him. Those who knew him soon saw his humble yet forceful powers of observation and persuasion. His reputation for plain speaking had been considered a potential advantage.

3) Senior Leader Boldun (Fatalist), Delphiope Faith Councillor. Boldun was an unpleasant, tall, thin, ratty man. Many were surprised to see him rise to the High Council so quickly. His father was a close friend of my father's, and they trained for the Legal Octon together.

> Many thought Boldun would follow his father into the Legal Octon. It was unclear why he entered faith training, and he often seemed bitter at his fate. His interactions with his fellow Councillors and his fellows of the Fatalism were always discordant.

This was not good news. With so few candidates, it would be easy to swing the majority vote. I contacted Elon again and petitioned him to submit his candidacy. If more candidates stood against Boldun, it would help dilute his poisonous dialogue. Unfortunately, Boldun had a way of finding favour in the most unexpected corners. He was adept at twisting words and had the most devious mind. The following days were full of passionate and compelling campaigns by Boldun, supported by Father, Professor Hog (Education Councillor), and Stratagon Wiklon (Militaria Councillor and good friend of Father's). It was expected that district Councillors would follow their High Councillor's vote. From the start, it was clear this election would not follow the usual pattern. I planned to make an opportunity to talk with Elon as soon as possible.

It came sooner than anticipated when I went to the Temple the following evening. Since Thea and the children left, I had found comfort in the familiar routine of the Temple. My feet were drawn to the doors most evenings. Sitting in the peaceful Sanctuary as the last note of song rose, I decided tonight was the night to talk to Elon. I knew he was in Thena for the many meetings related to the elections. Strictly speaking, it wasn't appropriate to talk to candidates unless it was a formal meeting. Records should be made of discussions to ensure there was no coercion. I was strangely liberated by the undercurrent of unrest and felt no guilt in approaching Elon after Evening Thanksgiving. He smiled warily but agreed to meet with me and led me from the Temple to the private sitting room for visiting

Stewards. After we were seated in the comfortable armchairs beside the fire, Elon looked up.

"Rush, we've been friends for a long time, and I know you well enough to know this is more than just a social visit." I choose my words carefully.

"Indeed, we know each other well, although we don't meet as often as we used to. How much our lives have changed in that time? We're both older and have taken quite different paths." I wish we hadn't drifted apart. I thought.

"Very true. Our lives are quite different now. I can't say I envy you in the Legal world. It was the best decision I ever made to go against Father and study Faith. Studying the three Faiths was very enlightening. I must admit I felt quite a pull to Quartive, although I remained with Singularity."

"Really? I had never considered you rebellious, but I may be mistaken. In that case, these elections must have you quite divided with candidates from each Faith." If he was sympathetic to Quartive, would he have divided loyalties? I may need to tread carefully. *This coffee was a great bitter blend and better than the usual trend for tea in the Temple. I wondered what it was.* Elon looked away for a moment before returning his eyes to mine, his expression open.

"Do you remember who set off the alarms at school to get out of Bloodline theory*?"* I did. Elon volunteered because he looked so innocent nobody would suspect him, not even if he stood right beside it. Jak and I would be taken for disciplining each time.

"Oh yes," we chuckled together as we reminisced before returning to the elections.

"Elon, you're right. I had several reasons to talk with you. The elections certainly form part, but not the most important element of what I wanted to discuss." I paused to frame my words.

"you've already heard from Mica about my family troubles, I believe."

"Mica and I have spoken. You have my interest piqued, my friend." He stood and went to the small kitchen behind me. "Do we need more coffee, or is it time for something a little stronger?" He waved a dark red bottle as he spoke.

"You have Cawsal Berry Brew? Isn't it forbidden in Thena due to the alcoholic rating?" *I knew it was, but I guessed he had his sources. I wondered if his connections to Cawsal were stronger than he admitted.*

"I do, and yes, it's illegal to buy or sell in Thena before you begin your legal lecture. However, what am I to do if a generous believer leaves a bottle in the Sanctuary? Steward Mica is not a fan of such potent brews, and it would be wrong to waste it now, wouldn't it?" he said with a wink.

"I agree that rejecting the generous gift would be rather ungrateful. I'd love a glass as well as some more coffee. We have a lot of ground to cover and may need our thirst quenching." Elon poured generous glasses of the thick red spirit. It swirled in the glasses as he brought it over with the coffee pot, now refreshed once more.

"Where would you like to begin as we sip this delicious brew?" he raised his glass with a nod and then took a sip. I raised mine and breathed in the potent fruity fragrance before sipping. It was thick and warm as it rolled around my mouth before making its way down my throat. I followed its journey in my mind as it settled in my stomach, bringing a warm glow that stretched through my whole body. I could feel myself relax in the chair and saw Elon doing the same with that familiar grin I remembered. I hoped the bottle had plenty in it.

"Do you remember my sister Amelie?"

"Of course I do, one of the prettiest girls in the school. She was a bit of a rebel, wasn't she? I remember the arguments.

What happened to her? She went to a college somewhere else, I seem to remember." I smiled sadly.

"Yes, she was a rebel, still is, I think, although perhaps she's mellowed a little with time. She's the other reason I wanted to talk with you, but are we secure to talk here?" *I hoped it was. I didn't know where else we could talk these days without being overheard.*

"We of faith are not subject to such observation as others in the district or the Council. I thank the Singular God for that every day." he smiled and raised his glass again. I raised mine and nodded at him in reply.

"You're lucky. I sometimes feel I should stand on the corner to tell the world of every conversation I have. It's good to know that the Temple is still sacred. Long may that continue."

"Indeed, my friend." he raised his glass again, and I replied, raising mine.

"Amelie didn't go to college initially, although she did later. She had fallen for a Cawsal boy and became pregnant before her sixteenth." I heard the sharp intake of breath. "Father was furious. He demanded the highest penalties for both Amelie and the boy. The boy was sent to the mines and died in an accident a year later. Amelie was locked in the attic, and we were forbidden to talk to her for the rest of her confinement. I spoke with Father for a long time, trying to persuade him not to flog her and leave her at the crossroads. Whatever she'd done, I couldn't have that happen to her." I paused and took a sip from my glass. Elon picked up his glass and nodded to me before taking a sip.

Then he spoke, "I'm sorry, Rush, I had no idea. Why didn't you tell us? Jak and I were, and still are, your friends. Surely, you could have told us. How it must have hurt to carry all that on your own."

He looked over compassionately.

"My father forbade anyone to talk about her from that day forth. After the babe was born, Amelie was taken from the house and from that day to this, he has never spoken her name." *I couldn't look at Elon. I didn't want to see his face and feel the shame that I could have done more.*

"What happened to the babe? Did it go with her?"

"No."

"No?"

"Thea and I took the babe as our own. We hadn't been lucky enough to bring a babe into the world. Millie, for that is what we called her, brought us luck, and we now have five more children."

"Millie? Wasn't that your name for Amelie?" Elon smiled. *I knew he would remember.*

"You're one of the few who know that. It was my private way to remember Amelie every day. Millie was a lovely babe, but I saw Amelie every time I looked at her. Knowing I couldn't see Amelie hurt so much, I grew to resent Millie."

"It must have been a very bittersweet time."

"Not having anyone to share the pain with was the worst punishment my father could have given. I'm sure he took pleasure in punishing me for supporting her as much as he relished punishing Amelie herself."

"How old is Millie now? She must be close to her sixteenth."

"She achieved her sixteenth anniversary two weeks ago. The day before, we had such a shock. An Invitation arrived for Millie from Amelie. When Millie was a babe, we made a Promisary Agreement as if she was our own. Father and I picked a boy child that would match Father's ambitions. I suspect you know how he works." Elon nodded, and I continued, "It seems my father hadn't anticipated Amelie making a Promisary Agreement, although she was legally entitled to do so as the birth mother. The Invitation arrived in the morning post addressed to Millie. Probably in case Thea or I prevented her from seeing it. As it was, I thought Thea might go into childbirth early with the shock. She knew who had sent it when she saw the handwriting. Father insisted they came to live with us to help Thea with the children. Of course, it was to ensure I stuck to the agreements I'd made when I bargained for Amelie's life. He forbade us from telling Millie of the Promisary Agreement until her sixteenth. He also forbade us from telling Millie of her true parentage. Until that day, she had regarded Thea and I as her parents. It was a terrible time, and she is distraught, as you can imagine.

I've since learned there is a boy from Pollo she's sweet on. If we hadn't taken precautions, she would have run away that night rather than go to the NIA. Taking her to the NIA the next day was the worst thing I've ever done, knowing how unhappy she was." I picked up my glass and drained it. The alcohol caught in my throat, and I coughed, *just like a novice drinker, I thought ruefully.*

"Can I refill your glass?" he was already on his feet and reached for the bottle.

"Definitely. It's been horrendous these past few weeks, and I've been unable to confide in anyone other than Thea." Elon returned and sat in his chair, raising his glass to me. I raised mine and nodded in reply before I took a sip.

"I wish you had confided in me sooner, but we are past that time now. Did you see Amelie at the NIA? How is she?"

"I did, and the boy she chose. She looks well. I've followed her quietly as she made a name for herself. It was the first time I'd seen her in person since the night she was discovered and faced Mother and Father. The years have been kind to her. She is the beautiful, successful woman I knew she would be. The only good thing about all this is that she has lived the life she wanted. Something she could never have done had she remained at home."

"I also have heard of her successes, but unfortunately, such things are denied to me. It's too light-hearted for a man of faith to seek such entertainment, but I'm glad she's well."

"We didn't talk then; it wasn't the time, and I was still angry and frustrated at how the day had arrived. It was another ten days before I went with Thea to visit Amelie and Millie. We told Father it was to take the rest of Millie's belongings, but it was more than that for us." I took a large sip. I need the warmth and numbness now. I felt foolish for letting Father rule my life even when I was way past my youth. Elon raised his glass and nodded in reply before he took a sip.

"I'm glad you feel able to talk to me. If I hadn't seen something of how your father works in recent years, I wouldn't have believed he could be so cruel."

"Thank you. It means a lot to hear you say that. When Thea and I visited Amelie and Millie, we had a fascinating conversation. Thea, for reasons too complex to go into, demanded I pushed for changes in law, Modernisation. There seems to be growing support in the other districts for easing the Bloodline laws." Elon's eyebrows rose dramatically, but he remained silent.

"Later, Thea and I spoke in private at home. Then she told me of a secret she had held for most of her life. You won't believe it, but her parents were Cawsal. When her mother died in a farming accident, Thea went to live with an aunt and uncle in Pollo. She wasn't told it would be forever, but it was. She was told never to tell anyone about her Cawsal family, only her family in Pollo. She kept that secret all these years. So, you see, we have three women, each with bad experiences of Thena Anlan laws. It has to stop." *Oh, I shouldn't have said that. This brew must be more potent than I remembered.*

"Mica explained some of this to me when he asked me to contact Kiron and Thea."

"It was the only way I could think of to warn them. I appreciate your help. I knew I could rely on you."

"What are friends for? But now, you also raise an interesting point about the Bloodline Laws. I can see they have driven some very undesirable behaviour. Surely they must still hold value in preserving the integrity of the bloodline otherwise why keep them?"

"How much do you know of Kiron, Healing Councillor?"

"I know him, but I've not had much to do with him other than meeting him recently on your behalf," I told him of my discussion with Kiron about the bloodline purity testing and his findings. The realisation is that the falling purity must be related to the hidden heritage of children. My family were evidence of that.

With a sigh, I swallowed the rest of my brew. I saw Elon had brought over the bottle, and even as I noticed, he was lifting it towards my glass. It reminded me of our college days when we would drink late into the night and then sleep late into the day for days. Eventually, we'd surface bleary-eyed and starving hungry. But we were too old for that now. This glass would be the last I decided. I watched the thick, rich brew swirling into my glass.

"Rush, how can I help? If Kiron already favours change, how many supporters do you need before you move to the Council?" that surprised me, but it shouldn't. Elon was always the most direct of us, and I loved him for it.

"Still as direct as ever, my friend, I see." I smiled at him, sitting relaxed in the chair opposite. He was still wearing his dark green robes. He had the black hair he always had, but unlike the sharp haircuts of our youth, he'd let his hair grow long, as expected for a man of faith. I saw it was tied behind his head at the nape of his neck. The Pennant had concealed it earlier. His face was smooth and clean-shaven with those bright, glacial green eyes that could hold your attention like no other I knew.

"What other way is there?" he asked with a mischievous grin as he raised his glass to me, and I raised mine with a nod in return.

"For you, there has never been another, and I wouldn't have it any other way. Although I suspect your father might have wished for it. Your tutors certainly did." we laughed, then raised our glasses together and nodded before taking a sip.

"We should do this more often. I'd forgotten how good chatting with an old friend is."

"Less of the old," I chuckled.

"But really, how can I help you?" he said as his face grew serious again.

"I need to discreetly find out who we can count on for support and votes on the Council. I think I know those who are supporters of Father and are not in favour of change. They are certainly not shy when it comes to telling everyone. There are those I suspect to favour AMBL, but there are quite a number where their allegiance is unknown. I have no idea which way they might fall, including old Prof Hog, although I think he may put his allegiance with Father. He must be due for retirement soon, anyway. The Industry Octon is the one with which I have had little involvement. Do you have any contacts there?"

"Well, as it happens, I do. The Thena Councillor for Industry is Folke. We were at college together before he decided faith wasn't his calling. Can you believe he preferred to stay tailoring with his father and mother? They own some of the water silk farms in Delphiope and a couple of weaving circuits there, too. It's unlikely he would be for change, but leave that with me. I may be able to sound out some others, too. Senior Leader Boldun of the Fatalists is definitely allied with my father, but Father Garten of Quartive would probably support AMBL. I'll sound him out." he sounded businesslike, and I was grateful to know I could count on him.

"Elon, I don't know how to thank you. Kiron is also quietly investigating the Councillor's allegiance. As you know, the first test of the water will be the Faith Councillor elections. Boldun has a strong campaign and has gained quite a lot of support. Mica would be a great candidate, but he's not strong enough alone, and neither is Father Garten. Boldon could still win. Fancy a new challenge? A way to redeem yourself in your father's eyes even? He couldn't argue that you hadn't achieved his lofty goals if you became the Faith Councillor, could he?"

"Now that is true, although I hadn't planned to put myself forward in favour of Mica's candidacy. Mica would be a great Councillor, and I'd hate to stand against him unless there is no other way to keep Boldun from the chair. His type of faith isn't a faith that should lead our Octon. That isn't a reflection on Fatalism but rather on him. He is the most objectionable man I've ever met."

"That's strong talk, Elon. From my few interactions with Boldun, I agree with your assessment. I believe we will need you to stand against Boldun. I know you have the strength of character and personality to drive a campaign. I accept your wish to support Mica, but I don't think it is enough to stop Boldun. Please consider putting yourself forward now. There's still time."

"I believe Mica is the best candidate for all faiths. I'll campaign on his behalf in the strongest possible way. If it becomes clear another candidate must stand against Boldun, I will reluctantly put myself forward. It would be a great opportunity, but I don't feel it's my time yet." *I was relieved. Elon understood the need to keep Boldun at a safe distance. Mica was the best candidate, but Elon would present a more substantial challenge against Boldun and hopefully reduce Boldun's advantage.*

"The time is now, my friend. Tomorrow is the last day for candidates." He must get his candidacy in.

Elon leaned forward and spoke urgently, his words beginning to slur.

"The three of ush should meet. You, Kiron and me, to compare notes? Have you thought of Jak? I know you're both preparing campaigns for Legal High Councillor. Not the right time? sh' your call."

"I'd the shame, same t'oughts. I wan'a call Jak, but ishnot good timing. Can you?"

"Greast, I'll call Jaksh. We should have a drink. I need another donasshion of this wonderful Cawsal Berry Bweww. Now may I order a conveyanshie for you? Later than I fought, and rain is forecasht."

"Thank you, good idea 'specially because I've had a few glasses of that beddy, berry brush. I fink it's gone to my, my shed, head, and I might be lost." we both chuckled. I had a notoriously poor sense of direction. We'd had some exciting excursions when I was leading in the past.

"Sho glad you came this evelling. Wasn't shh...scheduled but other Shhteward is sick. Fate for fatalists." We laughed again. *I'm a little intoxicated*, I think. I'd forgotten how strong that brew was and hadn't eaten this evening. Thankfully, Thea won't be home to see me and tell me how bad it was to consume alcohol.

"Yesh, we musshht do it more often. With Jak, like old timeses when you hasshh another bogle."

"Convelaayanice." He walked carefully to the telecom and made the call. I'd enjoyed this evening, but there was so much to do and so little time. It had been a relief to unburden myself.

30

Rush

As soon as I put my key in the door, I knew something was wrong. There was a flurry of movement behind the door as if someone had been waiting for me. It was no surprise to see Luzi there, but her expression and clasped hands told me I had been right to suspect trouble.

"Oh, Sir, it's good you're home," she said, relief evident in her voice. "That sister of yours has been calling, she's most keen to talk. I nearly called Mr Maxim, but then I heard the conveyance." I knew Amelie wouldn't have risked calling here unless it was urgent. Thank the Singularity, Luzi hadn't called Father.

"Thank you, Luzi. I'll get in touch with her. Did she say where she was?" I slipped my coat and hat off and hung them on the coat stand. The intoxication left my body along with my outer garments.

"She said she would be at The Moria in Delph until late, and you could call her there." She sniffed in disapproval. Being blessed with old-fashioned views, she disapproved of Thenan women in performing arts. She might not be of Thena Anlan descent, but she might as well be with her views.

"Could you bring some coffee to my study, please?" taking the key from my pocket, I slipped it into the lock and, with relief, entered my sanctuary. Here, at least, I was still master, although I've begun to wonder if even this room was safe in the past week. I sank into my desk chair and closed my eyes for a moment. *What could be so urgent that Amelie would risk calling here?* Pulling the telecom device over, I lifted the lid to expose the keypad. I found the number to contact The Moria and put the call through. Steady 'Bing bong' tones told me the call was active. I didn't have long to wait before a formal voice welcomed me to The Moria and asked how they could help. I asked for Amelie, and I was transferred without being asked for a name, which was a relief.

"Hello?" came a soft voice at the end of the line.

"Amelie?"

"Who's this?" she sounded as small and afraid as she had been as a child when she was in trouble.

"It's me, Rush. What's up? Are you in trouble?"

"Oh, Rush, I'm so afraid. I'm being followed. I think my house is being watched. I'm scared Father has found where I live and is having me watched. I don't know what to do. Every place I think of, he might guess..." she was rambling, her words tumbling over each other.

"Amelie, just hold it there. Can I come to you? We'll sort something out?"

"Where are you?" she asks tentatively.

"At home,"

"By the Gods, he'll be tracking you! Now he knows where I am. I have to leave now. Where can I go?" she was almost hysterical, and my mind went blank momentarily. Then it came to me.

"Where's Millie? Is she with you?" I was worried for the child I still thought of as my own.

"No, she's in Pol… She's visiting friends from school in Sorcia." She must mean either Yan or Thea. I hope that means she's safe.

"Do you remember the Councillor we were talking about? "I hoped she wouldn't give a name.

"Yes," she says cautiously.

"He told me of a woman who was visiting the Wernia Hub. Have you heard?" I hope she'll realise who I'm talking about and any listeners won't.

"It's been quite a talking point here," she said conversationally.

"Let me think about your predicament, but have you considered visiting the temple? It might be good to petition the Gods."

"The temple? I must confess I don't visit the Singularity often these days. It rarely seems to offer what I'm looking for. I prefer Fatalism, but the faith leaders here have some strong views, so I'm left with Quartive. It's quite good, and we have a visiting priest from Cawsal this week. It's been quite a draw for believers, although I haven't heard him yet. I had thought to drop in after I finish here." I guessed she was asking if Father Garten would receive her with understanding.

"That's a good idea. I've been to the temple most evenings since Thea went to her family in Pollo. It's lonely here without them. I don't think I appreciated Thea until now. This evening, I met Elon, and he told me how much he liked his fellow Councillor from Cawsal, Father Garten. Would that be the priest you mention, I wonder?"

"It could be. Perhaps I'll follow your example, but now I must go before the tr…." the line dropped.

What happened? *Have they been discovered? If they were following Amelie, had they found Thea too? What about Millie? Was I being watched as a person of interest now?* I realised long ago my movements were being tracked, but not as a person of interest until now. *How can I help Amelie? Who can we trust? I hope she will be safe if she reaches Father Garten. If Delph isn't safe, and Thena isn't, would Pollo be any safer? Could I risk travelling to Kiron again so soon without raising suspicion?* I decided to wait until the morning before trying to think any further. The brew was still swirling, my thoughts increasingly misty, and I was very sleepy.

Message from Councillor Maxim to Councillor Wiklon
Fugitives at The Moria. Description attached. Send guards. Clean up.

Message from Captain of Delphiope Guard to Councillor Wiklon.
Not at The Moria. Could be Quartive Temple. Watchers notified. Guards on way.

Message from Councillor Maxim to Father Boldon
Fugitives to Quartive Temple. Garten there. Distract and detain. Guards on way.

31

Amelie

After I'd spoken with Rush, I turned to Millie and saw my fear mirrored on the young woman's face. We were standing in the backstage restroom where the telecom unit was located. The theatre was growing quiet as the last few performers left. Sounds of cleaning filled the auditorium. It wouldn't be good to remain here if we were to have any chance of slipping away unnoticed. It was probably too late already. If only Rush had been at home when I first called.

"I think we should drop into the temple on our way home," I said. We pulled on our long coats and wrapped dark scarves around our heads to conceal our hair and face. As we stepped out into the cool night air, the conveyance was waiting, and we climbed inside the warm interior.

The Quartive temple had four distinctive panels of coloured stone. Each Quartane has a specific colour linked to the Gods of the Skies, Water, Earth and Life and an individual entrance door. Millie paused for a moment, taking in the impressive exterior. I led her to the door in the red stone panel and entered the Shrine of the God Sange. Inside was the rosy shrine with its rich gold candle sticks and central altar. The colours were warm shades from the deepest red to the palest pinky hues. Benches with dark red cushions were placed around the sides of the small shrine. Its central altar had a rich red cloth and the four candles of the Quartive, each in its colour, set in ornate gold candlesticks. The red candle was the largest for Sange, God of Life. Red signifies the blood of life running through all living things. Behind the altar was a large Ankh, the great symbol of life. Its oval loop stretched above two arms, reaching the sides and a lower pillar. The Ankh glowed gold in front of a rich red wall hanging from the ceiling to the floor. A sense of peace descended as we stood at the entrance, breathing in the shrine's warm, rich, spicy scent. It wasn't something I could put into words. Catching a glimpse of Millie, I could see she felt the same. We went further into the shrine and sank onto one of the benches. It was comfortable, and we exhaled a sigh of relief. It was a few minutes more before either of us spoke.

"What are we going to do now? We can't stay here," Millie said. She was frightened and tired, her words spoken in a harsh whisper.

"We'll rest here for a few minutes and thank The God Sange for bringing us here. I have a small offering to give. It isn't much, but I hope it will suffice." I slipped my hand into my bag and retrieved a small bundle tied with a gold ribbon. Stroking the red velvet bundle gently, I walked up to the altar and put it on the gold tray, where it joined a collection of other small bundles in different sizes, each wrapped in red material and tied with gold ribbon. Bowing before the altar, I stood with my arms out to each side, mirroring the symbol of the Ankh, as I prayed for my family. Then, with a nod, I walked back and sat beside Millie.

"What was in the bag?"

"Only money. It could have been a blood offering, but I don't like that. If I move to Quartive, I may see what others offer before this shrine. I've found money seems to be acceptable in all faiths."

"I was wondering about that. I had visions of you bringing some animal body part dripping with blood," grinned Millie.

I shuddered, “Urgh, no, I hope that won’t be necessary. Now, do you feel drawn to prayer?”

“I haven’t been in such a shrine before. It feels strange after our temple of Singularity in Thena.” she looked uncertain.

“That’s OK. I know what you mean. Let’s see if Father Garten is here. From what Rush was trying to say, I think he may be able to help.” I stood and offered my hand to her. We were the same height, but Millie looked like a child as she held my hand.

We walked back to the entrance together and took the door to the right, entering the shrine of Rapta, God of the skies. This shrine was a swirl of cool blues and wispy white clouds. The shrine was also empty and echoed as we walked to the door on the opposite side, which led to the inner sanctum. Here, all the colours swirled as they combined forces. The broad central altar had a pure white cloth on which four coloured candles stood in their rich gold candlesticks. The red candle was for Sange, the blue candle for Rapta, the green candle for Zuthor and the rich dark orange candle for Tera. Behind the altar were the four symbols of the Gods: The Great Ankh of Sange, the Ancient Circross of Rapta, The Rogalov of Zuthor, and the Great Tree of Life representing Tera.

In the sanctum, a group was gathered on benches around a priest in a brown robe. He had a stole with broadbands of the four colours winding up one side around the neck and down the other. We drew closer, and the priest looked up and indicated an empty bench at the back of the group. Sitting quietly, we waited for the priest to complete the study session. His voice was soft, and a sense of calm flowed from him as he spoke. Eventually, the last person received their blessing before they left the sanctum. The priest came over and smiled as he offered his arm.

"You must be Amelie. I've heard you sing. Your voice is a beautiful gift from the great God, Rapta. How can I help you this evening?" I took his arm and we embraced hand to elbow.

"Am I addressing Father Garten?"

"Yes, my child, I am Father Garten," he smiled, "I received a message from Steward Elon that you might visit. He explained a little, and I don't need to know more. Tell me how I can help." his face was full of concern as he looked at us.

"Is there somewhere we can talk privately?"

"Why don't we talk in my chamber behind the sanctum? Please, follow me," he walked towards the altar and opened a door hidden behind drapes. He held the door until we had passed before letting it close behind him. The corridor before us had pale green lighting illuminating roughhewn walls. I realised with shock that we were in an underground tunnel. The chill and earthy smell permeated the air, reinforcing my sense of foreboding.

Was Rush right to trust this man? Surely Elon wouldn't wish me ill, not after all this time. He was a steward of the Singularity and above such petty things, I thought. Father Garten stopped by a dark wood door as I mulled these things over. He extracted a long rope with a key attached from within his robes. He inserted the key and turned it, and there was a resounding clunk. The door revealed a sparsely furnished room with a table and three chairs, two chairs on one side and one on the other side of the table. A tall lamp stood beside the table, providing pale light to the room. The walls were unadorned and gloomy, and my sense of foreboding increased. I could see Millie sensed the same thing. Father Garten ushered us inside, and we turned as the door clicked behind us, expecting to see the priest, but we were alone.

I swallowed a moment of panic. *I had to be brave for Millie*, I told myself.

"Why has the priest locked us in?" Millie asked in a small voice. I walked to the door and turned the handle. It didn't move. A shiver ran down my back. Pulling all my strength into a positive response, I turned and smiled.

"I don't know. Your father, Rush, told me it would be safe here. He said he had spoken with an old school friend of his, Steward Elon of the Singularity. There's bound to be a good explanation. I'm sure the priest will be back shortly." *I hoped I sounded more confident than I felt.* Millie walked around the table, pulled out the chair, and then pushed it back. She looked around the room.

"This doesn't look like a priest's chamber. It's more like a prison cell," she said as she ran her fingers over the simple wooden tabletop. It was smooth to the touch, not a blemish or scratch.

"It does a bit, but maybe Quartive priests have a poverty vow?" I walked around the room's edges, my heels clicking softly on the stone floor. Finally, I took one of the two chairs in front of the table.

"Come and sit down, Millie. We're here now, and I'm sure the priest will be back soon to explain everything." Millie walked around and took the other seat.

"But what if he doesn't?"

"Let's not worry about that yet. Give him time." I said, trying to sound optimistic. Outside the room, it was silent.

The room's walls were rough in texture. *Was that to absorb sound? I've been in soundproof rooms rehearsing for performances, but none were like this.* The earthy smell was pungent here, and I was sure we were underground. Maybe we were inside the hill behind the temple. I hadn't realised how far back the temple stretched.

"What will we do if he doesn't come back? How will we get out of here?" Millie was starting to panic, her eyes wide in the pale light.

"I'm sure he'll be back. Perhaps he's making tea?" *I'd love that to be true, but I don't believe my words.*

"But what if he doesn't?" she persisted.

"Millie, it's only been a few minutes, come and sit down."

"It smells funny, doesn't it?"

"Well, I think we are inside the hill behind the temple. If you look at the walls, they've been dug out of the hillside and are probably left rough to absorb sound. It makes the room more private, as the priest said."

"But why lock us in?" she asked. It was a good question. The same one had been on my mind, too.

"To keep us safe, probably. Maybe he wants the room to look like no one is inside."

"But if there was a good reason, why didn't he tell us?" *she was right. It didn't make sense. There had to be a reason. There had to be.* We sat in silence until we heard the key in the lock.

The door slid open, revealing not Father Garton but another priest in the flame-red robe of the Fatalists. Senior Leader Boldun's tall, ratty frame entered the room. He had a smug grin on his thin face as he looked over at us. My heart sank. I knew of Boldun. He wasn't someone I'd expect help from. I was pretty sure he was allied with my father. *Had I misunderstood Rush?* I didn't think so, but there wasn't time to ponder further. Boldun came towards the table and took the seat on the opposite side.

"Amelie and Millie, how can I help you?" he said in a silky-smooth voice. His mouth stretched the skin of his thin face into an insincere smile.

"What happened to Father Garten?" began Millie.

"Shh, Millie, let Senior Leader Boldun speak," I said.

"It's an excellent question," he replied, turning his ratty face towards Millie. "Father Garten had to leave on an errand. A member of the Quartive was unwell. As I was here, he asked me to stop by and find out how we could help." My hopes fell, and my fears escalated as I saw Boldun's face.

"I want to learn more about the Quartive faith, Senior Leader Boldun. I've always been curious," Millie said with as much conviction as she could muster.

"Are you sure that was the only reason you came to see Father Garten this evening? I had the impression there might be something else. I want to help with whatever difficulties you may have." he said. His piercing golden brown eyes bored into us, and the sickly smile seemed stuck on his face.

"Millie's right, Senior Leader. I was brought up in the Singularity, but more recently, I've been looking into Quartive and Fatalism. Could you tell us a little about them?" *Millie was right; we needed to play for time,* I thought, as I smiled earnestly.

"Now Amelie, as a Thena girl, why would you look into Quartive or Fatalism?" he asked.

"I haven't lived in Thena for many years, as you know. I'm drawn to other faiths because they seem more relevant to my life than Singularity."

"It's good to explore your faith and find where you feel at home, but I wonder if that's the only reason you're here?" Millie and I exchanged glances. With a nod, as if something was agreed, I began.

"You're right, of course, Senior leader Boldun. We do have another motive for visiting today. I'm worried about my brother Rush. He no longer seems to be the brother I remember. He was always willing to help if I was in trouble, but now he's reluctant. It's very worrying and upsetting. I wanted to talk with Father

Garten because he might know Rush's friend, Steward Elon. Do you know him?"

"Ah yes, Steward Elon, odd you should mention him. He was arrested this evening by the watchers. It seems he was on his way to this very temple. What an odd coincidence, wouldn't you say? He also expressed concern about Rush. Rush is lucky to have so many people with his interests at heart." Those beady gold eyes continued to stare, but the smile had begun to slip.

"My brother has always been lucky with his friends." *what could I say?*

"So, it would seem. I'll talk with Rush and see if I can resolve these concerns." he stood and moved around the table. "I think you should stay here where you are safe. It will give you time to think further about what brought you here and whether anything else is troubling your soul. You may remain here as long as you wish," he said coldly. Then he turned to the door, and we heard the soft click as it shut and was locked again.

"We should be cautious here," I said as I looked around, hoping Millie understood my concern. If Boldun was here, there would be listening devices, too. I wished I knew more about the Council and had spoken with Rush, but there'd been no time. Now, it felt as if time was running out.

"I agree, perhaps Singularity was the best after all," Millie said. It seemed she had understood and was playing along. We fell into an awkward silence as we considered our surroundings.

Message from Father Boldon to Councillor Maxim
Fugitives detained at temple. Waiting for guard. Elon arrested.

Message from Councillor Maxim to Councillor Wiklon
Boldon has fugitives. Confirm when guards arrive.

We'd been alone for a while when we heard a rustling near the door, and something slid underneath the door. Millie jumped up and ran over to pick it up.

"Take care," I began, but it was too late. She'd picked up a piece of paper and placed it on the table.

"It's rather cryptic," she said as I read the words.

"In 10, it will begin. Prepare for the end." I guessed and held Millie's hand tightly, shaking my head.

"I hope Father Garten isn't too long," We lapsed into silence as the time ticked away. Suddenly, there was a scuffling in the corridor, and the door flew open, revealing a priest who stood grinning. Brother Lori, a student of Father Garten's, beckoned to us. We didn't need to be asked twice and hurried through the door. He closed the door behind us and locked it. We followed him as he led us along corridor after corridor until we had no idea which direction we were going. Finally, we began to smell the fresh air, and the light changed from the green of the corridors to a warmer golden glow. Arriving through a small door, we found ourselves in the temple of Tera.

Brother Lori didn't slow down but proceeded towards another concealed door. This time, it took us to a corridor leading from the temple to a small building on the outskirts of the grounds.

"This is our dry walk to the temple in times of poor weather," he said with a grin as they joined him in a cosy parlour. We sat on the settee opposite Brother Lori, who was in an armchair beside the fireplace.

"Sorry about the cloak and dagger stuff," he said with a grin. "It's rather fun, though," he looked like a schoolboy allowed to run in the corridor without being told off.

"Perhaps you could tell us what's happening and where Father Garten's gone. Is he OK?" I asked, sitting forward.

"All in good time. First, we must get you away from here. I fear we only have a short time before it's discovered you're gone. I've arranged for the pastoral team to take a bereaved wife and daughter to the cemetery to pay their respects. You are less likely to be stopped that way.

Now, you asked about Father Garten. Father Garten has been asked to provide evidence of the training for priests in all districts. It will be fine, but it has taken him away from the temple, which was the intention."

"Oh goodness, and what of Steward Elon?" I asked.

"He'll be released, I'm sure. His papers are all in good order." He stood, "Now, we must be ready when the pastoral team arrives." They followed him to the front of the little house, entering a room that was in darkness with deep shadows. In the deep shadows, they could watch the driveway unobserved.

"How do we know you're not with Boldun?" Millie asked, looking around suddenly, taking a step away from Brother Lori.

"I have a message for you. The invitation was yours. I hope you understand its meaning." Brother Lori said. He looked at the two women.

"OK, thank you. I think you know why we asked," I said.

"Yes, these are extraordinary times," he agreed.

"Ah, there are lights over there. It might be your conveyance but wait here while I check. I'll go and greet it and let you know if it's safe to come out." He moved towards the door into the hallway as a dark shape drew up outside the cottage. We heard his footsteps on the hall floor and the click of a door opening. There were muffled voices, and then we saw a figure step from the conveyance. Millie grasped my hand tightly, moving closer. We moved further back into the shadows, hardly daring to breathe. Then, we heard the door opening and soft footsteps coming towards them. The figure of Brother Lori appeared in the doorway.

"Follow me. The driver said there was another conveyance on its way. He saw it turn towards the temple as he came towards the cottage. Remember, you're a grieving mother and daughter, so you needn't say anything to the driver. Don't talk unless you have to." The two women nodded and hurried after him to the waiting conveyance. They bowed their heads and held hands tightly until they reached the conveyance.

"May the Gods be with you," he said, touching their heads in blessing.

Message from Captain of Delph guard to Councillor Wiklon

Fugitives escaped. Inside help. Searching for Evidence. Advise.

Message from Councillor Wiklon to Councillor Maxim

Boldon failed. Inside help. Release Elon?

Message from Councillor Maxim to Councillor Wiklon

Release Elon, under Watch.

32

Rush

I couldn't believe how fast things had escalated. I hoped my message reached Elon in time. Perhaps Amelie was right about the house having ears and eyes. It was a sobering thought, and I felt uncomfortable as I looked around the study. I packed a small bag. *Would it be safe for me to go to them? Would I put them in more danger? How could I ensure their safety? Should we go somewhere else? But where?* I began to pace the study, pulling out books randomly, flipping through the pages, then replacing and taking another. All the time, my mind was whirring. *Who could I trust? My brothers Max and Cid followed in Father's footsteps and couldn't be trusted. Maybe... yes, perhaps one of the twins, Barti or Brig?*

The twins lived on the other side of the town in Zenith Quart. I visited them as often as I could. They lived in Accam Drive, named after the famous Militaria Councillor Accam. Accam played an essential role in stabilising the country after the Bloodline wars. I named our oldest son after this great Councillor even though he was Militaria. Taking my bag, I added a few books and some essential papers from my desk before locking it. I slipped the key into my pocket. Locking the study door, I went to the waiting conveyance, instructing the driver before I entered the gently swaying vehicle. The journey was smooth, and from what I could see, I wasn't followed, but it didn't matter. A visit to either of the twins was not unusual.

On arrival at Accam Drive, I stepped from the conveyance and walked to the gate. It was a relief to hear Barti's voice through the telecom. The gate clicked open, and I went through, hearing it shut again with a resounding clang behind me.

Message from Watcher to Captain of Thena Guard
Conveyance in Accam drive. Passenger lost.

Message from Captain of Thena Guard to Councillor Wiklon
Fugitive in Accam drive. Advise.

Message from Councillor Wiklon to Captain of Thena Guard
Advise watcher - remain vigilant.

Message from Councillor Wiklon to Councillor Maxim
Fugitive Accam drive.

Message from Councillor Maxim to Councillor Wiklon
Brig secure. Barti unclear. Advise Watchers to be vigilant.

Barti's house was concealed from the road by a curving avenue of tall, dense trees. Reaching the white house with its bright red door, I was relieved to see it open, and my brother Barti stood there. His rotund shape filled the doorway, and as always, he wore a flowing tunic of dark purple with green trousers. His clean-shaven face looked slightly less full than when I last saw him, but his welcoming grin was as warm as always when he embraced me. Such open shows of emotion made me uncomfortable, but I accepted and returned the embrace. It was good to see him. Since Barti had left home, he had allowed his softer nature to flourish. I admired his courage to be himself. Barti led me through to the back parlour before he went to make coffee. While I waited, I put my bag down and took off my coat, throwing it over the back of a chair. The house was quiet and peaceful, but I craved company and joined Barti in the kitchen. Barti never wanted servants, so he and his wife managed the household tasks together. Their kitchen was a warm, rich buttermilk colour that toned with the creamy brown of the table and work surfaces. The effect was tasteful and refined, like Barti and Deeala.

"How are you?" I watched him brewing coffee. The aroma drifted towards me, rich and enticing.

"Oh well, I can't complain, you know. It doesn't do anyone any good to complain, I always say. How are you? I heard there had been some trouble over your side of town?" Barti turned towards me, his round face flushed from the stove.

"Yes, you could say that. I'm discovering there are more ears and eyes around these days. Even in our own homes if you believe the rumours." I said it as a joke, trying to bring a flippant tone to my voice and hoped he understood.

"You should be OK. Father living with you until recently should have validated you and your home. I've heard the rumours, but nobody would be interested in my business." He picked up the tray with the coffee and a plate of tarts and took it into the back parlour. We sat in armchairs beside each other, and Barti busied himself pouring the coffee. Then he picked up the plate and offered it to me.

"Do try the tarts. They're mulberry and delicious if I do say so myself." He grinned as he took one and bit into it. His eyes closed as he sighed with pure pleasure.

"I haven't had mulberry tarts since we were children. Cook made them when the berries were in season, didn't she?" I said, reaching out and taking one. Raising it to my nose, I inhaled the mouthwatering aroma before sinking my teeth into the soft berry filling. The pastry melted in my mouth; the juicy berry filling was heavenly. *As good as cook made, if not better*, I thought, as

I took another bite. I couldn't speak until I'd finished the tart and taken a sip of coffee. It had been a wonderful moment, quite out of time. I savoured the remaining flavours before setting down my cup and looking at Barti.

"How sure are you that the house is secure?" I didn't risk saying anything until I knew. Even that might be too much if the house was under the watch.

"Pretty sure. Deeala decorates regularly to keep the 'showroom look' for clients who visit our home. She would have seen something if there was anything to find. She knows what to look for and has seen them in other houses often enough." Barti's face was serious now. His dark green eyes looked at me, full of concern.

"I hope so. I don't want to cause more trouble than I've already caused. I'm afraid I was probably followed, spotted arriving here despite my caution."

"This room is one of the most secure, but there is the lower cosy room. No one other than Deeala and I use that room. Family members are unaware of its existence, except for you, now." he gave one of his brief half-smiles.

"You've always liked your secrets," I chuckled, "did you create it or was it already here when you moved in?"

"Oh, we created it ourselves in a moment of madness. Deeala had planned to take pictures and use a darkened room to develop them from the film. She never quite got round to that, but we decided to keep it and make it into a snug, cosy room."

"I'd love to see it in that case. Would you permit me?" it sounded perfect. I felt guilty dragging Barti into this madness but had few options. We stood, and Barti led me back to the kitchen, where he stooped and tapped a tile on the floor. The tile lifted, and I saw a rope handle beneath it, which Barti began to tug. As the section of the floor rose, I saw steps leading down into the darkness.

"You go first. On your left is a switch for the lights. I'll follow and close the door behind me," he said. Cautiously, I put my foot onto the first step and then the next, making my way down until I found the switch on the wall. The light illuminated the room below, flooding the area with a pale green glow. As I reached the bottom, I heard Barti pull the door closed above us and his heavy footsteps behind me.

There was a brown leather settee and two green armchairs on either side of what looked like a fireplace. *How could a secret room have a fireplace?* I wondered as I walked over to it. Barti joined me with a twinkle in his eye.

"Ah, you've spotted the fire. Great idea, isn't it? Let's get it lit, and we'll soon be snug down here." he squatted down and prepared the fire before he struck a lighter and put it to the kindling.

"Is it safe? Where does the smoke go?"

"Now that's the ingenious thing. The smoke goes up the kitchen chimney, so as long as we use the kitchen chimney, no one will ever suspect anything." Barti grinned as he took another tart from the tray on the table. I hadn't noticed him bring that down, but I was glad he had.

"Absolute genius!" I cried, genuinely impressed at the ingenuity.

"So, big brother, is this secure enough?" he asked.

"Yes, I believe it is, and I'm sorry to be so paranoid, but I have good reason to be these days."

"Tell me, you know you can trust me. Nothing will go to Father or the traitors who follow his steps."

"I fear this is life or death. It's not too late for you to ask me to leave. It would be far better for you not to become involved, but I don't know who else to turn to." I dared not look at him in case he was standing to see me out. I needn't have worried.

"You've always been there for me, and you should know you can trust me by now. How can I help?" I took a deep breath and told him about Amelie and Millie. About Amelie's fears and the hurried call from Elon telling me they'd been discovered. I told him about Thea's visit to her family in Pollo with the children and how I feared for them and myself. Stopping there, I fell silent and looked at the floor, all the words now spent.

"That's quite some story, dear brother. If it were anyone else, I'd fear you'd been drinking too much CB Brew (Cawsal Berry Brew), but not you. Father's corruption is no secret, but I can scarcely believe he would be out for Amelie's blood, not after so long. Were there other reasons watchers could be sent after you?" he looked thoughtful.

"I don't think so. It all started after Millie left, and Amelie was set on Millie choosing her future husband. She doesn't want to force her into honouring the match Father and Mother asked Thea to name on the Promisary Agreement. It was beneficial for Father, of course. The match Amelie found was good, and Millie also has a boy at school she's sweet on who would also be a good match. So, the lucky girl has choices, but it will be her choice. Thea and I supported Amelie in that. These archaic laws should have been modernised long ago to protect girls from political matches." I fell silent.

"These things are all tied together, Amelie and your radical views. Have you been seeking support too openly, I wonder?" Barti voiced what had been an increasing worry in my mind.

"I don't know. I didn't think so, but things seemed to change with Father after Millie left, especially when I asked them to leave our house."

"Haha, so you finally did it then. Father wouldn't have liked that. Do you think he had been watching you while they were there?"

"I've concluded that they might well have been. Thea and Amelie are both convinced that there are ears in the house."

"So, if I'm right, you need a way to meet up with Thea and the children. Then, passage to a safe place. Amelie and Millie need an immediate, safe place and a more permanent solution. If Amelie and Millie disappeared, would it be safe for you, Thea and the children?"

"I've thought about that too, but how can I ask them to go into hiding for the rest of their lives? We can't be sure of their safety until Father's gone and his network is destroyed."

"Well, what if they weren't in Anacadair? Would they still need to hide? For example, does Father's reach stretch across the border into Nicadair?"

"As far as I know, he doesn't stretch past Cawsal. The last time I heard him mention Nicadair, it wasn't very favourable. I hadn't considered them leaving Anacadair, but you have a point. For the moment, they need somewhere safe until we can make better arrangements. They're in a temporary place which isn't safe."

"Of course. Now, Deeala has some contacts in Cawsal who could help. They have connections with the Intercontinental Transport Route. Their transports are sometimes used by people who need a discrete way out of Anacadair."

He steepled his fingers and touched them to his lips, almost in prayer.

"Yes, I think that would be best for now. I'll make a quick call." He went to the telecom I'd noticed on the far wall. After connecting, he spoke quickly in abbreviated sentences that made no sense to me. Closing the call, he returned, sitting on the edge of his seat. His hands clasped in front, elbows on his knees.

"OK, so that's arranged. You said Amelie and Millie are in Delphiope, I think? If so, that's perfect. There's a transport leaving tomorrow evening. Is there a way to get word to them?" I shook my head.

"I don't know. I worked via Steward Elon. Do you remember we were at school together? and Father Garten, Cawsal Faith Councillor." I told Barti what I knew of the events at the temple. "Brother Lori helped them escape and may be the only one who knows where they are now."

"I can get word to Brother Lori. Do you have a passcode for them?"

"Yes, I had to find one they would recognise. We had no time to prepare one in advance. It's 'The invitation was yours'."

I dropped my head into my hands. It seemed so inadequate. *What if they didn't recognise its meaning?*

"OK, that seems fair, as long as they understand,"

Barti suggested that his transport manager visit Brother Lori. Amelie, the transport manager, and I have no connection, so that won't raise suspicion. Barti made another call to finalise arrangements. Then we waited. *What if they have already been found? What if Brother Lori or someone else has moved them, and they miss the transport?* So many what-ifs filled my head. I stood and began pacing the small room, trying to resolve the tension. Then it occurred to me, how did Barti have so many convenient connections? I was surprised to learn he had been working with underground groups to help people escape from Thena and Anacadair. Deeala was also involved. I was both so proud of him and equally afraid for them. What if Father found out? There would be no mercy for them or those involved; I was sure of that. Barti seemed unconcerned and waved my worries away.

"Relax, Rush, drink your coffee. Deeala will be home soon, and we'll make some food for your journey." I stopped my pacing and looked over at him.

"My journey?" a wave of panic rushed over me. "Where am I going?"

"You'll need to lie low for a little while. Why not visit some friends of mine in Cawsal? They're humble miners in Norwcan, North Cawsal, but they can be trusted. Their children have children now, so they have plenty of space. I know they'll make you welcome for as long as you need to stay." he smiled warmly at me. "Now, sit before you wear holes in the carpet. It was costly, you know." He grinned. We both knew the carpet was woven rushes that had been dyed and then painted. It looked far grander than it was. This very carpet had been in our great aunt's house, and we had both loved it. Barti was lucky enough to receive it when she died.

"Barti, I don't know how to thank you." I lifted the coffee pot for a refill, but it was empty. I was disappointed and tried not to show it.

"No need, we're family. I've always known the business with Amelie would rise again. I'm sorry you and your family have been caught up in it. You and Amelie were so close as children."

"But you have other things to worry about, Barti. Don't think I've forgotten." Barti had learned of a malignant being which had invaded his body just a year ago. The Healer had been treating him, but it persisted, flowing through his blood like poison.

"I'm fine, as you can see, don't worry about me. Now, that sounds like Deeala. Stay here while I go and talk with her." he went upstairs, and I was alone in the cosy room, my mind swirling. I didn't deserve to have such a brother, but I was very grateful I had. He had made arrangements for us, and I felt safe in his hands.

33

High Council Elections

The election for Faith Councillor proved to be a complicated and bitter battle after the announcement of Father Anberto's death. Senior Steward Mica and Senior Leader Boldun were the first to submit their candidacy, followed by Father Garten. There were fears that corruption would become worse if Boldun were elected. It was a very close campaign and began to turn nasty when rumours of foul play began to arise and suggestions that Senior Steward Mica was guilty of malpractice. Senior Leader Boldun seemed to be nudging ahead as accusations flew between campaign teams.

Father Garten appeared excluded from the battle at first until rumours began that he was too weak and his age was against him. It was a low blow and hard to contest since Boldun was the youngest candidate by several decades. Father Garten was quietly spoken, but so was Mica until needed. Then, both could hold their own. When the vote was counted, the tension was palpable. Max, Head of the High Council, announced Senior Steward Mica as the new Faith Councillor to cheers of support for Mica and jeers of disbelief from those who had supported Boldun. Humiliated, Boldon threatened to resign from the High Council, but after appeals from his supporters, he agreed to remain in his post while a recount took place. After two recounts, the second with witnesses from all Octons. It was confirmed that Senior Steward Mica had won the vote by an acceptable margin.

Steward Elon would cover Thena temporarily along with Pollo until a new candidate for Thena Faith Councillor was elected. During the elections, it became clear that the Council was deeply divided between those who craved modernisation and those who wished to keep the laws unchanged. Councillors who desired change were pushing for the Abolition and Modernisation of the Bloodline Laws (AMBL) to reflect current thinking and ease the pain and distress caused. It was difficult to determine precisely how voting on these laws might be resolved since many Councillors would not declare their support either way. They maintained that they would cast their votes secretly, as it should be with a secret ballot. For now, however, all the Octons had settled, and even the Faith Octon had reached a degree of acceptance.

Immediately after Mica was elected, two other Councillors announced their retirement along with Max. It was the most significant number of High Council vacancies to arise together in a very long time, and the administration was substantial. There were also two vacancies for district Councillors to replace Pollo Healing Councillor Kiron and Thena Faith Councillor Mica. With Max as one of the retirees, it also meant that it was to be an election in two parts. The first election would be to replace Stratagon Wiklon, Professor Hog, and the two district councillors. Their replacements could then participate in the second election for Legal Councillor and Head of the High Council. Even this caused dissent amongst some Councillors who would have preferred to vote on all vacancies in one election.

Amid this controversy, a district Councillor was quietly elected who might have otherwise caused even more division had there not been so much distraction. It was the election of Mother Plumb as Pollo Healing Councillor to the High Council. Mother Plumb was the first woman to stand for election to the Council, supported by Healers and wisewomen in all four districts, and the first woman to be elected outright. She replaced Kiron, who was now Healing Councillor. It was Kiron's support that was the primary force behind her election.

Rush should've played a leading role in these elections as the primary candidate to replace Max. Today was the last day for Rush to declare his candidacy, and still, there was no word from Rush. Max was furious at his son's rejection of his destiny to be the next Head of the High Council. Officers of the Militaria had been dispatched along with their watchers after he disappeared five days ago. He was traced to the road where Barti and Brig live, but he seemed to have vanished after that. Brig had been supporting his father's search for his brother. Barti and Deeala were out on the day in question and said they hadn't seen or heard from him. As the watcher hadn't seen Rush enter a specific house, there was no reason to suspect he had been there.

Max turned his attention to the witch, Thea, and her brats instead. He reasoned that if Rush went anywhere, it would be to join his family at Thea's parents' house in Sorcia. More watchers were dispatched to the area around Jonca's house. If the family tried to leave, they would be followed, caught, and dealt with. The watchers he had sent were ruthless and had been behind many a disappearance in the past. It was a risk, he knew, but to rid himself of the witch and her brats would be worth it. As for his traitorous son, he had shown his true colours, and there was no way back. There was the other matter, the tart and her bastard child. It was time to do what he should have done sixteen years ago if he hadn't listened to the traitor. The more he thought about it, the more he realised it was the only way to cleanse the festering wound. Once done, the Council could return to its smooth running again.

He bitterly regretted encouraging Rush to stand for election as Legal Councillor. Before Rush was elected, there was no opposition to his recommendations and proposals. Now, every time a new law was proposed, or an election was called, it was a battle to get the right outcome. Of course, it did bring the question of who to replace him as Legal High Councillor and Head of the High Council. Jak, Pollo's Legal Councillor, was a good candidate, but he had been at school with Rush. Where did his loyalties lie? A safer candidate would be Professor Anton, Delphiope Legal Councillor. He wasn't one of those headstrong lads who hadn't learned respect for the established law. The more Max thought about it, the more he realised it was the only option. He immediately began to set the wheels in motion to gain support for Professor Anton.

Message from Captain of the Pollo guard to Councillor Wiklon

Fugitives in Pollo, Sorcia Park.

Message from Councillor Wiklon to Captain of the Guard, Pollo

Send guard to detain.

34

Thea

The children and I had been enjoying a picnic in the parkland close to my parent's house this afternoon. Spending time with my parents had been lovely, but I longed to return home now. It was a bright afternoon, and after our picnic, we played games with a large ball. Now, though, it was cooling, and I was packing away the last picnic things while the children continued to run about. It was time to return to the house for dinner and get the twins ready for bed. Jami is getting difficult. He wants to go home, and no matter what I say, he doesn't understand why we can't go home now. As I watched the children run towards me, Elia suddenly stopped and put her hands over her eyes. At first, it looked like she was starting another new game. I was about to call her when she sank to her knees and slumped over.

"Elia!" I ran over and dropped to my knees in the damp grass beside her crumpled form. Drawing back the hair that had fallen over her pale face, I took in her appearance. Her blue-green eyes were open but looked far away as her lips silently formed words. I leaned down to hear, but I couldn't make out what she was saying. Carefully, I felt Elia's limbs, then lifted her head to my lap. *I had no idea what to do first. With the twins and a baby to think about, it wasn't that simple, was it?* Cam came over with the twins and Amillia in her carrier. Carefully placing the carrier down, he told the twins to stay beside her before he joined me. He was about to say something, but I cut him off.

"Cam, please collect the blankets and the picnic bag. Elia will be getting cold from this damp ground. Then, run to Father Jonca and ask him to come to us immediately." Gathering them up, he passed them to me. The twins moved close to me, and he put Amillia's carrier beside them. He was about to move when Elia raised her head from my lap and, in a faraway voice, said,

"Watchers will come. We cannot stay. We cannot return. We must go." She paused, then looked up, surprised to see us gathered around her.

"We aren't safe," she said as she looked intently at me. I nodded.

"You're right, it's time to leave. We've been here long enough, but I think Mother Plumb should come and see you to make sure you are ok before you move. Cam, do you remember the house next to the hospital? It's where we met Mother Plumb the last time we came to Pollo. You should be able to find her there. In case there are watchers around, pull on that coat Mother Lib sent us to sit on. Mess up your hair a little bit, too. No, don't look at me like that. You'll draw less attention this way. It's not far, just a few minutes from here." Cam looked at the old coat with disgust. It was muddy and had a musty smell as he opened it out. Closing his eyes in resignation, he shrugged it on. *Poor boy, I've spoilt him*. Reaching out, I took hold of the first button to do it up for him, but he pulled away.

"Mother, I can do up buttons even if they are totally revolting. Do I have to mess up my hair?" His shoulder-length dark hair was neat and brushed until it glowed like polished dark wood, glowing richly. Such is the fashion for young men today but now wasn't the time for fashion statements.

"Cam, please don't argue," I snapped.

“Seems a lot of fuss for nothing,” he grumbled, but he did as I asked. He rubbed his hands through his hair until it stood on end, looking like he’d slept in a bush.

“Ask Mother Plumb to come and check Elia over, please. I don’t want to move her very far in case she collapses again. We’ll go over to the river where it’s sheltered, and few people pass.” I said, “Go as fast as you can, but take care,” He left, running towards the closest gateway from the park.

I turned to Elia, who was beginning to stand.

“Are you OK? dizzy?” I stood beside her, brushing off as much mud as possible from my coat and the knees of my skirt. Elia began to do the same, and I helped her finish off.

“I’m OK, a bit tired,” she said, “shall we go to the river?” she asked as she took Jami’s hand. I slipped on the carrier with Amillia and took Edi’s hand. Holding the picnic bags in our spare hands, we walked briskly to the river. There was a seat surrounded by trees and shrubs, which I hoped would be free. It was a favourite spot for couples to meet in the summer because it was hidden away from prying eyes. As we approached, I watched Elia for any sign she might have another turn, but she walked confidently to the seat. She sat at one end with Jami beside her, Edi hopped up beside Jami, and I sat on the other. Slipping off the carrier, I put Amillia and the bag I had been carrying in front of me. The sun was now low, sending beautiful orange beams into the sky and over the river in front of us. It would have been worth discussing in other circumstances, but not today.

“Elia, has this happened before?” I looked into her clear, open face. *Why I hadn’t seen it before? Those blue-green eyes were far more blue than green, and her dark hair, with that hint of lilac, clearly suggested her Cawsal origins and possibly more. How could I have missed it?*

"It's always happened, as long as I can remember," she said. "I don't usually fall over. Sometimes it's more of a feeling." She spoke calmly, then her face clouded and said, "Are you angry? Grandma was angry, telling me off for being clumsy and stupid." I saw tears fill her eyes.

"No, Elia, I'm not angry with you." I broke off as we heard footsteps running towards us. I hoped it was Cam returning. A moment later, his face appeared flushed from his exertions. He stood, breathing heavily in front of us.

"Mother Plumb's on her way. She wants to see Yan's father on the way." he took another deep breath, "Edi, shove up a bit so I can sit between you and Mother." obligingly, Edi shuffled closer to Jami, who huffed, pulling a face. It was always the way. Edi was keen to please and happy to do as he was asked. Jami, however, was the opposite. He hated being asked to do anything, which was already proving to make lessons difficult.

"Thank you, Cam. Did you see anyone around that might be a watcher?" I was far more afraid than I wanted the children to know.

"I think there's one near the hospital but not by the door you told me to go to, a big, tall guy in the Pollo guard uniform of grey and green. I'm sure we saw him somewhere else; he had a red beard. Surely, he must be Delph with that red beard?" As he spoke, his hands pulled at the buttons of the old coat until he finally let it slide to the ground. Then, his hands worked through his hair, easing the knots. Finally, he took his comb and started running it through his hair. I watched him with a smile.

"I think you're right. The man you describe is like someone I've seen recently. He could be a watcher. Let's hope Mother Plumb gets here soon. I want to get Elia inside." Cam was still combing his hair; he wasn't vain, but he did like to look tidy. When he'd finished, he removed the collected hair from the comb's teeth, dropping it on the ground before he slipped it back into his pocket.

"She'll be OK. She usually is," he said in an offhand. I looked at him, surprised,

"Have you seen it happen before?"

"Yes, lots of times. We hid it from Grandma and Gramps because they got so angry." I saw Elia look across sadly. *I felt so sad she had been too afraid to tell me—a* deep pain seared through my heart. I wasn't surprised Max and Zillah didn't say anything, but for Cam to hide it from me hurt deeply.

"It's taken this terrible chain of events to discover such a secret. Please forgive me." I said with regret in my voice.

"That's OK, Mother. I'm clumsy, I guess, as Grandma says." she was light-hearted about it, and I decided not to say anything more until there *was* time for us to talk.

I was worried. It seemed like she had a premonition or warning that we were in danger. *Was I reading too much into what she said?* I was mulling this over when I heard voices approaching us and motioned to the children to hush. We sat, trying to make ourselves as quiet as possible, and hoped they wouldn't take the path past us. As the footsteps drew closer, we heard two voices. One was deep and masculine; the other could be a woman, but it wasn't easy to be sure. Was it Mother Plumb? I hoped so, but then I heard a third male voice, and my heart almost stopped. It sounded like Max. Standing, I picked up Amillia and my bag and moved behind the seat, indicating the children to join me as I quietly crept into the bushes behind us. I wish I'd thought of it before. The footsteps came closer, and I was sure one of the voices was Max. Then I heard what they were saying.

"The watcher said he saw the family here in the park," one voice said. It was the one I thought was Max, but now I'm not sure.

"They can't be far then if one of them was laying out cold on the ground." a second voice said. It was the one I'd thought might be a woman, but I decided it was another man. He sounded cruel.

"How far can a woman with a baby, two little 'n's and a teenage son drag the other one?" the first voice said.

"That babe will be howling soon; it's getting cold, isn't it." He was right, and I looked down at Amillia, sleeping soundly in her carrier. I hoped she would stay asleep until they moved away.

"We've almost covered the whole park now. How long since they were seen?" it was a third voice, deep and rasping.

"Half an hour, sir," the second voice replies.

"Why did it take so long to report it?" the third voice growled as they drew closer.

"The runner came to us as soon as the watcher sent word," the second voice said. He seemed to be junior to the other two.

"That runner will need questioning. He may be protecting them." the first voice said. It seemed as if they'd stopped and were talking on the other side of the small wooded area where we were hiding. What if they decided to search here? I glanced again at Amillia and then the twins. Jami looked wide-eyed and terrified as he sat with Elia, her arms tight around him. Cam's arms were wrapped securely around Edi, who had silent tears running down his face. Suddenly, I wished they would find us now or go away; the tension was unbearable. I didn't know how long we could stay hidden before Amillia or one of the twins gave us away. What if one of us sneezed? My heart pounded in my ears, and I was afraid our breathing might give us away.

"Unless they're down by the river, they must have gone. Jep, you go round that way and make sure there's no sign of them. We'll meet you on the other side." I looked towards the bench, and then I saw it. The old coat was still on the ground by the seat. Cam saw it simultaneously, and as he was closer, he stretched his arm under the seat. The footsteps drew closer as he grasped the corner and slowly pulled it towards him. The sleeve slid under the seat as a man walked past, glancing around. I didn't recognise him. He had the dark hair and shorter stature of a Polloman (A person from Pollo). It could be my imagination, but he doesn't seem to be looking too hard for us. Thank the Gods, it wasn't the other two searching this way, I thought before shutting that thought away. There was no need to tempt the fates. The footsteps continued past us until they met the other two once more.

"No sign of anyone that way unless they went in the river," he said.

"There's going to be trouble for this." the third voice said with malice.

"He could've been mistaken." the first voice said.

"The watcher and runner must be in it together. I'll bet they distracted us to let them escape," growled the third voice.

"We should get back before those two are released," Jep said.

"Well, there's nothing here, is there? Bloody waste of time," said the third voice angrily as the footsteps moved away.

I breathed a sigh of relief when I could no longer hear them. Cam carefully peered through the leaves and confirmed we were once more alone. We decided to remain where we were in case anyone else appeared. Reaching over, I wiped Edi's tears and squeezed Jami's hand. Elia had her arms around him and began gently rocking. She was so good with him, the only one who could manage his difficult moods. Amillia started to stir, and I saw her bright green eyes gazing back with a smile that stretched across her face as she saw me. Such smiles always lifted my heart, even now in this place. I reached over and felt her hands and face. She was still warm and cosy. The men were right about one thing: she would be hungry soon. I could feed her myself, but we'd be more vulnerable because I couldn't move quickly. However, she seemed happy enough to watch the leaves above her. I hoped Mother Plumb wouldn't be long.

"Cam, you did tell Mother Plumb where to find us, didn't you?" I trusted him, but I was beginning to doubt everything.

"Yes, I'm sure she will be here soon," he replied softly. I felt such a swell of love for him as he tried to comfort me. It should be me offering comfort to all my children, including him. *I was so proud of him and wished I told him more often.*

35

Thea

Just as I was beginning to give up hope, we heard more footsteps and the swish of skirts. I was sure it was Mother Plumb this time, but we remained hidden. I didn't want to leave our sanctuary until I was sure it was safe. My heart pounded when I saw the familiar red of a wisewoman's skirt approaching. Cam looked over, and I motioned for him to stay still for a little longer until we were sure it was safe. The woman sat down on the bench in front of us and was still for a moment before softly saying.

"Thea, if you can hear me, stay hidden a little longer. There's a watcher in the park. I'll sit here for a while, then go and see if he's gone." she didn't look round, but I'd know that voice anywhere, dear Mother Plumb.

"Thank you," I whispered, putting my finger to my lips as I looked at the children. Elia and Cam understood and once more surrounded their young charges with their arms. Jami was looking mutinous, and I guessed he was probably hungry. Slipping my hand into the picnic bag, I found the fruit loaf and pulled it out as quietly as possible. I passed slices around to the children and took a piece myself. We chewed quietly, the sweetness from the fruit giving us a boost and satisfying our hunger for a while. I wished I'd something for them to drink, but we hadn't planned a long excursion, and the fluid supply had gone. I hoped the twins could wait for a little longer. I anxiously looked at Amillia, but she still seemed content to look at the leaves above her. I gave a silent sigh of relief.

Presently, Mother Plumb rose and walked away. Cam looked at me and raised his eyebrows to ask if we should remain here. I put my finger to my lips once more and nodded. Footsteps were approaching, but they didn't sound like Mother Plumb's. Elia and Cam tightened their arms around the twins again. I didn't look at Amillia. I couldn't risk her chuckling or making a sound. A man came into view, strolling towards the seat. I couldn't see his face, but somehow, he looked familiar. I was so scared. *It couldn't be him.* The man stood by the bench, his face turned away towards the river. Then he turned and walked back toward the water, kicking at the grass along the edge. *I recognised that movement, but it couldn't be. Surely, he was in Thena.*

Then he turned, and I saw his face. I couldn't believe my eyes. It was Rush, his face grey with worry.

"Rush?" I whispered.

I can't believe he's here.

He looked around before saying, "Thea?" his voice was urgent and low.

"We're here." I couldn't keep the relief from my voice. I began to move when I saw his hand urgently motioning down as he turned his face to the right.

I froze, crouching and waited. My legs complained about the awkward position. Then I heard more footsteps coming towards us. My heart began to thud as I looked at the children and saw their eyes widen with fear. Cam and Elia tighten their grip on the twins again. Then I looked at Amillia, hoping she would wait a little longer before she asked to be fed. Her bright eyes showed she had caught the tension, and her little face puckered. Picking her up as quietly as possible, I held her tightly, hoping my closeness would soothe her. Then I turned and looked at Rush.

He was looking back along the path. His dark overcoat was as smart as ever, and those highly polished shoes gleamed in the twilight. He took a few steps from the seat towards the path before he stretched out his arm to greet someone. Then I heard urgent whispers as Rush returned with Kiron and another man.

"Thea, it's safe to come out if you're quick," he whispered. We didn't need to be asked twice. I slipped Amillia back into her carrier and covered her against the cold evening air. Behind me, I heard rustling as Cam and Elia got up and helped the twins. Carefully, we stepped out of our hiding place and walked towards Rush. I didn't recognise the third man, but I assumed he must be someone they trusted if he was with Rush and Kiron. Walking up to Rush, we nodded to each other. Too much had passed for us to embrace, and certainly not in public. I had to admit, though, I was more pleased to see him than I would like to admit.

"We've arranged for your travel to Norwcan. It'll take four days to travel by night for safety. They wouldn't expect you to travel by night with young children." His voice was low and firm.

"Oh Rush, that's so far. How will we travel? We'll need to eat and stop for personal reasons." it was embarrassing talking about such things, and I hoped Kiron and the other man couldn't hear.

"Thea, we must leave now. There will be time for talking later." his voice was urgent with that hardness I knew so well. I turned to the children, and we huddled together as I told them what was happening.

"Father has arranged a surprise trip! Isn't that fun?" I tried to make it sound exciting for the younger two.

"We must go." Rush's voice was firm. He came forward with the other man. "This is Frodel, your escort and driver for the first part of our journey. He's my usual driver, and I trust him with my life."

"Frodel, thank you for..." but Rush interrupted.

"Thea, go with Frodel and take the babe." Looking at Cam and Elia, he said, "You two, go with Kiron, the twins with me. We'll be less noticeable. There's a conveyance waiting for us just outside the park." the children looked at me, eyes still wide with fear.

"It's OK, we'll be together soon. Now go and make me proud." I smiled at the children. With Amillia on my back in the carrier, I watched Cam and Elia go to Kiron and then walk away.

My heart was in my mouth. *How could I let them go from my side at such a time?* Then Rush took my hand.

"Thea, Frodel will take good care of you and Amillia for the short walk to the conveyance. Relax and chat as if you know each other so you don't look suspicious. Kiron will take good care of Cam and Elia." I looked into his face and saw mirrored there the concern I felt. *Why had I not noticed how much he cared for his children?* It's like peeling a cape onion and discovering the different coloured layers. I'd called them rainbow onions as a child until I heard the real name. *This Rush was the man I'd married. He'd been there all the time underneath the layers*. I gave him a brief smile, and then Frodel was at my side, smiling kindly at me. He had a gentle, fatherly face, silvery facial hair and soft blue eyes. His hat had been pulled over his head, but I suspect his hair was also silver underneath it. He was no taller than I was and slight in stature, dressed in dark trousers and a long dark coat. We could make a good pairing as we walked across the park. I hoped any watchers would think so. He offered me his arm, but I turned and crouched down beside the twins. They were standing wide-eyed as they watched the proceedings. *How young they looked.*

"Edi, Jami, I need you to be very brave. Walk nicely with Father to the conveyance, and I'll see you there." Edi looked as if he might cry, while Jami looked mutinous. I could guess what was coming and continued, "Jami, would you take care of Edi and make sure you both stay close to Father?" he scowled, then nodded before standing taller and taking Edi's hand. They walked over to Rush. Rising again, I looked at Rush and nodded before turning to Frodel.

"We can go," I said, and he again held his arm out for me to take. This time, I slipped my arm through his, and we turned and began our walk across the park.

"Children can be such a gift, yet sometimes we find the beautiful gift also has thorns like roses in the garden," he said. His voice was soft, and I detected a slight suggestion of the Cawsal accent mixed with Thenan.

"How beautifully put and true," I replied. We walked across the park, keeping to the main paths. It avoided too much mud on our feet and drew less attention. Other couples were taking the evening air in the park, and I hoped we would blend in with them. As we drew closer to the tall hedge marking the boundary, I could see the gleam of a conveyance and hoped Kiron had arrived safely with Cam and Elia. Cautiously, I looked around, but there were no apparent watchers, although it was difficult to tell in the failing light.

It began to rain, and without a word, Frodel stepped behind me and raised the cover over Amillia's head to keep her dry. My hat covered my head; although it wasn't a rain hat, it provided some protection. We hasten towards the gateway. The rain fell gently, wetting our faces and hands and forming puddles along the path. As we left the park, Frodel led me to the left, where a conveyance waited. He casually looked around as we reached it before opening the rear door. I saw, with relief, that Cam, Elia and Kiron were already seated. Their pale faces watched as we climbed in; the conveyance gently rocked as we did so. Elia looked even paler than before, and my worry for her increased. I hoped Mother Plumb or Kiron could put my mind at ease soon. "Are you both OK? did you see any watchers?" I couldn't help firing questions at Kiron and the children. *I was so worried, and Rush was still out there with the twins.*

"No, Thea, I saw none. I don't know whether to worry more or be grateful. For now, let's be grateful." Kiron said.

"It's OK, Mother, we're OK. I was worried Amillia might be hungry, but I see she's asleep again," said Elia. "May I sit with you and Amillia?"

"Of course, take the seat there by the window." I was thankful the glass only allowed us to see out and prevented anyone from looking in. Elia stood and carefully moved to the seat beside the window so Amillia was between us. Outside, there were footsteps; we froze and fell silent. As we heard them draw closer, I thought I heard a softer scuffle alongside the footsteps. *Was it Rush and the twins*? The footsteps passed us, and we saw they belonged to a heavyset man with a grumpy-looking dog shuffling beside him. *Was he a watcher?* The footsteps faded into the distance, and we all sighed with relief. Frodel looked at Kiron, and they nodded.

"I've seen him before somewhere. That dog is very distinctive. If he was a watcher, he wasn't trying to be discrete, was he?" They exchanged glances but seemed satisfied there was no threat. I moved slowly to my seat, reaching for the chair back to steady myself. The conveyance swayed gently, moving like a boat on the water. Typical of Rush, I thought, to have a high-class model even for this occasion. Frodel helped me slip off Amillia's carrier and settle her on the seat beside Elia. She loved being in the carrier, and the movement of walking or travelling usually sent her to sleep. I sat down and looked at Elia.

"Are you OK? You look very pale?" I asked.

"I'm fine, just tired, I think," she said. I hoped that was all.

Shortly, Rush and the twins arrived. There was more swaying as they clambered in and took their seats. The twins were pale and quiet now. It had been quite an afternoon, and they were probably tired and hungry. We felt the conveyance move forward, and I sat back in my seat. I didn't know where we were going or how to get there, but I knew it would be a long night. The seats in the conveyance were comfortable but didn't allow us to lie down and sleep. Looking at the twins, I didn't think that would stop them from falling asleep.

"Rush," I said. He turned to me, smiling.

"Yes, we can answer your questions now. At least we'll try. Mother Plumb will collect your things from your parents. She will meet us in a while and travel with us to North Elwie near the border, where her brother has a farm. I can't tell you more now, and things may change." I was grateful to know at least a little of the plan for now.

"Thank you," I whispered before settling back into my seat and making myself comfortable.

"Mother," Cam's voice broke through my thoughts.

"Yes? Is everything OK?" My mind immediately began to spin, conjuring hundreds of scenarios before I heard him reply.

"Is there anything to eat? I'm starving; it's been a long time since lunch, and there wasn't much of that." Typical of Cam, always hungry, I thought with a smile.

"There's a hamper at the back behind your seat, young man," said Frodel. "Perhaps you can bring it forward for your mother to take a look. Mother Plumb did her best, but there wasn't much time." He sounded apologetic. I heard Cam reach behind his chair and drag something slowly forward.

"It's very heavy," he said, his shadowy face grinning. I grasped the handle of the hamper and was surprised at the weight. Cam shoved as I pulled it close enough to open it. Carefully, I unclipped the lid and saw why it was so heavy. There were bottles of fruit juice and water along with flasks of hot drinks. Carefully wrapped packages in all shapes and sizes, which contained food, filled the rest of the space. Mother Plumb had even included smooth cotton napkins. Without plates, we could fill the napkins as we would on a picnic. I opened the packages and found slices of meat pie, pieces of fruit, meat rolls, bread and slabs of cake of different kinds. Looking up, I described the contents of the hamper to everyone. The resounding groans confirmed that Cam wasn't the only one who was hungry. He came forward and distributed drinks to everyone while I prepared food napkins, which Cam then distributed. For a while, there was the sound of soft chewing and appreciation of food while the conveyance carried us towards Elwei. Mother Plumb had provided a great supper. There was plenty left over for breakfast, which I carefully packed in the hamper.

Frodel began to pass round blankets and cushions from the back of the conveyance. Then, we tried to settle as best we could for the night. Edi puts his head on Cam's shoulder, and Cam slipped his arm around his little brother. After scowling at Cam and Edi and pleading with Elia to swap places, Jami wriggled closer to Rush. He leaned his head against his father's shoulder. Rush slipped his arm around his son without hesitation, tucking the blanket around them both. He settled back and closed his eyes. My heart swelled with love. I couldn't believe it; Rush had never wanted anything to do with the children until they were Cam's age or older. This new Rush was a different man, one whom I might grow to like quite a lot. I looked down at Amillia, now settled at my breast, her rosebud lips gently moving as she suckled. Whatever the future might hold, my family would be together or would be when we met up with Millie and Amelie.

Despite knowing Amelie was her birth mother, I still considered Millie to be my child. I had nurtured her and brought her up, sitting with her through the nightmares and laughing with her at daft things that happened. I hoped we could continue to find our respective places in Millie's life and she in ours.

36

Amelie

Millie and I were at the Western Dock in Wernia, West Delphiope. We were waiting for a boat to take us north to Portho Nacon, the most northern port in Cawsal. Neither of us looked forward to being on a boat for six or more hours, but at least it might be warmer than standing here shivering. It had been a long two-day journey from the cemetery with only a few short breaks. We arrived here feeling queasy after a traumatic chase through the mountains as our driver tried to lose a watcher, which, thankfully, he did in the end. So here we stood, chilled to the bone from the icy breeze off the sea. Usually, I liked the salty sea smell that came in on the breeze, but it was just cold tonight. This was a working dock with no shelter for passengers. There wasn't even a coffee room or café. Instead, it was littered with heaps of nets and fishing equipment alongside shabby warehouses. Boats bobbed gently in the harbour, and, like music, the rigging clinked on their metal masts. Huddled together, I desperately wished we had somewhere else to go. *I was terrified a watcher would find us before the boat arrived. What would we do if the ship didn't come? Who could we trust here?* We pulled our coats tightly around us and clutched our bags as if to gain warmth from them. It could have been hours or minutes. We lost all track of time as we stood there.

Eventually, the gentle, rhythmic sound of water against a hull reached us on the breeze with the hum of a motor. Turning, we saw the large dark shape of a transport ship laden with crates heading towards the dock.

"At last," whispered Millie," I was more cautious. This was a massive vessel. I'd expected more of a fishing boat.

"Let's hope it's the right one," I whispered. We watched the boat make its way to the dock. As it drew close, several men sprung from the vessel, securing ropes to mooring posts on the dockside. The gangplank lowered, and smaller crates were carried off. Larger ones were lifted off with a hoist and lowered with a thump on the ground. Some of these crates must have had livestock, judging by the noises. The cries from the containers tugged at the heart. They were so pitiful. Millie wanted to ask someone to check if the livestock was OK, but there wasn't anyone to ask. It took quite a while, but eventually, the procession of crates ceased, and the hoist swung empty above us. Had anyone noticed us, I wondered? The answer came sooner than I expected.

"Are you ladies waitin' for someone on this lonely quay?" asked a gruff voice behind us. Hearts pounding, we turned and faced a small, swarthy man. He had a straggly beard and bushy eyebrows. Green beady eyes bored into us. He wore the clothes of a man of the sea, dark with a grubby grey jacket.

"We might be," I said. I wasn't sure if I liked the look of this odd little man with those piercing green eyes.

"Would you know anything about an Invitation? The invitation was yours?" he said with a wink.

"Oh yes," I said with a sigh of relief, squeezing Millie's hand.

"In that case, follow me if you will," he said, turning and heading towards the vessel. He rocked from side to side as he walked on bowed legs, setting a brisk pace. We hurried after him, reaching the gangplank as he stepped off it onto the boat.

Hesitating, we looked up after him and then at each other. Once we were onboard, there would be no turning back.

"Are you sure it's OK?" whispered Millie, her eyes wide with fear.

"Well, he knew the phrase," I replied, although I'm more than a little apprehensive. "Let's get on board; I'd prefer our chances on the boat than with a watcher." *Unless there was a watcher onboard,* I thought to myself.

There was a hive of activity on the deck as the crew prepared to leave. We followed the sailor to a door which he said we should enter.

"Capt'n Bard is waitin' for you in 'ere," he said before turning and walking away. I knocked on the door and, when a gruff voice called, 'Enter!' I turned the doorknob, saying with a grin.

"Let's go and meet Capt'n Bard,"

We entered a pleasant cabin with a desk in one corner and a screened-off area with drapes in the other. There were more drapes by the windows at the end of the cabin. Sitting behind the desk, taking in our appearance, was a thin man in a pale grey suit. His legs stretched under the desk and out towards us. He probably had to stoop in the cabin; he was so tall. His face was stern, with a dark, close-cut beard and hard, dark eyes.

"So, you're the passengers we're taking to Cawsal then?" he said in a matter-of-fact voice, emphasising the word *passengers*. He neither invited us in nor offered a seat, so we stood by the door.

"Yes," I replied equally matter-of-factly. I wasn't sure I liked or trusted this man.

"This isn't a pleasure boat. There's no fancy accommodation or leisure here. For your safety, I've assigned simple, clean quarters where you will remain until we reach Cawsal. This is a working vessel. The crew don't need you in the way."

"We understand. You are the captain, I presume?" I asked. He seemed to draw himself up as if to emphasise his importance as he said.

"I'm Captain Bard of the Cawsal Mercantile Transport Fleet and Captain of the Dolphus cargo ship. I don't need to know who you are. It's your business, not mine. Your passage has been settled in advance. Flit, here, will take you to your quarters and see to your vitals." I hadn't noticed the other person in the room standing behind the door. He now stepped forward and nodded at us. We thanked the captain and turned to Flit.

Flit was a small, neat man who seemed worthy of his name. His appearance suggested he could flit from one place to another in the blink of an eye. Smiling, he stepped in front of us.

"Ladies, follow me," He led us back on deck and opened another door beside the captain's cabin. This led into a corridor down the deck protected from the elements. We passed several doors to the right as we followed Flit. He paused by a door with the sign 'Galley' above it.

"Do you need vittals?" he asked. "It's simple fare, but I'd be happy to assist if you're in need. The coffee's good, but the tea isn't, not at all." Millie's eyes brighten at the thought of a hot cup of coffee. I felt the same and said so.

"A warm cup of coffee would be very welcome. We have some light vittals to eat." It was true. We had a little cornbread and cheese we'd been given as we hurried away from the cemetery.

"I'll get that organised once you're settled in your cabin." We followed him down the corridor until we reached the last door. He stopped and turned the handle, pushing the door into the room.

"Here you are, ladies, this is our guest cabin. It should have everything you need. Drapes can surround the cots if you wish for privacy. The other area with drapes is for your personal needs. Water is for washing only. I wouldn't recommend drinking it. It's a mix of seawater and reclaimed water from the boat. The Gods know what's in it, but they won't protect you from it. No, they won't, indeed."

"Thank you, Flit, this will be fine. How long is the voyage? I forgot to ask the captain."

"Around six or seven hours sailing against the tide. If the wind gets up, it could be a bit longer, yes, could. Oh, and if it gets too rough, I suggest you get onto the cot, I do. There's a bowl under each cot in case you get taken ill," he said with a knowing wink. Seasickness could be so unpleasant, and I was relieved this has been thought of. "If there's a storm, I'll nip back and make sure everything is secured, I will, including your good selves. Now I'll find that coffee for you." he disappeared, and we were alone in the tiny cabin. The cots on either side of the cabin had tired-looking drapes that might have been grey. The blankets on each bed were old and grey, but the sheets looked clean and almost white. In the corner was the third area with more drapes. It was probably the source of the unpleasant smell, like the smell from a farm. We sat on our cots opposite each other and looked around at the grey walls and dark floor. It certainly wasn't intended for comfort, but it would suffice. We were still sitting there when we heard a knock on the door. It opened to reveal Flit holding a tray with two mugs of coffee. Gratefully, we each took a mug, thanking Flit, who disappeared and closed the door behind him.

Message from Watcher at Wernia Western Dock to Councillor Wiklon

Fugitives onboard Dolphus. Heading to Portho Nacon. Advise.

Message from Councillor Wiklon to Councillor Maxim

Fugitives on ship to Nacon. Sending watchers and guards.

Message from Councillor Maxim to Councillor Wiklon
Advise when complete.

37

Millie

I woke with a start; it was claustrophobic in the small enclosed space, and I tugged at the drapes. *Where was I? My heart raced until I remembered where we were. The drapes around my cot swayed gently, bringing an odd smell.* Cautiously, I sniffed, relieved it wasn't me. Sitting up on the narrow cot, I pulled the drapes back to see if Amelie was awake, but her drapes were still closed. *It was no good; I had to relieve myself.* Reluctantly, I swung my legs over the side of the cot and slipped my feet into my shoes. I'd been avoiding the draped area in the corner, but I couldn't any longer without risking an accident. That would be far too humiliating. Holding on to my cot to steady myself against the boat's movement, I took the few steps needed to reach the corner.

The smell was much more pungent now, and taking a deep breath, I pulled the drapes. Inside was a washbasin, a clean drying cloth and what served as a toilet. It looked more like one of the oil barrels we'd seen on the docks with a seat and lid on top. *Ugh, this must be the source of the foul smell. I felt my nose wrinkling and tried not to gag.* Stepping inside, I dropped the drape, shielding me from view. When I lifted the toilet lid, the smell burst out, and I gagged. I took a deep breath through my coat sleeve and made myself comfortable. As I washed my hands, I heard movement in the cabin and guessed Amelie was stirring.

"Millie, Millie, where are you?" Amelie sounded worried as her voice rose.

"I'm in the draped corner," I said.

"Oh, thank goodness, I was worried seeing your cot empty with the drapes pulled back." The relief was evident in her voice. Amelie stood as I sat back on my cot, and I guessed she had the same need.

"It's not too bad if you hold your breath?" I grinned at her as I rolled my eyes. She didn't reply as she opened the corner drapes.

"Eww, I see what you mean," she said as she stepped inside and pulled the drapes behind her. I wondered how long we'd slept. It wasn't easy to know without a window to see out of. I didn't wear a timepiece, but Amelie did, I could ask her when she came out. My mouth was stale, and I wished I could clean my teeth. If we'd had more time to pack, I might have the right things now, but all I had was my comb. Well, I suppose I could start to work on it, teasing out the knots. I took out my comb and began. It would take time to get my untangled.

"How long did we sleep?" I asked Amelie as she sat back on her cot. In its engraved case, her elegant gold timepiece floated on a delicate gold chain around her neck. She lifted it, then slipped it back inside her shirt.

"Almost three hours. I didn't expect to sleep that long. We must be halfway there by now." she said.

"Good; I dreaded it was only an hour or so."

"Perhaps we can find Flit and get some more coffee?" Amelie said with enthusiasm.

"Oh, I'd love another coffee. Did you pack anything to eat? I can't remember when we last ate."

"I only have a little fruit, but we can share it," Rummaging in her bag, Amelie produced two orange papayas and passed one to me.

The flesh was sweet and juicy as I bit into it, the juice dribbling down my chin. I looked at Amelie and saw that, despite her dainty nibbles, juice dripped down her chin, too. We grinned, then began to laugh, and soon tears ran down our faces and mixed with the juice from the fruit. It was such a ridiculous situation, and the laughter broke the tension that had permeated the room. Eventually, our laughter subsided to the odd hiccup of a suppressed giggle. Tracks from our tears streaked our faces and mixed with the juice streaks.

“Well, that did us good,” said Amelie, “and if my face looks anything like yours, it needs a good clean. But not until we've finished our papayas.” giggling, my hands went to my face, I could feel the sticky mess on my chin and my damp cheeks.

“True,” I said with a grin. We continued eating, relishing the juicy fruit, which helped ease our thirst and hunger. When we'd finished, we began to look for something to clean our faces. Amelie found a pink embroidered handkerchief and passed it to me.

“It's clean,” she said. I took it with relief, wishing we had a mirror too.

“Do you have one for yourself?” She passed over a pretty green handkerchief with flowers embroidered in each corner.

I took both and ran water over them, squeezing out the excess. As I did so, I remembered what Flit said about the water and wished I hadn't. I passed her the now-damp handkerchief. We began systematically working from forehead to chin and around our necks. The dirt removed was shocking. Looking at Amelie, I saw a similar expression as she looked at her handkerchief. She was already rummaging in her bag and retrieved a good-sized green silk purse. Opening it, she expertly applied a little eye makeup and pale lip colour. *How does she make it look so easy? I wished I could apply makeup so quickly. Perhaps she would give me some tips when this was all over*. Taking out my small blue makeup purse, I used a little brightness on my cheeks and natural lip colour. I felt self-conscious as Amelie watched me. I tucked the damp handkerchief into my makeup purse and put it away when I finished.

"May I give this back to you when it's clean?" Amelie nods, and I see that hers has also disappeared. Resting my hand on my skirt, I realise some of the juice has landed on it, leaving sticky patches and sigh. Luckily, my skirt is dark, and it doesn't show.

"Now we have our faces on, let's see if we can find Flit?" Amelie said. I was grateful she suggested we went together. We picked up our bags and went to the cabin door. Stepping through the narrow doorway, I closed it behind us. Amelie walked confidently in front as we made our way down the corridor. Outside the galley, we paused and peered through the window. Crew members were sitting, eating and drinking at tables in neat rows. Amelie opened the door with a confidence I didn't feel. Head held high, she walked up to the chef behind the counter and waited for him to turn around.

When he did, she said in a clear, confident voice, "May we have some coffee, and what can you recommend to eat?"

The chef nodded before he spoke, "You the women Flit said were onboard 'til Cawsal?" His voice was rough, but his eyes suggested he wasn't unfriendly.

"That's right. Can we get some coffee and something to eat?" Amelie asked pleasantly with a beaming smile,

"Flit said he'd take coffee to you, didn't hear nofin' about food," he said in a low, rough voice.

"We haven't seen Flit since we boarded. He gave us coffee then, but that was many hours ago."

"Huh, now is that so. Flit is named so for that very reason. But I can't help you. I only serve the crew." my heart sank.

“Is there any way we can persuade you? Perhaps I can sing for you and the crew. I’m a singer.” she said with a flirtatious grin.

“Well, you'd have to ask the capt'n about that.”

“Where can we find him?”

“You can't go wandering about the boat bothering people. That's how boats sink, that is,” he said, his voice less friendly now.

“Come now, sir, we don’t need to bother the captain, do we? I'd be entertaining the crew. Surely that’s worth a little food?”

“You'd better get to your cabin. I'll tell Flit you was 'ere.” he said bluntly, turning back to the stove.

“Thank you for your time, sir,” Amelie said. We returned to the corridor, closing the door behind us.

“Well, he wasn't accommodating, was he,” she said, “let's see if we can find Flit or the captain.” Turning, she went down the corridor towards the deck. *I felt increasingly anxious. Flit told us to stay in the cabin, and he would attend us. Now, we were breaking the agreement and walking towards the deck. Amelie's offering to sing for our food was awful. It was a short trip, and we were already halfway through. I'd rather go hungry. I was discovering Amelie could be pretty determined when she set her mind on something and was used to getting her own way.* Reluctantly, I followed her.

“Is this a good idea?” I asked hesitantly, “We were supposed to stay in the cabin,” I knew I sounded childish. I wished Father was here; he’d know what to do.

“Oh, Psh,” she said, pulling a face. We won't be doing any harm, and we’ll stay out of the crew's way. Now, let's see what's going on deck.” In front of us was the door that led to the deck. She turned the handle and pulled the door towards us. Outside, it was pitch black, and the rise and swell of the boat seemed greater than it had inside. The crew were pulling ropes and checking cargo. Their waterproof coats glistened with sea spray that flew over the deck from one side to the other. *I didn't want to go out there. Please, Amelie, don't go outside. I silently begged.* But, after a moment's hesitation, she stepped out onto the wet deck, head held high. The door was snatched from her hand and thrown back against the side of the cabin with a hollow thud.

"Amelie! Come back," I hissed at her.

"Oops," she said as her hair flew around her face, making her look wild and slightly crazed. I felt the breeze tug at my own hair. The crew didn't notice us; they remained engaged in their work. I hung onto the door frame, afraid to let go lest I fall, but Amelie stood firm. Her sea legs kept pace with the churning seas beneath us. I heard movement in the captain's cabin and felt sick. He'd told us to remain in our cabin, and here we were on deck. The captain's door flew open, and Captain Bard glared at us. His face was dark and thunderous. I stepped back immediately to the safety of the corridor. Amelie merely turns to look up at him with a dazzling smile.

"Why, Captain Bard, we were just going to take a little fresh air," she said, smiling.

"I told you to stay in the cabin. No women on deck while we sail," he growled and took a threatening step towards Amelie, who remained unmoved. The sea spray was seeping into her skirt and jacket, and her hair was settling into wet ringlets. She seemed unconcerned about her appearance and continued to smile at him.

"Oh now, captain, what harm can it do? We aren't in anyone's way here, are we?" she purred.

"Zuthor doesn't like women on board. Especially not on deck," He growled, oblivious to her charm.

"I'll make an offering to the Great God Zuthor. I'm sure it will be OK," she said, but a little uncertainty had crept into her voice.

"Zuthor most likely would like an offering as penance for carrying you. Maybe I'll give him one of you!" he snarled, stepping forward again. Taking Amelie by the arm, he pushed her back through the doorway. Catching my arm with his other hand, he drove us back to the cabin. Amelie struggled to free herself, but his grip was too tight.

We resigned ourselves to the indignity of being taken back to the cabin. Captain Bard deposited us inside and shut the door. Then, to our horror, we heard the sound of a latch. Grasping the handle, Amelie turned it, but it won't move. It was stuck firm,

"Hey, you can't lock us in here!" she cried, and we heard a deep chuckle.

"Oh yes, I can girlies. You will stay locked in there until we arrive, and I can get rid of you." we heard the sound of his boots on the wooden floor as he walked away, still chuckling. We looked at each other before embracing tightly. *I was so scared. Her arms around me were reassuring, but I felt her fear. I wished Mother or even Father were here right now.*

Message from Captain of Pollo Guard to Cawsal Road Checkpoint 3

Thena conveyance approaching. Detain.

Message from Cawsal Road Checkpoint 3 to Captain of Pollo Guard

Received, lights approaching. Stand by.

38

Thea

We were passing through a rural area of Pollo, although I couldn't see much because it was so dark outside now. I sat with one arm holding the carrier where Amillia slept and the other arm around Elia. Everyone else seemed to be asleep or in deep contemplation. The silence inside the conveyance was thick and lay like a blanket around me. *I wished I knew where we were heading. There had been talk of meeting Mother Plumb at a farm on the Cawsal border. I hoped we would get there before morning. The twins would need to stop when they woke. I wished someone else was awake to talk to. It had been a long time since anyone had spoken. Judging by the snuffling and snoring around me, I'd be alone with my thoughts for some time yet. I wondered if Millie and Amelie had reached their destination. Would we join them? I wondered, or were we going somewhere else? Rush and Kiron were rather vague when I asked them earlier. It relied on further information getting to... ah, now, was it Frodel or the other driver? I couldn't remember. How did they get information when there was no way to send messages? What would happen if Mother Plumb wasn't there to greet us? What if watchers were following us? So many questions and no one to talk to.* As I mulled these things over, I glimpsed a light moving in the darkness. It seemed to flicker up and down before disappearing and then reappearing. The conveyance slowed, and I heard soft voices behind the privacy screen. Turning, I saw Rush was making his way to the front.

"What's happening? Why have we slowed?" I whispered.

"I don't know, I'm going to find out. It's probably nothing," he said softly before tapping the privacy screen. It moved down, and a whispered conversation took place. I waited, anxiety frizzing around me until he returned.

He motioned for me to join him in the rear of the conveyance, where some seats were set further back. We sat close together and leaned in so our heads were touching as he whispered.

"Frodel has seen a light signalling ahead. We have to find another way. It's not safe to go on this route. Frodel and the other driver are working out a new route."

"But what if there isn't another way? What if they find us? What then?" I could feel the anxiety rising.

"Shhh, we're prepared for this and have our own watchers who watch their watchers."

"But..." I began, breaking off as the conveyance suddenly threw us to the left as it made a sharp right turn into a tiny road. Bushes scraped the sides of the vehicle as we squeezed down the narrow track. The movement caused Elia and Amillia to shift in their seats, and Amillia began to stir, making little whimpering noises. As I began to rise, Rush took my hand.

"Elia can take care of her for a moment." I perched on the seat as Amillia's whimpers began to escalate. *My anxiety climbed as I felt the maternal urge to go to my baby.* Then I heard Elia's soft voice crooning, and the whimpers began to subside. I sat back in the chair once more.

"What else is there to say?" *I was weary and wanted this endless journey to be over. To feel safe.*

"We have another hour or so to travel. A little longer than planned before we can stop."

"Will we still meet Mother Plumb?"

"We should, unless there are complications." his voice was firm, exuding confidence, and I relaxed a little.

"When we arrive, we'll meet Mother Plumb and the others. Then, Cam and Elia must look after the twins and Amillia while we finalise plans for the next part of the journey," he said.

"Rush, there's something..." I began, then stopped. *Was I imagining things, making something out of nothing? I wondered.*

"What?"

"Nothing." It could wait unless something else occurred. "I should get back." I rose, and this time, he let me return to my seat, where Elia had Amillia on her lap. Both were curled up together in the corner of the seat, securely wedged. Smiling, I wrapped a blanket over them, tucking it under securely. Then I took another blanket and sat close beside them. I tried to relax and clear my mind.

I was beginning to feel drowsy when I noticed the conveyance slow to a stop. Then, the conveyance swayed as someone went to the door, followed by the sound of doors opening and closing. I remained where I was; I had no inclination to move. I was finally warm and comfortable. My eyes stayed closed, but I listened, straining to hear the voices outside. They were indistinct, but it sounded as if we had stopped to look for someone, but I couldn't catch the name. Then, the conveyance swayed again as someone climbed back on board. Footsteps came towards me, and I felt a hand on my shoulder. Rush's warm smell, mixed with another colder odour, drifted like smoke around me.

"Thea, there is a problem. One of our watchers should have been waiting to greet us, but nobody's here. With the earlier diversion, we aren't sure we are on the right road. Frodel has sent a communication to our contact to get more details." I nodded. "Cam's out with me. He's old enough. Remain with the children. The twins are asleep on the seats across the way there." I looked over and saw two bundles wrapped in blankets, each with a dark mop of hair at the top. "We'll be outside, but we won't move away from the conveyance." his voice was soft, but I knew he was worried despite his calming words.

"Are we safe?" *I didn't want to know, but I had to ask*; my voice was no more than a whisper.

"These are uncertain times, and the roads are unfamiliar. Father seems to have his watchers everywhere, far more extensive than…" he stopped, realising he'd said more than he'd intended.

"It's OK, I understand. Go, be with the others, but keep close." *I want to get going again, and if Rush can help, he should be out there.* Lifting my head, I looked sideways at Elia. *At least she was asleep.* Although I closed my eyes again, I knew I wouldn't sleep until we began moving again. Outside, I heard footsteps moving away. I strain my ears to listen again. *It sounded like Frodel and the other man, Malic, but I couldn't hear their words.* Rush and Cam were close to the conveyance with Kiron. Their voices were soft, but I could hear them talking, planning our arrival. *They didn't seem too worried, which was a relief.*

Before long, I heard a shout and boots thudding on the ground towards us. It must be Frodel because Rush and Kiron remained where they were. A few minutes later, Frodel said they had received a reply from the contact. I sat up and stretched my limbs before standing. Gently, I tucked the blanket around the girls, ensuring Amillia was safe with the sleeping Elia. The door opened behind me, and Kiron came over.

"The watcher is up ahead on the left. He's near a burial patch marked with four stones facing towards the four winds." Kiron was tall and could only stand stooped over in the conveyance. His face was etched with worry.

"Is there something else I should know?" I whispered. *I was sure there was, but will he tell me?*

"The message Frodel received was a little odd..." he stopped, looking at the girls. *I want to know what's happening but don't want to worry Elia or leave them alone.* Kiron must have seen my dilemma.

"Why don't you take the opportunity to get some fresh air while we consider what to do," he said." I'll sit with the children for a while." *Kiron was the only person other than Rush I trusted to be with my children.* Reluctantly, I stepped from the conveyance.

It's good to put my feet on solid ground once more and breathe the fresh air. I joined Rush and Cam, and Frodel and Malic joined us.

"...but I'd be back shortly," finished Malic.

"you're needed here; you're a driver, and we need to be ready to leave at a moment's notice." countered Rush.

"a point well made," agreed Frodel.

"I could go," offered Cam.

"No, lad, not this time. You should stay with your mother and sisters to keep them safe." Malic said. Cam pulled a face.

"Frodel, it must be you or I," Rush said, his voice low, "Do we know who the watcher is? Is there a code word or something?"

"Well, that is the problem," said Frodel. "In the reply I received, part of the code was right, but part of it was muddled. It's either a warning, or their watchers have discovered part of our code."

"I see, so what are we to do if the watcher is compromised?" asked Rush.

"Does that mean the meeting place with Mother Plumb might also be compromised?" I asked. Silence fell between us like iced water, and a chill ran down my spine. *That must be what Frodel was trying to say.*

"I'm afraid we must assume the worst," he sighed. "There are options, none ideal, especially with little one on board. We could go inland and around the farm into Cawsal, cross Low Lowri and onto the fishing village where we would have stopped next. Alternatively, we could head down to the coast and try to hire a boat."

"Do we have any contacts in the fishing villages along the coast? We're still in Pollo, aren't we? Perhaps Kiron might know?" asked Rush as he moved towards the conveyance. "Cam, go sit with your sisters while we work this out," he said. Cam began to speak, then thought better of it and returned to the conveyance. Shortly afterwards, Kiron came to join us. We discussed whether hiring a boat from a fishing village was possible. A few villages are on that part of the coast, but Kiron has no contacts there. He suggested a less well-travelled route that would take us via the tip of Ankpoli. Then we could cross into Low Lowri and on to a fishing village. We talked a little longer before deciding that was the best option. It meant turning back and taking a road we passed a little while ago. That slight diversion would be worth it if we remained ahead of the watchers.

We returned to the conveyance and took our seats. I sat back with Elia and Amillia, slipping my arms around them and felt the soft rise and fall as they slept. The conveyance purred into life, and we were thrown to the side as it swung round and began to travel back along the road towards the turning to Ankpoli. My arm tightened around the two girls, holding them securely. It wasn't long before the conveyance swung sharply to the right again, and we were thrown to the left. This road was an even smaller track if that was possible, and soon, we were passing through dense forest on either side.

"We must not go right," a ghostly voice beside me said, and I looked at Elia and saw her eyes open, staring ahead of her.

"Elia, are you OK? did you have a nightmare?" I asked, but I knew it wasn't even as I spoke.

"Mother, I... we should leave as soon as possible. I can't explain why." I nodded and lifted my arm from her before standing and moving towards Kiron. He might not be as surprised as Rush when he heard what I had to say.

"Kiron, I must speak to you," I said. He was talking with Rush at the back of the conveyance, and they looked up as I approached. With a tiny nod, I saw Cam understood what I was not saying. He joined us and began talking with Rush, allowing Kiron and I to move to the front of the conveyance where we could whisper discretely.

"We need to take the next left and not turn right," I whisper.

He looked at me. "I must tell you something in confidence that is not fact or confirmed." he nodded.

"Elia seems to have warnings. Cam says she's always right. They hid this from me until recently."

His eyes widened as he took in the implications, and as he looked over towards Elia, he said, "Does she know?"

"No."

"She should be told, guided as soon as possible. Then there's her age too..." he broke off. I know what he meant. She might not have long if she was. He would have been more shocked if he hadn't known the truth about my heritage. Now, he understood the implications and the danger. He knocked on the privacy shield. Frodel lowered it, and there followed a whispered conversation. Frodel's eyes widened and flicked towards Elia.

"It was agreed," Kiron said, "We'll take the turning on the left shortly. Please let me know of anything else I should be aware of." He returned to the back and began talking with Rush and Cam. I could hear them chuckling as they looked towards me affectionately. I took my seat once more beside the girls. Elia seemed to have dropped back to sleep again, and I'm grateful I don't have to explain my actions to her. The twins were still asleep, which was a relief, too.

Message from Cawsal Road Checkpoint 3 to Captain of Pollo Guard
Conveyance turned before reaching us Watchers on mountain road at Q Burial site.

Message from Captain of the Pollo Guard to Councillor Wiklon
Fugitives heading to Watchers at Quartive Burial Site.

Message from Quartive Burial Site to Captain of Pollo Guard
Conveyance heading your way.

Message from Councillor Wiklon to Councillor Maxim
Fugitives have twice avoided Watchers. Do they have help?

Message from Councillor Maxim to Councillor Wiklon
Activate plan.

The small road we were now travelling along was even narrower. Dense woodland rose on either side. Bushes brushed the sides of the conveyance, and some even knocked on the roof. I watched anxiously through the window as the forest flashed past. *It must be quite a large forest. I wondered how far it stretched.* Thena was primarily low-lying plains with few forests. *I wish we'd travelled more as a family, but Rush said that before we travel outside Thena, we must visit all the Thenan Quintareas.* A moment later, I was nudged, and my eyes flew open, my heart racing.

"Caught you sleeping, did I? Amillia's deafening us with her cries," Cam said, grinning. *How did I miss her cry?*

"Where is she?" I said in a panic as I started to rise from my seat. *I've never missed her cry,* but I needn't have worried. She was happily gurgling with Elia.

"Oh Cam, you scared me half to death." I reached out to bat his arm, but he stepped away lightly. It was lovely to see him smile, breaking the tension of the past few days, and we both laughed. Then Amillia began to grizzle, and I knew it was time to feed her. Taking her gently from Elia, I cradled her in my arms, enjoying our reunion. Then, switching places with Elia, I fed her, enjoying that special bond as I looked down at her face. It was such a precious moment. My heart filled with love, and I knew I would fight dragons for her and each of my children. The conveyance was full of soft voices. Kiron and Rush murmured at the back, and Cam was catching up with Elia. Fortunately, the twins were still asleep. *I wondered how they could sleep with this noise around them*, but I was grateful they were. The privacy screen was down at the front, and I heard Frodel and Malic murmuring. At this moment, I felt safe, cocooned in the conveyance with those I love and trust. *If only Millie was here too, I'm worried about her. Would Amelie be able to take care of her and keep her safe? Millie's* so young and naïve, *and Amelie is inexperienced as a parent. It was a lot to take on with everything we had learned in the past week.*

39

Amelie

We had been locked in the cabin for what seemed like hours. I was hungry, thirsty and frustrated, and I was sure Millie was too. Conversation had dried up, and we had been sitting silently on our cots for quite a while. Suddenly, there were footsteps in the corridor and a tap on the door. We exchanged a glance before calling out in unison.

"Yes?" the lock slid back, and the door opened, revealing Flit with a severe look on his face.

"'Ello ladies, I 'ear you was on the deck. Big mistake, if you don't mind me saying so. A big mistake. Now you've upset the capt'n, and an upset capt'n is not what we need. No, indeed, it isn't. I might add that I've persuaded him, at great risk to myself, that you should have some vittals. So, 'ere's more coffee and some stew 'n' bread." he stepped into the cabin with a flask and two mugs before retrieving two pots, each with a hunk of bread and a spoon sticking out.

"It's not fancy fare, but it's good. The cook is well respected, he is." he began backing out of the cabin.

"We're sorry. We didn't realise it would cause so much trouble. We just wanted some air," Millie began, but Flit cut her off,

"Plen'y of air down here, there is, plen'y of air down 'ere. Better use that 'til we make land. Stay locked up now; you will. For your own good, it is." Turning, he shut the door, and we heard it lock again.

With a sigh, I poured the coffee. At least we had food and coffee now. Then, we both began to tentatively poke at the contents of the pots with our spoons. It smelled pretty good, and I touched the spoon to my tongue. The sauce was rich and savoury, well-seasoned, and delicious. I smiled at Millie.

“It's delicious.” Then, realising how long it had been since I'd last eaten, I began to eat, dipping the bread into the stew. After a hesitant taste, Millie started eating hungrily. I saved a little of the bread to indulge in a childhood treat - mopping up the last of the gravy. I saw Millie do the same, and I smiled,

“I always loved to do this, but I was only allowed if I ate with Nanny or Cook. Father was furious if he ever caught me, and I would have to eat dry bread and water for a week as punishment.”

“That's horrible. We were told that, too. But I never dared find out if it was true. I thought it was just words.” Millie said.

“I was more rebellious than you, Millie. It's not good for the health, though. Far better to be you.” Later, our appetite satisfied and thirst quenched, we began discussing plans. Arriving in Portho Nacon was the first thing, of course, but how would we reach the place in the mountains? Would someone meet us, or would we have to find our own way? We wondered. Then what about Thea and the rest of the family? How would we find them? Then, the conversation turned to reminiscing and catching up on the missed years. We enjoyed the opportunity to discover more about each other’s lives.

Sometime later, Flit reappeared with more coffee and bread.

“Now, we migh' be stoppin' for a while, we might. Imperative, it is very imperative, you're not seen nor heard. The capt'n ‘as some business to attend to, he 'as. Remember, not a sound, it’d be bad, very bad for yous if you was heard. If you know what's good for you, you’ll do as ol' Flit says.” his face was etched with lines of worry, and I saw genuine fear on his face.

"But..." began Millie, but Flit cut her off.

"I can't say more, I can't," he said as he locked the door behind him. We heard his footsteps disappear along the corridor. I busied myself, pouring the coffee while I tried to make sense of what Flit had said and not said. Millie was frustrated, and after consuming the coffee and bread, she began pacing the cabin. I tried to reassure her but was afraid and didn't know how to comfort her. Being locked in wasn't helping either. A short while later, we heard shouts echo along the corridor. One voice sounded like Flit, the other was probably the cook. I couldn't hear what was said, but after our brief meeting with the cook earlier, I wondered if we were the cause. Flit's warning had sent cold shivers down my spine. I wanted to avoid becoming involved in whatever the captain's business was. All I wanted now was to get safely to Portho Nacon.

Not long after the row, we noticed the motion of the ship change and guessed it was slowing or stopping. Millie stopped pacing and sat opposite me on her cot, her hands tucked under her legs. Muffled voices drifted along the corridor, and then we heard other voices with an accent I couldn't place. I had travelled throughout Anacadair and a little in Nicadair, but this didn't sound like an accent I'd heard. The ship swayed. Was cargo being loaded or unloaded? There could only be one reason to do that in the ocean: smuggling. I had heard of the dark market and the types of trade: food, goods, and, I hardly like to say the word, flesh—trade in people. Millie stared wide-eyed as I mulled it over out loud. She didn't know smuggling still happened.

At school, they were taught that it was part of history. I shook my head. I was shocked at how much of what was taught by Thena schools was wrong or inaccurate. Millie was confused and upset that the school hadn't told them the truth. She couldn't understand why tutors would do that. I agreed, although I had my own thoughts on why. For now, I kept my opinions to myself. It wasn't the right time or place for such a discussion. Bangs and thuds rose from the hold below, accompanied by shouts, until finally, the noise subsided. Soon, we felt movement again, and we were on our way. Thank the Gods, I thought. Later, Flit appeared with a flask of coffee and dry-looking ship's biscuits. He looked flustered and dishevelled.

"You're to stay 'ere an' keep quiet, you are," he said abruptly before locking the door behind him. We didn't have the chance to ask him about the noises in the hold. Occasionally, as we lay on our cots, we heard muffled noises that seemed almost human coming from the hold below. *Was there live cargo down there*? The noises stopped as suddenly as they started. *Perhaps something wasn't secured?* Flit didn't return until much later. We guessed a night had passed when he arrived with two mugs of coffee and more bread. He didn't speak, putting his finger to his lips before he turned and quietly locked the door behind him.

When we heard an increase in activity on deck, we both hoped it meant we were close to port. Flit reappeared, slipping in quietly and again, putting his finger to his lips.

"We're coming into Portho Nacon. Capt'n says you're to stay 'ere 'n' keep quiet, you are, stay 'ere 'n' keep quiet. You're safe 'ere you are," he said in a hushed whisper. "Better safe than out too early, you are, better safe 'ere," he reiterated.

"For how long?" I whispered almost inaudibly.

"Shhh," he put his finger to his lips again, "no talking." Then he hurried out, silently closing and locking the door behind him. It was odd, but maybe it was to allow the crew to unload the hold and go ashore. Fewer people would be around to see us leave, and it would be safer. We hoped so, or maybe it was to allow time for our contact to arrive. Until then, we must wait a bit longer.

40

Thea

After I'd fed Amillia, I passed her to Elia and asked Cam to sit with them. I needed to talk to Rush. I'd had a growing feeling we might have a spy with us. *Who could it be? Who will they betray? Rush, my husband and father of our children, would he betray us? I think not, and not Kiron, which left Frodel and Malic. We relied on their local knowledge and expertise to get us to the meeting point. Would they betray us? They were the only ones with access to communications. Who recommended them? Ah, yes, Rush said Frodel was his usual driver, so could it be Malic?* Rush was sitting on his own, so this was my chance. I learned long ago to trust my intuitive instinct when it arose, and so I sat beside him, and we exchanged pleasantries. Then, with a deep breath, I began.

"Rush, a while ago, as I was feeding Amillia, I'm sure I saw several men in the forest on the right. They seemed to be heading in the same direction as us." I watched his face darken and worry lines spread across his brow.

"Why didn't you mention this sooner?" he asked abruptly.

"I was feeding Amillia," I said, lowing my head.

"If they were watchers and stopped us, what would you have done then? Ask them to wait while you fed her before they shot you both?"

"Rush, please!" His words hurt me.

"These are not cosy times. We are fleeing, and our lives are in danger," he whispered harshly.

"I know. I'm sorry," I said gently, hoping it would be enough.

"Let's hope you're wrong," he said curtly. I decided to risk continuing.

"We've had several narrow escapes, and there are watchers where they shouldn't be. Can we be sure there isn't someone with divided loyalties among us? I strongly feel someone will betray us, someone travelling with us." he looked away. He was silent for a while, and I watched his face as his expression changed. Finally, his face pale, he turned and put his hand over mine.

"We've had our times, Thea and I've not always appreciated your intuition, but that changes today." He stood and began walking down to the front before turning back and kissing my forehead. It surprised me. We're not a couple who show affection openly and not at all for a long time. I watched him return with Kiron. The two men sat beside me, and I repeated what I told Rush. My eyes flicked to the secrecy screen, but it was closed. Kiron looked between us, and I saw the concern on his face mirroring our own.

"You could be right," he said. "there've been rumours of spies for some time."

"What can we do?" I asked. I was afraid to hear what he might say.

"Unless we know who it is, we can do nothing but hope we remain ahead. It's impossible to know who's betraying us or how messages are being sent. No one is alone long enough to use the communications in the driver's compartment. Whoever it is, they're very clever," he said softly.

"What are we to do?" I turned to Rush, his face dark and angry.

"We find out who puts my family at risk," he said savagely, turning to Kiron. "We'll need a personal break soon. We'll find out who it is then. Only we three know we have a spy. Let's keep it that way." he glared towards the secrecy screen.

"Rush, remember that although it could be a deliberate betrayal, it could be innocent. A valid attempt to communicate that gets into the wrong hands. Until we discover the nature of the communication, we should keep an open mind." Kiron's voice was calm and confident.

"Huh" was Rush's reply. We fell silent as Kiron returned to the front and tapped on the privacy screen. He spoke with Frodel and Malic, who nodded. Kiron stayed at the front, taking the seat closest to the screen as Frodel began to talk. I couldn't hear what was said, but I was on high alert. It wasn't long before the conveyance slowed, and Kiron stood.

"We're stopping for a short personal break. I'm sure you'll appreciate the opportunity to stretch your legs. Please don't go out of sight and stick together or have someone with you. I apologise we don't have facilities on this conveyance." There was a sudden swaying as people moved, stretching, then gathering jackets and coats. I went back to Cam and Elia.

"I'd feel happier if we stayed together." It was true. I couldn't bear to let them out of sight. Cam and Elia nodded.

"Is Amillia coming out with us?" asked Elia.

"Yes, the fresh air will do her good, too." it would do us all good, but that unease was still there. Rush joined us as we stepped down from the conveyance.

"What about the twins?" Cam looked back at the sleeping boys. They really could sleep through anything!

"Err, good question," I looked at Rush, "Rush, would you watch the twins for a few minutes, then I'll take them as well?" I expected him to say no, and I was ready, but instead, he nodded and sat in the doorway of the conveyance.

"Cam, do you want to join Kiron and me for a short walk in a minute?" he asked.

"I've asked Cam and Elia to stay with me," I said quickly. "But when we get back, he can, while Elia and I take the twins," Rush shot a glance of annoyance at me but said no more. Frodel and Malic had paired up and were walking down the track, for that is what it is, not a road at all. *Who suggested we went this way?* I tried to remember, *of course, it was Elia,* I felt a little easier. *Why hadn't Rush and Kiron tried to split up Frodel and Malic*, I wondered. *What if one of them was the spy? Or could it be Rush or Kiron? What about Cam or Elia? I've heard the rumours of child spies. Both are old enough to be swayed by the Anti-Modernisation Pact. I was sure they wouldn't be turned. They were my children, and I would know, wouldn't I?*

"Mother, can we take turns to visit over there?" Cam suggested, interrupting my thoughts. He was pointing to a shrubby area just off the track. It was a good choice away from the others, offering privacy.

"Well spotted, Cam, yes. Do you want to go first?"

"Really? Do we have to go behind a bush?" cried Elia. She was particular about such things.

"I'm sorry, love, but yes, if you need to go, that's all I can offer." She huffed in disgust and stood, arms folded, scowling as Cam disappeared into the bushes. He reappeared shortly with a grin.

"It's a better spot than I thought," he opened his hand to reveal several dark blue berries. "There are wild blueberries ready for picking on one side."

"EWWW!" cried Elia. "You pick berries after you have done whatever round there? Great Gods, anything could be on those berries?" Cam looked down at them, grinning.

"You're right, except they were not quite in the same area and were well above the dodgy level. Take a look if you don't believe me." his grin broadens as he rubs a berry on his top before popping it into his mouth. "Mmm, ripe, juicy, crisp skin, crunchy seeds and a hint of natural seasoning." he burst out laughing at her horrified face. Soon, he had tears running down his face as she slapped his chest, and he had difficulty fending her off. It was a few minutes before he could add, "There's a little mint growing beside the berry bush." he dissolved into giggles again. Elia turned away with tears of frustration in her eyes. She hated him getting the better of her.

"Elia, why don't you take a quick look while I change Amillia's napkin? Cam, can you help me? There isn't anywhere I can put Amillia down. Lean against the tree, and I can lay Amillia on your back. It'll help you get control of yourself." He hated this punishment. I didn't use it often, but it was good when we were out and quickly brought him back down to earth. There was the practical point, too; there wasn't anywhere to put Amillia down while I changed her without returning to the conveyance.

Elia stalked off, kicking bushes and leaves as she went. When she reappeared, her face was dark like thunder. *Goodness, I could see Rush in that expression!* Elia walked up to Cam, now relieved of his duty. She shoved something into his face, leaving brown streaks down his cheeks, then stalked away. A startled Cam put his hands to his face. His fingers return streaked brown. Gingerly, he puts them to his nose. He was ready to run after her, but I put an arm out to restrain him.

"Cam, you shouldn't tease her. Let her win this round. It's only mud, I expect, isn't it?" he nodded. He had caught the earthy smell with no trace of any other odour. Even so, he was annoyed. He wasn't so good on the receiving end of a prank.

"Here, use this cloth to wipe your face. It's clean. I didn't need it for Amillia." He took the damp cloth and wiped his face in irritated swipes. I sighed. It will become increasingly challenging to keep the peace between these two. While they were great together most of the time, they needed their own space, too. *I'll ask Rush if he could occupy Cam or if Kiron could help*. I wanted to keep Elia close to me in case she had any more turns, and of course, I had Amillia, too. Then I heard the twins chatting inside the conveyance and saw Rush helping them out and directing them to me. I sent them one by one to the bushes to make themselves comfortable. Then, I told them to run over to Rush and back to me a few times. At least it would give them a little exercise. Hopefully, the motion of the conveyance would send them to sleep again when we were moving once more.

Back in the conveyance, Frodel passed around drinks and refreshments. It was primarily dry biscuits and fruit now. I asked Kiron to watch the twins while he chatted with Cam, then left Amillia with Elia while I joined Rush at the back of the conveyance.

"We need to keep an eye on Cam and Elia. This journey is so long and stressful for them. I don't want arguments flaring in here. Can you keep Cam occupied, perhaps?" He looked at me and then at the children. Cam was sitting with Kiron, and Elia was with Amillia.

"They look OK," he said dismissively.

"You missed their antics outside," I said. He had no idea. They were his children, yet he didn't understand them at all.

"Hmm, well, we'll see. I'll talk with Cam if you like." he smiled, expecting me to be grateful. It was so infuriating.

"Talk to him about his future and what college he wants to go to. That sort of thing." he brightened.

"That's a good idea. There hasn't been time to talk, but we have time now," he said and made as if to rise, but I caught his arm.

"Rush, did you and Kiron find out anything?" I whispered in his ear. He shook his head before he stood and walked to Cam.

Message from Watcher Port.Nacon to Captain of Pollo Guard

The Dolphus docked. Unloaded. No passengers.

Message from Captain of the Guard Pollo to Watcher Port.Nacon

Remain Observant, intelligence good.
Passcode 'The Invitations yours'.

41

Amelie

It had gone quiet on the ship, and I was afraid we'd been forgotten. The unpleasant smell from the draped area in the corner was becoming unbearable. Its tendrils stretched through the cabin like a poisonous vine attaching to our clothes and choking our throats. We had both resorted to holding our sleeves to our faces as we breathed. It didn't help much, but doing something felt a little better than doing nothing. Finally, footsteps sounded in the corridor, and the relief was almost overwhelming. The lock clicked, and the door swung back to reveal Flit.

"Let's be 'aving you now, ladies, it's time for you to leave, it is. Time for you to take your leave. You'll be glad to leave that 'n' all." he nodded at the corner. "Them pottys really honk on a voyage, they does, really honk." I feel hot with embarrassment at this deeply personal comment. It was bad enough we could smell our business, but for a stranger to point it out was too much.

"We will be glad of fresh air," I said, picking up my bag and leading the way from the cabin, followed by Millie. Flit shuffled past in the corridor, leaving his musty male smell in his wake. We followed him back along the corridor and onto the deserted deck, past the gaping black hole down to the hold, and onto the gangplank. Carefully, we made our way down to dry land once more. Turning, I was about to thank Flit, but he had disappeared.

It was almost dark, a few workers still hurried about their business near another ship on the otherwise deserted dockside. We walk towards what looks like a road away from the harbour towards the town. I couldn't see a signpost, but it looked like a road to somewhere. A stiff breeze came in from the sea, and we tugged our coats tightly around ourselves as we walked. It was a relief when we turned away from the dock and the breeze dropped. Unlike the darkening dock, a few streetlights were here, making it all the more appealing. It was just wide enough for one vehicle to travel at a time. *Perhaps it's one way, but which way?* I wondered. Our footsteps echoed on the stone road. Walking down such a poorly lit road with no one else around was disconcerting, and certainly not friendly. Even the houses that lined each side of the road had closed their drapes, allowing no light to escape. There must be a dampener on all sounds because I heard nothing but our footsteps. There were no sounds of voices, animals, vehicles, or anything. The further we walked, the more uncomfortable we began to feel. The road stretched out as far as we can see, with no town in sight. The scattered lights did little to ease our discomfort. Several times, I felt someone was following us and glanced back but saw no one. The hairs on the back of my neck prickled as if eyes were on me, but I couldn't see them if they were. I didn't want to worry Millie, but I picked up the pace. I hated walking the streets at night, especially in an unknown place when I didn't know where I was going. Millie touched my hand as she looked back along the road.

We turned and saw a figure standing beside a house, looking right at us. He appeared to be wearing a long dark coat and a wide-brimmed hat pulled down on his head, his face hidden in its shadow. For a moment, we stood looking at the stranger, who looked steadily back at us. Then he seemed to shrug off the darkness and began walking towards us. We stood our ground hand in hand. *Is he a watcher? Have all our efforts to escape been in vain*? I hope not.

"Are you the sister of Rush?" came a rough voice. I was about to answer when I remember there should be a password. I squeezed Millie's hand as I glanced at her.

"Who wants to know?" I asked.

"I do. I suppose you want to know if I have a message for you," he said. His voice was condescending and unpleasant, but I played along.

"Do you have a message?" my tone was matter of fact. Neither pleasant nor unpleasant aiming for neutrality.

"The invitations are yours," he said confidently. I almost sighed with relief and was about to speak when Millie squeezed my hand, and I realised the message was wrong. It was very close but not right.

"I'm sorry, your message must be for someone else. It means nothing to me," I said.

"Oh, I'm sure it must be you, ladies. You just came off the boat, the only ladies that walked off," he said with a nasty grin as he took a step closer. We stepped backwards at the same time.

"We did travel on a boat, but it docked hours ago," I said.

"Naa, you were on that boat, kept quiet while cargo was offloaded to protect your dainty eyes, I 'spect," he said, taking another step forward, and we stepped back.

"Who might you be, and what makes you think you know who we are?" I decided to see if I could discover anything about the man.

"You need a guide to Norwcan, and I'm your guide, Al. Your pal Al," he said, stepping forward. We repeated our step backwards. *How can he know so much? Did he get the passcode wrong by mistake? I don't know, but something doesn't feel right.*

"If what you say is correct, who sent you?" I asked.

"Someone called Boldun gave me the nod to meet you. Nice man with nice ways," he said with a sly grin as he stepped forward again. *Boldun, I might have guessed. So, Al must be a watcher. Now, what were we going to do?* My mind raced as we stepped back. *Could we outrun him long enough to reach the main town? I hoped we were going the right way.* I tighten my hand on my bag and squeezed Millie's hand as I glanced at her bag. Then I swung it back and let it fly from my hand straight into the man who staggered back. Millie's bag followed, catching his head and sending the hat flying, revealing a dark face with a full dark beard. His thick, dark hair now flowed around his head like a puddle. *I hoped that was hair and not blood.* Turning, we ran for our lives down the street. Behind us, we heard him cursing as he threw off the bags, then heavy footsteps, stumbling at first, gaining speed behind us. We ran faster, I didn't dare look back in case I lost my footing on the stony road and stumbled. His footsteps didn't seem to get closer, but they weren't getting further away either. *How long could he run for? How long could we run for? Were there others further along the road?*

42

Thea

Finally, the conveyance emerged from the trees into an open area with fields on either side. *Were we still in Pollo, or had we crossed into Cawsal?* I could hear Kiron and Rush murmuring in the back. Poor Cam was standing hunched over to stretch his legs. He was finding it uncomfortable now, and I wondered about Kiron and Rush, who were also too tall to stand in the conveyance. The twins continued sleeping soundly, soothed by the motion of the conveyance. Amillia had been feed and was now settled her in the carrier to sleep. I wanted to join Rush and Kiron to see if they'd discovered anything, but I was afraid to leave Elia and Amillia alone.

"Cam, can you sit with Elia and Amillia for a while? I'm going back to your father." He huffed but moved to the seat I had just left. As we swapped places, I smelled his stale, unwashed odour and wrinkled my nose. We'd been travelling so long that the conveyance was beginning to smell musty and stuffy. Wafts of unwashed bodies and the smell of fear flowed around the interior.

As I took the seat beside Rush, I asked softly, "Do we know anything more?"

"No, not really," whispered Rush, "but we're due to meet a new driver shortly who'll take us into Cawsal. We're near the border now."

"How do they know where to meet us?"

"We have a way to communicate in emergencies," Kiron said almost silently. He was hunched over with his arms wrapped around himself, looking cold.

"Are you OK, Kiron?"

"Yes, I just need some fresh air, but no point stopping now until we meet the new driver," he said. I looked more closely at him. *He looked very pale indeed. I hoped he was OK.*

"Thea, when we stop, keep the children away from the drivers, Frodel, Malic and the new one. We feel it's safer for you all." Rush said in a flat, emotionless voice. His head held in his hands.

"Is there that much danger?" I asked.

"Kiron has been telling me more about the Council's activities and my father's involvement. There's a whole layer underneath the official one I had only guessed about. A few like him sit in both camps. His allegiance is to us, but he has found a way to be part of the core group close to my father. We must be wary of others like him until we know their allegiance."

"Do we know who they are or what they do?" It was a terrifying thought.

"No, that's the problem. We know Watchers are part of a second layer, but we don't know who directs them. I can't say more and may have already said too much." I looked around, but Frodel and Malic were still in the front, and the privacy screen was closed. Suddenly, there was a shout from the front as the conveyance lurched and came to a stop.

Rush and Kiron hurried forward, and I followed, returning to the children. I squeezed onto the seat beside Cam and Elia. Cam has Amillia on his knee, her bright eyes taking everything in. Elia was looking out of the window, and turned to me.

"Elia, did you see why we stopped?"

"It was too dark to see anything. There was a bump. Did you feel it?" At that moment, Rush came back, followed by Kiron.

"Are we stopping here? can we get out and stretch our legs?" I asked.

"It's not safe," he said sharply before turning to Kiron. Kiron left the conveyance after a few hushed words, carefully closing the door. Rush sat beside it like a guard.

"Why can't we see out?" came a panicky voice. Elia's face, eyes wide with fear, looked back at me.

"Frodel must have changed the crystal to protect us. We don't want anyone to know who's inside. We must keep quiet and still until they tell us it's OK." I said.

"I thought the windows did that anyway, but we could still see out?" Cam said in a soft voice.

"What are they hiding from us? Why can't we see out?" her voice rose as she looked wildly around.

"Elia, calm down. It's just to keep us safe while they see what's happened." I stood and went behind her seat, and draped my arms around her shoulders, trying to reassure her. Elia's shoulders began to shake as she started to cry.

"Why did Kiron go out? He's a Healer. Why did he go outside? Is someone hurt? Did we hit someone or something?" she stiffened and then slumped against my arms. Her face went blank, and her eyes closed with rapid movement under the lids. She was heavy against my arms as I leaned over the back of the chair. *I couldn't stay like this for long. Thank goodness Rush remained with us. What would he make of this?*

"Rush, I need your help," I turned my head as far as possible. "Can you take Amillia from Cam? Elia's fainted. If I move, she'll slide to the floor." *I'd wondered how to tell Rush about my fears for Elia. Now, he would see it first-hand.* Thank goodness Cam had been holding Amillia and not Elia. Elia would have been devastated if anything had happened to Amillia while she was holding her. Cam turned and handed Amillia to Rush before squeezing past to join me behind the seat. Carefully, I let Cam take my place and squeezed past Rush to sit beside Elia. *I wished Rush would sit down; he seems frozen to the spot, holding Amillia. He wasn't used to holding babies. He didn't hold any of his other children. Millie was the only one he held, I thought sadly.*

"Sit, Rush. It's easier in case the conveyance rocks." I said. He sank into the seat behind him as I slid in beside Elia, gently taking her wrist and feeling for a pulse. I'd seen Mother Plumb and Healers do it, but wasn't as easy as it looked. Eventually, I felt a fluttering under my fingers. Despite the terrible pallor on her face, it felt like a regular beat. *I wish Kiron was here. Although, if this is one of her episodes, do we want anyone outside the family to witness it? It was bad enough that Rush was here.* With Cam's help, I pulled her towards me so she was lying across the seat with her head on my lap. I hoped she was more comfortable, *but how do I know if I'm doing the right thing moving her? I wasn't trained for this, and felt so inadequate.*

"Elia, can you hear me?" I said, "It's OK, I'm with you. You're safe," *I hoped my voice could reach her wherever she was and bring her back to me. I can't bear it. I cradled her head in my arms, desperate for a movement to indicate she was coming back.*

"Cam, how long does this last?" I glanced over and saw Rush sitting stiffly, holding Amillia against him.

"Rush, you can relax. She won't break. Why not slip her back into her carrier? Then you can settle the carrier on the seat beside you." he looked back at me before slowly sliding the little child into the carrier. He lifted it onto his knees, wrapping his arms tightly around it. He looked like a fish out of water. It was so odd to see him out of his comfort zone. Cam turned to stand beside him and gently helped Rush settle the carrier beside him.

Watching father and son in such a tender moment was rather touching. I couldn't remember ever seeing such a moment before. Rush always avoided the children until they were much older and independent. Cam now put a hand on my shoulder, and looked down at Elia.

"It's usually a few minutes, not longer than that. She should be coming out of it soon," he said as he leaned over and hold of her hand and gently rubbed it.

"Elia, it's time to come back. We need you here," he said as he took the other hand and rubbed that one too. It was a moment or so later before she began to stir. At first, it was a fluttering of the eyelids, then her breathing deepened and finally, her eyes opened. She startled as she saw us crowded around her.

"He's dead, he's dead, we can't stop. No time to fish, just mine." Then her eyes closed, and she seemed to go to sleep.

"She'll be fine in a little while now. She needs to sleep." Cam said as he came round and took Amillia's carrier. Rush seemed to sag with relief before recovering himself.

"What's happened? What did she say?" he said, standing up and moving closer. I was as unpleasantly aware of his body odour as I had been of Cam's, but it wasn't the right time to mention it. I probably didn't smell any better.

"I'm not sure, but she thinks someone's dead. She says we can't stop, no time to fish, just mine. Does that make any sense to you?" He moved away towards the door. "Rush?"

"I have to talk with Kiron," he said, opening the door and stepping out, leaving us rocking.

I looked at Cam, whose face mirrored my own, at that moment. *I was afraid and confused. Who was dead, and what did she mean about fishing?*

"Did it make sense to you, Mother?" he said.

"No, I wish it did. Your father seemed to gain something from it, though. I wish he'd explained."

"So do I. He's probably afraid you'll ask him to hold Amillia again." his voice was harsh and resentful. He was so good with his younger siblings, far better than their father. I hadn't realised until now how little time Rush had spent with the children as babies. There was truth in what Cam said, I thought. Looking over at the twins still sleeping, I hoped they wouldn't notice the conveyance had stopped and wake.

"Your Father wasn't able to spend much time with any of you as babies. You're lucky times are changing, and it is more acceptable for men to show their tender side. Thank you for helping your father just now. It was a very kind thing to do." I was so proud of my son. He was growing into a kind and sensitive young man. I hoped one day he would meet his match and marry. He'd be an excellent husband, of that, I was sure.

"He looked as if he would drop her if he moved even one finger from its position," Cam said with a cheeky grin.

"You're right there. We'll have to encourage him to spend more time with Amillia when this is over." I heard footsteps approaching the conveyance and the door opening. It was Kiron. He stood behind Elia's seat and leaned over to examine her, taking her wrist and feeling for her pulse. He put his hand to her face to feel for heat.

"She seems to be sleeping now. If she doesn't wake in the next half hour, we should try to wake her," he said. "In the meantime, we must talk. Cam, you should join us, I think. We all need to be aware of what to expect as we continue our journey." he looks over at Cam, who stood beside Rush as we huddled around my seat. Behind them, the twins stirred as Rush and Kiron nudged them but quickly settled back to their slumbers.

"I want us to agree that Elia is delivering some prophecy. She's right; someone's dead, but I'm sure he was dead before we struck him. It's likely to be a trap. So, we need to change our plans again. We were heading for a fishing village to replenish our food supplies. Now we must push straight on for the mountains in Norwean. Max has less influence in Cawsal, but there's still a risk in Central Caws. Frodel has family there, so stopping and getting more food and fluids might be worth the risk.

"By all that's Singular, let's hope it's enough to keep us safe until we reach our destination," said Rush.

"I will not disclose our final destination for now to reduce any further risk to us all," Kiron said.

"Elia has always been right in the past," Cam says quietly added, looking down at Amillia. She was making soft, gurgling noises as she grinned up at him.

"You can't really believe she's prophesying?" Rush began dismissively, but Kiron interrupted.

"I'll explain why I believe this to be so at a later point when we have time. Until then, please accept that I have good reason and facts support them."

"I can't..."

"Can we wait until there is time to talk? It won't hurt if we arrive sooner. Let's take the shorter route and miss one stop. We've been travelling for so long, and I can't wait to be able to wash properly. It's beginning to smell sour in here," I said firmly. *I hoped the practical talk would direct his attention away from Elia.*

"Well, I suppose you have a point," he said, "I thought we would be able to stop along the way to freshen up, but that hasn't happened. But it's a bit much to suggest we're all beginning to smell, Thea," he said with a note of irritation. The distraction worked, and we moved back to our seats.

When Elia stirred, I heaved a sigh of relief. She sat up, rubbing her eyes and looked around. The windows were still deeply tinted, but we could see shadows again as we passed through the farmland of Low Lowri. It was an oddly peaceful landscape with fields and farm buildings dotted around. Some fields had crops, and others have animals grazing. The serene landscape permeated into the conveyance, and we relaxed a little. Closing my eyes, I let my thoughts wander.

Message from Watcher Cawsal Woodland Way to Captain of Pollo guard
Body on the road. No vehicle. Footsteps suggest several people. Could fugitives.

Message from Captain of Pollo guard to Watcher Cawsal Woodland Way
Remain Vigilant.

Message from Councillor Wiklon to Councillor Maxim
Discovery needed.

Message from Councillor Maxim to Discovery
The time is now.

43

Millie

We hurtled down the road, turning left into a wider street with more lights. With relief, we saw people here and slowed a little to blend in. Amelie pointed to a bookshop on the right, and glancing behind us, we slipped inside. Immediately, we felt the atmosphere change and a sense of calm flowed around us. Moving over to a bookshelf that allowed a little concealment, we watched the street. The books in this section were all related to travel and explorers. Those brave navigators who mapped the world when it was still a mystery. Travellers by land and by sea. Our small peninsula was so tiny when we looked at world maps. My eye fell on a book about the mountains north of Cawsal between Anacadair and Nicadair. It told of mythical beings and magical places. I wished I had time to read it. Children hear stories about Cawsal people with mythical powers in children's books, but my Cawsal friends at school were very dismissive. Professors suggested it was some deformity or illness, but I've always been curious to know the truth.

"Do you see anyone?" murmured Amelie. I looked out, but there wasn't anyone who looked like the man following us.

"No, you?" Amelie looked back up the street to the left, and I looked to the right.

"No,"

"Let's give it a little longer."

"What about our things?" I didn't have anything valuable in my bag, but there were two books that I treasured. One was my favourite book, telling the story of the last princess of Adair before the Blood Wars. It was so romantic the princess fell in love with the gardener. Her father, the king, forbade their love. Of course, in the end, they ran away and married. It brought a lump to my throat. It might be a story, but how close it was to my life now. I couldn't marry the person I loved either. The other book was my Singular Prayer book, signed by everyone on the last day of school. I won't miss the prayer book itself, but it was a treasured memento of school. That said, I'm not going back to look for it, not with a watcher on our tail. Then, a worse thought struck me: maybe he was, at this moment, going through our stuff. I was about to turn and say as much to Amelie when I saw him.

The man was walking down the road with my bag in his hand and Amelie's over his shoulder. His head swung round from left to right as he walked, taking in each side of the street. My heart began to pound as I turned to Amelie.

"He's here." I hissed, moving further into the shop. Amelie followed me, and we stopped by another bookshelf to watch the shop door more discretely.

"What shall we do?" I asked my eyes wide. My heart was pounding so loudly I was sure the whole shop could hear it.

"We go to the shopkeeper, and with luck, he might have a place where we can hide. I haven't been to Cawsal for a while, but in Delph, it isn't unusual for a bookshop to have such a place." *I couldn't believe it, shops with hiding places?* I would've laughed if you'd asked me if such a thing existed even a weeks ago. I would never have considered the need until today. After all we had been through in the past few days, I understood the need only too well.

"He's outside, he's stopped, he's peering in... what do we do?" I was *terrified. Had he seen us? could he see us now? I felt sick.* Cold sweat trickled down my back. Amelie clasped my hand, leading me further into the shop. I tried to walk with her, but my legs were shaking so much I could barely walk. She guided me into an alcove with a reading seat and sat me down.

"Wait here, take a book and hold it up to read. Don't, for any reason, peek until I get back," she whispered before returning to the aisle. I grabbed a book and held it up.

"Turn it round..." she whispered. I turned it around. I'd no idea what it was about, and my eyes wouldn't focus on the words in front of them. I strained my ears to hear the door opening or footsteps approaching me. The book shook as I held it, and the writing moved across the page, making me feel even more nauseous. I closed my eyes, then open them again. *It was even worse when I couldn't see.* Faith had never been important to me, but now I prayed to the Singular God as I had never prayed before. *Deliver us safely from this place, oh most Singular God.* Amelie was taking so long, and my sweaty hands were slipping on the book's glossy cover. Footsteps approached the alcove several times, only to continue past, leaving my heart pounding like a drum. Then I heard what can only be Amelie's footsteps. Soft, like tiny fairy steps approaching me.

"Millie, the bookseller has a privacy room we can use. He knows some of the watchers and will try to find out what happened to the person who should have met us. He also said he may be able to find out where Rush and Thea are." A slim, perfectly manicured finger appeared on the top of the book and gently pushed it down. My arms had frozen in place, holding the book in front of my face. She slipped the book back on the shelf before taking my hands and pulling me into a warm embrace. Her arms were reassuring, reminding me of Thea, who had always been there when I needed comfort. Then I felt disloyal to Thea and pulled away. She said nothing, taking my arm and linking it with hers. Together, we went to the bookseller, who directed us through a small door at the back of the shop behind the counter. It looked like a stock room from the outside, and when we entered, we found, to our surprise, that it was precisely that. A stock room full of boxes of books except for a small area at the back hidden from sight by the stacks of boxes. Here, there were several comfortable chairs around a small coffee table. Behind was a place to make refreshments. My mouth watered at the thought of coffee. I sat in a comfortable chair next to Amelie. It was warm in the room, and I soon felt drowsy, sliding further down into the chair. I was almost asleep when my foot was nudged sharply, and I jerked awake.

"No time to sleep, Millie. We must be ready to go at any moment," she said. She was tired, too. Despite careful makeup, dark shadows under her eyes were clear to see. Her once immaculate coat and trousers now looked crumpled, and I wondered what I looked like. I hoped I didn't meet anyone I knew, although that was unlikely. Most Cawsal students from school that I knew were from Central Caws and Low Lowri. I can't think of anyone from Norwcan. Amelie went to the door and listened for a moment before coming back. She was on edge, prowling the room like a caged animal, picking up the odd book from the top of a box and flicking through it before putting it down again. She was on her third circuit of the room when the door opened, and a large man bustled in. He closed the door behind him. His eyes were wide, and his presence projected fear and concern.

"Dear Friends, there is no time to lose. You were right. It was a watcher from AMP (Anti Modernisation Pact). He's well known here and knows some of our hiding places, including this one. We must find a safer place without delay. He turned without waiting for a reply and, moving with surprising speed, led us back through the shop to another door that took us into a loading area that served several shops along the road. The bookseller continued through an open gate into a side street at the back of the shop. He hurried along, and we follow in his wake, hoping he was taking us to a place of safety. At the end of the street, we turned into another small street leading away from the main road. It was narrow and unlit, reminding me of the one where we met the watcher. *This person couldn't be about to trap us, could he?* I caught Amelie's arm and tried to convey my worries with my eyes as we hurry along. Pressing her hand over mine, she nodded briefly but said nothing. *What did that mean? Was that supposed to be reassurance or agreement?* Meanwhile, we hurried after the rotund man. Finally, he stopped and knocks on a door. He tapped twice, then again, then three taps together, followed by a single one. It must be some sort of code. The door opened, and a woman looked out before beckoning us inside. She glanced up and down the street before shutting the door and sliding the bolts firmly in place.

Message from Watcher Portho Nacon to Captain of Pollo Guard

Fugitives escaped. Watching Bookshop. Owner under Watch.

Message from Captain of Pollo Guard to Councillor Wiklon

Fugitives escaped Nacon Watcher. Bookseller suspected. Sending Guard.

44

Millie

"You poor things, it's not a good night to be out with a watcher on your tail, no, indeed it isn't. Let me take your coats. I'll hang them, I will," We gratefully slid our coats off and handed them to her. The hallway was narrow, and we stood awkwardly close to our hostess and the bookseller.

"You'll want to freshen up, I'm sure you will. Upstairs, door on the left. Everything you need, there is. Clean clothes in sizes, first door on the right. Make yourselves at home. If you can't find something, press the call button. I'll make you something to eat. You must be hungry, you must." she gently ushered us to the stairs.

Upstairs, there was, indeed, a small, well-laid-out bathroom with everything we needed to freshen up. Amelie suggested I went first while she investigated the bedroom with clean clothing. I smiled, *typical of Amelie to think of clothes first.* As for me, I couldn't wait to take a rain shower. I knew I was beginning to smell and hated that anyone might notice. I couldn't wait to remove the clothes I had been wearing for the past two or three days now. The washing gel was fragrant, and soon, the room was filled with a steamy fresh smell. The feel of the raindrops drumming on my skin, hot and cleansing, was heavenly. There were clean blue towels laid out, which I used, and then I investigated the deodorising hygiene creams to freshen myself further. Finally, I wrapped the large blue towel around myself and secured it firmly. Emerging from the bathroom, holding my bundle of dirty clothes I went into the first bedroom. Amelie was standing beside the bed with several sets of clothes laid out. She looked pleased with herself.

"We're in luck. There's a complete change of clothes for each of us. Luckily, we're a similar size, so I didn't have to guess. You can take the blue, and I'll take the green unless you prefer the other way round." Looking at the two sets of clothes, I immediately saw the blue set was perfect for me. It had a lovely overdress in a small daisy design with dark blue slim trousers and a navy coat. The green outfit had dark green tailored trousers, a matching jacket, pale floral blouse, and even a hat. The green is perfect for her, so I agreed. She disappeared with her prize into the bathroom while I closed and locked the door so I could dress in the clean clothes. I left my dirty clothes in a pile on the floor. I was relieved to see Amelie had even found undergarments and stockings. It was like being in a fashionable shop trying on clothes. Once dressed, I looked at myself in the looking glass by the window. The whole effect was elegant yet appropriate for my age. Several clean hair combs and brushes were on a table near the looking glass. Cautiously, I inspected them before selecting a wide-toothed comb. I began to ease out the tangles from my damp, curly hair. It was great to feel clean and groomed once more.

Hearing the bathroom door open, I unlocked the bedroom door. Amelie walked in, looking immaculate as if she had just stepped out of her dressing room. I grinned at her, and she smiled back.

"This feels much nicer, doesn't it.?" she said.

"What should we do with our clothes?" *I was worried about leaving them, but how would we carry them without bags if we took them with us?* I picked up my clothes, wrapping my undergarments inside the bundle I place on my coat.

"Let's leave them here for now and go downstairs," Amelie said, placing her neat pile beside my clothing bundle. I stood beside her, catching the scent of a floral fragrance. She must have found some perfume in the bathroom, how like her. Her face had received some attention, too, I noticed. The tired makeup has gone, revealing a fresh face underneath, revitalised and youthful. We followed the most enticing smell downstairs. It was savoury, spicy, fragrant, and delicious. My mouth was watering by the time we entered the large kitchen.

The bookseller, Ollee, sat at a big table, rapidly spooning something into his mouth. The woman turned and smiled. She was motherly, not like mine, but like the mothers of some of my friends. She had a comfortable figure to embrace a child and bring comfort. The woman was wearing a green woven work dress with a cream full apron over the top. A rich gold plait flowed down her back, shot through with silvery threads. Her round face had a warm smile that reached up to her grey eyes.

"Now, you look better, you do, all refreshed. My name is Katja. Ollee has been telling me of your predicamentie."

"Katja, thank you so much for your generous hospitality to two outsiders. We are most grateful. My name is Amelie, and this is Millie." She extended her arm, and Katja clasped her elbow in greeting. I was hurt. Why didn't Amelie acknowledge me as her daughter?

"Come now, come and sit. You must be hungry, you must. Sit, sit here by the fire. I'll fill your bowls, humble Cawsal fare it is, meat stew with herbs from the garden and my own vegetables. It's good and filling, it is. Will you take tea with me, perhaps?" We sat at the table beside the fire. The warmth and gentle crackling relaxed us.

"Katja, you are most kind, thank you. We accept your generous offer of food and tea." Amelie spoke again using her formal

Thena accent. It sounded too formal so far from Thena, but I supposed she must have her reasons. Katja began ladling stew into two bowls from a large pot on the cooking fire. She brought them to the table and placed spoons beside each one.

"There's no fancy stuff here, there isn't, just bowls and spoons." Taking the large black pot beside the fire, she poured tea into mugs and sets them before us. The bowl of stew smelled divine. Picking up my spoon, I dipped it into the bowl. There were pieces of meat and vegetables in a thick, dark gravy. My mouth watered and I filled the spoon and brought it to my lips. The hot gravy scalded me, and yelping, I dropped the spoon back into the bowl, splashing a few drops onto the table.

"Oh, be careful now, dear, be careful. It's hot, it is, just made and bubbling in the pot. You mind your mouth, dear. Blow on it a little." she chuckled. I flushed with embarrassment as I picked up my spoon again and took a much smaller amount. Raising the spoon, I blew across the delicious spoonful before tasting it. It was just as good as it smelled. The meat melted in my mouth, and I tasted carrots, paroots (purple vegetables shaped like a carrot with a sharp, intense flavour), and other things I couldn't identify. It tasted so good. My spoon dipped rhythmically in and out of the bowl. I was completely lost in the moment and unaware of anything around me for a while. When I reached the bottom of the bowl, I was feeling comfortably full and satisfied. Looking up, I found with embarrassment that all three faces were looking at me.

"What?" I muttered as I saw Amelie smiling at me with a twinkle in her eyes.

"You've been so engrossed in your meal I don't think you heard Katja ask if you would like a little more. Oh, and you have a trickle of gravy on your chin. Here, use this." She handed me her handkerchief, and I self-consciously wiped my chin and mouth. I hoped I hadn't dripped any on my clothes.

Surreptitiously I glanced down to check and couldn't see anything, thank goodness.

"Thank you," I said quietly to Amelie, then looking up, "Thank you, Katja, I've had sufficient. It's delicious, the best I've ever had." Katja smiled warmly.

"I'm glad I could do this much, I am. Now, we must talk," she looked over at Amelie, who nodded.

"You ladies are in a predicamentie, yes you are. I can shelter you, but only tonight, just tonight. We've sent word, we have. You need a guide to take you where you're going, you do." she smiled at us, looking pleased with the arrangements.

"You've been so kind, Katja. Please tell us how we can repay you. We should also find a way to clean our clothes or something to carry them in. You've been so kind to lend us these fine clothes, but I'm sure you'll wish to have them returned." Amelie's soft Delphi lilt had returned, which suited her better than the stuffy Thena tone.

"You don't need to worry about your clothes, you don't. They can stay here for the next person they can. I'll clean them. I will."

"Oh, that's very kind, although..." Amelie broke off, looking over at me.

"It's OK," I said, I liked being asked. It made me feel grown up, which, of course, I was. As they continued talking about practical things, my mind drifted. I was warm, safe and comfortable, and I thought of Yan for the first time that day. *I missed him so much. What was he doing right now? I wondered. Did he miss me? Does he even know what happened?* Everything had happened so quickly, and I wondered if anyone had told him. I wish he'd come with us. *Would I ever see him again?* My heart ached, and a bubble of pain rose in my chest. I felt tears well in my eyes and looked up, taking a deep breath and pushing all thoughts of Yan away again. I tried to focus on the conversation once more.

"... but whatever you do, don't leave this side of the house. Keeping away from windowsies is best. It is," finished Katja. The Cawsal drawl was becoming stronger as she relaxed in our presence. It was a comfortable reminder of my friends from school.

"Thank you, Katja, we don't want to intrude unnecessarily and will certainly provide reimbursement for your trouble..." began Amelie, but Katja interrupted.

"Now, that isn't necessary, it isn't. I knew you'd come one day, I did. I've seen that day approaching. You're the girl my Kayden fell for, aren't you?" Amelie drained of colour, swayed, then slumped to the floor, taking me with her.

45

Millie

"Oh, Dear, dear!" cried Ollee as he moved quickly to take Amelie's weight from me. He swept her into his arms as I scrambled back to my feet. I froze when I saw her. All colour had drained from her face. *What happened? Why was she so pale?* I didn't know what to do, I was very afraid.

"Katja, we should move to the back parlour, we should. She needs more comfort, she does. It's the shock, it is." he walked towards the door at the far end of the kitchen with Amelie in his arms. Her arm flopped down, and her hair spilled over his arm. Katja went ahead of him, her face now a dark plum hue.

"Dear, dear, I never meant to upset her, I didn't. I wanted her to know she wasn't blamed, not her fault. Oh, dear dear," she kept saying as she led us down a short corridor and through another door on the right. Ollee gently laid Amelie on a dark red settee with her head resting on a cream flowery cushion.

I slipped round and knelt on the floor by her head. The floor was hard on my bony knees, but I ignored it. Taking her hand, I caressed it softly.

"Amelie, Amelie... please wake up." tears sprung to my eyes, and I looked up at Katja. "What should I do*?"* I really had no idea. Mother cared for such things or cook or nanny, but never me. I felt so helpless. Then Amelie stirred, her head rolled from one side to the other before her eyes opened and came to rest on me.

"Millie? "I was so relieved to hear her soft voice, tears trickled down my cheeks.

"Yes, it's me." I threw my arms around her and felt her arms surround me. A swell of emotion filled me, and I buried my head in her shoulder, sobbing.

"It's OK, Millie, I'm OK, love," she murmured in my ear as she gently rubbed my back.

"Amelie, I'm sorry, I am. Sorry, it was such a terrible shock. I never meant to upset you, I didn't." Katja stood beside me, wringing her hands, her face a picture of misery. Ollee put his arm tenderly around her.

"Come now, Kat, my love, you weren't to know she'd have a turn, you weren't. She'll be right as rain in a minute, she will. Go and make more tea, then we'll talk, go now," he said. She looked at him with such love in her eyes.

"Ollee, you're a good man you are. You're right, as always. I'll be just a moment while I make the tea," she said as she hurried from the room.

"Come now, ladies, this won't do, it won't. Kat's only trying to help, she is. When she knew who you were, she had so much to say, and it just tumbled out too fast, it did." he said fondly as he took a comfortable armchair beside the fireside. Soft light from lamps around the room made it feel cosy. Amelie eased herself into a sitting position, and I knelt back on my heels as she stood and straightened her clothes. Sitting down, she patted the seat beside her.

"Come, Millie, sit with me." wordlessly, I stood and sat beside her. My head was spinning. *Where have I heard that name before? Kayden, Kayden? I can't remember. Was it someone at school? I know I've heard the name recently.*

Katja returned with a large tray. She placed a generous plate of sweet treats on the table before us, then busied herself, pouring tea and passing round cups.

"Now then, have some tea and some sweet treats. Sweet is good for the shock, it is," she said. *The tea smelled good as I took my cup and sniffed it. I wasn't good at guessing tea infusions. I only liked camomile tea, it was nice to relax with before sleep. I didn't know other infusions, though. Coffee was another thing. I preferred coffee, and I missed its bitter taste. Cautiously, I took a sip, wincing as it burned my already scalded lips. It tasted soothing and comforting, but I'll have to wait for it to cool.*

"Katja, I'm so sorry for my weakness. Please forgive me. You have offered nothing but kindness and hospitality." Amelie's voice was soft and gentle. She was sitting cradling her cup, gently blowing across the surface, something we were never allowed to do at home. I did the same, which made a surprising difference when I took my next sip. I'd expected to feel another burn on my scalded lips, but the burn didn't come, although it was still hot. I smiled to myself. *What a discovery.*

"Amelie, I'm very sorry..." began Katja.

"No, Katja, it's I who should apologise. Please continue with what you want to tell me about Kayden. I'm ready to hear what you have to say." her fingers tighten around the mug as she says his name.

"Well, Kayden was my brother, older than I by five minutes he was," Amelie gasped.

"Your brother, your twin brother? I never knew he had a twin, only that he had a sister," she said.

"Yes, well, in those days, it didn't do to make much of relationships, it didn't. I went to live with my mother's sister in Pescari, I did. Moved here to Norwcanie when I met Ollee. He was fleeing from Thena, he was. Wanted to take shelter near the harbour in case we had to leave Anacadair. He has family in

Nicadair, and somewhere else further away, he has. Kayden told us of this beautiful girl he met at school with fiery hair. He wanted to marry you, Amelie, he did. He loved you, he said, loved you he did." Amelie began to shake, and I took her cup, and placed it on the table with my own. Then, I put my arm around her.

"When it happened, our parents fled here to the mines, they did. Most don't know this area, the mines, or other places people can be safe. They thought you didn't care for him, they did. Poor little Arte was caught, though and has never been the same since prison, poor kid. My parents thought you would be married off to some fancy Councillor when they found out who your family was, they did. Someone who would support your father's ambitions." She paused to sip her tea.

"I met Silph, a dreamer, the one you met, she was. She told me you'd come looking for the family, she did. I knew then my parents had been wrong. You did care, said so to them, but they wouldn't believe me. Silph told me what you said, she did. Told me about the babe too," Amelie looked at me and then at Katja, tears brimmed in her eyes and spilled down her cheeks.

"What happened to the babe? will you tell me?" Katja said, her eyes glistened with tears. Amelie gulped and gripped my hand tightly before nodding. I knew what was coming next. I'd remembered where I heard the name Kayden before.

"This is the child, Katja, this is Millie. Brought up by my brother and his wife, she was," Amelie said quietly, patting my hand.

"Ohh!" Katja knelt and wrapped an arm around each of us in a tight embrace. "She has his eyes. I knew it when I saw her, I did. Couldn't believe it, thought she'd be dead, I did." her voice was muffled with emotion and tears as she spoke into my shoulder, and I awkwardly placed an arm on hers. The whole thing was becoming so weird and overwhelming! *was I supposed to say something? What should I say?* But I needn't have worried.

"If it weren't for my brother, she might have been," Amelie said, her voice trembling. "He persuaded Father to let him raise her as his own. Father threw me out the day after Millie was born. Banished me from the house, and Thena, he did." I could hear the pain in her voice as the old wound opened. It was as raw and angry as it had been on the day I was born. Amelie crumpled forward, her body shook with the tears she could finally allow to fall. Katja moved to the side of the settee and wrapped her arms around Amelie as she wept, her arms joined mine as we held Amelie between us. We sat in silence for a while until Amelie's tears subsided.

Finally, she raised her head, wiping her tear-swept face with the cloth Katja had given to her.

"I'm sorry, it's such a shock, brought so much back. I haven't thought of those days for a very long time," she said weakly.

"I understand. I've had grief in my life, too, I have. You've held that in too long. It grows like a canker. You must let it out. If you don't let it heal, it will destroy you." she said gently.

"Millie and I have only just begun to get to know each other. My father forbade me to see her, write to her or even know what she looked like until her sixteenth anniversary. The only thing I was allowed to do was make a Promisary Agreement. He couldn't take away my right as the birth mother, although I suspect he would have done so if it wasn't written in law. I made one because I had to know I'd done all I could to ensure we would meet. When the day came, I didn't know if my brother, Rush, would honour the agreement. There was no response to the Invitation I sent to Millie. Father had become so powerful we could assume nothing. It was the most wonderful moment when I finally saw her and could see how beautiful she was. You're right. She does have Kayden's eyes, and I see she has your nose too. For too many reasons to go into now, my father has gone back on his agreement with Rush. Now, he wants the full extent of his legal rights carried out for my disgrace. He wants me and Millie... um, I believe he wants us dead." she squeezed my hand as she said the last part. I'd guessed, but hearing the words aloud was painful. Tears trickled down her cheeks, and I felt my own eyes fill and overflow.

"Oh, my dears, your father has a lot to answer for, he does. Such a wicked thing to wish his flesh and blood dead, it is. What will you do now? I know you're heading north, I do, but will you be able to return?"

"I don't think so. Father rarely goes back on a decision. It would be a loss of face. While he's head of the High Council, we have no choice but to disappear. Even when he steps down, I'm sure he will remain powerful while he lives. He's building a network to sustain what he has created and looking for a successor to continue his work. I don't know what to do; we haven't had a chance to think further than escape from watchers. We hope to meet Rush and his family in the mountains. Then we can work out what to do."

"I can take you north. I can. Do you know where you are meeting them?" Ollee spoke for the first time, and we looked over at him.

"Oh, Ollee, we can't impose on you," Amelie said. Was he fit enough for a trek into the mountains? He doesn't look as if he exercises much. I was worried about the trek myself.

"Well, there's always young Kayde there is," he said, looking at Katja. "Kayde is our oldest, and he's good, strong and reliable, he is."

"Yes, Kayde will help. I'm sure he will, especially as it's family. Millie and Amelie are family, you are," she said firmly. "Go call Kayde, Ollee, quickly now, go call him." she stood, ushering him out of the door, closing it softly.

“Are you sure, Katja? I hate to impose on a young man, but I don’t know what else to suggest, I don’t.” Amelie said.

“Young Kayde is old enough to take you, he is. He often helps when people are in difficulties, he does.” she smiled proudly, “Nobody suspects a young 'un they don't. When he hears who you are, he’ll want to help. I know he will.” I was curious to meet this boy. He couldn’t be much older than I was, yet they trusted him to be a guide. It seemed very strange to me, but then I'd had so little freedom in Thena. I wished my life had been different. Maybe it would be now.

We heard muffled voices approaching the door, and Katja went to greet Ollee and Kayde. She returned looking pale, followed by Ollee and another person. A tall person in a long black coat, my heart began to thud. *Had the watcher found us?* Amelie caught my eye, and our hands moved together, and clasped tightly. Only when the person entered the room did we realise it wasn’t a watcher. It was a tall young man with striking fair hair who looked vaguely familiar. Amelie took a sharp intake of breath.

“But...” she began.

“Yes, he's the image of Kayden, the image of Kayden,” Katja said proudly.

“Yes, yes he is,” Amelie whispers. “I thought I'd seen a ghost, I did. Gave me quite a shock.” She stood and held out her arm. The young man stepped forward, and they clasped elbows.

“I'm Amelie, I'm honoured to meet you,” she said.

“Kayde, pleased to meet you, I am. Mothie and Porthie have told me about you they have.” Amelie turned to me.

“Kayde, this is Millie, Kayden's daughter and your cousin. Please welcome her as family.” I stepped forward and shyly offered my arm. It felt a little awkward. Usually, formal greetings weren’t used by young people, but this was far from normal. Kayde took my elbow, and I took his, feeling the warm, strong arm beneath the coat. *I wondered what my arm felt like to him.* It wasn't unpleasant, yet I felt compelled to break away as soon as appropriate. Raising my eyes, I looked into his face and was surprised to see a big grin as he looked back at me.

"I know who you are. I've seen you at school with the smart set. I left school this year with you, although I don't think you noticed me. You only had eyes for Yan." I felt my cheeks redden.

"Er, yes..." I muttered. *That was why he looked familiar.*

"I knew it, I did. Meant for each other, you are, I said to myself. Is he with you?" My eyes filled with tears, and I turned away. I didn't want him to see me cry.

"Millie misses Yan very much. He isn't with us. We aren't sure when we'll see him again. Perhaps we can talk about what we must do now and keep chitchat for later," Amelie said. I was relieved but, at the same time, humiliated. She was covering for me, when I should be able to do that myself. I swiped at the tears until my face felt dry once more, then raised my head and turned to stand with Amelie.

"Amelie is quite right, she is," said Ollee, "The watcher is still prowling about, he is. We should leave as soon as we can, we should." Katja looked up.

"Ollee, are you going with them?" she said sharply. They locked eyes, then he looked at us.

"I'm going as far as the mountain, I am." he turned to Katja. "We need the walking clothes and a small hamper, we do. I think the trail is best considering how persistent this creature is," he said.

"OK, I'll take the ladies upstairs and get them ready. Kayde, can you take care of the hamper? There is the usual food in the kitchen, there is, and put some of the sweet treats in, too." she said with a chuckle as she led us to the door.

"Come now, I have some walking clothes that will be better than those for the route into the mountains, I have."

We follow Katje back upstairs, where she pulled out the clothes we needed: stout walking trousers, warm shirts, long waterproof coats, hats and thick socks.

"These are great, Katje, but what about boots? We don't have any boots for walking." Amelie comments as she surveyed her appearance in the looking glass. She looked, as always, perfectly turned out. I often think she could look good even in a sack with a rope belt. As for me, well, the trousers were too long as always and a little big, but they will do with the belt I'd been given and the hems rolled up.

"Yes, yes, don't you worry, we have boots downstairs in sizes. You can leave yours or take them with you as you like, but you will be carrying everything you take, so you will. Best don't take too much. My Kayde will carry the food and anything else to keep you safe for the journey." She sounded businesslike and efficient. *How many others have they helped to have all this spare clothing in so many sizes? I wondered.*

We followed her downstairs, through the kitchen, into the boot room, it really was named perfectly. It was filled with shelves of boots in every size and description. I'd never seen so many pairs of boots. Katja began pulling boots from shelves and returning them until she found what she wanted. She repeated the process until two pairs of long boots, sturdy and well-worn, stood before us.

"There you go now, there we are," she said as she indicated the bench on the far wall. "Sit there and try these on. They should be OK for you, they should."

"Thank you, Katja. You've done so much for us I don't know how we can repay you." Amelie said as we sat on the bench.

Katja smiled, saying family helped each other. No repayment was needed. *I liked Katja, she was so warm and friendly.*

I looked at the boots. They were well-worn, which meant other people's feet had been inside them. *Ugh, someone else's feet, leaving sweat, and what else? My toes curled up instinctively as I pushed back on the bench. I couldn't go through with it.* I looked at Amelie. She was slipping her feet into the boots, her trousers firmly tucked into the thick socks. My heart sank. If Amelie could put them on, then I'd have to try. I pulled on the thick socks and tuck my trousers into them like Amelie. Taking one of the boots, I cautiously sniffed, then sniffed again. *I could smell stale boot leather but nothing else. When they're worn, they must be cleaned afterward, that must be it. That counted for something, didn't it?*

"Come on, love, slip your boots on. You need to get going, you do," said Katja, kindly passing the other boot to me. Reluctantly, I took it and pulled them both on, lacing up as I had seen Amelie do. I hated to admit it, but they felt comfortable as I took a few steps in a small circle. Amelie had just done the same thing and smiled at me. *How did Katja guess our boot size? I could scarcely remember my own.*

"Good, now you are ready, you are," Katja said, folding her arms and looking like a proud mother hen.

"Kayde, are you finished with that hamperie?" she calls, and he appeared in the doorway with an enormous bag on his back. He had two smaller bags in his hand, which he passed to us.

"We'll all carry something, we will," he said. Katja looked at us.

"We're happy to carry our share, we are," Amelie smiled at Kayde, then swung her bag over her shoulders. I did the same.

"We should go, we should," Ollee said. Rilec is keeping watch and has signalled all clear for the path to the edge of

Portho Nacon." Kayde walked to the door at the far end of the boot room and looked at us.

"We go now, OK?"

"Yes, let's get moving," Amelie agreed. She gave Katja a quick hug. "Thank you so much, Katja. I wish we had more time to talk." I didn't want to leave this warm, comfortable house, but I knew it wasn't safe for us or our new family while we remained.

Kayde led us down narrow streets and pathways until the houses thinned out. We moved through fields towards a small copse and the mountains ahead.

"It's open here, so go as fast as you can until you reach the thicket," Ollee said, "I'll keep watch until you're out of sight, I will. The Gods go with you, and the fates keep you safe," he said, it was the Fatalist blessing. We walked quickly through the fields until we entered the cool, dark shade of the thicket.

"We can take a few minutes here, we can. We have quite a way before another safe place to stop. It's not a well-known route, but it's best to be cautious." Kayde said.

"How long is it before daylight is upon us?" Amelie asked. I hadn't thought of that, of course travelling in this half-light was better than in full daylight. I was glad to catch my breath. One of the shoulder straps of my pack was hurting, and I took the opportunity to try and rearrange it.

"Uncomfortable?" Kayde asked, deftly running his fingers underneath the shoulder straps, identifying the problem. Tugging my coat, he lifted the pack and then lowered it. "Better now, I think?" he said. It was, and I thanked him.

Message from Watcher Portho Nacon to Captain of Pollo Guard
Bookseller closed. Request watchers for mountain route.

Message from Captain of Pollo Guard to Watcher Portho Nacon
detain bookseller.

Message from Captain of Pollo Guard to Watcher Team Beta Norwcan border
Fugitives approaching, detain.

46

Thea

I jerked awake as the conveyance swayed violently. *I was back in the place of my nightmares, and I couldn't get out. As the scream rose in my throat, my eyes opened, and I remembered where I was. We were in the conveyance heading to Cawsal.*

"What's happening?" I asked, looking around. Elia was gazing out the window holding Amillia, and Cam was sitting close by with the twins. Rush was talking urgently at the back with Kiron, their heads together. Nobody answered my question. I stood, then grasped the seat for support as my legs gave way. They had turned to jelly; it was a minute or so before they held me. I glanced at the twins and smiled. They were asleep on either side of Cam, each resting a head on his shoulder. I joined Rush and Kiron at the back and sat down.

"Where are we, and what was that bump just now?" I said, keeping my voice low. They looked up and exchanged glances. "Come on, Rush, please," I said, frustrated. "Don't treat me like a child." but I could see it was no good. It was the Thenan way to keep women in their place by only telling them what they needed to know, but I'd had enough. Kiron looked at me, his face drawn and worried, and it was he who spoke.

"We've passed into Norwcan. That bump was a trap probably set for us. It failed because we rose above most of it but caught the highest point. We have avoided a few previously, but this was a serious attempt. If traps were being laid, watchers would be close by. The conveyance should be OK, but it would be too risky to stop and check." Rush took my hand and gently squeezed it.

"We're OK for now, but we're certain someone with us is communicating with the watchers." I was grateful to have some of the truth, although I was sure *more would still be* kept from me. For now, it was enough. Confirming I was right about a spy meant he took me seriously. Then the words finally registered in my mind, *a trap laid for us by all that's Singular; what was to become of us?*

"Do you know who it might be?" I whispered. They brought their heads as close to mine as was decent before Kiron spoke.

"We're unsure. We've watched the family and seen no unexpected absence or concealed behaviour. As we said before, our concern is with Frodel and Malic. Frodel has been with Rush for a long time, but not Malic. Ever since we started our journey, there have been times when we have been too close to watchers for comfort." I nodded in agreement. The same thought had crossed my mind.

"I suppose the early encounters could be coincidence or external influences," I suggested. "Before we left Thena and Pollo, there were so many ways we could have been identified and many more watchers." The two men looked at each other.

"Yes, that could be the case," Rush said. "We've wondered the same, which suggests Malic is the leak. Until we're sure, we can do nothing to raise suspicion that we are aware. The closer we get to our destination, the greater the risk to the network helping us."

"Do we need Frodel and Malic? can we let them go, and you two drive the conveyance?" I wondered aloud.

“Unfortunately, neither of us can drive a conveyance such as this. It’s a good suggestion, though. I don’t think we will change drivers now, either. It brings even more risk.” Kiron said.

We heard movement behind us and saw Cam gently easing away from the twins and moving to Elia. He grabbed his sister as she collapsed against him, still holding Amillia. I couldn’t get there fast enough. The conveyance rocked as I hurried to my children. Taking Amillia, I slipped her into her carrier and put it on the floor where she would be safe. Looking up, I saw Kiron standing behind Elia's seat with concern on his face. He leaned over to support her as Cam, and I gently laid her back on the seat. She was so very pale. These episodes were happening more frequently. There had been several already on this journey. I was worried for her, but at least we had Kiron with us. Cam and I moved back, allowing him to come around and examine her.

“She's OK in that her heart and breathing are fine, but if I'm right, that may not be the biggest concern anymore.” he looked meaningfully at me.

“Cam, has it been happening as often as this in the past?” I asked.

“Um, it was only, like, every month or so until now,” he said.

“Do you know what’s happening, Cam?” I asked. I wondered if they had worked it out between them or if they assumed it was something that happened.

“We thought, well, we thought she could be a dreamer, except she didn’t have Cawsal blood. I guess we know differently now. Could it be possible?” he asked hesitantly.

“I'm afraid it might be,” said Kiron. “Do you know much about dreamers?”

“Not really. They weren't spoken about much at school. The tutors didn't like us asking questions about things that weren't

Thena or Anlan history. They said dreamers were make-believe, invented by Cawsal storytellers."

"Elia may have these episodes more frequently as she approaches her sixteenth. She's how old now?" Kiron asked.

"She'll be thirteen next anniversary," I reply, my heart sinking. I am trying to remember what I knew about dreamers. They were usually children, but I had thought they grew out of their ability as they aged.

"This might not be the right time, but I think you need to be prepared." he looked around as Rush joined us. I was relieved the twins were sleeping. This wasn't a conversation for the very young.

"What are you trying to say?" asked Rush, his voice low and challenging. Kiron joined us as we stood in a tight group.

"Dreamers have this special ability to see the future, but it comes with a heavy price. We don't know why, but it's very rare for them to continue past their sixteenth. Many don't even reach their teens."

"Do you mean they lose the ability?" I asked hopefully, but he slowly shook his head.

"I'm sorry, but it seems this ability drains their life far sooner than expected."

"You mean she'll die? Is that what you're saying?" Rush said, his voice rising with emotion. Kiron put a hand on his arm, but Rush shook him off.

"I don't believe it. She's just exhausted from this bloody journey. By the God in whom all things are singular, this journey is enough to exhaust anyone." his voice exploded from him, and that warning flush began to creep up his neck. I stepped in. I didn't want the twins to be woken.

“Rush, can we, for now, agree that she needs to rest? When we are safe, we can confirm what's wrong with her. Right now, we have more pressing concerns.” his eyes flashed in anger.

“Thea, I don't think you have the right to speak on this. If she's unwell, it's your Cawsal blood that's poisoned her. We can only be grateful that it wasn’t Cam or the twins. They can still fulfil their destiny on the High Council and in Thena.” he spat his words at me, and Kiron's head snapped up.

“I can give Thea something to help her for now. There is a Healer in Donic village. He's part of the Healer and wisewomen hub. We should be able to trust him. I'll see if we pass close to the village on our way.” He turned and went to the privacy screen and tapped on it.

Too late, I saw the hand move towards me, but Cam blocked it and was thrown onto the twins by the blow.

“Rush!” I cried in shock and went to the twins. They were awake now and beginning to cry as Cam rolled off and turned to face them.

“Edi, Jami, are you OK?” I asked as Cam stood up. Kneeling beside them, I began to check them over.

“Cam, are you OK?” I asked as I felt him standing close beside me. I didn't know where Rush was and didn't care right now. My children needed my attention and reassurance.

“What's happened?” Drawn back to us by the disruption, Kiron rose from his seat at the front.

“Cam, the stupid, clumsy boy, fell on the twins.” snapped Rush, glaring at Cam and I, daring us to contradict him.

“Are they OK, Thea?” Kiron asked as he moved closer.

“I think so, just a little shaken. No harm done,” I said.

“They're attention seeking. Ignore them. There’s nothing wrong with them.” growled Rush as his fingers clawed into my shoulder.

“Cam, are you OK,” Kiron asked, looking directly at him. Cam nodded. He’d seen enough of Rush's temper and knew to keep quiet and out of the way at home. Here, we had no choice but to weather the storm and hope it passed.

“The movement of the conveyance can take us off guard at times, can’t it?” Kiron said kindly, then he looked at the twins and me. “How about the twins?”

“They'll be OK.” Rush's fingers dug further into my shoulder painfully, and I knew I couldn't say any more. Kiron’s expression was unreadable as he looked at Rush’s hand on my shoulder, and the pressure released.

A moment passed before Kiron spoke again.

“It seems that we will pass close to Donic village. I've told Frodel that Elia's been taken ill. She needs the help of a Healer with more equipment than I have with me. It's partly correct. I only have emergency equipment with me. It's all I dared take without raising suspicion.” He looked at us. I stood and faced him, not caring that Rush was behind me. Taking Cam's hand, I squeezed it.

“Thank you, Kiron, I understand. It’s fortunate the Fates are shining on us. The Gods are indeed Singular in their favour towards us today.” I smiled, although it was the last thing I felt like doing.

“Indeed, Thea, we are fortunate.” he turned to Elia and crouched again beside her. He felt her pulse and touched her forehead before looking up. “she's a little cold. Can we find a blanket for her?” Cam immediately passed over a blanket, and Kiron wrapped it snuggly around her.

“Is she OK?” I was afraid to ask, but I had to know.

“I think so. If she doesn't rouse shortly, I'll try to rouse her,” he said. *My poor Elia looked deathly pale lying there. She was so thin, too; why hadn't I noticed that before? I was sure she wasn't so thin before we left. Why hadn't I noticed she was getting thinner? Was I so wrapped up in other things I had forgotten my children? Am I failing to be a good mother? What of the twins? Have I missed something there, too?* I turned and sat between them in the seat Cam had vacated, putting an arm round each one and pulling them close.

“That was a bit of a shock, wasn't it? Are you OK?” I said.

“Cam's heavy. He sat on my hand and squashed it flat,” Edi said, holding his hand as if it was fragile. It looked perfectly normal, but I kissed it to make it better.

“Cam's a big lump. He banged my head on the window and did it on purpose. Now my head hurts a lot,” grumbled Jami. He’s a complainer, but I kiss his head and hug them both.

“Poor Cam, he didn't mean to land on you. He lost his balance when the conveyance turned suddenly. He's much bigger than you because he's older. He’s not a big lump, Jami, that's a bit harsh, don't you think?”

“He did it on purpose,” Jami said sulkily, his face grimacing. “Now my head's banged and hurts.” I have to look away. He looks so like his father when he doesn't get his way.

“I don't think he did. He's very fond of you both and wouldn't hurt you on purpose. You know that,” I said gently.

“He did so...” his petulant voice threatened tears.

“Jami, I'm sorry if I knocked your head. I didn't mean to.” Cam said, crouching before the twins. “Where does it hurt?” Jami rubbed his hand all over the back of his head.

“All over,” he said. Cam gently put his hand on Jami's head and stroked it.

“There, is that better?”

“A bit,” mumbled Jami, but I could see that the crisis was past. Cam continued to surprise me.

"Edi, I'm sorry I squished your hand," he rubbed Edi's hand and then Jami's head again. "There, all better now." *When did Cam become so good with the twins? I felt a swell of pride.*

"I can sit with the boys if you want to sit with Elia," he said as he stood. We changed places, but as I was about to sit, Kiron stopped me, looking over my shoulder as he did so, and I guessed he was looking for Rush.

"Is everything OK, the boys, OK?" he asked, his eyes full of concern.

"Yes, we're all OK. I was going to sit with Elia, will she be alright? I don't know how to help her." he looked at me, then looked away as he stepped before me to crouch beside Elia. He puts his hand on her forehead for a moment before taking her wrist and feeling for her pulse again.

"She's strong. We should try and rouse her." He began to rub her hands, first and then the other, as Cam had done. Then he took each foot, gently slipping off her boots one by one. Kiron began gently rubbing each foot in turn before returning to her hands. He repeated this pattern several times before her eyes started to flutter. As he continued to rub her hands and feet, he said, "Elia, return to us. You are needed and loved here. It isn't your time."

"Donic, Petia." Her voice seemed far away, thin like a reed. She went quiet again and seemed to slip back into that silent place. Kiron rubbed her hands and feet rhythmically, speaking the same words at the end of each cycle. After the third cycle, her eyelids fluttered and then open.

"Cam?" she said, looking round. "Amillia?" her eyes widen with horror. "I… did I drop her? Is she all right? Where is she?" she looked around in panic.

"Elia, it's OK. Amillia is fine. She's in her carrier. Are you OK?" Assisted by Kiron, she slowly rose to a sitting position.

“I'm OK. I had a weird dream. It felt like we were going through a very dark place but heading towards somewhere lighter. Has something happened?” she looks at our faces. “Just tell me, please,” she says with a hint of exasperation. I knew she hated to be protected. She was so independent.

“Well, we hope we're heading towards a place where we can rest a little while before the final part of the journey,” I said to her.

“OK, I guess maybe that's what the dreams meant then.” she said, “I just thought, well, never mind,” She tucked her hands under the blanket.

“Is anyone hungry? I think there are still a few treats left in the hamper,” I said, changing the subject. Food was always a good distraction for the children.

“Yes,” chorused the twins and Cam together. We all laughed. It was a welcome relief from the tension a few minutes ago. Pulling out the hamper, I shared the last of the treats. *At least there was enough for the children to have something. Elia took a small biscuit and nibbled on it without enthusiasm. I watched her for a minute. It felt like she was going through the motions of eating because it was expected. She didn’t want to draw attention to herself. We adults would have to wait a little longer. I hoped it wouldn’t be too long before we arrived in Donic*. As I looked away, I saw her discretely passing the biscuit to Cam from the corner of my eye.

Message from Discovery to Councillor Wiklon
Donic.

Message from Councillor Wiklon to Captain of Pollo Guard
Fugitives heading to Donic, advise Watchers. Permanent authorised.

Message from Captain of Pollo Guard to Councillor Wiklon

Confirm permanent.

Message from Councillor Wiklon to Captain of Pollo Guard

Confirmed permanent.

47

Amelie

The climb through the mountains was challenging. Pain shot through my feet with every step as the boots rubbed blisters upon blisters. My leg muscles screamed at the unaccustomed exercise, and my shoulders ached from the weight of my pack. *I felt so unfit as I puffed along behind the two youngsters.* Millie walked ahead with determination, each step steady and even. *Did she have blisters? I hoped not. She was chatting with Kayde, and I was happy for her. At least it would bring a little distraction from everything.*

"Kayde, how much longer before we can stop and rest?" I gasped. "Please say we can rest soon." *I really didn't know how much longer I could keep going.*

"There's a little way to go, there is," he called over his shoulder. He was like a mountain ghoastil. Ghoastils seem to float across impossible rock faces like ghosts, hence the name. A ghoastil has mottled grey fur that blends with the rocky crags around us, camouflaging them until they move. Then I have a thought. If they were camouflaged and moved fast over the rocks, there must be a predator... by the Gods, I hope we don't meet that predator.

I stumbled on behind Kayde until we crested the top of the mountain and saw the valley opening out before us. It was beautiful. I'd barely noticed the scenery, with my eyes focused on the ground before me. Finally, Kayde paused, and I caught up with them. Breathless, I took in the view. The valley below had farms dotted amongst fields, some of which had crops, others grazing animals. On the valley sides, there were deep gashes. *Mines perhaps? Where were we heading?* I was about to ask, but Millie got there first.

"Are we heading to one of those mines?" she asks, hopefully.

"Yes, but not one you can see, it isn't." his face split into a broad grin at our puzzled faces.

"How much further?" she asked. I could now see how tired she was and wondered if she had blisters or sore muscles, too.

"Not far. We can stop soon, we can." he began walking down the mountainside, seeming to hop from rock to rock. Millie went next, carefully following Kayde, trying not to slip on the loose stones. It was a rough track, and I placed each foot down hesitantly, trying not to cry out. I was sure we must be following a ghoastil track. Focusing on the ground before me, I lost sight of Kayde until I looked up and realised, he wasn't there. Millie was standing on the path beside a bush, smiling at me.

"Kayde? Where's Kayde?" I cried out. Then his head popped up from behind the bush on the right. *Oh!* I felt my face grow warm, and then I saw his mischievous grin and felt foolish.

"We're here, we are," he said before disappearing again. Millie followed him behind the bush. I tried to hurry the last few steps but was so afraid of falling that I could barely do more than a slow walk. When I finally stepped around the bush, I saw a concealed mine entrance.

Kade grinned as I came inside the entrance.

"I have the fire ready to make tea. I have." he gestured to a fire neatly laid with a structure over it holding a pan of water. The fire was burning, but no smoke rose that could give us away. I was too tired to ask why and gratefully sank to the floor beside Mille. Kayden poured the water into the pot to infuse the tea before pouring it into our mugs. It was warm and soothing, and

I felt my muscles easing as the warmth spread through my body. He passed around food, cheese, bread and fruit, and we ate hungrily.

"How are your feet?" he said, looking at us both. Millie spoke first.

"A bit sore, but OK, I think," she said. I wondered if she was trying to be kind because the boots were borrowed.

"I have a few blisters and some sore places. But I'll be OK," I said as brightly as I could. Kayde began rummaging in his pack until he found what he wanted. Carefully, he unlaced and removed my boots with practised ease. Then he removed both pairs of my socks, revealing my feet. Thank goodness there wasn't an overwhelming stink rising from them. The skin had deep indentations from the pattern of the socks and the bootlaces. Bulging blisters bubble around my toes, and a large one around the back of my heel. Even the soles of my feet had deep blisters. Kayde gently tended to the blisters and applied a balm before slipping on a pair of silver silk socks of such fine weave. Finally, he replaced the thick socks and pushed my feet back into my boots, lacing them firmly.

"The silver socks help with healing; they will. Protect your feet, they do," he said. Then he turned to Millie, who meekly stretched out her legs. *I couldn't believe how much better my feet felt, although I had yet to stand on them.* Millie didn't have as many blisters as I had, for which I was grateful. Kayde worked quickly, and Millie soon pulled her socks back on and relaced her boots. My blisters were nowhere near as tender as they had been, and when I cautiously stood, I was pleasantly surprised.

"Kayde, how did you guess, and where did you learn such Healing?" I asked. He smiled as he doused the fire. Then, he collected and rinsed the mugs before drying them and returning them to his pack.

“I've been travelling these parts since I was tiny I 'ave. Always my job to help Mothie and Porthie. Only when I could lead those wanting to journey on foot and take care of them could I become a leader myself.” he smiled shyly at us. “Now, we should keep moving for a while longer, we should. We can reach the village near the mine before nightfall, we can. Dangerous by night, it is. Animals hunt at night, hunt people too, they do.”

“What animals?” asked Millie as she stood and shouldered her pack before turning to help me with mine.

“Well, there are the great bears, there are. The great brown and less common great gold bear. Packs of lufel (creatures somewhere between a wolf and a cat, green-grey stripes with glowing red eyes). Lufel can climb trees and hunt like a wolf. Know them if you see them, you will, but few see them and live.” I gave a little shiver.

“What do they sound like?” asked Millie.

“It's an eerie sound like the cry of a vixen but more of a howl. The first time you hear it, you will think someone is being torn limb from limb.”

“Oh wow,” she said. “I'd love to hear it, but perhaps somewhere safe, not out here.” He shook his head slightly, then turned towards the entrance. He gestured for us to wait while he checked to see if it was safe.

Our journey continued down the mountainside and across the valley below. A gorge was hidden at the far side, and we were heading towards it. I felt exposed as we crossed the fields. Even though farmers were working their land, it still felt very exposed. Walking on the flat was much easier, which was a relief, and we crossed the valley floor with impressive speed. The sun was lower in the sky now, and farmers were finishing their day. They called to each other as they returned to their farmhouses. Lights were beginning to appear in windows, welcoming them home. Kayde kept up the pressure, and we hurried along as best we could. *Whatever the salve on my feet was, it had worked wonders, along with the silver silk socks.*

My mind strayed to Rush. H*ow was their journey going? Would we meet them at our destination*? I still didn't know, but I hoped so. The evening fragrance from the hyacintias and moon flowers was powerful. I inhaled deeply, appreciating their scent. The hyacintias glowed in shades of yellow and green alongside the track. Fields of moon flowers were beginning to open, ready to greet their namesake as it rose. Stunning glossy black petals and silvery centres glistened across the fields, resembling a great dark lake, its waves gently ebbing and flowing with silvery highlights. I was growing tired and needed to catch my breath for a moment. I wanted a sip of the sweet mountain water Kayde was carrying, but with his warning of dangerous animals, I wondered if I dared ask. He must have read my mind because as we reached the end of the village near the gorge, he stopped. Swinging his bag off his shoulders, he pulled out the water and passed it to us. We both drank deeply before passing it back.

"We go through the gorge, then the village will be there, it will," he said smiling, "in the gorge, we go with no stops. Not safe in the gorge, it isn't," he said, looking at each of us in turn. He didn't need to warn us twice. We understood after his talk about the animals who prowl by night. But then he added.

"There are bad men in the mountains at night, bad men," he emphasised. A shiver went down my spine. We didn't need any bad men when we were so close. As we walked into the gorge, I tried to focus on the lovely soft bed I was looking forward to. The light was failing now, and shadows took the shape of wild animals and evil men. I jumped at every noise, my heart racing. Every stone we disturbed as we walked echoed like a rockfall, making me even more anxious. We walked in single file along the narrow track. Kayde was in front, Millie in the middle (to keep her safe), and I was at the back.

It was a relief when we saw the opening ahead of us and emerged into another smaller valley surrounded by a wall of mountains. At the foot of the mountains ahead of us was a small village.

"Iltanic village." he smiled, pointing ahead. "Those who wait for you will be there, they will." I hoped he was right and they weren't watchers.

"Are there watchers?" Millie asked.

"No watchers here, there aren't. Farmers signal if there are," he said. "We rarely see them here, but we know what to do. They won't find those who don't want to be found, they won't," he said proudly as we walked along a broad track towards the village. It wasn't a big village, but as we drew closer, I saw more houses than I'd first thought. They bloomed around the central ring of houses in small circular groups. From what I'd read of them, it was a typical mountain village in Cawsal. Daylight had faded, and seeing the track ahead became more difficult. Millie and I stumbled as we hurried after Kayde.

The houses were simple, perhaps just a few rooms inside, but they looked cosy with warm glowing lights in the windows. As we passed the first cluster, I caught the most delicious aromas, and my stomach growled in response. I hoped there would be something to eat when we arrived. Millie grinned wearily at me. I could see the same thought on her face. Kayde entered the centre circle of houses and walked around the edge. He seemed well-known here, judging by the smiles and waves he received. We took a path between two houses and arrived at another circle of houses hidden from sight. There were only five houses, and a woman waited at the door of the second one on the left. She waved at Kayde, who waved back, but they said nothing until we reached her doorstep. Opening her arms wide, she welcomed us into her house, closing the door firmly behind her and bolting it. Kayde walked through the back of the house and opened a hidden door on the right. This took us into a tunnel with swaying lights hung from the ceiling and a slightly musty smell. At the end was another door which opened into a cosy room. There were comfortable chairs near the fire on one side and a table set for dinner on the other. The most mouthwatering smell was coming from the table, and I longed to run over and take up a spoon. Millie and I stood near the comfortable chairs, uncertain what was happening.

"Welcome, welcome to my home. I'm Dorca. Put your packs and coats down here and come to the table. You must be hungry, you must." she said.

"I'm..." I began, but she interrupted.

"I'll call you Alana and Betha. Dangerous to know too much, it is. So, Alana and Betha, please join me," she smiled. I looked at Millie, and she grinned.

"Come, Betha," I said, returning her grin. Gratefully, we sat at the table, and Dorca ladled stew into our bowls and encouraged us to take some bread. She poured mugs of light ale that tasted like honey, sweet and warming. It was heaven. We ate and drank until we were satisfied. After our meal, Dorca showed us into comfortable rooms where, finally, we could wash and climb into soft, warm beds. I remembered nothing more of the room that night, drifting into a deep, dreamless sleep as soon as I lay down.

Message from Councillor Wiklon to Discovery
Guard on way. Meet H Watcher.

Message from Councillor Wiklon to Councillor Maxim
fugitive 3 arriving Donic. permanent confirmed.

Message from Councillor Maxim to Councillor Wiklon
Permanent needs evidence. Critical.

48

Thea

It was getting dark as we arrived in Donic. The conveyance drew up alongside a long, low building with a light outside shrouded by a red cover, indicating it was a hospital. I watched the door open, and a wisewoman in her red uniform emerged. She was tall and thin with a severe face. Frodel and Malic were the first to leave the conveyance, which swayed gently as Kiron followed. After exchanging a few words with them, Kiron approached the wisewoman and began an earnest conversation, glancing our way several times. The twins had woken up and were getting restless. I hoped it wouldn't be long before we could let them out. They'd been so good, sleeping much of the journey. Unfortunately, it also meant that while we were all exhausted, they were full of energy. I gritted my teeth as I heard Rush snap at them.

I saw Kiron return accompanied by the wisewoman who looked like she had a bad smell under her nose. Kiron opened the door and asked me to join them.

"Thea, this is Mother Kron. She's willing to allow Elia and yourself into the hospital but not the rest of the family. The Healer is away at present and due to return shortly. He may know where we can stay tonight." *I'm relieved Mother Kron will see Elia.* I stepped back into the conveyance.

"Rush, the wise woman will see Elia, but the rest of you must remain here. I'll go with Elia. Cam, will you look after the twins?" Cam nodded.

"I'll stay with Rush and Cam to make the arrangements. You know what information Mother Kron needs and can talk with the Healer when he arrives." Kiron said as I got out, and a moment later, a pale Elia joined me. She breathed deeply in the night air, brightened a little, and smiled at me.

"Elia, this is Mother Kron. We're going with her to talk about these episodes." I smiled reassuringly at her.

"Mother Kron, this is my daughter Elia. Thank you for agreeing to see her." I held out my arm, but her arm remained firmly by her side, and I dropped it again. *So, it would be like that, I thought. I hoped we were doing the right thing.*

"Follow me." Mother Kron said curtly before turning with a sniff and leading us towards the hospital. I glanced back at Kiron, who smiled encouragingly. Then, taking Elia's hand, we followed Mother Kron.

It was bright inside, and I winced as my eyes adjusted. We were in a short corridor with a red floor and pure white walls. We passed two red doors before reaching another at the end, which Mother Kron pushed open. She held it as we walked through. She then bustled past in a waft of antiseptic and lavender. She led us down the corridor and stopped by the third red door on the left. Taking a set of keys from her pocket, she selected one, inserted it into the lock, turned it, and pushed the door open. We followed her into a consultation room with a desk and chairs on one side and an examination bed on the other. She closed the door behind us and turned the key. I looked around in alarm and saw a nasty smile stretch across her face as she walked towards us.

"So, you think you can arrive late and expect me to tend to your spoilt child," she said. "You Thenans are all the same. But you aren't in Thena now, and I don't have to bow to your airs and graces. This is Cawsal, and we do things differently. I agreed to see you because Kiron is well respected here despite being from Pollo and on the High Council. He has always supported the wisewomen." she stood behind the desk, and we moved to the two seats in front.

"Mother Kron, please, I beg you to listen to what I say before judging us too harshly..." I began, but she interrupted.

"Elia, Kiron says you are having fainting fits. Have you been eating properly or skipping meals to lose weight?" Elia turned pink with embarrassment and looked at me in alarm.

"It's OK, Elia, just tell Mother Kron what's been happening." she looked uncertain but turned back to Mother Kron, sitting erect opposite us, a superior air oozing from her.

"Um, I don't remember when they started, but it's been going on a long time."

"What did your Healer say?" said Mother Kron.

"Nothing, I…I didn't tell him. I haven't told anyone about them. Cam, my brother knows because he found out when he saw it happen years ago." My heart ached for her, and I felt so sad she hadn't been able to come to me.

"Why didn't you tell anyone?"

"I… er, I thought I'd be in trouble."

"And why would you be in trouble? Because you're starving yourself, perhaps? I know about you girls who always want to look like sticks," she said unpleasantly. Elia's embarrassment deepened, and she turned to me.

"I didn't, I didn't. It wasn't like that. It wasn't like that," the anguish in her eyes was so painful to see. I looked over at this hateful woman with disgust. *How dare she torment my child like this?* Standing, I looked over at her.

"Mother Kron, if you had no intention of helping us, why did you invite us in? I think now is the time for us to leave if you'd be so kind as to unlock the door. We will not trouble you further." Mother Kron remained seated with that hateful smile on her face.

"Thea, I have no intention of helping a spoilt child who is fainting for lack of food. She has just admitted that's the problem. It's clear on her face for any mother who takes the time to look at their child." The barb struck like a knife through my heart.

"Who do you think you are, telling me how to raise my children? You have no idea what you're talking about. You make judgements without understanding the facts. Insulting my daughter and I, do you know who I am?" It wasn't something I'd planned to discuss, but it seemed the only thing that might persuade her to help. I couldn't have been more wrong.

"Oh yes, I know who you are. You're the wife of Rush, son of Maxim, head of the hated High Council. Your kind has been the cause of so much pain and suffering to Cawsal. I do not intend to help you or your spoilt child. You can stay here until the watchers come for you. They can have you and your spawn." she spat. My blood boiled, and I turned on her; rounding the table, I stood over her. Putting my hand under her chin, I forced her to look up at me and spat my words into her face.

"My father is the Cawsal Industrial Councillor to the High Council. My cousin is the Cawsal Militaria Councillor. I'm sure both will be pleased to know how kindly you received us." She looked at me with a new understanding and fear in her eyes. My blood was boiling. I was losing control, and a new energy began pulsing through my veins as I hissed.

"Give me the key." at that moment, a noise from my left distracted me, and I saw Elia collapse in her chair and slide to the ground as her body shook.

My rage evaporated, and I stepped back, removing my hand from under Mother Kron's chin. There were spots of blood where my fingernails had pierced her skin and an odd look on her face. Quickly, I began moving the chairs away, then eased Elia's body from the desk so she couldn't hurt herself. Feeling movement beside me, I saw Mother Kron reaching for Elia's hand and touching her forehead.

"I'm sorry, I have misjudged you. May I examine Elia?" she asked, her voice soft now. I moved back and let her examine Elia. The adrenaline was still coursing through my blood, but a deep fear had replaced the rage. Elia hadn't shaken like this before. It seemed to be getting worse each time now. Mother Kron turned to me, her face full of concern.

"We should get her to the bed as soon as we can once the shaking has eased." She squatted, holding Elia's head gently as her body shook, but the intensity slowed. I watched her give a final shake before lying still. For one horrible moment, I wondered if she had died; there was no movement from her chest. Then she took a ragged breath, and I let out the breath I'd been holding.

"Thea, can you support her legs and lower body? I'll take the upper part and her head. Together, we can lift her to the bed." Gently, I slipped my arms under her slight body, and Mother Kron did the same. Carefully, we lifted Elia, transferred her to the bed, and turned her onto her side.

Mother Kron's hands moved swiftly along Elia's body, checking her limbs. Then she moved to her head, her hands hovering above Elia's hair and moving around its shape. I'd never seen any Healer or wisewoman do that before and asked what she was doing.

"I can feel her energy inside. It's a gift from the God Sange, God of Healers and life." she said, "Those with gifts have an energy I can feel. Sometimes I can help ease the distress of energies. Elia is a dreamer. Did you know?" she looked at me with a new respect that had been absent earlier.

"We were coming to the same conclusion. Elia and her brother had guessed some time ago. As she said, they concealed it from me. The reasons are too complicated to go into."

"I understand. To be a dreamer in Thena would not be accepted as it is here, I think," she said sadly. "I'll do what I can. Concealing her abilities for so long has distressed her spiritual energy and reduced its ability to return after a vision, it has." She placed her hands over Elia's forehead, closing her eyes, which fluttered under their lids. Now lying still, Elia seemed to take a deep breath and sigh. Her face had lost the earlier anguish and now had its usual serene expression. Mother Kron stood over Elia for a few minutes, motionless. Her expression twitched as if trying to resolve a complicated puzzle. Eventually, she lowered her hands and opened her eyes.

"I've done as much as I can. Elia is calmer now, she is."

"Yes, she's looking more comfortable now. Thank you," I said. "How long will she need to be here? We're… we're on our way to stay with friends." *I hoped I was convincing enough.*

"It would be better if she remains here for the next few hours. When will you continue your journey?"

"I'm not sure. My husband and Kiron were going to look for food. We planned to continue our journey and arrive later this evening."

"Expected tonight, are you?" she asked as she stood beside Elia.

"We had some unanticipated delays, so we are later than we hoped." It was close enough to the truth, at least. My mouth was getting so dry now, and I longed for coffee, tea or anything. It had been so long since we last had vittals.

"Is there somewhere I can find a drink? Some water, perhaps?" I asked. "Elia will be thirsty when she wakes, too,"

"We have a small facility for staff, but as it's the end of the day, I'm sure nobody will mind if I make you a drink. Would tea be acceptable?" she asked, stepping towards the door. "Please remain close by Elia. If she wakes, encourage her to remain lying on the bed until I return." Gliding smoothly to the door, she slipped the key from her pocket and unlocked it. She closed the door behind her, but this time, it remained unlocked, and I immediately felt more relaxed. It was turning out to be a very peculiar day indeed. I wondered how Rush and Kiron were getting on. Had they found a place to stay or food? I hope they have rather than travelling through another night. We can't be too far from our destination. Frodel and Malic must *surely know the destination and route by now*. Even if they were responsible for our encounters with watchers, how do we know they haven't told the watchers our final destination?

While I pondered these things, the door opened, and Mother Kron entered, her footsteps silent as she crossed the floor. She placed two steaming mugs of tea on the desk before coming to look at Elia.

"She's awake now, you know," she said with a smile, looking down at my pale daughter. "Come, child, it's time to wake and sit up. We have much to talk about." she gently placed a hand on Elia's arm. Elia opened her eyes, looking at me before looking up at Mother Kron. Her eyes grew wide, and she began to struggle up.

"It's OK, Elia, it's OK. We're safe here. Mother Kron has been trying to help you. Just sit for a moment." I said, standing in front of her and placing my hands on her thin forearms, crouching to look into her eyes. I could see the fear and pulled her into me, wrapping my arms around her. Poor child. It had been such a difficult time for her. She must be exhausted.

"We're not safe here. We are not safe here. We'll never be safe," she said, tears welling in her eyes. I hugged her tight, her small body shook as she wept. Looking up, I caught Mother Kron moving closer.

"Elia, would you like something to eat or drink? Then you can tell us what you have seen, you can." her face was kindly now, and her voice so gentle, unrecognisable as the woman we first met. Elia looks at her.

"Why are you being nice when you were so mean?" she said through tears. Mother Kron took her face gently, looking deep into her eyes.

"Elia, I'm sorry I didn't understand. Now I can see you have a wonderful gift. I see it now. Can you see mine, I wonder?" Elia looked into her face for the first time, and I saw the moment their eyes met. For a split second, they were motionless before Elia looked away.

"But I don't understand. How can you do that? I can see you have the ability, but how can you show me? I've never had anyone do that before." she said, her voice shaking slightly as the sobs still bubbled up. Then she asked me, "Have you heard of such things?"

"Elia, I only learnt of your ability on this journey. You and Cam hid it so well from me that I didn't know. I've heard of children who can see visions but never met anyone. Cawsal people have long been rumoured to have abilities, but visions are the only ability I know of. As I told you, you've inherited Cawsal blood through me." I don't know what else to say. I felt so inadequate and unprepared. There had been no time to prepare for this discussion.

"I thought I was a freak. Grandma and Gramps said anyone who thinks they can see the future is a freak. They said freaks should be sent away or put to sleep like deformed animals. That's why we didn't say anything after the first time. I was so afraid, and so was Cam." My heart broke as she spoke, and tears tumbled down my cheeks.

"Elia, I'm so sorry you had to go through all that alone. I wish I'd known, but I understand your fears. From now on, both your father and I understand and accept you as you are and love you just as much. I promise I will never put you in such a terrible position again as long as I live." I hugged her tightly, and she wrapped her arms around me, hugging me back.

"Can I see Cam? I want him to know it's OK. That it's OK with you and Father?" her voice held a note of confidence it had lacked earlier.

"You can, but we need to check you're OK first." I turn to Mother Kron. "Do you know why Elia has these episodes? What can we do to help her?" she smiled and led us to the desk where we first sat.

"First things first, Elia, you should have something to eat and a drink. It will give back energy; it will," she smiled. "Now, is it something sweet perhaps or some fruit? what do you like to drink, tea or coffee?" Elia looked at me, and I nodded.

"Well, I like fruit but not honey apples or blue pears and perhaps some tea," she said. She was sitting up in the chair formally as I'd taught her. Her dark coat and trousers were crumpled, as were mine, but their tailored origins still show.

"Now I think we have some dewy plantains and some pink figs. What do you think?" Elia's eyes lit up at the mention of pink figs; she loved them, but they were an expensive delicacy in Thena.

"I'd love a pink fig," she said with a big grin, "they're delicious. We don't have them very often at home." Mother Kron smiled.

"They grow here in the mountains where the pure sun and mountain dew bring the sweetness. Would you like some fig leaf tea to go with it?"

"I've never had fig leaf tea. What does it taste like?"

"It tastes a little like a sharp fig, it does. I prefer coffee to drink, though, I do," she said with a wink.

"I think I'll have coffee then," Elia said, giving a conspiratorial wink back. I couldn't believe how much she had brightened with just a few minutes of understanding and acceptance.

"I'll be just a few minutes, I will." Mother Kron said. I saw the moment of fear cross Elia's face as the door closed and watched it disappear when the lock didn't click.

"Mother Kron is different now, isn't she? She wasn't very nice when we arrived."

"I'm glad you sense that too," I said, and I was. Somehow, I knew we were safe with Mother Kron.

"Can I tell you the vision I had? It's important?" she said. I put my hand on hers.

"Do you think it affects us here in the hospital?"

"I think so. Someone will give us away, but I don't think it's Mother Kron. I..." She stopped as the door opened, and Mother Kron appeared carrying a steaming mug and a plate with two pink figs. She put the mug and plate before Elia and returned to her seat.

"There you go. That should bring back your energy. It is best to eat something after you have a vision. Something sweet has the best properties to revive your spirit."

"Mother Kron, we've just met, but I must ask you something." I hesitated. *Did I want to begin this? Can we trust this woman? Had we any choice?* I made a split decision and hoped it was the right one.

"We are in something of a difficult situation."

"I guessed that might be the case, I did. Hiding from watchers perhaps, you are?" she said.

"Yes,"

"Follow you here, did they?"

"I don't know, but we may have someone with us who's leaving a trail for them."

"I see." she laced her fingers together, resting her arms on the table. "You are heading to Iltanic, I think, are you?" I looked up in surprise. *I hadn't expected her to know that.* "there've been many fleeing from AMP, there have. You should leave now you should. Not safe here, not safe it isn't."

"I knew it wasn't safe!" cried Elia.

"Yes, my child, you're correct. What did your vision say exactly? Important to keep you safe." Elia's eyes turned to me questioningly, and I nodded.

"I saw us here. A man came with two others. I think one was a Healer. They, they... hurt Mother, and they were coming to hurt me when it went black." Mother Kron turned and locked eyes with me. *I could hear her voice clearly in my head, saying what I had guessed. Elia had seen her own death in the vision.* She stood and nodded at me. *I had no idea such a thing was possible, but there was no time to reflect on the experience because she began speaking.*

"We must leave immediately. Our Healer, Oldron, is due back shortly, he is. Best if you aren't here, it is." She moved so fast to reach the door that I scarcely saw her move. We follow her deeper into the hospital, travelling down corridors and through locked doors before she stops and turns to us.

"We're far away from where the Healer will go. Safe for now, we are. Where are your family?"

"My boys are with my husband. Our Healer, Kiron, went into the village looking for food and perhaps drivers." My voice was shaky. *I felt panic rising. Were my boys safe? What about Kiron? Was a watcher here already?*

"Will you trust me?" she asked. *I don't know, but what choice do we have?* So, I said yes.

"I know someone who can help you, I do. As Elia's vision saw men, I will call on a woman I know. She's helped those seeking refuge in the past, she has. She can be trusted. May I leave you here? You should be safe. It's a part of the hospital not used at the moment; it is. It has been closed for new equipment, it has. The Healer has no reason to come down here. I'll give you two keys. One to lock or unlock the door we came through. The second will open the door on the other side that goes into an alley behind the hospital. There are places you could hide if you needed to, there are. You should be safe here, I think." she said, fiddling with her sizeable key ring. Selecting two keys, she separated them and passed them to me. She repeated her instructions before returning to the door we entered through. We heard it lock behind her.

We looked at each other, then looked around the room. It had probably served as a ward at some time. Bays were on each side, but no beds, curtains or other furniture now. The floors were red and dirty, and the walls were probably grey but very dirty. There wasn't even a chair or table to sit on, which was a shame. I hoped Mother Kron wouldn't be too long. Elia decided the usual rules didn't apply and sat on the floor with her back against the wall by the far door. She dug into her pocket and pulled out a small package wrapped in a handkerchief. With a grin, she showed me one of the pink figs.

"I couldn't leave them both behind," she said. With a sigh, I joined her and sank to the floor. Leaning against the wall, I accepted a small piece of the pink fig.

Message from Discovery to Councillor Wiklon
Arrived Donic, seeking Health Watcher.

Message from Councillor Wiklon to Captain of Pollo Guard
Conveyance at Donic Hospital. Send Guard. Permanent authorised. Discovery and H Watch in area.

Message from Captain of Pollo Guard to Councillor Wiklon
Confirm permanent.

Message from Councillor Wiklon to Captain of Pollo Guard
Permanent confirmed.

49

Betha/Millie

Drowsily, I stretched, and as I did so, I sensed something wasn't right. With a start, I remembered where we were and sat up. Looking around, I took in the empty bed where Amelie had slept and felt a rush of panic. Then I saw she was already dressed and brushing her hair by the looking glass.

"Morning," I said, yawning, stretching, then drawing the bedcovers around me again and lying back down. She smiled.

"Morning, sleepy Betha. It's time for you to rise and dress. The sun is up, and I smell coffee," she said.

"Oh, coffee," I groaned. "I'd die for a good cup of coffee." Reluctantly, I threw back the covers, then gave a sheepish smile when I realised I'd only removed the outer layer of my clothes and slept in the rest. *Ugh, the state of my clothes.* I wish I'd removed my clothes and folded or hung them. *How did Amelie manage to look so smart?* Her clothes looked as if they had been pressed. Did I miss something last night?

"How do you keep your clothes so clean and pressed?" I tried to brush off the worst of the dust and dirt from my trousers.

"A trick from my performing days when I was travelling. Always brush your clothes off at night and lay them out under your bedding before you go to sleep." she grinned and helped me brush off the dust and dirt from the back of my clothes.

"There, much better. Now, take the brush and run it through your hair. That needs some work before it looks like its normal gorgeous self." I pulled the brush through my hair until every knot had gone. It looked much better. Gathering it up in my hands and pulling it behind my head, I considered how it changed the shape of my face. *Would short hair look good on me? It would be much easier to manage, I thought.*

"You look beautiful," Amelie said, standing before me. She gave me a quick hug, then straightened my bed. "Try to leave your room as you'd like to find it. You'll either appreciate your attentiveness later, or the maid will when she changes the bed." she winked.

We followed the smell of coffee to the kitchen, where we found Kayde and Dorca deep in conversation. They looked up as we came in.

"Did you sleep well?" Dorca asked, "Would you like some coffee and something to eat?"

"Yes, we did, and definitely yes to coffee for both of us," Amelie said.

"I'm right pleased I am. I'll pour your coffee. I have barley porridge or fresh eggs for breakfast. What would you like?" she poured dark coffee from a large black pot on the stove. The aroma was heavenly, and she brought over the two steaming mugs, placing them on the table before us. I said I'd like porridge, and so did Amelie. Soon, we were dipping our spoons into large bowls of porridge with sweet honey apple syrup poured over the top. I've never had honey apple syrup before, but honey apples were a lovely autumn treat at home. After trying a little, I poured a generous measure over my porridge, telling Dorca how delicious it was.

"I'm glad you like it, I am." Dorca said with pleasure, "We press the honey apples ourselves each year to make the syrup." Kayde looked up.

"After you've finished your vittals, we must talk. There are things to finalise." He stood, went to the stove, and poured another mug of coffee. “Thank you, Dorca, it's excellent coffee.” he gave her a cheeky grin.

“Young man, you should ask first, you should,” she said, tapping his head fondly. Grinning, he ducked away.

After breakfast, Kayde led us to a cosy parlour at the back of the house and shut the door. It was easy to forget that we were the same age as he went through everything with us meticulously. The primary decision was whether to wait for my family or continue on our own. I hoped Amelie would agree to wait a few days. I missed Mother and the children. I couldn’t think of going on without them. *Were we safe here? Would it be OK for us to stay? Kayde said we weren’t restricted to our room and could leave the house, but the risk was our own. They couldn’t be sure there were no spies or watchers here. That was easy. I didn’t want to go outside if it meant I might meet a watcher. I've had enough of running.* Amelie decided we would wait for two days, then go on. There would be more decisions to make, but we could delay those for now. Kayde went to tell Dorca, returning with more coffee and some news.

“A fancy conveyance arrived in Donic last night. It's a village not far from here. Seen outside the hospital, it was. The wisewoman met two women and went into the hospital with her, they did. Two men were asking about food and drivers to the mountains. Two others left the village and came back with another they did. Rumour is he might be a watcher.” A cold chill ran down my spine.

“Do you know who the men were? Surely that conveyance must be what Rush and Thea were travelling in?” Amelie said, sitting forward, clasping her hands together. *I hoped it was my family, but the thought of a watcher so close was terrifying. I was so afraid of what he might do to them or us.*

"One of the men who came back may be the Healer. The wisewoman is one of us, but it's unclear where the Healer's loyalties lie."

"What can we do?" Amelie asked.

"I don't know. Dorca asked me to stay here until we know more. She's sending word to my family so they don't worry." All at once, he was a boy again, not the man he'd seemed to be earlier.

For the rest of the day, we remain in the back parlour. Dorca and Kayde kept us supplied with food and drink. Dorca was an excellent cook, and the fresh fruit was lovely, juicy, and sweeter than I'd ever tasted in Thena. It wasn't until the evening, when we were in the kitchen for our meal, that someone knocked at the door. As Dorca went to see who was calling so late in the evening, we returned to the parlour with Kayde. We could hear voices, two men talking with Dorca. Eventually, she appeared with a worried look on her face. She explained that callers had brought further news from Donic. It was believed that the men asking about food and drivers were from the conveyance. They'd mentioned a baby, two young children, older children, and three adults needing shelter. *That had to be my family,* I thought. Dorca said someone would make contact with them and get them to safety. The two men who met with the Healer were definitely from the South, Pollo or Thena (the accents were similar). These three men were believed to be watchers or spies. I went cold at the thought. We talked for a while before returning to the kitchen and our meal.

50

Thea

We waited for a long time, growing numb and uncomfortable on the cold floor. We got up when we could bear it no longer and walked a little, easing our stiff muscles and trying to keep ourselves warm before sinking back down again. When Mother Kron returned, she looked worried. The Healer had returned with two men from the South. From the descriptions she gave, they must be Frodel and Malic. She said there had been rumours that the Healer could be a spy for some time. Until now, there has been no confirmed connection between the Anti-Modernisation Pact (AMP) and Cawsal. Now, it was confirmed action must be taken. Spies were usually executed or made to disappear. The Legal Octon should judge high-profile spies, but with a corrupt Legal Octon, the highest-ranked official not associated with AMP may decide within the district. She asked whether Rush might be able to assist. I couldn't answer. She would have to speak with Rush. Another problem was that Oldron was the only local Healer, and they needed a Healer. He would need to be replaced. For now, it has been decided to continue close observation. There was no reason to delay dealing with the other two. They would be executed, I guessed, although I didn't like to think about it. *Suddenly, it all became rather like war, and I was terrified.*

Mother Kron brought a large bag full of clothes with her when she returned. They were more typical of the area and would disguise us for the next part of our journey. The fabrics were simple and felt rough against our pampered skin. We were used to the finest weaves, but at least they were clean and comfortable. Mother Kron asked me to let my hair run loose to be more easily hidden under the hood. Elia's hair was loose, and we wove it into a simple plait falling down her back. She still looked pale, although she had a little more colour than before. We followed Mother Kron from the hospital using a side door. She led us through a series of narrow alleys towards the mountains. It was quiet, and nobody was around, which was a relief. My senses were on high alert for any sounds behind us that would suggest we were being followed, but I could only hear our soft footsteps.

Eventually, Mother Kron stops beside a small dwelling with a simple wooden door. She rapped twice, then twice again. A few moments later, the door opened, and a face appeared, a face I recognised. The woman at the door was my cousin Bogdo's wife, Petia, whom I met months ago at the council dinner. She invited us in, and we entered the hallway, but Mother Kron remained in the doorway. She said a quick farewell and disappeared back along the alley. Petia led us through to a cosy back room. *How much we could trust her? Mother Kron wouldn't have brought us here if it wasn't safe, would she? I thought.*

"Thea, you are most welcome to our humble dwelling, you are," she said softly. Petia was a small, neat woman with long dark hair pulled into a simple plait flowing down her back. When she smiled, her whole face lit up. It was strange how a face that appeared plain could change so much with a smile.

"Thank you, Petia, may I introduce my daughter, Elia. Elia, this is Petia, my cousin Bogdo's wife, Bogdo is Cawsal Militaria

Councillor." Elia shyly offered her arm to Petia, who grasped her elbow warmly.

"Hello, Petia," she said quietly.

"Petia, is Bogdo here?" *I didn't know how much I could trust Bogdo or whether I wanted to see him. I feel so vulnerable.*

"Oh no, never here he isn't. Stays in Thena, he does." she said a little sadly, "don't see him very much now he's on the Council, I don't." While I understood her sadness, I was relieved he wasn't here or expected to return. It made things less complicated.

"How much did Mother Kron tell you of our situation?"

"Told it all, she has," Petia said. "she'll try and find your children and bring them here. Others look for the men. Don't worry, we'll find them, we will. Your father is a great favourite of the people he is. His rise to Industrial Councillor brought prosperity to Cawsal, it did. We are proud to do our small part for you and your family." she said.

It was strange to acknowledge my family connections openly. Two family members on the High Council besides Rush was quite a claim indeed. It had been so long since I'd seen my father. I wondered what he looked like now. Rush had said my father wasn't often at the High Council offices in Thena, preferring to work in Cawsal when he could. Was that intentional to avoid our connection being uncovered? How would he feel if we met? Would he be pleased to see me? It had been a strange meeting with Bogdo. He was distant, initially becoming more open as we spoke. I realised Petia was still talking and tried to tune back to her voice.

"...welcome to stay here you are," she finished.

"I'm sorry, Petia, my mind drifted for a moment. Would you mind repeating what you said?" *how embarrassing to admit I wasn't listening.* Elia looked at me and grinned.

"Petia says we can stay here. There's somewhere to wash and a room where we can sleep," she said. *I was exhausted and smiled gratefully*. Petia offered to prepare a meal for us, but I declined. *I was too tired to eat.* Elia must have felt the same as she nodded in agreement.

"You poor things, you must be exhausted after your journey. I'll show you the room where you can wash and your bedroom, I will. It isn't much, but it's clean. We live a simple life here, we do." She led us down a short corridor and up a steep flight of stairs to the second floor. There were three bedrooms and a bathing room. The bedroom she showed us was simple and comfortable. There was a bed on the left with a pretty blue flowery cover. At the end was a second bed with a matching cover. On the right was a window with a table and looking glass beneath, and next to it, a tall wardrobe where we could put clothes if we had any. Elia sat on the bed at the end of the room until Petia left. Then she slipped off the outer garments Mother Kron gave her and got into bed. She was asleep before I had time to suggest she removed another layer. It wasn't long before I fell asleep, too.

Sometime later, I was aware of a gnawing hunger that woke me. I realised that it had been a long time since we last ate. Glancing over at Elia, I saw she was also stirring. We rose and went downstairs. When we reached the hallway, Petia appeared with a smile.

"Sleep well, did you? Some vittals perhaps now, yes?" she asked.

"Petia, thank you. We did sleep well. Some vittals would be lovely," I replied. *She must have seen the hunger on my face, I thought.*

"Come through, come through," she said, waving us into the kitchen. The delicious aromas of coffee and something spicy assailed our senses. My stomach rumbled loudly, and Elia grinned at me. *It was good to see her smile. She had a better colour now.*

“Come, sit by the fire, sit here,” Petia indicated to the table near the fireplace. The fire was softly crackling in the hearth, giving warmth. *What time was it? I couldn’t see a window to know whether it was day or night.* Were we underground, perhaps? At that moment, Petia brought over two bowls of something steaming. It smelled delicious.

“Here you are. It's just my aromatic vegetable stew, it is. Will you take some bread with it?” She placed the bowls in front of us. I inhaled deeply, closing my eyes with pleasure.

“Yes, please, Petia, some bread would be lovely,” I said, and she disappeared behind us again. I dipped my spoon and tasted the stew. Suddenly, I was overwhelmed by a memory from my childhood. I was sure I'd had this before or something similar. It was a long time ago. My mother cooked it for us, perhaps. I saw her face smiling down at me. It was the first time I'd recalled her face for a very long time. Closing my eyes, I felt tears flooding my eyes. How ridiculous to feel such emotion just from a memory. A tear escaped as Petia approached, and I tried to wipe it away discretely.

“Thea, is everything OK?” she asked tenderly.

“Yes,” I said, my voice almost a squeak. I cleared my throat and tried again. “Yes, just a strong memory of my mother cooking a similar dish. I haven't tasted this since childhood, before my mother died.”

“It's a traditional Cawsal dish. Since your mother was Cawsal, she would know it,” she said. Her voice was gentle and understanding. *How much does she know of my mother? Bogdo was five years older than me and would have known about the accident.*

"My mother was killed in a farming accident when I was twelve. I grew up in Pollo. My memories of Cawsal and my mother are not usually very strong." Petia looked at me before nodding briefly.

"Bogdo told me about that. Very sad for you it was," she said. "Would you like coffee or tea, perhaps?" Her expression puzzled me, but it wasn't the right time to ask. I said we would both like coffee.

We were finishing our meal when there was a knock at the door. Petia closed the kitchen door behind her and went to answer the front door. We heard voices, some male and one female. Then I realised I recognised one of the voices, and my heart flipped. I was sure it was Rush. If so, my boys must be here too, yet glancing at Elia, I saw caution on her face.

A few minutes later, the kitchen door opened, and two men entered. They were immediately recognisable as Rush and Kiron. I was out of my chair and moving towards Rush before he saw me. We embraced warmly, and a third pair of arms slipped around as Elia joined us. It was spontaneous and would never have happened even a week ago in Thena. Here, it felt right and natural.

"Father, I'm glad to see you," Elia said as she buried her head in the space between us.

"Where are the boys and Amillia?" I asked as we broke apart.

"In the conveyance, I left them there," he said, the worry rising as he spoke. Turning, he looked back at Mother Kron, who was already moving to the door. "Mother Kron, my children..." he began, but she interrupted.

"There's no time. I'm returning to the hospital and will bring them to you as soon as it is safe. Please remain with Petia for one day, then go with her to Iltanic. Petia can take you a safe way. Do not go near the hospital. It is not safe." She left before they could respond, and Petia took her place in the doorway.

"Please sit. You must be hungry and thirsty, you must. May I offer you vittals? Simple fare, but good." Gratefully, the two men sat at the table near Thea and Elia. Realising their hunger and thirst, they graciously accepted Petia's offer. While she turned to dish up their meal, they looked at Thea and Elia. There was much catching up to do, and they began to relate their adventures.

Message from Discovery to Councillor Wiklon
Contacted H Watcher. Silence active and present.

Message from Councillor Wiklon to Councillor Maxim
Do we have Silence Watcher?

Message from Councillor Maxim to Councillor Wiklon
No. Silence uncovered and retired.

Message from Councillor Wiklon to Councillor Maxim
We may have a problem. Discovery and H have Silence active and present.

Message from Councillor Maxim to Councillor Wiklon
Proceed with permanent.

Message from Councillor Wiklon to Captain of Pollo Guard
Proceed with permanent.

51

Cam

I wished someone would come back: Mother, Father or even Kiron. The twins had had enough, and Amillia was crying again. I was so scared a watcher would find us. I didn't know what to do. Then, the twins started to run from one end to the other, and the conveyance began to sway gently. I was just about to distract them when there was a knock on the door, and we all froze except Amillia, who continued to cry. Nervously, I looked at the shadowy figure standing by the door. It was the wisewoman who took Mother and Elia into the hospital, but where were they? Cautiously, I opened the door a crack.

"Wisewoman, may I help you?" I used formal Thenan. *I was terrified. Where were Elia and Mother? What has happened to them?*

"I come from Thea and Rush. May I enter your conveyance that we may talk?" her voice was so soft, and I strained to hear her. As I tried to decide what to do, Amillia's cries escalated. I sighed. My instinct was that she was safe, so I waved a hand for her to enter. When she stepped inside, the conveyance rocked, and she looked uncertain before sitting beside Amillia.

"Do you have food for the babe?" she asked as she opened Amillia's carrier. Amillia was lying inside a cosy nest, but her angry red face showed frustration and hunger. She slipped her hands under Amillia's arms and gently lifted her out. My heart sank when I saw she needed changing, and I turned to find the necessary things. The wisewoman laid the babe on her lap and was ready when I turned back. Her face was gentle and kind, putting me at ease.

"I'm Mother Kron," she said as she deftly changed Amillia's napkin. "May I know who I'm talking to and who this lovely babe is? Then perhaps you can introduce me to the two young men sitting quietly there." she nodded to the twins, sitting perfectly still. She wasn't Thenan, I was sure. She could be from Delph or Cawsal. Never mind, it must be OK if Father and Mother had sent her.

"I'm Cam, the babe is my sister Amillia, and these are my twin brothers Edi and Jami." I hesitated, then added, "Thank you for taking care of Amillia. I was preparing to change her as you knocked." it wasn't entirely true, but I would have done it if I'd had to.

"Well now, Cam, I'm glad to meet you, I am. Do you have milk for the little one?" Leaning over, I took a bottle from the bag.

"This is the last one. Mother Kron, well..." how should I say it? It wasn't something we talked about. "Mother feeds her, but she's been gone a long time."

"Don't worry. Your mother's safe with your sister, father and Healer, Kiron. When this little one is satisfied, we'll join them. Do you have snacks for the boys, perhaps?" I glanced back at the boys and saw their faces light up.

"I'll have a look." digging into the hamper, I found two pieces of bread amongst the empty wrappers, "This is all we have left, boys." Their faces lit up as they took the bread and began to eat.

When Amillia had finished, Mother Kron turned to the three of us.

"Now, we're going on an adventure, we are. We have to dress up to surprise your parents. Do you think you can do that?" Edi grinned immediately and gave a great whoop of excitement. Then, he clamped his hand across his mouth and looked at me. Jami nodded slowly. Mother Kron slipped Amillia back into her carrier and reached down to the medical sack she had brought. Opening it, she began pulling out clothes and piling them on the floor before her.

"So, which of you is Edi and which is Jami?" she asked with a smile. The two boys stood and moved to the pile of clothes. One of them was already reaching out while the other pulled him back.

"I'm Jami, and this is Edi. Why do we have to dress up?" Jami said, and I caught the note of disapproval in his voice. He hated this type of thing. I wished Elia was here. She always knew how to get Jami to do something.

"Well now, Jami, we're in a difficult situation. Some people want to cause you harm, so we must disguise you."

"Are they watchers?" he said, sounding much older than his years.

"Yes. Can you disguise yourself so they won't recognise you?" He stood with a serious expression on his face before he said.

"I think we should wait for Father. He should be back soon." His voice was brittle yet defiant.

"Your father is with your mother and Elia. I will take you to them as soon as we're ready. Now, quick, quick, there are watchers nearby," she repeated.

"Jami, it's OK, we should go with Mother Kron as she asks. Let's try these disguises. It might be fun to look like someone from Cawsal." I grinned, hoping they would take the hint.

Edi, who had been silent until now, said, "Come on, Jami, let's dress up. It will be fun."

He begins pulling at a coat, digging his hands into the pile of clothes. He pulled and pulled, then suddenly rolled back followed by the coat which covered him. The conveyance rocked with the sudden movement, and I froze before warning them to be more careful. Giggling, Edi said, “You can't see me. I'm in disguise.” I had to laugh. It was a welcome break from the tension in the conveyance.

“Edi, I think that might be a coat for me,” I said, taking the oversized coat from him. “Why don't you try again and see what else is in the pile.” Still giggling, he dug his arms deep into the pile up to his shoulders before taking hold of something else and pulling. This time, it was a small dark coat, which he slipped on, grinning.

“That's better, Edi,” I said as I slipped on the larger coat. “Now, find another coat for Jami and see what else is there.” Happily, Edi rummaged in the pile again. This time, he found a pair of trousers and a coat that would fit Jami. He passed them to his twin, who stood holding them at arm's length, a disgusted look on his face. Then Edi pulled the leg of another pair of trousers. It went on and on before the rest of it arrived. He held them up against himself, his face red with the effort, and was about to try them on when I leaned over and snatched them,

“Those are far too big for you,” I laughed and began to put them on. “Come on, Jami, slip those clothes on,” I said as I caught sight of his face. Scowling, Jami began to put on the trousers and coat. Edi found a coat for himself, which he slipped on. Lastly, I picked up three hats, pulling one on and passing the other two to the twins. Mother Kron was satisfied that the twins would do as long as they kept their hats on. Such dark hair was unusual in Cawsal, where fair hair was far more common. I've strapped Amillia to my chest in a sling Mother Kron gave me, and she's snuggled up happily. The oversized coat fastened over us so she was completely concealed.

“You look huge!” giggled Edi as he pointed at where Amillia was lying against me.

Mother Kron peered through the shaded windows and, seeing nobody around, opened the door. She told the boys not to talk until we reached our destination. If we met anyone, they must keep their eyes on the ground and not speak. I repeated the instructions and warned them again of the watchers. We followed Mother Kron away from the hospital in single file, with me bringing up the rear. Later, the two boys slipped a hand into each of mine, and we walked together through the alleyways. I could feel the boys tiring as we turned yet another corner. They were dragging on my arm and had begun to stumble a little, poor things. I was relieved when we stopped beside a door. Mother Kron looked sternly at us before knocking four times and twice more. A moment later, a woman stepped back to let us inside. I looked at the twins, raising my finger to my lips and gave what I hoped was a stern look as we entered the house.

The woman led us into a warm, cosy kitchen, and I was relieved to see Mother and Elia. Mother stood when she saw us enter, and the twins ran over to her, hugging her tightly. I almost wished I could join in, too. To feel Mother's arms around me would be so comforting after all we'd been through, but I'm not a child now. Mother suddenly looked up in alarm, and I realised she was looking for Amellia. Smiling, I walked over to her, unbuttoning my coat to reveal Amillia curled up asleep in the sling against my chest.

"Oh, Cam, I'm so glad to see you all. Have they been good? Did you have enough milk and napkins for Amillia?" the questions tumbled from her lips. "I'm sorry, I've been so worried about you all, especially when we heard there were watchers. Probably Frodel, Malic or both are spies." She took Amillia from me, and I went to sit with Elia. It was so good to see her. She'd had another episode recently; I could feel it. There was a strange quiet about her that wasn't there before. I couldn't place it. It was something to do with Mother Kron, perhaps. Elia nodded as I thought this, and I knew she agreed. It was strange, but there were times when we needed no words. We were being observed, and I saw Mother Kron looking at us. It was odd, but I knew she meant no harm.

"Are you well? I was worried." I whispered, "She looked like a nasty piece of work when she took you away with Mother." I nodded over at Mother Kron. Elia smiled.

"Yes, but when she realised we had Cawsal blood and saw me have an episode, she changed. She said I shouldn't hide them because they wear out my spirit." We sat back together and caught up on our adventures.

Father, Kiron and Petia joined Mother and Mother Kron. We heard them talking about the next part of our journey to Iltanic. They want to avoid taking the conveyance, but how else would we all get there? The twins couldn't walk far, and what about Amillia? We looked at each other as we listened. Finally, Mother Kron stood. She was going to make arrangements for us. Petia went with her to the door.

Message from Discovery to Councillor Wiklon
Fugitives gone to ground. Suspect destination Iltanic. Watching sympathisers.

Message from Councillor Wiklon to Discovery
Received. Advise Silence may not be secure.

Message from Discovery to Councillor Wiklon
Received.

52

Thea

Later, Mother Kron returned with a farmer, whom she introduced as Roklid. He had a cart and would take us to Iltanic, but we must leave now. We needed very little preparation and were ready in minutes. What was left on the conveyance was now lost. It was too dangerous to return for it. Quietly, we went out to the alleyway and climbed aboard the cart. We would be in the covered back section where he usually carried food to market. There was still the odd leaf and root strewn across the floor. There were no seats, but some small half-bales of straw had been provided for us to sit on. The twins and Elia were small enough to sit without reaching the canvas roof, but Cam and the rest of us had to slide down so our heads would not cause bumps that could give us away. With a jolt, the cart began to move, and we were on our way. It wasn't the most comfortable journey, bumping and bouncing along the track, but at least we weren't walking. Elia was in her usual place next to Cam, still looking pale. They were deep in conversation, and it warmed my heart to see them so close. I had hoped Millie and Cam would become close, but it never happened. They were close but didn't have the same bond as Cam and Elia. I hoped Edi and Jami would be close. It was likely since they were twins.

I was left to my thoughts with the twins asleep on either side. Rush, Mother Kron and Kiron were at the back of the cart, deep in hushed conversation. I wanted to know what *they were* saying, but I didn't have the energy to ask. Amillia was lying quietly in the sling against me. She wasn't asleep, and I'd moved her so she could look around if she wanted to, although there wasn't much to see. She was happily gurgling away, which usually made me smile. Today, I was so tired and worried I didn't have the energy for anything else until we reached our destination. At least we could stay here for as long as we needed. I was increasingly afraid we might never be safe with watchers so close, not even here. If we couldn't stay here, where could we go? How long could we keep moving around? What would we do for coin? I was still running these things through my mind when Elia slid to the floor, shaking and moaning.

Mother Kron turned as she heard the noise and moved swiftly along the strawbales to where Elia was lying. As she'd done at the hospital, Mother Kron took Elia's head and held it momentarily before asking Cam to take over. After freeing Elia's arms so they could move unhindered, she put her hands over Elia's eyes. Closing her eyes, Mother Kron remained still for an agonising few minutes as we bumped along the road. Then she looked up and over at me with a worried look.

"She's a long way away. I'm not sure if I can lead her back, but I'll try," she said, "Cam, will you assist and do what you usually do when it happens? Perhaps between the two of us, we can reach her." She closed her eyes. I saw a look flicker on Cam's face as he looked down at Elia before stroking her hands and feet, alternately muttering softly to her. I looked at Rush helplessly. I wished we were anywhere other than on this bumpy track in the back of a cart. I was so tired of being afraid. Afraid of seeing watchers, afraid we'd be caught. Afraid we'd be separated and afraid for Elia. I'd never heard of anyone caught by a watcher who had ever been seen again. Elia's episodes were now every day, and I didn't know how much longer her petite body and spirit could keep going at this rate. I heard Cam softly whispering to her. As I watched Elia, the shaking eased, and her body became still. *Was that a good thing? I hoped so.*

Mother Kron sat back on her heels and took one of Elia's hands, feeling for a pulse. She put a hand on Elia's forehead and then over her heart. Finally, seemingly satisfied, she looked up at Cam with an odd look before she looked at me.

"She'll be OK this time, but she needs to be somewhere safe as soon as possible. She cannot do this much more. Cam knows how to help her and can do so very well. If they stay together, she'll have all the support she needs." she gave Cam another questioning look before clambering back to sit with Kiron and Rush. Elia was now stirring and beginning to speak softly. I strained my ears to hear what she was saying.

"Not here, not here. Mine, mine, mine." She repeated the last word with increasing volume until she was fully awake. She looked around, surprised to see she was sitting on the floor. She struggled back onto the straw seat beside Cam and leaned against him.

"Elia, what did you see? Can you tell us?" I had to know. She seemed so distressed. Her face was deathly pale now, and her blue-green eyes looked out from dark hollow shadows.

"We will not be safe where we're going." She whispered, "We can go somewhere else in the mines. A dark tunnel to somewhere where we can be safe, I think." I looked around and saw Kiron and Mother Kron listening. Mother Kron gave a nod.

"I understand, I think," she said, and Elia's face relaxed.

"Do we have much further to go?" I asked. Edi and Jami will wake soon, which could make things more difficult.

"We're almost there." Mother Kron smiled and went to the front. Opening a flap in the canvas, she moved out to the bench where the farmer, Roklid, was sitting. As she did so, the cart slowed briefly and lurched, and I realised someone had jumped on board. I heard a new voice, and my heart began to pound. Then I realised the driver and Mother Kron were chatting comfortably with the new arrival. It sounded like a young man. His voice cracked now and again, suggesting it had yet to find its adult pitch.

The straw bales were prickly to sit on after a while, and I was tempted to try sitting on the floor, but there wasn't much room. The cart took another turn to the right and finally stopped. I breathed, wondering if this was our destination or another temporary stop. A moment later, the driver appeared at the back of the cart and let down the flap. A young man stood with Mother Kron and helped us down from the cart. Cam jumped down, and Rush handed the two sleepy boys to him. Kiron and Mother Kron helped Elia, and finally, I was left alone, wondering how to get down with Amillia. I needn't have worried. Rush was there holding up his arms for his little daughter. It was strange to think that I wouldn't have given any of the children to him just a few weeks ago. Now, I saw what a good father he could be if he had the opportunity. I took in his handsome face as he reached for his little daughter. He needed to shave, I noticed. His beard was beginning to show. Finally, Kiron helped me from the cart as a fine rain began to fall. The drops caught on the fibres of our clothing, giving them a coating of gems that sparkled like magic in the morning light. Mother Kron walked up to a door and knocked. A woman opened the door with a smile.

"Come in, come in, why don't you?" she stood back to let us pass. When we were all crowded into the small hallway and the front door was closed, she called,

"Door at the end, at the end, go through, go through." Cam, who was nearest, opened it and peered in before throwing it wide and entering crying.

"Millie!" he rushed in to embrace her. We're not usually an emotional family or used to physical contact. It warmed my heart to see such evident pleasure in their reunion. When I thought about it, only a few weeks had passed since they last saw each other, yet it felt like a lifetime. It was on that fated day of her sixteenth when everything changed. As I entered, I saw the other person standing in the room and realised it was Amelie. She came forward and pulled me into an embrace. After the initial surprise, I found it curiously comforting, conveying so much more than words. Then I joined Millie, hugging her tightly. Hesitating briefly, she hugged me back. She'd changed in these past few weeks, becoming quite the young lady.

After a somewhat chaotic reunion, Dorca appeared and asked for our attention. She had refreshments, and as we passed them around, she said we must not use our real names in her hearing, so she could not say who had been here if she was questioned.

When we'd all had refreshments, Rush came over with Kiron, Amelie, Mother Kron and Kayde.

It was Kiron who spoke first, "We have some important decisions to make for your family. We've told Amelie of Elia's visions. In turn, she has confirmed that Frodel and Malic are suspected spies. They will likely know where we are heading and will have passed on that information by now. It would only be a matter of time before watchers appeared in the village. It was also now known that watchers had a mandate to capture and imprison the male members of the family. They'll receive re-education. Female members are to receive no mercy. Simply put, your body will never be found."

My eyes widen. Hearing it said so plainly sent a cold shiver down my spine.

Rush began to talk, "Mother Kron has agreed to stay with the female members of the family. Kiron will remain here, too.

When the Cawsal rebels had taken care of matters in Donic, he had agreed to act as Healer at the hospital so they are not left without a Healer in this area." What would happen to the High Council? That could wait until we were safe, and I could talk with Rush.

"He may be able to retain his place on the Council, which will be a huge advantage, but it depends if Max has discovered the full extent of his involvement in our escape. Only time will tell." We nodded in silence.

Mother Kron asked Cam to stay with the female family members. Elia needed his calming presence. We had to decide whether to stay together as a family or split up. It was impossible to say when we would be reunited again if we split. If we stayed together, we were much more visible wherever we went."

"It's an impossible choice. Of course, I want the family to stay together. How can I think of being apart from even one of my children or you?" I cried, tears poured down my face. Rush took my hands.

"If we stay together, we have to leave Anacadair. I believe that's what Elia's vision meant. She talked about mines. Kayde says there are tunnels from the mines here that reach Nicadair. They are used by those who must escape guards or watchers. Smugglers also use tunnels through the mountains, but those are closer to the coast, away from the ones we will use. Kayde agrees this must be what Elia's vision means."

"I want us to stay together, Rush." How can I make any other decision?" Tears stung in my eyes as Amelie touched my arm. I could see she understood the impossible decision I'd been given. "I cannot bear the thought of the twins being caught and imprisoned, Rush. They're only five. We cannot agree to such a monstrous thing."

"If it were just me, I would accept imprisonment, but you're right, Thea, not the twins," Rush said.

"Mother Kron, would you really come with us? I'm so sorry for turning your life upside down. Having you with us would be reassuring." I asked.

"My motivations are two-fold. They are. Fold one - I need to disappear for a while, I do, until Oldron has gone. It's a little matter of some coffee and a sleeping draft. It was for a good reason, so you and Elia could escape." She gave a wicked grin and winked, "Fold two - I've family in Nicadair; I'd like to visit. Now seems to be an opportune time, it does. Young Kayde will show us the way. For such a young'un, he's very mature. He is," she said.

"Well, that's settled," I said brightly, "so when do we leave? Is there time for vittals?

"Yes, but after vittals, we must leave. Sooner the better with watchers so close, it is," Mother Kron said. We agreed, and she went to speak with Dorca. After she left, Kiron took me to one side.

"Thea, Elia's condition is far more serious than I believe has been explained. Dreamers rarely reach their sixteenth, as you know. The frequency of Elia's visions and the urgency of their message are straining her spirit and body beyond what normally occurs. I fear you should prepare yourself for the worst." I looked over at Elia as she sat with Cam and Millie. She was talking brightly with them but was still deathly pale. She was losing weight too. As if Kiron had read my mind he added "the weight she is losing also indicates the extreme strain on her body. She must be removed from this situation as soon as possible if there is any chance. Despite the episode on the way here, we must leave immediately." I digested his words, shocked by the implication. Was my poor Elia only a short way from the end of her life? I couldn't bear to think of such a bright light extinguished so soon, but I knew deep inside he was right. I'd known her light would go out early for some time. I'd seen it in my dreams, although I'd never tell anyone.

"Why did Mother Kron ask Cam to come with us?" I was puzzled, even though we had all decided to stick together.

"She's not sure, but there seems to be a close bond between the two that she's not seen before. It would be best to keep them together until there's time to assess. He knows how to reach her and help her back after it happens." Having seen him with Elia during our journey here, I realised that was probably true. After we'd taken vittals, we assembled, ensuring we had coats, shoes and woven trousers for walking. The twins insisted on keeping their own trousers underneath; they said the woven trousers were too itchy. I knew what they meant, but the everyday woven material made us less noticeable.

The tunnels were entered from a shed behind this dwelling, which made it easier to slip away unnoticed. Kayde would go first with Amelie and Millie. Mother Kron was next with Elia, Cam and the twins. Rush and I would follow with Amillia. In our groups, we quietly slipped out of the back door. Rush and I pause momentarily, thanking Dorca for her hospitality and help. Then we embraced Kiron, who promised Millie would see Yan soon. It was Millie's condition when she agreed to leave Anacadair. Kiron, Amelie and I agreed they were meant to be together, and we were all happy with the match.

The small grey shed was just a few steps from the back door across an overgrown path. It was still drizzling, and I covered Amillia as we hurried to the shed and slipped inside, closing the door behind us. My heart was beating fast as we made our way to the back of the shed and, as instructed, pushed the back wall, which moved up to reveal a narrow opening. Rush held the wall for me as I stooped to go through before he followed me, letting the wall drop behind us. We were the last to leave and picked up the last lantern, which threw a pale light along the tunnel. Walking carefully along the tunnel, we followed the voices ahead. This was the day our lives changed forever. There was no going back.

Acknowledgements

So many have supported me as I embarked on this project. Michele Powponne Osborne must come first. Without her encouragement in our Creative Writing group sponsored by Mary Frances Trust, I never would have begun this book. I'm thankful Mum and Dad read the original short story, which became the first few chapters of this book and inspired me to write what happened next. Sadly, neither of my parents will see the final book, but I know they would be proud.

Michael Heppell and Write that Book Masterclass was the nudge I needed to believe I could write my book. The fantastic Team 17 provided so much support and encouragement when Mum died. Thank you for keeping me writing through such a difficult time. The wonderful talents of Mattew Bird deserve a special mention for his work on cover design, typesetting, and so much more. I'm indebted to my beta readers for helping me focus my editing: Judy Brulo, Claire Delgano Todd, Eleanor Baggaley, Lynn Morland, Alison Hares, Deborah Brown, Anna Rushton, Dawn Booth, Stefanie Lillie, Sara Roome, Amy Mann, Olivia Wheatley Hince. Thank you all.

Lovely Ladies! You know who you are. Without your encouragement, where would I be? My son Ben Fryer created the map of Anacadair, and I'm so grateful for his artistry in interpreting my doodles and bringing the country into being. Without the support from my family this book would never have been completed: my husband David for his patience and encouragement to keep writing and my children Amy Mann and

Ben Fryer for their enthusiasm in my new writing adventures. There are many more friends and fellow writers who have encouraged me through support groups too numerous to list, but without you all, I couldn't have finished this book. Thank you.

About the Author

Clare grew up in Guildford surrounded by books. Her father was a poet and author who inspired her to write. She began doodling poetry in her teens and loved writing stories at school. She continued to doodle poetry throughout her life, although yearned to write novels but never had the time. When not reading, Clare enjoys gardening, crochet and cross-stitch and always has several projects on the go.

In 2022, Clare took early retirement and finally had time to realise her dream. The Invitation began as a short story inspired by a writing prompt. It won the monthly writing competition in her creative writing group. Clare's mother and several friends asked what happened next, and so she began to write the rest. That short story became the first three chapters of this book. Clare has always been curious about the stories hidden behind the veneer of normality, whether created by culture or something more sinister.

Clare and her husband David have been married for over 30 years. They have two children who are both married, and a delightful granddaughter. Clare and David now enjoy time together with their beautiful Burmese cats, Rosie Posie and Poppy.